TWELVE STEPS TO Normal

TWELVE STEPS TO Normal

FARRAH PENN

FOREWORD BY JAMES PATTERSON

JIMMY Patterson Books
Little, Brown and Company
New York Boston London

Copyright © 2018 by Farrah Penn
Foreword copyright © 2018 by James Patterson

JIMMY Patterson Books / Little, Brown and Company
Hachette Book Group
1290 Avenue of the Americas, New York, NY 10104
jamespatterson.com

First Edition: March 2018

JIMMY Patterson Books is an imprint of Little, Brown and Company, a division of Hachette Book Group, Inc. The Little, Brown name and logo are trademarks of Hachette Book Group, Inc. The JIMMY Patterson Books® name and logo are trademarks of JBP Business, LLC.

The publisher is not responsible for websites (or their content) that are not owned by the publisher.

The Hachette Speakers Bureau provides a wide range of authors for speaking events. To find out more, go to hachettespeakersbureau.com or call (866) 376-6591.

Library of Congress Cataloging-in-Publication Data
Names: Penn, Farrah, author.
Title: Twelve steps to normal / Farrah Penn; foreword by James Patterson.
Description: First edition. | New York; Boston: JIMMY Patterson Books, Little, Brown and Company, 2018. | Summary: Upon returning from a year in Oregon to Texas and her alcoholic father, Kira is distressed to find three of her father's rehab friends staying at her home, while her own friends seem distant.
Identifiers: LCCN 2017048468 | ISBN 978-0-316-47160-2 (hc)
Subjects: | CYAC: Alcoholism—Fiction. | Fathers and daughters—Fiction. | Interpersonal relations—Fiction. | High schools—Fiction. | Schools—Fiction. | Single-parent families—Fiction. | Grief—Fiction.
Classification: LCC PZ7.1.P44713 Twe 2018 | DDC [Fic]—dc23
LC record available at https://lccn.loc.gov/2017048468

10 9 8 7 6 5 4 3 2 1

LSC-C

Printed in the United States of America

In memory of my grandma Clara,
who taught me to write, and my dad,
who encouraged me to never stop

foreword

WHEN I FIRST READ *Twelve Steps to Normal,* it was one of those stories that stayed with me long after I turned the last page. Farrah Penn manages to capture the joyous highs of love to the blackest lows of despair with her writing, in a way that made Kira and her life feel incredibly heartfelt and real.

From personal experience, I can say that living with any kind of addiction—even if it's not yours—changes you in many ways. But in the end, this isn't a story about alcoholism. It's about a girl who just wants to be normal, not realizing at the start that there's really no such thing. I think we're all on the journeys that we're meant to be taking. For Kira, hers begins with twelve remarkable steps... each one vital to reaching her destination.

I hope you enjoy the journey.

—*James Patterson*

TWELVE STEPS TO Normal

ONE

I USED TO THINK THE worst moment of my life happened in eighth grade when I got caught stealing the latest issue of *Cosmopolitan* from 7-Eleven because I didn't have four dollars to learn all the secrets of being a great kisser.

I was wrong.

From several thousand feet in the air, our plane shakes. I try not to take it as a universal sign of my slowly accumulating bad luck. It doesn't help that Aunt June put me on a flight to Austin on what is probably the rainiest day in the history of Portland. This delayed my departure, which forced me to text my dad to inform him I'd be arriving later than expected.

I've been unraveling the tight knots in my earphones for the last half hour to take my mind off my impending doom. The woman beside me watches as I do this. I've noticed she's already read through her paperback romance and since there aren't any movies playing on this flight, I must be the next best form of entertainment.

My fingers work through the last knot and break it free.

"Wow," she comments. "Must have been really tangled in your pocket."

I don't respond. Instead, I take the white cord and begin looping it back into tiny knots, making sure I pull hard. She gives me a puzzled look before glancing away.

Our plane hits another spot of turbulence. I tell myself to concentrate on undoing the knots. I hate planes. I don't particularly trust anything designed to defy the laws of gravity, nor do I enjoy being trapped in such a close vicinity to strangers who are all breathing the same recycled air. We have another hour before we're scheduled to land, and then I'll be home.

As much as I wish this were a celebratory occasion, coming home was not my decision. I thought I was accepting my permanent fate when I was sent to live with Aunt June in Portland. I'd learned to put up with the noisy city voices and the uncomfortable fold-out bed and walking a block and a half to do laundry. All of this was better than living with my dad.

But last week Aunt June broke the news that he was officially released from Sober Living Alcohol and Drug Rehabilitation Center. She even brought home lasagna to celebrate—the slightly pricier frozen kind from Trader Joe's.

"Of course I love having you here, doll," she told me, squeezing me tight in the middle of her tiny kitchen. "I'm going to miss you something fierce."

"But you want me to go back?" I mumbled into her crocheted top.

She pulled away, but I noticed a weight of emotion fall over her features. "I really think it'll do you good to be home. I've talked with your daddy over the phone, and Margaret's had a few meetings with him. I wouldn't be telling you this if we didn't think it was a good environment."

Margaret is my social worker who always wears big Audrey Hepburn sunglasses to our meetings. She was a big believer in this rehabilitation center, but I was skeptical. Alcoholics Anonymous meetings hadn't been enough to help my dad, so I doubted this would, either.

"He'll be home Sunday morning," Aunt June continued, handing me a plate before sitting down next to me. She took the broken chair—the one that rocked slightly if you leaned the wrong way. "I've already submitted your transcripts back to Cedarville. That way you can be back with all your friends in time to start junior year together."

I could tell she expected me to be more excited. Going home meant that I could go back to my old life. The life that contained my best friends and boyfriend (well, *ex*-boyfriend now). I'd been on the dance team and participated in National Honor Society and Earth Club. I grew up going to school with everyone in my class, which was comfortable more than it was congested. Cedarville was a small town, but it was *my* small town.

Aunt June would have lost her job if she'd come to live with me in Texas, which is how I ended up in Portland. It wasn't that I was unhappy with the situation, but I wasn't exactly happy having to start over, either. My grades made it clear I wasn't trying very hard in school. In the entire eleven months, I'd only made one friend—Katie

Jones, who was obsessed with the movie *Borat* and had memorized all the national capitals of the world.

It wasn't my best friends or ex-boyfriend that was making me hesitant to return. It was my father.

"Sounds good," I told her, but there was very little enthusiasm in my voice.

She put her fork down. "You know you're always welcome back here, doll. If you go home and decide it's not where you want to be, you call me. Anytime, day or night. Okay?"

I promised I would, and that was that.

When she sent me off to the airport this afternoon, she gave me a long hug. I breathed in her scent of jasmine that had become one of my only comforts over the last several months. There were tears in her eyes when she pulled away.

In the row across from me, a dad watches his kid play some game on his Nintendo DS. The glow of the screen lights up their faces. He gives an encouraging "Good job, buddy!" when his son levels up. The entire exchange makes my gut twist in nervousness. I wish coming home to my dad would be that easy.

I pull tighter at my knots.

Six hours and one layover after taking off, I finally land in Austin. I'm jittery, like a rattling car engine on the verge of breaking down. This is home. I should be breathing sighs of relief. So why does being here feel so . . . foreign?

I go through the motions of shuffling off the plane, then make my way to the baggage claim. My two huge suitcases are patterned with silhouetted birds in flight, so they're easy to spot on the carousel.

I'm channeling all my inner Hulk strength—*Why did I bring so many shoes?*—as I lift the last one from the belt.

And that's when I hear it.

"Goose!"

I am not actually named after a particularly ill-tempered bird. I should find comfort in the longtime nickname my dad gave me, but a part of me doesn't want to be his Goose. I just want to be Kira.

"Hi," I say as he comes toward me. I'm sort of glad I have my luggage in my hands, because it's an excuse not to hug him.

The first thing I notice is that he's lost weight. His naturally dark hair is peppered with more gray than before, and he has traces of bags under his brown eyes. Most evenings he would drink himself to sleep, but maybe the detox threw off his internal clock.

My dad steps through my barrier of luggage and leans in to hug me. I breathe into his soft button-down out of habit. Smelling alcohol on him was always a giveaway, but all I smell is unfamiliar laundry detergent and a bit of musky cologne.

"Here, let me get that." He takes the handles of my two heavy rollaways in each hand. "How was your flight?"

"Good," I lie.

Small talk. I'm sure he doesn't care to hear about the weather and the plane that shook us around like a Magic 8-Ball.

"Good, good," he repeats, and then we walk out of the airport and into the balmy Texas night.

I spot his cherry-red Nissan as we walk to the parking lot. Old dents and dings and scuffs litter the body, but I find myself inspecting it for new scars. Which is stupid. My dad wasn't allowed to bring his car to Sober Living and he hasn't been home long enough to inflict new damage.

He places my bags in the trunk and then we get inside, ready to make the forty-minute drive to Cedarville.

My stomach flips in a nervous sort of way. I shouldn't be so anxious to go back. Maybe it's because I haven't contacted Lin or Whitney or Raegan, three of my best friends since elementary. It's not that I didn't want to let them know I'm back, because I definitely do. I guess I wanted it to be real for me first.

I begin to type a group text to them.

"Good to know not that much has changed," my dad jokes, glancing at my cell.

It's an attempt to break the ice, but I don't reply. I'm not in the mood to try and put forth any type of conversation. Even though he's written me dozens of apology letters, that doesn't make up for all the time I lost being without my friends and boyfriend and my own life.

I finish typing and hit Send.

My dad takes a small breath, like he's gathering up the courage to speak. Then he does. "Sober Living is a great facility. Really great, supportive people. I'm feeling really good about this, Goose." When I don't respond, he continues. "The ranch was beautiful. I took some pictures, but I still need to figure out how to get them off my SD card. There were horses—it reminded me of when you were a little thing. When I took you to the petting zoo near Austin?"

I nod, remembering the brochure from Sober Living all those

months ago. It talked all about how the *twelve-step program could explore and empower their lives* and how they used *equestrian therapy to create connection and personal fulfillment.* I didn't quite understand how riding a horse was supposed to enforce sobriety, but whatever.

"We made a lot of ceramics, too," he continues.

Arts and crafts. Brilliant.

I don't want to come home with a terrible attitude toward his progress, but it's hard to trust his optimism when Alcoholics Anonymous hasn't exactly worked for him in the past. He'd commit to it for a while with the help of Michael, his sponsor, and the twelve-step program, but then he'd ultimately fall back into his excessive drinking routine.

I was thirteen when my dad came home from his first AA weekend retreat. He brought a present for me, poorly wrapped in newspaper. When I opened it, I discovered a pale green ceramic mug he'd made by hand. At the bottom was a decal of a cartoon pug, his floppy tongue hanging out.

"Because you love pugs!" he said.

He was so proud of himself. It made my heart ache. My pug obsession had ended in like, second grade. It was like he barely knew me at all.

His creation sat in the china cabinet, displayed for all to see, but when he wasn't home I took it out and hid it in the back of the pantry. It was embarrassing—something a little kid should show off, not a grown adult.

I wonder how many ceramic mugs it took to help him stay clean this time. I say this aloud because a part of me feels like being spiteful. Silence falls thick between us. I'm not sure if he heard me. I tell myself I don't care.

We clear through dense clusters of oak trees and emerge into the flat, wide landscape of Cedarville. It's a running joke that there are more cows than homes out here, but I've always loved how everyone on the farm town outskirts owns so much property. Whitney is the only one of my friends who lives a few miles outside the suburbs of Cedarville. When we were younger we would take turns riding her go-kart on the expanse of green acres in her backyard.

"Mr. Buckley offered me a janitorial position at Cedarville Elementary," my dad says. "I guess we'll both have big days tomorrow, huh?"

I shrug. This time he gives up on the small talk. We stay silent for the rest of the ride home.

It never used to be like this. Before Grams died, we had our own Wednesday night tradition where we'd bake homemade pizzas and watch an episode of *Crime Boss,* a show similar to *Law & Order* (with a whopping fourteen seasons and counting) that always replayed on various networks. He used to scribble awful puns on napkins—*ORANGE you glad it's Friday?!*—and slip them into my lunch sack. I'd always pretend it was so lame, but I was secretly pleased when my friends found them hilarious.

Sometimes he'd text me selfies he took in the milk aisle of the grocery store, mock-terror on his face as he captioned it with, **I CAN'T REMEMBER WHICH % WE BUY HELP.** He'd buy ingredients for dinners he found on cooking blogs and together we'd whip up homemade ziti and falafel.

We're a long way away from those days now.

When we pull in the driveway, Dad gets out to grab my bags from the trunk. I reach in the backseat for my purse, but I'm fumbling blindly in the dark. I flip on the overhead light so I can see. That's when I spot it. There, lying in the middle seat, is a mug-shaped gift wrapped in newspaper, tied neatly with a turquoise ribbon.

TWO

MY DAD HAS THE KEYS in his hand, but he doesn't let us inside right away. I step around him and make my way up the porch. If I had my own key with me I would let myself in, but I don't. It's inside along with the rest of my interrupted life.

Our house looks the same. The rusty red brick exterior held up without us during tornado season last spring. I notice the plants in the front look a little wilted, but with unsurprisingly hot summers, that's to be expected. Grams's white porch swing gently sways in the night's breeze, and a familiar emptiness falls over me. I remember her sitting out here every morning in her terry cloth robe before I went to school. How she'd kiss me on the cheek and tell me to *Be good, darlin'*.

It's been two years since she unexpectedly passed from a heart attack, but some days it feels like yesterday. Being back here at her house, where her memory lives so strongly, brings back the dull ache of her loss.

I wait for my dad to catch up to me, noticing that he takes his time hauling my suitcases up the porch steps.

"Listen." He hesitates, thumbs over the house key. The floodlight is on, and I can see spiderwebs of wrinkles near his eyes. "We have some company."

"Company?" I repeat, wondering if it's my social worker Margaret, or if he'd already contacted Lin and Whitney and Raegan.

Or Jay.

My heart squeezes tight. Leaving my friends was hard, but leaving Jay was harder. Because I was falling for him, and being forced to leave someone you're falling for is kind of like having to throw away a chocolate swirl cone after one bite.

In Cedarville, you grow up with the same group of kids. You know birthdays by heart and whose parents are on the PTA and who's allergic to nuts or latex. I knew Jay Valenski, but I'd never *noticed* Jay Valenski.

I did, however, start noticing him in history class.

He'd gotten his braces off and started taming his puffy hair with the magic of hair wax. He was always giving these super intellectual responses in class discussions, but he'd litter his replies with humor and always make the whole room laugh. I'm not exactly a world history fan, but I found myself poring over our assigned reading so I could contribute. I figured the more I talked in class, the more he'd notice me.

Of course it didn't occur to me that it would be much easier to just talk to him *outside* of class.

I was right behind him when we were leaving history one

afternoon. He was opening a packet of those fun-sized M&M's, so I seized the opportunity when he turned in my direction to throw the packaging away.

"Did you know red M&M's were taken off the shelves at one point in time?"

I regretted the words the moment I said them. He just stared at me. Oh god. He thought I was a total dork. I could feel the heat in my cheeks. My skin burned.

But he laughed. In this completely charming, nice guy way. "For how long?"

"Like, ten years."

"How could an entire decade of chocolate lovers be deprived of one of the most important primary colors?"

An ease of relief let up in my chest. "Good thing they came to their senses."

We became closer friends after that. He started sitting by me in history, and sometimes we'd walk to the Sno Shack after school. He told me about his obsession with Sudoku and putting together those classic model car kits. I told him about my obsession with pineapples and how I had all sorts of vibrant knick-knacks decorating my room.

He was on the freshman basketball team and I'd joined the Wavettes—our school's dance team. On Fridays, he started coming early to football games to see me perform.

I always loved spotting him in the crowd.

I loved other things about him, too. Like how he'd call me *Kira Kay,* a nonsensical nickname he made up because it rhymed with Jay. Or how he complimented the rare occasions when I got up early to straighten my thick mass of dark hair.

"I have something for you," he said to me once at lunch.

I raised a speculative eyebrow. "Oh?"

"Yup. Prepare to be impressed."

"I'm fully prepared. Hit me."

He unfurled his hand, revealing a small tin of canned pineapples.

I laughed. I had recently argued in favor of pineapple on pizza and commented that our cafeteria never put enough on the slices they sold. But he revealed he couldn't get behind that topping. I believe his actual words were, *It's a tragic way to ruin a pie.*

"For the next pizza day," he clarified, smiling. Oh, his smile was *so* charming. "Go to town."

I was attracted to him. I loved his earthy brown hair and taut, long arms. When we saw each other before school, I'd yearn for him to hold my hand. I would get this deep, erratic sensation in the pit of my stomach just thinking of how it would feel to have his fingers twined in mine. It felt stronger than simply a *feeling*. It was a sort of *VOOSH* that shot right up my spine and into my heart.

After Friday football games, Whitney, Raegan, Lin, and I would meet at Sonic with him and his friends, Colton and Breck. He always sat by me, and he always ordered the same thing: a blue raspberry slush. We'd talk until we were the last two people sitting at the plastic picnic tables.

We were there so late one night that he offered to walk me home. I was still in my uniform from performing earlier, and he was wearing his red and white Cedarville basketball T-shirt. I liked the way everyone stared at us when we left. It felt like we belonged together.

He walked me all the way up to my porch, where my stomach was cramping from laughing so hard at his impression of our history

teacher, Mr. Benet, who dragged out certain words when he spoke
to the class.

"Who can tell me about the Treatyyyyyy of Cahuengaaaaa?"

"Stop!" I snorted. "You're awful."

"Then whyyyyy are you laughingggggg?"

I playfully slapped him on the chest. He took my hand and pulled
me closer to him. My breathing grew rapid, my pulse quickening.

"I like you a lot, you know."

I didn't know much about anatomy, but I was pretty positive my
heart somersaulted.

I smiled. He stared right into my eyes, his tongue running over
his bottom lip. He was nervous. I was nervous. But, oh god, I wanted
this *so* bad. I saved screenshots of his texts when he sent me heart
emojis or when he typed that he was thinking of me. I tallied up the
number of times we'd held hands and how long we hugged and if he
ever took an extra second to smell my hair. But this? This was something I didn't even have to think twice about wanting.

He leaned close. Our lips brushed.

Contact.

VOOSH.

His lips were soft and cool and tasted like raspberry. I spent the
entire weekend playing it back in my mind.

I was the one that started the inconspicuous hangman games
in history class. I'd draw the tiny diagram with blank lines on
the corner of my notebook and scribble a hint at the top. Movies.
Teachers. Sports. After an entire week of playing together, I solved
the best hangman puzzle in the history of hangman puzzles:

go out with me?

Of course, I said yes.

We dated for a long time. When I found out I was moving to Portland, I stayed in my room and cried for the entire weekend. I tried to be hopeful at first. I figured that we could stay together through texting and video chat, but I knew it wouldn't be the same. Eventually we'd grow apart. Or worse, I'd start becoming jealous of every girl who was closer to him in physical distance than me. What I had to do seemed inevitable.

I broke up with him in the school parking lot after practice. It turned out he was more hopeful than me, promising my situation was only temporary. The truth was we both didn't know that. I had no idea when—or if—I was ever coming back to Cedarville.

There was a knock on my front door later that night. I flipped the porch light on to answer it, but no one was there. When I looked down, I saw a simple greeting card with a rolling green Texas field on the front. I opened it and instantly recognized Jay's slanted handwriting.

Don't forget about me, he'd written.

It killed me that he was still so optimistic.

I never said good-bye to Jay, but I hoped he understood. I couldn't selfishly keep him as mine when I didn't even know if I'd be coming back. My friends knew I didn't want to break up with him, but he was still another part of my life that I lost when I was sent to Portland.

But the way my dad's looking at me tells me that Jay isn't the one inside.

"I have company staying from Sober Living."

I'm jolted away from my thoughts of Jay. Wait—what? Some-one from the rehabilitation center? I'm confused. And annoyed. It's almost nine o'clock at night. Why would he have company over so late? Besides, aren't there post-rehab rules? I'm sure there are. I bet one of them says *no hanging out when it's over* or something.

"Okay." I blow out a breath. "I'm kind of tired. I didn't know you were going to have someone over tonight."

I hope he doesn't expect me to play the Good Daughter this eve-ning. I'm not in the mood.

"Well, um." He looks uncomfortable. "It's actually more than one person. We all became so close at the ranch, and I told them if they needed time to get their lives in order..."

I feel my stomach drop. No, no, no no no. Please, *please* don't let this be true. It *can't* be true. Because there is no way my dad—my supposed newly sober and responsible father—has brought home a bunch of other alcoholics to live with us. How could he ever think that was a good idea? Margaret certainly wouldn't.

"So," I start slowly, hoping I have this all wrong. "They're inside now?"

"We're taught to help and support each other." There's more authority in his voice now. "They need a little time to get back on their feet. I promise, Kira, if I had even the slightest feeling that they were a threat I wouldn't have invited them. But they aren't. They're really great people. You'll see."

Great people? Is he serious? Opening our home to these recovering addicts is the last thing we both need.

I'm opening my mouth to tell him this, but the front door swings open. A woman in a navy dress stands there with a radiant smile on her face.

"I thought I heard someone!" I notice right away that she's one of those women who have a naturally loud voice. "Come in! What are y'all still doing outside?"

I stand there, staring from her to my father. He heaves my luggage up the porch and steps around me. I follow behind. What else can I do?

"This is Peach," my dad says by way of introduction.

The woman called Peach beams at me as I set my purse on the entryway table. I guess that maybe she's in her late thirties. There's a smudge of pink lipstick on one tooth. Her pale hair is piled on top of her head and tightly secured with one of those giant clips. There are slight creases around her tired eyes.

"A true pleasure to meet you," Peach tells me. "Your daddy talked so much about you at the ranch!"

"Uh," is the only thing I can think to say.

A guy wearing dozens of leather bracelets on each arm steps toward me. "You must be Kira."

I blink up at him. His long hair is pulled back into a ponytail and he's wearing a black T-shirt that has the word *namaste* in cursive on the front. When he smiles at me, I notice a gap between his teeth. He can't be older than twenty-five. Or maybe it's his gawkiness that makes him look young.

"I'm Saylor," he tells me, sticking out a hand.

Warily, I take it. His skin is slightly chapped.

Before I can even process my overwhelming thoughts, an older lady appears in front of me. She's wearing a neon-pink sweater that has blue jaguars (*jaguars?*) patterned all over, and on her feet are two giant…cats? Confirmed. She is definitely wearing fuzzy feline slippers. Her gray hair is in giant rollers. She squints as if her vision is troubling her, peering at me through her turquoise frames.

"Kira! Oh, it's so nice to meet you." Her rollers bob up and down as she speaks. "Call me Nonnie."

My breathing is shallow. I feel light-headed. I think I might be sick. Or claustrophobic. This was *not* the homecoming I expected. I'm sure everything was all *kumbaya* at the ranch, but bringing a group of alcoholics here? Into our lives? Into *my* life?

I consider calling Aunt June. There's no way she knew about my dad's plans. She would honestly think this whole situation is completely bananas.

Plus, how are we supposed to house three extra people? I mean, sure we have a fold-out couch and—

Wait. No. There's no way Dad would offer up Grams's room. But when I look over at him, I can tell he's already made the decision. My blood boils, fueled by heat and anger and betrayal.

I grab my purse and the closest suitcase to me. "I'm going to bed."

My dad nods gently. "Of course. You've had a long day." He steps forward to hug me, but I step back. He looks hurt. I pretend I don't notice. "We'll see you in the morning."

Saylor motions to my other suitcase. "I'll get this one."

Before I can say no, he grabs it and begins taking the stairs two at a time. Sighing, I follow.

We reach the top landing, and I make a right toward my bedroom. Saylor starts to follow me inside, but I snatch my suitcase from him with more force than the both of us were expecting.

"I got it. Thanks." My words are clipped and ungrateful, but I don't care.

Saylor gives a little shrug and smiles. "Okie dokie. Have a good night."

I don't say anything as I forcefully shut the door behind me.

My room has always been my sanctuary. The yellow pineapple lamp Lin bought for me sits on my IKEA nightstand. Strands of twinkle lights zigzag across my ceiling. It'd taken two hours and three extension cords to make it happen, but the result makes it look like a starry night. My yellow throw rug, aside from all the nail polish stains, matches the little yellow pineapple trinkets I have lined up on the shelf above my desk.

My pineapple obsession has been a reputable part of me ever since I was younger. It was usually Whitney, Raegan, and Lin who gave me pineapple-themed presents for Christmas. Aside from my lamp, I also owned three pineapple candles, two golden pineapple bookends, a knitted pineapple tissue holder, and a pineapple-shaped clock radio.

I leave my suitcases in the middle of my room and flop face-first into my bed. It smells like home—like my coconut lotion and clean linens and a little bit like the warm, dewy evening. I think of Grams's room being invaded by strangers and try not to cry.

I hear my phone buzzing excessively in my purse. I completely forgot about the group message I'd sent Lin, Whitney, and Raegan.

Aside from my room, they're the next closest comfort to me right now. I dive into my bag and retrieve it.

LIN: ARE YOU REALLY BACK IN CEDARVILLE?

WHITNEY: i had no idea you were coming home

RAEGAN: so happy, love!!!! xoxo

LIN: SUPER happy! Omg. It's been forever. Can I see you?

WHITNEY: are you coming back to school

LIN: Well duh, Whit. It's not like she's dropped out.

RAEGAN: i could use more help with Leadership Council stuff! 🙏 🙏 🙏

LIN: BFF REUNION. LET'S GET MILKSHAKES.

WHITNEY: nothing is open now!

RAEGAN: love ya, K. so excited to see you tomorrow!! ♥

LIN: I'm coming over now then!

Frantic, I type a quick reply to all three. I tell Lin not to come over, that I'm exhausted and I'll see her at school tomorrow. She sends back a frowny emoji, but disappointing Lin is the least of my worries. Because a small town like Cedarville loves gossip. And my life feels like it's spiraled enough to make headlines.

My cell phone rings.

I expect to see Lin's name appear across the screen, but it's not her. Instead, I read: **MARGARET—SOCIAL WORKER.** I freeze, debating whether I should answer, but quickly decide it would probably be a good idea.

"Hi, Margaret."

"Kira, hello!" Her voice is chipper. "I'm so sorry to call so late, but I figured you must be home by now."

"No, it's okay. And you're right. I'm home." I glance around my room, feeling the comfort of being in a space that's so purely *mine*.

"Listen," she says, adopting a more serious tone. "I just wanted to check in and say that if you sense that there's anything unusual about your father's behavior, don't hesitate to call me, all right?"

She continues talking, but my brain zeros in on those words: unusual behavior. I wouldn't call my homecoming usual, exactly, what with three alcoholic strangers staying here for the foreseeable future. But that's not what she means.

Is it?

"—we'd rather your dad continue getting help and have you with your Aunt June if things escalate again."

I try and stop the uncertain thoughts spinning through me. "I understand."

"Excellent. If you need anything, I'm just a phone call away."

"Thanks, really," I say more confidently than I feel.

Once we hang up, I stare down at my phone. Calling Aunt June to tell her everything seemed like a good idea before, but now I'm not sure. If June tells Margaret about this living situation, or worse, if Margaret decides to schedule a check-in and finds out, there's no question about it. Because my mom is out of the picture, I have no other choice. I'd have to go back to Portland. And that's not what I want. Now that I've texted my friends, I realize just how much I'm looking forward to seeing them. If I want to stay in Cedarville—if I want my *old* life with my dad again—then the answer is easy. I can't let anyone find out these people are staying here.

If I'm lucky, they'll be here a few weeks. A month, tops. How long does it take to get your life together, anyway? I thought that's what Sober Living was for. Why would they need to invade our house to get it together?

There's a knock at my door.

I'm hit with a sudden burst of déjà vu. Most nights before I went to bed, Grams would come in and chat with me for a bit, usually as I was picking out my clothes for school the next day. It was nice talking to her about things, like what I should wear to homecoming and if I could see a dermatologist because my pimples were getting out of control—things that were awkward to talk about with my dad.

Once she'd come in as I was getting ready to perform with the Wavettes at a Saturday game. I was frustrated because I couldn't get my eyeliner to match perfectly with both eyes, and I really wanted it to look even.

"Here," she'd said, her hand gesturing for my bottle of liquid liner.

"I'm running late," I'd replied, somewhat annoyed. Grams didn't ever wear eyeliner, and letting her attempt to apply it would only hold me up.

"Trust me." She took the bottle from me anyway, so I gave up and closed my eyes. I felt the cool tip glide onto both eyelids. "Now, look."

I did. It wasn't perfect, but it was way more even than my prior attempts.

"Wow," I said, surprised. "Thank you."

"See?" She was smiling, and her tone was only somewhat smug. "Sometimes you have to take a step back. Let someone else help out."

I blink away the memory, but it doesn't stop me from feeling her absence all over again.

It would be polite to answer whoever is on the other side of my door, but I don't feel like putting on a smile and entertaining someone named after a piece of fruit. I just want to be left alone.

I hear descending footsteps. Whoever it was gave up.

Exhausted, I set my phone alarm and crawl into bed. I'm about to turn off my lamp when the collage of pictures taped on the wall catches my eye.

There's one of Whitney and me pushing up our nostrils and flaunting unflattering pig noses. I find the one of Jay and me posing in my front yard before homecoming freshman year. There's another of Raegan, Whitney, Lin, and me on our front porch swing with popsicles in our hand. It's all evidence that my life is here, that I belong here. Even if it doesn't feel like it.

THREE

THE INTRO TO "WE WILL ROCK YOU" bangs through my skull and into my brainwaves when I wake up the next morning. I'm disoriented for half a second before remembering I'm back in my old room. But the music doesn't quiet. And it's unnecessarily LOUD.

I stagger out of bed, my tired eyes still adjusting to the morning light. I didn't sleep well. I'm nervous about starting school again, which is ridiculous. I should be bursting with joy. Last night I tried to tell myself I was worrying for nothing, but my mind didn't drift off until around one in the morning.

I wander down the upstairs hallway only to discover that the music is accompanied by very loud, very off-key singing. The source is coming from my bathroom, where I hear Nonnie belting lyrics from under the blasting water.

"Morning!"

Peach is walking up the stairs. She looks like she started her day hours ago. Her pale hair is tied back in a French braid and she's wearing a crisp floral blouse with a knee-length, conservative green skirt. She's even wearing magenta heels that match her lipstick.

"You look like you could use some coffee," she says, placing an armload of clean towels in the linen closet.

"I don't drink coffee." I've tried, but it tastes like bitter sludge. I prefer mine blended with massive amounts of sugar and mocha, which is less like coffee and more like a milkshake. A milkshake that's socially acceptable to drink in the morning.

The music stops and the bathroom door swings open. Nonnie emerges in a pink, zebra-print bathrobe. A shower cap covers her massive curlers, and her glasses are fogged from the lingering humidity.

She smiles, gesturing toward the door. "All yours!"

I lock myself inside, eager to make my escape. The digital clock on the counter reads 6:52. Crapsticks. I'm behind schedule. I flip the shower on, annoyed. I make a mental note to tell my dad that since these are *his* friends, he can share *his* bathroom with them.

I'm not in the shower for even five minutes when the water turns cold, further cultivating my irritation. Do these people know our water heater is older than this blessed country?

When I'm done, I rush to my room and throw on some makeup, keeping it as natural as possible. Unfortunately for me, a colony of zits has invaded my forehead. I consider cutting my bangs to hide them, but then decide against it. With my luck, I'll end up at school sporting a hack job.

I turn to the suitcases I'd shoved in the corner of my room. I can't wear any of the clothes in there. They're all wrinkled. I resort to my closet and rifle through the outfits I left behind. Most are winter clothes, which definitely won't work since my weather app is reporting temperatures in the high nineties today.

The tops I do have aren't super trendy anymore, but I settle for a coral button-down that allows my lotus charm necklace to peek out. It was a gift from Grams on my tenth birthday, and I rarely ever take it off.

I'm reaching for my hairbrush when my fingertips accidentally knock the lid off my jewelry box. Amid the thin sterling silver chains and delicate rose gold rings lie tiny notes written on Starburst wrappers from middle school that I'd carefully tucked away. All from Alex.

I've known Alex Ramos since kindergarten—which is about as long as he's had a crush on me. Even though he was always lousy at hiding it, it never made things awkward. Our friendship was instantaneous.

Because of alphabetical assigned seating, we sat by each other in almost every class and always got in trouble for talking about *Supernatural* reruns in the middle of lectures. When we were younger, we'd borrow each other's *A Series of Unfortunate Events* books and e-mail each other about our favorite parts, graduating to texting when we both got phones in seventh grade.

But I don't want to think of Alex right now. I'm stressed enough as it is.

I close the lid of my jewelry box and let the sound of my blow dryer drown out my thoughts. When I finish, I'm hit with the scents of salty bacon and warm pancakes. If my father thinks he can win me over by cooking me breakfast on my first day of school, he's mistaken. Besides, pancakes on the first day of school were Grams's schtick. She would always make mine with chocolate chips, arranging them into the shape of a smiley face.

Thinking about how things were sends pangs of nostalgia through me.

My stomach gurgles with hunger. I went to bed without dinner last night, and now I'm starving. I don't want to give in to the pancakes, but they smell heavenly.

In the end, my appetite wins. As I walk down the stairs, I hear waves of commotion coming from the kitchen. I take a deep breath and remind myself that I'll be at school during the days, so for the most part I won't have to deal with them.

I round the corner, expecting to see my dad at the stove. But it's not him flipping flapjacks. It's Peach.

"I hope you're hungry!" She says this with enough cheer to fuel a small city. "Your dad's getting ready for his big day back, too, so I decided to make my famous pancakes."

"They're really delightful," Nonnie adds. She's sitting at our kitchen table pouring a glass of orange juice. Her hair is free from the rollers, a curly mass that looks like a gray raincloud sitting atop her head. "Almost better than sex."

Peach nearly drops the spatula. "Nonnie!"

She's probably worried about corrupting my sweet, innocent ears. I grab a bowl from the cabinet and suppress the urge to roll my eyes. "Don't worry, I'm familiar with the concept."

"This isn't exactly the breakfast conversation I wanted to walk into."

Peach's face drains of color as my dad joins us in the kitchen. He's wearing a nice blue button-up and khaki pants. His face is clean-shaven and, if I'm being honest, it's the healthiest he's looked in a long time.

I decide to make this as uncomfortable as possible. If I play it up, maybe they'll leave faster. "Yeah, I know from experience. I had *loads* of sex in Portland."

Nonnie's face lights up, clearly amused by this, but Peach looks appalled. My dad takes one look at my deadpan expression and says, "She's kidding."

I don't bother clarifying. Instead, I grab a box of cereal from the pantry. Bran Flakes, gross. But I'm determined not to give in to the niceness of pancakes. I don't want to enable them to stay any longer than they have to, and I won't be bribed with delicious breakfast food.

I feel Peach watching me as I pour my cereal. To make up for my behavior, my dad decides to lay it on thick. "Oh man, *mmmm*. This looks phenomenal."

Peach grins. She hands my father a stacked plate and passes him the syrup.

I gulp down my cereal like it's the most delectable meal on this good earth. Nonnie watches me. She's still wearing her floppy kitten slippers.

"Is it your plumbing that's backed up?"

I shoot her a confused glance. "What?"

"You know." She gestures to her stomach. "Constipation?"

I almost choke on my cereal.

"Because Bran Flakes are good for that, you know."

Oh my god. I have to get out of here.

"Fiber helps," she adds.

I let my empty bowl clatter in the sink. Like I'd ever take advice from someone who still wears kitten slippers.

My backpack is sitting by my desk upstairs, but when I come back downstairs I notice my keys are missing from the key rack. Weird. That's where my dad leaves my set for the old Corolla. After he upgraded to the Nissan last year, the Corolla was promised to me once I earned my license. Since I passed my driving test in Portland, I am now legally allowed to come and go as I please.

I look on the side table, but they aren't there, either. They're also not on the coffee table in the living room. Sighing, I check the clock. It's almost eight, which means I have thirty minutes to get to school and pick up my schedule. But more importantly, I have to find Whitney, Lin, and Raegan. I know when I see them the craziness of these last twenty-four hours will dissolve.

I pop my head back into the kitchen. "Where are my car keys?"

My dad chews his bite of pancakes before answering. "I don't want you driving with your Oregon license. Everything on that car is registered in Texas." He sets his fork down. "I'll take you to the DMV and then you can start driving yourself. How's that sound?"

He must be joking. I'd rather consume Bran Flakes for the rest of my life than sit through a torturous trip to the DMV with *my father.*

"Besides," he continues, "I let Saylor borrow it this morning. He has an interview."

"That's *my* car." I know I sound ungrateful, but I don't care.

His face grows serious. "Driving is a privilege, Kira."

Now he chooses to play the authority card? Right. He didn't seem to care how I got to school all those months ago. I'm surprised he even knows I have my license. Aunt June must have told him. She's the one who enrolled me in Driver's Ed over the summer.

I cross my arms. "You could have asked me."

His eyes harden. I know I'm pushing it. "I figured I would drop you off on the way to work."

Anger slides up my veins. I'm going to be the only junior whose parent still drops them off curbside along with the rest of the freshmen and sophomores. No way. I refuse to look like a loser on my first day back. Besides, juniors and seniors have their own parking lot. That's where everyone hangs out before school starts. I can't just waltz up without a vehicle. I'll look pathetic.

This was my one opportunity of freedom. I can already picture my dad hounding me at the DMV about everything I learned in driving school. And—oh no. Will I have to retake the test? If I do, it'll just be another hassle that he's caused me.

"I'll give you a ride after breakfast," he tells me.

I am so not ready to endure another car ride with him. "I'm walking."

Before he has the chance to argue, I head out the door, slamming it loudly behind me.

FOUR

I DON'T WALK. AT LEAST, not all the way. I text Lin from the bus stop, and she happily agrees to come get me.

As I wait for her in the humid morning sun, I can feel my hair frizzing in the damp air. What a waste of a blow dry. I use a hair tie from my wrist to pull it back into a ponytail. Trickles of sweat fall down the back of my neck. I silently curse my dad. If he'd let me drive, I wouldn't be standing here melting like the Wicked Witch of the West.

It doesn't take long for Lin to arrive, and when she does I seek haven in her air-conditioned Explorer. It's her mom's car, but Lin's allowed to borrow it if her mom doesn't need to run errands.

Lin squeals and launches over the armrest to pull me into a hug. I squeeze back, swelling with happiness. Her straight black hair is a few inches shorter than the last time I saw her, and she's wearing the same deep-purple cat-eye frames that she's worn for ages. She also has on a blouse that's patterned with daisies. For as long as I've known her, she's loved wearing anything with a fun pattern. Her lips are slathered in a sassy shade of pink lipstick and her eyes are lined in heavily winged eyeliner. I remember how strict Mr. Pham used to be about her makeup, but I wonder if that's changed since I've been gone.

"I'm so glad you texted!" She pulls back onto the road. "What happened to your car?"

"My dad won't let me drive until I get my Texas license," I say. It's part of the truth, anyway. "How have you been? And everyone else? I feel like I'm so behind."

Lin's smile fades a little. "Uh, well, same I guess. Raegan is President of Leadership Council this year—oh, but you probably knew that. She posts, like, a zillion status updates about it. But I'm still a part of Academic Decathlon and Earth Club. Oh, and the dance team is getting new uniforms this year—at least that's what Whitney and Raegan told me."

I nod along, but something feels off. Lin nervously flicks her gaze over at me every few seconds like I'm a chemistry experiment and she's studying me for a reaction. It feels awkward. I don't want it to feel awkward. WHY does it feel awkward?

"What about you?" she continues. "How was Portland?"

"Lonely," I admit. "I made one friend the entire time I was there. It wasn't home, you know?"

"Yeah." Lin has lived here her whole life, too. We've never found Cedarville's small town constraining. "How's your dad? Is it weird being home with him?"

Weird is an understatement. The current state of my living

environment is borderline bizarre. For half a second, my brain wants to spit out the truth. I want to tell Lin how Saylor stole my car and about Nonnie's funky cat slippers and how Peach's personality is like a creampuff, sickly sweet. I wish I could tell her how strange it is having a dad who's acting like, well, an actual dad.

But I don't.

"Yeah," I say instead. "It's weird."

Lin adjusts the collar of her daisy-covered blouse, suddenly growing quiet. I can tell something else is on her mind. Or is it me? Maybe I *should* have texted her sooner. I guess I expected things would naturally pick up where they left off.

When she pulls into the parking lot, I'm relieved to see a sea of people I know. Familiar faces! Recognizable territory! I never thought I would be so happy to see the plain brick walls of this school again.

Lin parks, but she doesn't get out right away. "Um," she starts, her voice hesitant. "Before we go in . . . there's something you should know."

Lin is suddenly serious. Lin is *never* serious. Well, except when she's running through her decathlon flashcards. I wonder if she's worried that I won't be in National Honor Society with her. I'm pretty confident I can bring my grades up this year. That's the plan, anyway. Or maybe she thinks I won't be rejoining Earth Club? But that's ridiculous. We had tons of fun freshman year.

"What is it?" I finally ask.

"Whitney . . . kindofstarteddatingJay."

She says this all in a rush, like ripping off a Band-Aid. I feel my jaw go slack. No. I can't have heard her right. My hearing must be temporarily impaired from Queen's greatest hits blasting through the hall this morning.

I stare at her. Her expression hasn't changed.

"She—*what?*"

Lin turns off the Explorer, but she doesn't look at me when she repeats it. "She started dating Jay."

My heart sinks like a brick in a bathtub. That absolutely cannot be right. Whitney used to make fun of Jay's buck teeth in sixth grade, and then she made fun of the crush I developed on him freshman year. It seemed like she only approved of him because he made the basketball team. But, to be fair, this did put him on the radar for a lot of girls at school.

That's why I know she would *never* in a million years date Jay. I mean, he's my boyfriend. Well, ex-boyfriend. But still. Isn't that girl code or something?

"How did—wow." I shake my head. I'm pissed. Did they not think I was ever going to come back? "I can't believe she'd do that."

"Well," I catch the defense in her voice, "I mean, you *did* break up with him. Before you left and all."

There's hurt in her words, as if I moved to Portland and left everyone behind because it was my choice.

"I never wanted to break up with him. What was I supposed to do? Make it long distance?" She knows how I felt about that. Even *she* agreed it wouldn't work. "I didn't know when I was coming back."

"So you can't really be surprised that he moved on," she argues.

My stomach feels like it's been drenched in battery acid. I understand her point, but I didn't expect it to hurt this much.

Lin sighs. "Look, I'm sorry. I know it sucks."

"Nobody was going to tell me?" I wonder how long they've been together without me knowing. Does he hold her hand in the dark movie theater and make tiny circles on the inside of her palm? Do they send each other good night texts? Have they made out? Or worse—

I swallow. No. I can't think about that.

"It's not like you told us anything, either." Lin folds her arms. "After you left, you pretty much dropped off the face of the earth. You never replied to our texts or answered our calls or anything. It was like you were suddenly too cool for us."

Hurt creases Lin's features. She's not wrong. I did stop replying, but only because it hurt *me* too much to see them moving on without me.

I'd sulked alone in my misery when Lin texted me details from homecoming. The pictures that Raegan and Whitney would send from dance practice made me physically ache. The "we miss you" group texts that came through when they got together at the mall on weekends made me seethe with jealousy. I wanted to be there so badly, and I thought distancing myself would make the pain easier to deal with. Turns out, it just made me a crappy friend.

"I'm sorry," I say softly.

Lin shrugs. She won't look at me.

"I am. I never thought I was too cool for you guys. It was just hard seeing you have fun without me. I didn't know how to deal."

Lin picks at her light-pink nail polish. "I guess I understand that. The whole situation with your dad . . . it sucked."

Lin was with me the morning I got the call from the police

station. We'd been in the kitchen making cinnamon rolls per our usual tradition when she spent the night. My dad wasn't home, but I didn't think twice about it. He'd been drinking less the last two weeks, which was why I asked Lin to spend the night in the first place. I assumed he was on a coffee run.

When the officer told me to come down to the station, I panicked. My anxiety levels skyrocketed, and I couldn't process anything else he was saying. But Lin gently took the phone from me and when she hung up, she told me we needed to go. All I could think was *please don't be dead, please don't be dead.* I'd already lost Grams. I couldn't imagine losing anyone else.

I don't know what I would have done if Lin hadn't been with me. She took me up to my room and threw me a pair of clean jeans as I changed out of my Muppet pajamas. Then she called Jay. I heard her explain that his mom was on her way. She would take me to the station.

Don't worry, she kept repeating.

How could I not?

Jay's mom didn't pry as she drove. When I got in she leaned over and squeezed my arm.

"It'll be okay, sugar."

I realized these are things people said when there was nothing left to say because they think lies are better than silence.

Even though the entire situation was awful and shameful, I was thankful Jay's mom stayed to talk to the police with me. My dad had been found standing in the middle of the McCarthy and Jettison intersection—a congested area that was always clogged with traffic as cars merged onto the highway. He was drunk, they told me. Mumbling nonsense. Stumbling to stay upright.

The officer said someone had called in for help. They saw a dog in his arms, a tiny poodle. She was shaking, clawing at my dad's arms as vehicles whizzed past. That's the part that sank the knife deep in my heart. I knew the poodle was Millie, who belonged to Mrs. Jenkins next door. But that wasn't what broke me. It was that this innocent dog couldn't escape. She must have been so scared—terrified—and the only person she could depend on for her safety was the person who'd carried her into danger in the first place.

The cops had to block the intersection for a few minutes to get my dad and Millie safely to the sidewalk. They'd arrested him for being drunk and disorderly in public. My dad tried to tell them he found Millie in our yard that morning. He was certain he was only trying to return her back to Mrs. Jenkins's house.

He was two miles from home.

They questioned me about his drinking habits, but I was too shocked by this situation to answer. The last several months I'd told myself that he wasn't that bad, that it only seemed bad on the outside because no one understood the pain he was going through after losing his mother.

Jay's mom had sat me down in the two empty chairs in the station's lobby. "Honey," she started. "I've arranged for you to talk with a social worker. She'll be here in a few hours." Her concerned expression was the first of many pitying looks I received after that. "If you want, I can stay with you until she arrives."

I shook my head. "That's okay, but thank you."

She nodded. But before she went home, she gave me a long hug.

Margaret, my social worker, contacted Aunt June once my dad was released. My aunt flew out the next day, but I didn't go home after I left the station. Lin let me sleep in her room on her trundle bed. She didn't pressure me with questions. Instead she took my mind off it by talking about Harry Styles and showing me funny YouTube videos.

Even after months of me ignoring her texts, she's still here for me. She still picked me up with no questions asked.

There's a hard lump in my throat. I didn't think it was possible to feel so lousy this early in the morning.

"Are you okay?" she asks me. "I mean ... you feel safe at home and everything?"

Even though there are three strangers living in my house, *I'm* the one who feels like a stranger. Although it's ironic, I don't feel unsafe.

A tiny thought of uncertainty digs its way into my brain: I'm not sure if Margaret would feel the same way.

"Yeah," I tell her. The letters my dad wrote me during treatment were heavy with apologies. Even though that doesn't change anything between us, I believe he's sorry enough to not let anything like that happen again.

"Good." Lin fiddles with the strap of her lilac book bag. "Are you going to join Earth Club again this year? If we don't have at least twelve members, Principal Lawrence is pulling the plug."

Since I was a part of exactly zero clubs at my school in Portland and completed a whopping total of zilch extracurricular activities, rejoining Earth Club will help fluff up my college applications.

Besides, I need to spend more time with Lin. It's clear I've knocked her down a few notches on the importance pole.

"Count me in."

She smiles, and her approval makes me feel good. I think of all the things she used to tell me that she didn't share with Whitney or Raegan. About liking David Cornwell, who was a red flag in Whitney's book because he told the faculty they should invest more of the school's budget in Academic Decathlon versus the dance team. Or about how she actually loves going to engineering conventions with her parents, even though she says otherwise in front of our friends.

I want to get back to the close, unbreakable friendship we used to have. I promise myself I'm going to be a better friend from now on, no matter what it takes.

FIVE

I PART WAYS WITH LIN in the auditorium as we line up according to our last names. The plan is to quickly get my schedule so we can continue to catch up before first period. I'm not excessively eager to see Whitney anymore, which sounds horrible, I know. But swiping my boyfriend—*ex*-boyfriend, whatever—and not telling me is a lot to process first thing in the morning.

"Um," I say as soon as I'm handed my schedule. SENECA, KIRA is printed neatly at the top, but the classes are definitely not correct. For one thing, English I is a freshman class. I need English III. And Geometry? I took that sophomore year. "This isn't right."

The attendant sighs, as if this isn't the first time she's heard this today. "Main office. Go talk to your guidance counselor."

Of course. I should have expected this with the kind of morning I'm having.

I step out of line and attempt to find Lin in the crowd, but it's impossible with the whole school in here. I'm stopped multiple times by old Wavette teammates and other students in my grade who say they're happy I'm back and ask a few polite questions about Portland. It's nice to feel so welcome, especially after my abrupt departure, but I don't want to be late to my first class, so I try and hurry along.

If this were any other day, the grayish-blue walls and scuffed linoleum would depress me. But today I let myself soak it all in. I'm enthralled by the rows of navy lockers and the slightly cheesy motivational posters tacked to the walls. I relish the echoing of the morning announcements that are being ignored by groups of friends loudly comparing schedules. I'm obsessed with the normality of it all. I will never again refer to this fine institution as prison.

When I walk into the front office, I immediately spot dozens of students in the waiting area. A stressed secretary barely acknowledges me before grabbing my schedule and jabbing her keyboard like it recently wronged her.

"Let me guess." She pushes her rimless glasses up the bridge of her nose before looking up at me. "Your schedule's wrong?"

I wonder if she can read minds.

She lets out a frustrated sigh. "Our system bugged out last night. Have a seat and I'll call your name when your guidance counselor is available."

I look around the waiting room for a place to sit and quickly realize that's not going to happen. All the chairs are taken, and a lot of students have already claimed the corners as standing space. I don't recognize many of them, so I figure most must be freshmen.

I end up standing awkwardly next to the front door. I'm tempted to pull out my phone and text Lin or Raegan, but I don't want to risk having it taken away on my first day. The secretary looks like she's ready to snap at anyone who steps out of line.

"Ramos?" she calls.

I freeze. Wait, Ramos? Alex Ramos?

My eyes fly to the back corner of the room just as Alex stands up. His gaze falls on mine, and his eyes widen in surprise. But before either of us can say anything, the secretary ushers him toward the guidance counselor's office.

Here's something I haven't mentioned about Alex Ramos: At one point in time, I had a crush on him.

But then freshman year happened.

Alex was unofficially inducted into the theater kid clique while I became a part of the Wavettes, but we'd always meet out front after school to wait for our parents to pick us up. And because my dad was constantly late, Alex's mom began to offer me rides home, which I gratefully accepted.

This wasn't a big deal at first. During those car rides I'd tease him about getting paint on his Converse from painting theater props and he'd threaten to tell my friends that I still listened to One Direction. But there was one Friday where my mood had turned sour. My dad had stumbled home late the previous evening reeking of beer and causing me to worry even more about his emotional state over Grams.

"What's wrong?" Alex had asked when he sat down on the brick wall next to me. I noticed today his Converse were splattered with streaks of gray.

"Nothing," I replied, the same thing I'd told Raegan and Whitney and Lin.

He just stared at me.

"What?" I finally snapped.

Instead of getting defensive, his eyes softened. "It's okay if you don't want to tell me."

I looked at him, realizing just how much he paid attention. Even though my friends knew about Grams passing, he was the one who continued to text me every evening to help ease my mind away from my sad thoughts. I wasn't as guarded as I thought I was, at least not around Alex. It'd always been easy to talk to him.

So I took a deep breath.

"It's just...my dad." Then I told him about his occasional binge drinking and how he was always late to get me because he'd usually go straight for the beer after work and pass out.

"Anyway," I'd finished. "He's still torn up about Grams. It'll be okay."

"Well," Alex kicked the heels of his sneakers against the wall. "If you need anything..."

A new kind of warmth spread through my chest. "Thank you."

He tugged on the back of his beanie, a small smile forming at the corner of his mouth.

Later that night, my phone chimed with an incoming text. My heartbeat tripled when I saw who it was from.

ALEX: you watching Crime Boss?

Face flushed, I typed:

ME: Detective Fay's season 6 acting is lazy. and these explosions are WEAK

Seconds later, another chime.

ALEX: lol

ALEX: you know I meant what I said earlier?

The warmth in my chest was back, a strange new feeling that made my heart flutter. I believed that he cared for me, and that meant more than I could even begin to say.

ME: I know

I tried to fall asleep later that night, but my mind spun in circles around Alex. I'd always brushed aside his crush like it was a pair of pants he'd soon outgrow. I never expected I'd return the feelings he'd had for me for so long.

I kept these emotions to myself for the rest of the week, but the original brushfire quickly burst into a white-hot flame. I yearned for the moment when he'd slip beside me in English and turn toward me to say hi. I found myself wanting to prolong our conversations before we had to part ways for our next class. When I spotted him waiting for me by the brick wall after school, my tumbling heartbeat wouldn't quiet until the moment I stepped through my front door.

I made the decision to ask him to our freshman Sadie Hawkins dance a week later. I could picture him sputtering through his response, that modest smile spreading across his cheeks as he said yes.

This would have gone perfectly if he hadn't said yes to Lacey Woodward's invitation first.

I found out on our ride home together. He explained that she'd cornered him after theater rehearsal and asked.

"Oh," I said, my initial shock turning to numbness. "And you—?"

"Yeah, um," Alex looked at the car floor as he said this. "I said yeah."

It was scary how quickly my hurt turned into jealousy. He said yes to Lacey? *Lacey?* Did he forget that she totally made fun of him in fifth grade after he had to go to the nurse for his asthma? Or that she'd called us losers for always obsessing over *Supernatural*? On the Richter scale of anger, I was a nine.

One of my biggest regrets was texting him to tell him I didn't need rides from his mom anymore. But because he was Alex, he texted me twice to see if I was sure. At the time I was. I couldn't sit in a car and pine for him knowing he had feelings for Lacey and not for me. It wasn't until later that I realized he'd been in this exact same position with me for the last few years. Without any success, *of course* he'd moved on.

So I became preoccupied with dating Jay and after the weirdness of Sadie Hawkins was over, Alex and I ended up staying friends. Even if we weren't as close as before, we'd still sometimes pass notes to each other on discarded Tropical Starburst wrappers and text about *Crime Boss* and the small snippets I told him about my dad. Things I never bothered telling Jay.

I stare at the closed door of the counselor's office. Alex looked surprised to see me. Was it a good surprised? Bad surprised? My stomach sinks. Of course it's the latter—especially after what he told me right before I left for Portland.

I'm so engrossed in my thoughts that I don't hear the sound of the door bursting open behind me. Before I have time to step aside, it hits me on the side of the head with a *thwump*.

"Oh shit—" a voice says.

Pain sears at my temple. I groan, immediately enraged. Maybe

I shouldn't have been standing in the way, but who the hell swings a door open with that much momentum?

"I'm so—*Kira?*"

I glance up when I hear my name.

Oh god.

There he is.

Jay.

I'm clutching the side of my head, but through the spots I immediately recognize his concerned eyes and neatly cropped hair. I blink. He's still there. He wears a slightly amused smile on his face, complete with a tiny mole on the edge of his lip. Definitely Jay. My Jay.

Wait. No. Not *my* Jay.

I blame being caught off-guard for my brilliant reply, "Ow."

"I'm sorry." He takes a step toward me and reaches out like there's something he can do to stop the throbbing. When he realizes there's not, he drops his hand. "I didn't see you."

I shrug it off and lower my own hand. "I was in the way."

He's staring at me, not bothering to hide it. I feel a stirring deep down in my stomach, remembering all the times he used to look at me that way.

"I'm not going to lie. You're the last person I expected to accidentally hit with the door." He has an easygoing smile. It's effortless for him. "I didn't even know you were back."

He looks different. Of course he looks different. It's been eleven months. He must have grown at least two inches. The same Cedarville basketball shirt he always wore freshman year fits him slightly tighter, showcasing his very, *very* nice arms. Basketball has certainly been good to him.

I can't stop staring at him.

I need to stop staring at him.

I blink and say, "I got in last night."

The secretary clears her throat, an obvious gesture to gain his attention. Jay glances over at her and then holds his schedule up to me. "They put me in art history instead of basketball."

"They gave me mostly freshman classes."

"Holding you to your true potential?"

Without thinking, I give him a playful shove. He laughs, but I'm alarmed by my extent of physical contact. Heat flushes from my toes to the very tip of my brain, but I don't think he notices because he's already walking over to the front desk.

My gaze drops to my outfit. I should have tried a little harder this morning. All of a sudden, my coral blouse feels boxy and unflattering. And—oh god. We were standing so close. Could he see the unfortunate breakout across my forehead? Wait, what does it mean if I'm worried about my zits around Jay? I wasn't worried about it around Lin.

I'm debating whether my butt is comparable to the size of Jupiter in these jeans when Jay comes back and stands next to me.

"So," he says, sliding his hands in his pockets. "Your dad is back?"

"Yeah," I say, and we fall into an awkward pause of silence.

Jay knows my family. When my dad first started AA and seemed to be doing better, Jay would come over for dinner and watch all my *Crime Boss* with us. One weekend he even helped us assemble my

IKEA nightstand I ordered online and laughed at all my dad's tool puns.

"I'm so glad we didn't *screw* this up."

Jay high fived him. "You *nailed* that joke, Mr. Seneca."

"STOP," I yelled, but I was laughing. "You're worse than him!"

But when my dad's drinking binges worsened, I stopped inviting Jay over. I knew Jay was concerned, but I played a role of overconfidence. *Of course* I was okay. *Sure* my dad was attending his AA meetings. Everything was fine.

It wasn't, obviously. I was juggling dance practice and my schoolwork and making sure there were groceries in the fridge and a hot dinner on the table. The nights my dad downed three or more six-packs, I would set my phone alarm for midnight, two a.m., and four a.m. so I could make sure he hadn't fallen asleep on his back in case he threw up. I started hiding his car keys when I noticed there was nothing but beer cans in the recycle bin.

Jay found me at Lin's house after I left the police station that day. His mom told him what happened, and I was so ashamed and embarrassed over my dad's worsening behavior that I burst into tears. He wrapped his arms around me as we stood out on Lin's front porch. In that moment, that was all I needed.

"It's supposed to be better this time," I say, but my words are laced with cynicism.

Jay shifts his weight. I don't want our first exchange to be uncomfortable so I say, "Anyway. I'm glad I'm back in Cedarville."

He leans toward me, just slightly. "Yeah? Too rainy for you up there?"

Subject change. *Finally.*

I grin. "No one even carries umbrellas! I felt like such a tourist."

"Let me guess. You decided to ditch the umbrella to try and blend in?"

"I invested in a very fashionable raincoat."

Jay laughs. "Fashionable raincoat? That sounds like an oxymoron."

"They exist."

Jay stares at me. A beat passes. Two. "I'm really glad you're back."

My heart warms for half a second. He's probably only saying that to be polite. Definitely not in an I'm-glad-you're-back-let's-pick-up-where-we-left-off sort of way.

Right?

"I am, too," I say.

"Are you trying out for the Wavettes this year?"

"Yeah." I fiddle with the strap of my shoulder bag. "I actually wanted to talk to Raegan and Whitney about tryouts, but I haven't seen them yet."

Jay's amused grin dissolves as if he's swallowed something bitter. That's when it hits me. There will be no picking up where we left off with Jay. Not when he's dating Whitney, whose name suddenly tastes like charcoal.

I cringe at my own thoughts. *She's one of your best friends.*

"Right." Jay distinctly appears uncomfortable. He won't make eye contact with me. "I'm sure they'll help you with the new dances and . . . whatever."

I'm losing him. Whatever connection we had minutes ago is gone. I have to say something to fix it.

"Definitely missed all those high kicks."

Jay's eyes move to my legs, then he flushes. OH GOD. I can only imagine the mental image I've just provided him. I need a subject change.

"And those—uh—BIG comfy Wavette sweatshirts," I blurt.

Jay gives me a confused stare.

"AND SWEATPANTS."

That should do it.

"Uh, you miss . . . the sweatpants?"

I give a very enthusiastic nod.

"I remember you were wearing those when I came over that one Christmas," he says. "When it snowed, remember?"

I nod, surprised he actually remembers. We had a very rare white Christmas, and Jay came over to give me a present. I was a little disappointed at the thoughtlessness of the iTunes gift card, but I tried not to let it show. We ended up sitting on the porch swing drinking hot cocoa and watching the short-lived snowfall that had graced the town. It all felt very magical.

"It seems like forever ago," I say without really thinking.

"Yeah," Jay agrees.

We make eye contact. I want to tell him I miss him, but I think of Whitney. Lin is right. I can't expect things to be the way that they were. Especially since I neglected my friends for so long. And Jay. Obviously he moved on. I mean, he's one of the most attractive guys in Cedarville. It doesn't hurt he's grown a few inches, too.

I want to tell him that I hope we can be friends. Before I can get the words out, the secretary calls, "Kira Seneca?"

I turn to Jay and give a light shrug of my shoulders. "That's me."

"The one and only." He smiles. Ugh. Why can't his smile be less attractive? That would help. "See you at lunch?"

My mood instantly soars. Lunch! That's one shred of normalcy I can grasp on to. It's comforting that he still wants me to sit at our usual table. Maybe some things haven't changed that much.

"Okay," I say, then smile. "See you."

SIX

IT TAKES THIRTY MINUTES TO fix my schedule. The process would have been much faster if they could access my Portland transcripts, but the system sucked those down the technological black hole. Everything had to be redone by shuffling through my files and inputting them into the computer. Nightmare.

All in all, my schedule isn't the worst. I missed first period English III with Mrs. Lee, but that's fine by me because I've heard she's tough. I don't have any of my friends in second period Spanish class, which is a bummer. I try not to fall asleep listening to Señora Martínez read us our syllabus word for word. She even makes us tape them on our binders so we "never miss turning in an assignment," as if we're six instead of sixteen.

The irony of all ironies happens when I walk into third period AP US History and see Jay. I remind myself the divine powers of destiny are not interfering with my life as he motions for me to sit by him. Despite the stares from my classmates, I do. I keep my body language casual because I am *so totally cool* with Jay and Whitney, even though I haven't seen her yet.

I'm starving by the time lunch rolls around. Lin texts me as I'm walking to the cafeteria, letting me know she's waiting for me in the pizza line. Relief eases through me. I'm thankful that our small lunchtime rituals haven't completely disappeared. I tell her I left my money in my locker, but I'll be there ASAP.

I make my way through crowds of students until I reach my locker. It's a lower locker (ugh) so I have to squat to open it. I pull out a few bills that I keep in my dance bag. I don't know why I brought it today. I haven't tried out for Wavettes yet and I didn't know if my Dance III elective would be approved (luckily it was), but it was sitting by my backpack like it belonged there, so normal and familiar. I would have felt naked leaving the house without it.

When I enter the lunchroom, I notice not much has changed. The walls are already covered in this year's hand-painted cheerleading posters. Drama flyers are taped to the double doors promoting the fall play. The circular tables designed to fit eight (but *can* fit ten— we've done it) stand before me in their blue plastic glory. Even the weird, mixed-food cafeteria smell is unenticingly the same.

Our table is in the left-hand corner near one of the many windows. I'm relieved to see Jay, Raegan, Whitney, Lin, Colton, and Breck already sitting there. From afar I notice Breck's braids are tied back with a recognizable red-and-black Cedarville cheerleader's ribbon, and I wonder if he's begun dating someone on the squad. It's a minor detail, but it's a subtle reminder of how much I've missed.

As I walk closer, I realize Whitney occupies the seat next to

Jay—my unofficial seat. It makes sense. They're dating now, so she should have the seat next to him. I can't help the tingle of irritation that courses through me. Am I that easily replaced?

No. I'm being too sensitive.

"Kira!" Raegan leaps out of her seat, bumping the table with her hip as she reaches to hug me. She's wearing a black skirt and a floral top with a pale green cardigan over it—one of many she owns. Cardigans have always been her thing. "I'm *so* beyond happy you're back!"

I squeeze her tightly. Raegan is one of my oldest friends. We used to play together with our Betty Spaghetty dolls when we were little, and she would always make hers run for president. But Betty Spaghetty pantsuits didn't exist, so she had to dress her up in the standard neon short-shorts. In middle school, she wrote an outraged letter to the Ohio Art Company suggesting they should highly consider evolving Betty from a fashion queen to a strong, independent woman figure for little girls to look up to. That's just the type of person Raegan is. So it doesn't surprise me that she's made Leadership Council President this year.

Through her springy coils I see Whitney. She looks uncomfortable. Is it bad that I feel justified? Maybe.

But it's *Whitney*. She's the one who half-carried me to the nurse when I sprained my ankle at dance camp in middle school. When we were eight, she talked my dad into letting us go to her uncle's ranch so I could finally learn how to ride a horse like a true Texan. She's been there through all my fallout crushes and tears over failed tests and through all the frustrations with my dad.

I can't hold Jay against her. We've been through so much. Besides, I was the one who cut off communication. It's a miracle they're all still talking to me.

When Raegan releases me, I bounce over and hug Whitney. I feel her tension dissolve, and I wonder if she can sense my own relief.

"I'm glad you're back," she says when she lets me go. Then she gestures for me to sit in the empty seat between her and Lin. "How was Portland?"

Lin slides a paper plate with a large pepperoni pizza slice on it. I thank her and hand her three bucks. "Uneventful," I say truthfully. "I missed you guys."

"We missed you, too," Breck says, but he's not looking at me. He's staring at his own reflection using the front-facing camera on his phone and stroking his smooth, dark skin near his cheek.

"Breck is growing a beard," Whitney explains in a very unenthusiastic voice.

Breck looks up at the sound of his name. He leans closer to me in case I need to further inspect his patchy facial hair, which is not even close to a beard. "It's coming in nicely, see?" He stares back at his phone. "I'm going to keep growing it."

Whitney rolls her eyes. "Don't. You look diseased."

Breck ignores her, looking at me. "I'm trying to appear more distinguished. A beard is a sign of maturity and—" He glances at Lin. "I'm trying to convince this one to let me on Academic Decathlon."

Lin appears unmoved. "We already have enough for Varsity."

I know from Lin that decathlon is ranked by your GPA, the

top-tier being Honors, then Scholastic, then Varsity, and you have to have a mix of all three in order for your team to compete.

"Ah, but I'm a Scholastic student." Breck leans over the table. "And I know you need a replacement since Araceli graduated."

"Yeah, we need a *dedicated* replacement."

While they bicker about Breck's commitment to both basketball and decathlon, Whitney turns to me. Her wavy brown hair has been cut into layers that frame her face, and she's ditched her heavy concealer for a more natural-looking powder. I didn't think it was possible for her to get any prettier.

"Are you going out for Wavettes this year?" she asks me.

"You *have* to!" Raegan squeals. She digs her fork into the packaged salads we swore we'd never buy because the chicken in them looked like cow brains. But I notice she and Whitney are both eating them. "I'm co-captain, did I tell you that? The team voted for me!"

"Only because nobody wanted Brianne Bossy-Ass as co-captain," Whitney says. Is that jealousy in her voice?

Raegan lets the comment slide. "Tryouts are next week."

Although I was never a fan of the grueling practices, I loved performing Friday nights with everyone. The bus rides to the games were the best part. We'd blast music and make silly faces for pictures we'd later post on Instagram. I wonder if this is Whitney's way of letting me know she still wants me to be part of that.

"I'll be there," I tell them.

"She's definitely joining Earth Club," Lin brags. She's never been on dance team with us, and sometimes I think she feels left out. Earth Club has always been our thing.

I smile at Lin. She looks so happy. How could I ever have stopped talking to her? It was stupid. I was so self-absorbed in my miserable life that I didn't realize they were only trying to stay connected to me.

Colton leans over, trying to steal one of Lin's pepperonis off her pizza. It's an unsurprising maneuver coming from him. He was always doing this freshman year, even *after* eating two entire burgers by himself.

She pulls her plate away just in time. "Eat your own food."

He looks glumly at his empty tray. "I did."

Colton has been Jay and Breck's friend for as long as I can remember. He's one of the poor souls who's had the misfortune of wearing braces for the last three years and counting, and he's always wearing obscure band T-shirts with a long-sleeved flannel over them. Today's shirt reads BLOODSPURT, which almost makes me lose my appetite.

I try not to lose my appetite *even more* when he starts picking food out of his braces.

Raegan makes a grand gesture of flipping her spiral open.

Jay groans. "Already?"

I have no idea what's going on.

Whitney elbows him in the ribs. "Be nice. She's president this year."

Oh. I get it. She's in charge of the Leadership Council agenda.

"Thank you," Raegan tells Whitney, then she sweeps her gaze over the table. "You all better be nice to me, or I'm not inviting you to the White House when I'm the first black female president."

Colton's head shoots up. "Will you have a personal chef?"

Whitney gives him a look like, *duh*.

Colton elbows Jay. "Yeah, man, be nice."

"I can't fall behind." She taps her pen on the empty page. "We're starting to plan the homecoming dance."

I find myself repeating Jay's question. "Already?"

Raegan gives me an exasperated look. "It's so much planning! I didn't even realize how much." She scribbles something in her notebook. "You'll be on decoration committee, right? Whitney and Lin already told me they would."

"It's a lot more fun than it sounds," Lin promises, swatting Colton's hand away as he unsuccessfully attempts another pepperoni. "Last year we brought our dresses with us and got ready in the girls' locker room when we were done setting up."

"I almost forgot about that!" Whitney's eyes go wide with amusement. She leans over and grabs Lin's arm, her cluster of thin silver bracelets tinkling into each other. "Oh my god! Remember how Bethany Weaver forgot her bra? And we had to cut her sports bra into a bandeau so she could wear it with her strapless dress?"

Lin laughs, adjusting her glasses. "Because she refused to NOT wear one!"

Raegan looks up from her notebook. "And remember we made Vanessa run to Walgreens because we all needed extra bobby pins? But she also came back with that giant bag of gummy bears—"

As I listen to the three of them reminisce over last year's memories, I can't help feeling like a sock left behind in the dryer. But I fake a smile and pretend I'm interested even though it pains me to hear about all the fun I missed.

I'm so deeply involved in my self-induced pity party that I don't register what Raegan asked me and she has to repeat it.

"I asked if you wanted to come over this weekend and help make posters for Spirit Week." I know this isn't for another month, but Raegan likes to be ahead of the game. She starts studying for exams at the end of October even though they aren't until mid-December. "Then you guys can sleep over after."

Colton pumps his fist in the air. *"All riiiiight!"*

Raegan rolls her eyes. "Not you."

He shrugs like he gave it his best shot.

It's been so long since we've all had a sleepover. We would spend most of the time scrolling through Netflix looking for a show to binge on but we'd end up not watching anything, choosing to gossip and lurk on classmates' Twitter accounts instead. That sounds like exactly what I need right now.

"I'm in," I say.

"Ugh, I have pre-calc next," Whitney moans, staring at her schedule. "Do you think it's too late to switch into Algebra II?"

"The office is a nightmare," Jay says with a mouthful of baked potato. "Kira and I were stuck there for thirty minutes this morning."

Whitney's eyes slowly travel to mine, then back to Jay. This is the first time he's acknowledged me. Well, indirectly acknowledged me. I wonder if lunch is as weird for him as it is for me. Not too long ago, it was me sitting in Whitney's seat. I try and suppress those thoughts, but I can't help feeling a sting of jealousy underneath the surface.

"You guys were in the office together?" Whitney says, her words careful. I can tell Jay didn't share this information with her before lunch.

Jay doesn't seem to notice her tone. He shovels another forkful of baked potato into his mouth, so I'm forced to speak for the both of us. "The system went down last night. It messed up our schedules and we had to wait to fix them."

Whitney nods, but she doesn't say anything else about it. Instead she rests her hand on Jay's arm. This gets his attention. I have to look away.

"We still on for after school?" she asks him.

They've already made plans. Just the two of them. This shouldn't send throbbing pangs through my chest, but it does.

Jay chugs the rest of his Gatorade, then says, "Can't. We have practice."

Whitney frowns. I know it's horrible of me, but I feel oddly satisfied.

"We have our Wavettes meeting anyway," Raegan says, then throws an apologetic look my way. "Don't worry. You'll be on the team in no time."

Lin smacks her head. "Crap. I just remembered the first decathlon meeting is after school." She glares at Breck. "See? Your basketball schedule is already interfering with decathlon, and you aren't even on the team."

Breck gives her his most charming grin. "I could work it out. Trust me, Linny."

"Don't call me that." She looks at me. "Sorry, Kira. Will you be able to catch a ride home?"

"Sure," I say confidently, but my throat's gone tight. I don't know why I feel like crying. Maybe it's because everyone else has lives after school and I don't. Or because no one has brought up our post–first day of school tradition of getting Slurpees from 7-Eleven and binge-watching bad sitcoms while we procrastinate doing homework.

Raegan takes a huge bite of her cow brain salad.

I cringe. "Why are you eating that?"

"It's not as bad as it looks." She stabs some lettuce with her fork. "Besides, I'm trying to cut out greasy food. It makes me break out."

I glance down at the rest of my pizza. Was that a hint? Has she noticed zit city on my forehead? I should have cut my stupid bangs this morning.

No, I'm overanalyzing things. But still. We never cared about stuff like that before. It makes me wonder what else I've missed.

SEVEN

I END UP BUMMING A ride home from Colton of all people. His truck is littered with toothpicks from his disgusting teeth-picking habit, and he has a bloodied zombie air freshener dangling from his rearview mirror. I'm tempted to ask what scents zombies come in, but ultimately decide I don't want to know.

I'm still wallowing in self-pity, so I don't mind when Colton cranks up his screamo music instead of making conversation. He shakes his head to the whines of the guitars as he drives, his long hair flying into his eyes. I clutch my armrest in case I need to brace for impact.

"Left on Rosebrush?" he asks when the song ends.

"Actually, can you drop me off at the 7-Eleven?"

Colton nods and makes a right. I don't want anyone near my house. Not when Peach, Nonnie, and Saylor are around. I can't chance anything getting back to Margaret, especially since she has the final say in sending me back to Portland with Aunt June.

When Colton pulls up to the 7-Eleven parking lot, I get out and shut the door. Before he drives off, he rolls down his window and sticks his head out. His light-brown hair is tangled from his elaborate thrashing.

"You sure you don't want a ride home?" His fingers drum on the body of the car. "I can wait."

Offering is beyond chivalrous for Colton, who doesn't think twice about calling girls *dude* and publicly refers to his man-part as the Socket Rocket. But I know he wants to get straight to his band practice where he can re-create the same thrashing music that I had the pleasure of listening to on our short drive.

I wave him off. "Nah, this is perfect."

"Oh, hey." Colton leans over on his arm. "Our first show is coming up in October. You should come. I'll text you the details."

"Yeah, okay," I hear myself say, my mind still processing everything that happened today. More specifically, Whitney and Jay. Jay-and-Whitney. Jitney?

My stomach roils.

I give him a small wave. "Thanks again."

Colton nods, then blasts his music before driving away.

I'm only a five-minute walk from home, so it's not a big deal. I know it's pitiful to honor the Slurpee tradition by myself, but I'm in a mopey mood and don't feel like going straight to my house. I still feel the blow from the Jay and Whitney news. It was wrong of me to neglect my friends, but isn't going out with your friend's ex wrong, too?

I wander down the cool aisles of 7-Eleven. I have to be okay with this. Everyone else already is. If I'm not, I won't look like a good friend—and I already earned that label when I didn't keep in touch with them in Portland.

I reach for the waxy, plastic cup and watch the dispenser distribute my red slush. I pay, then step out into the sticky afternoon and make my way home.

When I open the front door, I'm greeted by a warm, garlicky scent. It has to be my dad's homemade marinara sauce. I would always beg him to make it for me when I was little, and he'd tell me that if I ate too much I'd start growing noodles out of my nose. The nostalgia catches me off guard.

Loud laughter erupts from the kitchen, immediately bringing me back to reality. I consider which would be less painful: walking into my kitchen that's full of weird strangers my dad has brought home or rubbing chopped onions into my eyeballs.

"Is that you, Goose?" my father calls.

My shining opportunity to sneak unannounced upstairs is gone. I set my bags by the front door and head into the kitchen.

As expected, my father is leaning over an enormous pot of bubbling tomato sauce. Peach is beside him slicing a loaf of French bread. Her hair is pulled back in a giant clip and she's wearing a floral apron. And heels. I don't know a single person who could possibly be comfortable cooking in heels.

It's strange seeing so many people in Grams's kitchen. I used to find her in here after school cooking dinner. I'd start to tell her about my day, but instead of letting me stand there talking to her she'd put me to work chopping up whatever vegetable she needed.

"Hope you're hungry!" my dad says once I'm in sight. "Dinner will be ready in the next hour or so."

I wonder if I can fake cramps and avoid dinner altogether.

Nonnie is sitting on one of our barstools, transfixed by my dad's laptop screen as she watches some video on YouTube. Her navy blouse has neon-green cheetahs printed all over in an eccentric pattern. It's clear she has an obsession with multicolored safari animals. At least she's ditched the cat slippers.

"How was your day?" Peach asks, smiling. She's still wearing that too-bright magenta lipstick.

"Fine." Although I really want to just say, *Why do you even care?*

Nonnie swivels around on her barstool to face me. "What is that?"

I follow her gaze and look down at my Slurpee cup. "I stopped by 7-Eleven after school."

She frowns. "All that sugar in your teeth will have you looking like a jack-o'-lantern."

It's a joke, but it feels like an accusation. I make a huge gesture of slurping down the last bit of liquid at the bottom before throwing it in the trash.

Nonnie plays another video, and immediately I hear music starting up. From over her shoulder, I see she's watching one of Queen's live performances. As if I didn't hear enough of it this morning. When Freddie Mercury takes the stage, Nonnie claps and hollers as if he can hear her. I wonder if anyone's told her that the internet doesn't work that way.

"Peach is teaching me how to make her basil marinara sauce," my dad says. "She's a chef."

"Oh, stop." Peach swats him with the dishcloth in her hands. She turns to face me. "I'm not. I'm just a big foodie."

Nonnie waves her off. "She's being modest."

I stand there with my hands in my pockets. They're going about this so casually, as if they've lived here for years. I never thought I'd feel so awkward in my own home—a place that was once my sanctuary. Now I'd be lucky to ever find a moment's peace to watch *Crime Boss* in my ratty sweats.

The back door swings open. Saylor walks in carrying my old boom box that I haven't seen in years. His face is beaded with sweat, but he's smiling as if it's seventy outside instead of ninety.

Peach looks up from rubbing roasted garlic on the slices of bread. "How was your practice?"

I look at him, wondering what he could possibly be practicing.

"Awesome." He notices me, his face brightening. "Hey, Kira. Your dad told me you dance. You should join next time if you want."

"*You* dance?" He doesn't seem like a pirouette kind of guy.

Saylor laughs. "No, yoga. I mean, I practice yoga. But it helps with flexibility and technique and inner strength. Balances your chakras and all that."

"Sounds very . . . Zen," is all I can think to say.

"We did a lot of yoga at the ranch," my dad explains, then turns to Saylor. "You hungry?"

He grins. "Like an ostrich!"

I look from my dad to Peach, wondering if this is some inside joke that I'm not in on.

Saylor must sense my confusion because he looks at me and says, "Ostriches have three stomachs."

I blink. "Right."

After Saylor heads upstairs to shower, my dad turns to me and says, "Can you set the table, Goose?"

As much as I would rather hide out in my room, I begrudgingly obey. I grab five plates from our cabinet and start placing them around the table. The faster this is all over, the faster I can escape.

It's strange. After Grams passed away, the house felt smaller. Emptier. I never expected it to feel crowded again without her.

When I was little, way too young to remember, my dad obtained full custody of me. He met my mom in college during their senior year, and from what Grams shared with me, they'd only been seeing each other for a few months when she became pregnant. He supported her through it, but not too long after I was born she got herself in trouble selling drugs and served a hefty amount of jail time.

After she was released, she didn't have any interest in getting to know me, and the feeling was mutual. I had Grams and my dad. That was enough.

You'd think an unplanned pregnancy would result in a lengthy sex talk, but my father's version involved awkwardly setting a twenty-four-pack of condoms on my dresser when I started dating Jay. Which—OH MY GOD—we hadn't even *kissed* at that point.

My dad moved back in with Grams to take care of me, completing his last few university credits online and skipping his graduation ceremony altogether. Grams had done her best to fill the void of my absentee parent. I remember she used these colorful Styrofoam letters to help teach me the alphabet, and she'd let me prepare tea parties using her antique tea set. Birthdays were always momentous occasions with family trips to water parks and

Six Flags. I could talk to her about things I couldn't talk to my dad about: boys and bras and the proper application of eyeliner.

When Grams died, my dad wasn't the only one who'd lost someone close to him.

I was lucky to have Whitney, Lin, and Raegan to turn to after she passed. I'd sleep over at Whitney's house a lot, and her parents always went out of the way to make me feel comfortable. They even bought a toothbrush for me and kept it in her bathroom. Raegan made sure I stayed involved with school activities to keep my sadness out of my mind, and Lin was there whenever I *did* need to break down. The three of them, in their own way, helped me heal. But there were moments when I'd catch myself wondering what things would have been like if she was still alive.

Michael, my dad's AA sponsor, would come around sometimes. Twelve years sober, Michael was a divorced IT technician who'd dedicated much of his life trying to save others from destructive behavior. My dad talked about him constantly. Sometimes he was happy with the twelve-step program and Michael's help, and other times he was defensive and reclusive.

When Michael first started sponsoring my dad, he reached out to me through e-mail. One part in particular stuck out in my mind.

> Alcoholism is a disease. I know that can be hard to understand—it's not like cancer or diabetes, and people are less sympathetic toward it, but it is. You need to know that he would have struggled with his addiction even if your grandmother didn't pass.

He was right. It was hard for me to understand. It still is.

I push aside the heaviness in my chest as I finish setting the table. A live rendition of "We Are the Champions" erupts through the computer speakers. I turn around to see Nonnie watching Freddie Mercury strut across the screen. It's clear she's enamored by his majestic presence, but I'm starting to wonder if she knows YouTube contains more than just Queen videos.

"How're all your friends doing?" my dad asks. "I bet it was nice to see them."

I sloppily drop forks on each napkin. "They're fine."

"You're welcome to have Jay over for dinner anytime."

I freeze at the mention of Jay. Did his brain jump in a time machine and forget to bring along the rest of us? I didn't talk to my dad much after the intersection incident, but I assumed he knew that leaving behind Cedarville also meant leaving behind Jay. It wasn't like I was gone for a few days. I was gone for almost *an entire year*.

I slam the last fork in place on the table. "We're not going out anymore."

"Is Jay short for Jason?" Nonnie asks, still staring at the screen.

I suppress the urge to roll my eyes.

"Oh, Goose, I'm sorry. I didn't know."

"Well," I say, desperately not wanting to talk about this anymore. "Now you do."

Peach slides the tray of garlic bread into the oven. "Boys care more about food than feelings, anyway. Best not to waste your time with them at this age."

I feel my defenses rise. I didn't ask for her advice. Besides, she doesn't know anything about my relationship with Jay.

"I have homework," is all I say before darting upstairs.

But I don't get any homework done. Instead I lie on my bed and think about Jay and Whitney because apparently I've turned into a masochist. I can't get rid of the mental image of her hand on his arm at lunch, and I'm tortured by the thought of them kissing. I don't know how I'm supposed to get over this, so I send a text to Lin.

ME: how serious are they?

LIN: Who?

ME: jay and whit

LIN: Oh. Maybe 3 months? It happened over summer.

Three months is definitely enough time to get past first base with the possibility of second.

WHY am I TORTURING myself with this?

ME: oh.

LIN: Kira . . .

ME: i know. it's fine. i'm fine.

LIN: It IS a little weird, but you know how fickle she can be with guys. Just ride it out. I doubt it's going to last forever, you know?

Ride it out. Like I'm riding out this whole Sober Living strangers thing because of my dad. But Lin does have a point. Whitney's known for quickly losing interest in guys and moving on to the next. So if it's just another thing I have to ride out, I can pretend I'm okay with it. It shouldn't be too hard.

Right?

I decide a subject change is necessary.

ME: what's up with breck wanting to join decathlon?

LIN: Valerie Martinez is on the team and I'm pretty certain he has a thing for her

While it's not implausible for Breck to want to go out of his way to impress a girl, the time and studying commitment seems like a *lot*. Even for him.

LIN: BUT . . . ugh, I can't believe I'm about to say this, but he texted me a picture of his transcript and he wasn't lying. His GPA would make him a perfect Scholastic student for the slot we have open.

ME: you could give him the chance?

She fires back with a string of stressed-out and eye-rolling emojis.

Dad calls me down for dinner. I'm too hungry to make a valid excuse for skipping, so I trudge back downstairs.

"That's just ironic," Peach is saying as I reappear in our dining room. She's occupying Grams's usual seat, which is weird, but I doubt she's aware of it.

Saylor nods across from her. "More ironic than the Mall of America being owned by Canadians, which I told him—"

"You *told* the president of this company that his new mascot is ironic?" Peach interrupts, shocked.

Nonnie laughs, her gray curls shaking as she does. "While you were at it, did you alert him if his toupee was crooked?"

Saylor does not find this funny. I notice that he's swapped his ribbed yoga tank and sweats for a clean yoga tank and sweats. I wouldn't be surprised if that's what he wore to the interview.

"If they wanted to hire me to rebrand the company, then they need to know that placing a chicken mascot on a *vegetarian* product makes no sense."

My dad brings the bowl of spaghetti into the dining room, and I slide into the only empty chair, across from him. "Saylor was going to OSU for graphic design," he tells me. "A company wants to bring someone aboard who could help out with its new redesign."

I heap a pile of spaghetti on my plate. I don't know why he's trying so hard to involve me in their lives when they aren't going to be here long.

Saylor is still adamant about his case. "On what planet is it okay to put a chicken on a vegetarian patty box?"

Nonnie reaches for the noodles once I'm done. "Maybe it was a metaphor?"

"Consumers don't tend to have deep, metaphorical thoughts when walking down the frozen food aisle."

"Unless they've been smoking the Mary Jane," Nonnie points out.

Peach leaps in to quickly get the conversation back on track. "So the interview was a bust?"

"Basically," Saylor replies, looking down at the leather and beaded bracelets on his arms. There are so many that they practically reach his elbows.

"Hey," my dad says in his best rally-the-troops voice. "You still have an SS today. You were offered the interview in the first place."

"A what?" I blurt out before I can stop myself.

My dad looks pleased with my interest in the matter. Which I'm not. The only thing I'm interested in is seeing them leave before Margaret finds out.

"Small Successes," he explains. "Instead of dwelling on the negative, we're encouraged to talk about any SS's we experience each day."

Oh. Right. Yet another takeaway from Sober Living.

Peach catches my eye from across the table. "Do you have an SS you want to share?"

Does getting through this dinner count?

"Uh," I say. "No."

"What about making it through your first day of eleventh grade?"

I cringe. Okay yeah, it *is* eleventh grade but nobody calls it that. It sounds so young. We're juniors.

I grab a piece of garlic bread. "Sure."

"I found some animal shelters who need extra help," Nonnie replies.

"Excellent." Dad passes me the marinara sauce. "You have to try this, Kira. It's way better than my own recipe."

I stubbornly drizzle the tiniest bit of sauce on my pasta. There's nothing wrong with his recipe. It was perfectly fine before she showed up and changed it, but he watches in anticipation as I try a bite.

"Good," I mumble, and I hate that it's true.

I barely register what my dad's saying as he talks about his first day of janitorial duty at the elementary school. This is the old Dad I'm used to—the encouraging, positive Dad who comes home from work, puts dinner on the table, and makes an effort to be involved with my life. I wouldn't be here if Margaret thought he was unfit to take care of me, but that doesn't mean I automatically trust him again.

We were both in denial for a long time after Grams died. One night when he was on the back patio finishing off a handle of whiskey, I googled *alcohol addiction*. There were bullet points that neatly described when someone should get help. *Neglecting responsibilities. Escaping reality. Repeated disorderly conduct. Frequent, extreme mood swings.*

I'd closed my laptop, telling myself I was overreacting. My dad was just upset because Grams was gone. He'd come out of it, but until then I would make our dinners and clean up his beer cans and place a glass of water by his bedside. If that's what I had to do to make sure our days went smoother, then that's what I did.

I don't remember much of what Margaret told me at the station, but I do recall one thing she said to me.

"It's okay, honey. Don't blame yourself. You didn't know."

But that was the thing. I did know.

I haven't been following anything they've been talking about through dinner, but Peach feels the need to bring the conversation back to me.

"So, wow, eleventh grade? That's a big year."

I take a huge bite of garlic bread. I'm not feeling up to small talk.

My dad speaks on my behalf. "Yup, I can hardly believe it." He turns to me. "Do you need to sign up for the SATs soon?"

"Everyone takes them first semester of senior year." I'm annoyed he doesn't know this.

"What about pre-SATs? You do the practice test, don't you?"

I give an indifferent shrug. "I guess."

"Well, good. Okay then." He lifts a forkful of spaghetti to his mouth, then stops. "Should I get you an SAT study book?"

"I—"

"I'll get you a book," he decides.

"Veronica might have one," Peach jumps in.

The table goes quiet with the exception of scraping forks. I don't know who Veronica is, but I don't want her books. I don't want anything from anyone at this table.

"You don't have to reach out if you're not comfortable," my dad says.

Nonnie leans over to me, her turquoise frames slipping down the bridge of her nose. "Veronica's her daughter. Went off to college last year."

I give the slightest nod, but I really don't care.

"No, I should." Peach sits up a little straighter. "It could be a good ice breaker."

Saylor grins at her. "Maybe it'll be tomorrow's SS."

Peach gives a hopeful smile. "It could."

"Again," my dad says. "No pressure."

I let my fork clatter on my plate. I'm entirely over talking about embracing positivity through acronyms like it will solve all our problems. "Can I be excused?"

Peach looks at the mass of leftovers on the table. "I think we made too much."

My dad pats his stomach. "I could *pastably* eat more for lunch tomorrow."

He looks to me for a laugh, but I don't give him the satisfaction. Instead I clear my plate and leave it in the sink. Before I can head upstairs to my room, my dad joins me in the hallway.

"Listen, Goose," he says, lowering his voice a bit. "I know I wasn't a father to you those months after Grams died. And I'm working on that just like you're working on trusting me. But while you're under this roof I expect you to respect my rules and authority. Okay?"

It's a reasonable request. I nod curtly, but all I want to do is go up to my room and be by myself.

"You don't have to like these people, but they're my friends. All I ask is that you treat them with respect." He looks me in the eyes for a moment. "They're all here for you if you need anything. Don't hesitate to ask. I promise they're good people."

I glance back into the dining room. Nonnie's using her napkin to wipe a splotch of sauce off one of the neon-green cheetahs on her blouse. Peach has another gash of magenta lipstick across her top teeth, and Saylor's humming with his eyes closed, rocking side to side as if he's gone into deep meditation at the dinner table.

I can't possibly imagine what I'd need from any of these people.

"I'll be fine," I say, scooting past him. "I have homework."

"All right."

There's hesitancy in his voice, but I pretend I don't hear it as I take the stairs two at a time. Once I'm in my room, I close the door and sit down at my desk. It was a yard sale find from a few years ago. The white paint needed to be retouched, but instead of repainting, Whitney, Raegan, Lin, and I Sharpied every inch of it.

The surface is covered in Lin's cartoon bunny doodles and Whitney's inscription—DANCE 4 EVA—in bright purple. There's an Eleanor Roosevelt quote in Raegan's handwriting near the center. I drew stick figures of the four of us in different neon colors, but that's not what catches my eye. In bright green, we'd written our names in big, bubbly letters. Lin had scrawled, BESTIES BETTER THAN THE RESTIES in block lettering around it.

I know it was only the first day back, but I hate feeling so far removed from them. The memories they've made without me make my stomach twist. If there was a way to make things go back to normal, I'd do it in a heartbeat.

Wait.

I dig through my book bag until I find a spiral notebook. I open it to a blank page and grab a pen from the collection in an old mason jar on my desk. It's not enough to *wish* for something to go back to normal. If I want my life back, I need to do something about it.

Aunt June was the one who told me about the twelve-step program after my dad attended his first few AA meetings. They're a set of twelve principles that present a guided path toward recovery that involve bettering yourself by admitting your addiction, fixing situations with people you've wronged, and committing to eliminate all bad behaviors that led to the addiction in the first place. If these principles were followed and practiced, a person would be able to go back to living their life the way it was before addiction.

I know the steps didn't work for my dad the first time, but it was like his grief over Grams prevented him from really trying. I have to believe he's trying now. He's made progress, and if the steps *did* contribute to his sobriety, then maybe abiding by my own steps could help me, too.

This is what I need. Principles. Rules. A process that I can easily follow to get my life back on track.

I pick up my pen and start writing.

EIGHT

KIRA'S 12 STEPS TO A NORMAL LIFE:

1. Forgive Dad

2. Learn how to be a family without Grams

3. Make amends with Whitney

4. Be a better friend to Raegan

5. Make sure Lin feels appreciated

6. Reconnect with Jay

7. Talk to Alex about that text

8. Help Breck get on the decathlon team

9. Support Colton's music

10. Convince Nonnie to move out

11. Push Saylor to leave

12. Make Peach go home to her family

These twelve people are a significant part of my life now, whether I want them to be or not. If I focus on each of these steps, my life should revert to how it was before I left Cedarville. That's all I want, really. For things to be how they once were.

And I'm certain this is the way to do it.

After Grams died, my dad's addiction, neglect, and lack of communication drew us apart. While I was able to cope with my grief over Grams when I was living with Aunt June, it still doesn't make coming back any easier. I'd almost hoped nothing changed—that Grams would be here, in this house, waiting to hear all about my time in Portland. Learning how to be a family without her, when that's all my dad and I have known, is going to be a challenge of its own. But if we're going to ever try and get back to the type of father/daughter relationship we had when she was alive, it has to be an important part of the list.

Of course, there are some major problems. Obviously, I want Peach, Nonnie, and Saylor to leave, but it's not purely because they've caused an unexpected disruption in my home life. No, because if *they* don't leave, Margaret is going to make sure *I* leave. Again. And being back has shown me that this is where I belong. It's not only my home—my whole life is here. My dad. My friends. My school. If I truly want things to go back to how they were, I can't risk exposing the fact that we have other recovering addicts here. The only way to extinguish that threat is to get them out.

In the meantime, I can make sure nobody—especially Margaret—knows they're living here. They may be a bit odd, but I don't think they're a bad influence on my dad. But after speaking with Margaret the night I arrived, it seemed that anything she found out of the ordinary would get both me *and* my dad sent away.

I won't let that happen.

And then there's the questionable: reconnecting with Jay. Okay, *maybe* I still have feelings for him. But what if he has feelings for me, too? Shouldn't we see where it can lead?

It's a thought that's layered with guilt. He's dating one of my best friends. I wouldn't make any moves on him, but I could leave the door open for the possibility of an *us* again. Like Lin said, Whitney is a serial dater. Their relationship may not last. If I reconnect with him on a platonic level—that wouldn't be so bad, right?

And yet, I *want* to make amends with Whitney. I know I hurt her with my silence, but if I can prove that I can be a trustworthy friend again, maybe we could pick up where we left off. Lin and Raegan deserve the same treatment. I mishandled friendships with people who truly care about me, and I'm determined to make up for it.

Even though I was never *super* close with Breck and Colton, we still hung out nearly every day. Thankfully there's no weird tension in the air with either of them, but I'd like to show them that I can be as good of a friend as Lin, Whitney, and Raegan. Supporting Colton's music and potentially helping Breck get on the decathlon team—depending on Breck's motives—seem like the best ways to do that.

Then there's Alex, who sent me That Text the weekend before I moved to Portland—after I'd already broken it off with Jay. Which he knew. Everyone knew. And even though I deleted the text, I still remembered what it said:

ALEX: i know my timing is off, but i wanted to tell you i've liked you . . . a lot. for a while.

My heart stopped when I read it.

His timing. Was. *Awful.*

I didn't know it was possible to be flattered and hurt and enraged all at once. Why was he telling me this *now?* Didn't he already know having to leave Cedarville was painful enough? It's not like I could do anything about it. Why did he decide to say anything at all?

I never replied. And after seeing him in the office, I regret not saying something. Because I miss his friendship. We always had a natural rhythm, and it was always so easy to talk to him. If I'm lucky to even get that much back, I'll consider it a success.

Then there's quite possibly the most difficult step: Forgiving my dad. He's trying. I can *see* he's trying. He's not drinking, he has a steady job, and he's building his trust with me. The very least I can do is be open to forgiving him, but that's something that takes time. And it's hard not to be difficult when he's brought home strangers to live with us when he should be focused on fixing our relationship.

It's even harder not to harbor the resentment I've held on to.

As the next week goes by, we fall into our own routines. Nonnie typically keeps to herself in Grams's room, yet she's unsurprisingly forward about blaring Queen every single morning. Peach has been sleeping downstairs on the fold-out couch and keeps her arrangement of conservative skirts and boxy blouses in the hall closet.

Aside from rearranging the living room furniture to create an open practice space, Saylor does little to disturb anyone. Although, I'm convinced he doesn't own a pair of shoes because he's always walking around barefoot in his loose yoga pants. I've started going straight to my room after school to avoid him asking me if I want to practice with him.

On the upside, despite a slightly rusty performance during Wavettes tryouts (we had thirty minutes to learn and rehearse a thirty-second routine in small groups and I'd accidentally stepped right instead of left, throwing the routine off for a moment), I'd earned my old spot back on the team.

Raegan was the first person standing in front of the list when Coach Velasquez posted it. She threw her arms around me and jumped up and down, and I couldn't help but bounce back in excitement. Even Whitney congratulated me at lunch.

My dad was ecstatic that I'd remade the team, but that enthusiasm faded when I politely told him I didn't want him at the games. I know his presence would only draw attention from my classmates, and I'm trying to put that part of my life behind me.

One afternoon, I come home after school to find Peach cooking in the kitchen. I try not to let it annoy me too much that she's taken charge of dinner. That used to be something my dad and I did together. Sometimes we would even imitate *Chopped* and pull random ingredients from the kitchen and attempt to make a dish from it. Whenever it came out tasting horribly, we'd order a pizza and laugh about where we went wrong.

My dad isn't home yet. I decide this is a good opportunity to work on step 12 and push Peach toward going home to her own family.

I sit on the barstool, casually flipping open my history book. "Brisket?" I guess from the savory smells wafting from the oven.

She glances up. "Absolutely."

"I bet your family misses your cooking. What's your daughter's name? Veronica?"

Peach pauses for an instant, and I can see a wave of sadness fall over her delicate features. "Yes." Her tone is soft for once. "And Bailey. Who's a sophomore this year."

I let silence hang over us for a moment. Before I can chicken out, I say, "They'd want you to come home, right? You should, you know, talk to them."

The edges of her mouth jump into a frown. Her gaze is distant, and I can see I've dug my way into a sensitive topic. I try not to feel bad, but if I don't get them to leave, then things won't go back to how they were before.

Peach excuses herself. When she returns a moment later, I notice her eyes are a little red.

I tell myself it's better this way, but the guilt clings to me like a static garment all through dinner.

The next week at school is better, but not easier. Especially during lunch. Jay barely makes eye contact with me, yet he's always more than happy to talk to me during history. Whitney only directs attention toward me when I ask her a question. It's not like she's pushing me away—it's worse. She's basically attempting to ignore my existence.

But with my twelve steps in the back of my mind, I'm attempting to right things with my friends. So I sit and listen as Raegan freaks out about presidential responsibilities and while Lin stresses about the decathlon team. I've only genuinely laughed once, and that was when Colton started throwing tater tots at Whitney to make her stop talking about a Kate Spade purse she was obsessing over. He quickly shut up when she threatened to chuck his iPhone across the cafeteria.

I tell myself that if I keep making an effort, it can only get better from here.

It's Friday. I'm feeling pretty confident in my toffee oxfords and speckled navy top that I've paired with my favorite jeans. I've even accessorized with a pair of golden pineapple stud earrings.

Today I'm focusing on step 5—making sure Lin feels valued in our friendship—which is why I got up extra early to help her hang Earth Club posters throughout the school before first period. I find her standing on a step stool she borrowed from the theater department. She's placing a piece of tape over the first flyer. I read it as she slaps it on the wall.

Earth Club!
Let's do our part to help our environment
Tuesdays at 3:50
Room 208
(Free cookies during 1st meeting)

"We're not beneath bribing people with food?" I ask.

Lin scoots the stool over several feet. "I'm not letting Principal

Lawrence cancel the only club I care about." She places another flyer on the wall. "So I'm hoping my cookies will bring the boys to the yard." After a brief pause, she adds, "And girls."

"I didn't know Earth Club was so sexual."

"Oh, shut up. Hand me another piece of tape."

I do, then we move another few feet down the hall. "Are you coming to Raegan's on Saturday?" I ask. It's not unlike Lin's parents to spring a family gathering on her at the last minute.

"Yup," Lin replies. Today she's wearing a knee-length flouncy skirt with a white V-neck that has a giant recycle symbol printed on the front. She pushes her frames up the bridge of her nose before saying, "I haven't been to her house in a while."

"You haven't?" I assumed the three of them stayed close over the summer.

Lin shakes her head. "Raegan's mom is pregnant—"

"WHAT?"

"I know!"

"How—?"

"Are you really asking me that?"

I shake my head, shocked. Raegan's always been an only child, and she certainly acts like an only child. She's always been confident in her personal achievements, but she can be a little self-centered. Like the time she made Whitney and me help her find the classiest pair of heels to wear to her cousin's wedding when she knew we both had a major biology exam the next day. She would have outright refused if the situation were turned around, which makes it hard to picture her as a big sister.

"Sorry, I just—wow. That's a surprise."

"I'm pretty sure it was a surprise for them, too, but they're embracing it," Lin says as we round the corner at the end of the hall. "I didn't see her for most of the summer because she was working as a counselor at Camp Bridgeport. She wanted a summer job where she could escape her mother's hormonal episodes. Plus, Whitney was super busy with dance camp." I hand her a piece of tape so she can secure the next flyer. "Meanwhile I signed up for an online pre-SAT class because I was *that* bored without you guys."

I won't lie. This makes me feel a little better.

"Hey, so," I say as we move into a different hallway. "Have you figured out if you're going to let Breck on the decathlon team?"

Lin lets out a deeply annoyed sigh. "It's just—" She thinks for a moment. "I don't understand *why*, you know? It makes no sense. And I don't want him screwing up our chances if he's not going to take it seriously."

I nod. As much as I want to work toward step 8 and be a good friend by helping Breck out, I also understand Lin's concerns. She's really put her heart in this over the last two years.

"I can find out," I offer.

She raises an eyebrow, skeptical. "Yeah?"

I shrug. How hard can it be? Breck is pretty transparent.

Ten minutes before the bell rings, the halls become more congested. We've successfully hung three dozen flyers down three different hallways. I'm putting the extras in Lin's binder as she collapses the step stool.

"Hey, Alex!"

I turn to see Lin waving at him from across the hall. My pulse sputters for a quarter of a second. We have algebra together and have already been through the polite, *Hi! Hey! You're back for good? Yeah. That's awesome. Yeah, it is,* routine. This is the first time I'll voluntarily be in his presence, and my stomach is all nerves.

You need to talk to him.

He waves before changing direction and walking toward us, but I shake step 7 and the entire list out of my head. It's not the right time.

His text pops back into my head. **i know my timing is off—**

Lin's voice interrupts my thoughts. "Do you have tech first period?"

"Yup," Alex replies. He's not wearing his beanie today, but he is wearing a navy deadCenter Film Festival T-shirt with a long sleeve black tee underneath. The double shirts are typical Alex Ramos attire. His hair is slightly damp and curling at the ends, as if he rushed out of the shower to get here in time.

Lin holds out the step stool to him. "Would you mind running this back with you? I have to deliver the extra flyers to Mrs. Dwight's room before the bell rings."

"No problem." He takes it from her, then glances at me. "Are you rejoining Earth Club this year?"

His tone is friendly. If he's holding a grudge against the whole text thing, I can't tell. But it's his smile that throws me off kilter. It's a sincere smile, something I didn't expect.

I find I can't look away.

"Yeah, I am."

"Cool." He looks back at Lin. "See you guys later."

I watch him head down the hall, adjusting his backpack as he goes. I never told anyone about the text—not even Lin. My friends knew about Alex's obvious crush on me in middle school, but since we'd gone our separate ways freshman year I'm sure they assumed those feelings evaporated.

As I watch him disappear down the hall, a strange feeling of loneliness lingers in the corners of my heart. But as fast as it comes, it fades just as quickly when I turn away.

I'm in a surprisingly good mood when I walk into Algebra II after lunch. Raegan had a Leadership meeting and Whitney had a dentist appointment, so it was only Breck, Colton, Lin, Jay, and me at the table—which meant Jay made eye contact with me on more than one occasion. He even offered me some of his cheese fries without doing that weird jaw-clenching thing he does when he feels uncomfortable. It was as if we were both relieved Whitney wasn't the barrier between us having a friendly conversation.

On the flip side, I feel guilty that I spent all lunch feeling relaxed without her there. I felt even guiltier when Jay pulled his notebook out in AP US History and drew us up a hangman game to play as Mr. Densick explained today's Data Based Question. Even though we stuck to movie titles, I couldn't help overthinking it. I mean, this *was* our way of flirting with each other before he officially asked me out. But he has Whitney, so this definitely isn't flirting. Or is it sub-flirting?

Then I'd caught him staring at Jana Nelson's cleavage while thinking of a letter to guess in the puzzle and decided that I was *surely* overthinking it. Did he do that when we were dating? Stare at other girls? No. I mean, I would have noticed. At least, that's what I tell myself.

But a tiny part of me questioned how much he'd changed since I've been gone.

The warning bell rings just as Alex flops into his assigned desk next to me. My eyes catch his profile. He looks tired, as if he didn't sleep well last night. I didn't notice it this morning, but there are dark circles under his eyes. Alex has never been one to party. I guess the stress of this week has caught up with him.

When he catches me staring, he pulls his beanie out from his back pocket and tugs it over his hair. He rests his head on his arms, then pulls the beanie over his eyes. Well. Okay then. I grab my spiral and flip it open to a fresh page.

Mrs. Donaldson walks into the room and begins scrawling something on the board. I hate math even more because of Mrs. Donaldson. She never slows her pace, which makes it hard for me to keep up, and she hates when students ask too many questions. Whitney and I had her freshman year for Algebra I, and I barely passed with a low C. I don't know what I did to disturb the karmic gods to have her *again*.

"Good afternoon, class." She taps her dry erase marker on the board where a sequence of numbers is written. "Today we're talking about radical numbers and square roots."

Riveting.

I open my textbook and do my best to pay attention to the for-
mulas she scribbles, but my mind wanders back to Jay and Whitney.
This week she made it very clear that they're already planning on
going to homecoming together. It's obvious that she wants my past
with Jay to have nothing to do with her present relationship. I guess I
can't blame her, but I wish it were easier to get my head around.

For now I'm going to focus on Whitney. I can't control her relationship with Jay, but I can control my friendship with her. That's
why I'm glad Raegan invited us over to her place tomorrow. Maybe
if it's just the four of us without the guys, things won't be as awkward.

I copy the example problem from the board. I try and understand
it, but I'm already lost in the terminology. I wish Mrs. Donaldson
would go easy on us.

Next to me, Alex twitches in his seat. He's asleep on his arms
again, head on top of his notebook. I stare down at my own spiral
and realize nothing I've written down makes sense.

Mrs. Donaldson sets a wicker basket full of Jolly Ranchers on
her desk. "For the last ten minutes we're going to do some Radical
Races."

I sink in my seat, anxiety swelling in my chest. This is not a game
I enjoy. At all. Two people are called up to the board to solve a problem
from today's lesson, and whoever solves it before the timer stops wins
a Jolly Rancher.

Blood rushes to my head and whirs in my ears. I know she thinks
it's good practice, but it's too nerve-wracking for me to be put on the
spot. I never won any rounds, but at least I had Whitney to laugh
it off with after class. Sometimes she would even give me her Jolly

Rancher, and I never thought it of as a sympathy gift. She was just being a good friend. This year I'm completely on my own.

"Mr. Ramos." Mrs. Donaldson is looking straight at Alex. He startles in his seat before lifting his head to look at her. "Perhaps you'll join us at the board?"

The whole class is staring at Alex. He blinks away the tiredness in his eyes and says, "Uh—"

"Now, please."

Alex sighs, then slowly shuffles to the front of the room. With his back to the class, he chooses a blue dry erase marker and waits.

Mrs. Donaldson's eyes scan the room. I pretend to look really, *really* interested in the textbook in front of me.

"Miss Seneca?"

Crapsticks.

"Please join him at the board."

My chest tightens. A cold panic falls over me. Every single nerve in my body is on high alert. I stare down at my spiral one last time, hoping something sticks, but all I see is a blur of numbers and letters that don't make sense.

I stand next to Alex at the board. God, I hate this. I hate her. I would rather endure a pop quiz, because that way I would be able to fail in privacy.

I pick up a purple marker and stare at the whiteboard in front of me. I try to slow my racing heart by taking a deep breath. It doesn't work. I know I shouldn't care what the class thinks, but I do. I remember the look of relief on my classmates' faces when they were called up to race against me freshman year. They knew it was basically guaranteed they'd win, and they wouldn't bother hiding their smug looks when they did.

I don't look at Alex.

Mrs. Donaldson reads the problem to us. As soon as we finish writing it on the board, the timer starts. I stare at the jumble of numbers in front of me, wishing I could somehow decipher how to solve it. I raise my marker, but I can't make my brain understand the functionality of the problem. I need to write something—God, *anything*—at this point.

I hear Alex's marker tapping the board beside me. My anxiety intensifies. I feel my mouth go dry. I'm about to lose to someone who spent the entire class *sleeping*. And everyone knows it. A lump builds up in my throat. Instead of concentrating on the problem, I blink back tears of frustration.

"Time," Mrs. Donaldson calls. "Please face the class so they can see your work."

I hang my head and cap my marker. From beside me, Alex doesn't make any effort to move, either. I resist the temptation to look at his work.

"Please face the class," Mrs. Donaldson repeats.

I do. As slowly as possible. From my peripheral vision, I can see Alex turning to face the front as well. Instead of looking at the class, I stare down at my oxfords. I pretend I'm anywhere but here.

A few students let out surprised gasps. That's followed by a few chuckles. My throat tightens. And then I'm mad. Really mad. I refuse to play a part in this stupid game just to get mocked by my own classmates. I can't be the only one who doesn't understand this, but it's *my* humiliation that Mrs. Donaldson chooses to put on display.

Mrs. Donaldson's voice booms across the room. "Now, *what*—?"

Before I can fully comprehend what I'm doing, I march to my desk and grab my things. I don't have to put up with Mrs. Donaldson belittling me by explaining that this problem was *so easy* and that I *really needed to pay better attention*. I refuse to be made a mockery in front of my classmates just because I can't solve one algebra problem.

"Miss Seneca!"

A few hushed whispers fall over the room as I sling my book bag over my shoulder and push my way out the door. Mrs. Donaldson is still calling my name, but I don't care. There are only a few minutes of class left anyway, and I can't stand to be in there another second.

I rush to my locker before the bell rings and grab everything I need for my last three classes. Then I think better of it and grab all the books I'll need to do homework this weekend. I'm embarrassed enough as it is, and now the entire class knows I'm *still* an incompetent idiot.

I slam my locker closed and wander down C hall right before the final bell rings. Crowds of students press around me, and I try and pretend I'm invisible. I allow a few tears to fall down my cheeks before wiping them away, taking a deep breath, and pushing my way into the chemistry classroom.

NINE

I'M LOADING DISHES INTO THE dishwasher after dinner on Friday, which is a not so pleasant indication of my current social status. Since there wasn't a game tonight, Raegan and I grabbed limeades from Sonic after school, but she was spending the rest of her evening developing the Leadership Council agenda for next week. Lin's parents were dragging her to her cousin's birthday dinner, and Whitney and Jay went to go see the latest end-of-summer blockbuster. I only know this because at lunch I asked Jay what he was up to tonight and he stumbled awkwardly through his reply.

I tell myself it's fine. Good for them. I mean, it's not like I *don't* have plans. I need to practice next week's Wavette routine and start on a paper for AP History.

The only reason I'm not holed up in my room right now is because my dad bribed me with allowance money if I helped with chores around the house. And since allowance money equals gas money, I can't say no. I'll have my car back soon, which means I'll be able to escape whenever I choose.

I can hear muffled conversation coming from the backyard. Short bursts of laughter follow every few minutes. I didn't make it home in time for the formal sit-down dinner, but Peach saved me a bowl of her stew in the fridge along with a note written in her loopy cursive: *Kira! Missed you tonight. Enjoy!*

I'd inhaled it before she could see. I didn't want her to think she was winning me over because I thought her food was delicious.

After I turn on the dishwasher, I creep to the back door and peer outside. Saylor's doing some kind of arm balance on his yoga mat, his long ponytail flopped into his eyes. Nonnie watches from the hammock—*When did we get a hammock?*—and cheers him on. In the dim lighting, I can see she's wearing a multi-colored cheetah print head wrap with a bright-orange muumuu.

"They're close."

The voice startles me. I whirl around to find my dad standing behind me.

"Sorry, I didn't mean to scare you," he says.

I shrug. He holds out a blue and silver bag and offers me a chocolate-covered peppermint square. For as long as I can remember, he's always had a stash of them hidden somewhere around the house. He hid other things, too, like liquor bottles, but part of me wants to believe he's done with that. Whenever I was upset over silly fights with Whitney or if I'd bombed a test that was worth a large chunk of my grade, he'd slip a silver-wrapped square under my bedroom door. It meant he was there if I wanted to talk. That simple gesture always made me feel a little better.

I stare at the bag. He's trying. Step 1 is learning to forgive him, and I can't do that if I don't hear him out.

I accept one.

"They met at the ranch," my dad continues. I unwrap my chocolate and take a small bite. "Saylor's parents kicked him out when he was in college."

"For drinking?"

"Among other things." He stares at Saylor as he twists himself into a backbend. "He started living with Tessa. That was his girlfriend at the time. She's the one who suggested AA, but when he stopped attending meetings she told him to leave."

I can't find the sympathy to feel bad for him. If he wanted to change, to fix the relationships he was ruining, then he'd have to *try* to do it.

"Anyway, he ended up dropping out of OSU so he could work full time at a grocery store to afford rent." My dad finishes chewing. "But he was evicted after spending nearly all his paychecks on alcohol. Eventually, his friends wouldn't let him couch crash anymore, and he was spending his nights on park benches. That was his rock bottom, I think. After that he went to the library to use the wi-fi and found Sober Living."

I'd expected him to say that Saylor went back to his parents for help, that they were the ones who sent him away. The fact that it was his decision surprises me.

"Nonnie was the first person at the ranch who didn't go easy on him," he continues. "On the first day, he cut in front of her in the breakfast line. Oh, *man*. If there's one thing everyone learned that morning, it was not to mess with Nonnie. She called him out in front of the entire room, and I don't think he was used to anyone telling him that he couldn't get what he wanted."

Saylor kicks his legs up, going into a handstand. Nonnie waves her hands in the air, her mouth moving as she tries to control her grin. Saylor ends up on his back with his hands clutched to his stomach, laughing.

"Sober Living is a huge support team, and that's what he needed. He really has come a long way."

I crumble my foil wrapper into a tiny, silver ball. The chocolate feels heavy in my mouth. I know what he's doing. He's trying to convince me that his friends are good people. That maybe if I have a little bit of empathy, it'll make it easier for them to live here. But learning to live in the absence of Grams means attempting to be a family on our own, and that's not easy to do with three strangers living under our roof.

I fold my arms across my chest. "Then what?"

My dad's forehead wrinkles in confusion. "What do you mean?"

"I mean, what's the next step? Interviewing for jobs he obviously doesn't want? Won't that just make him even more miserable than before?"

My dad shakes his head. "He wants to become a certified yoga instructor, but he needs to find a job so he can pay off his rehab first. It's a step in the right direction." He stares back out the window. "Now that he has a goal, he's more positive about the outlook of his future."

I watch Saylor kick himself up into a handstand. It's selfish, but I hope he lands a job soon. That way I'll complete step 11—getting him to leave.

I point to the hammock. "Does he sleep out there?"

"Yeah. Says it brings him peace, being out there with nature and all. The first night he got eaten alive by mosquitos, so I bought him a net. But he says he's comfortable. I guess that's all that matters."

Nonnie struggles to get out of the hammock. After a moment, Saylor stands up and helps her.

I turn away from the screen door. My stomach twists in uncomfortable knots. I can't really explain why. Maybe it's because I used to have the same comfort and familiarity with my dad and Grams as everyone here has with each other, and now I don't have either. They support each other. Trust each other. It's everything *I* want with my own dad, which makes step 2—learning how to come together as a two-person family without Grams—all the more important.

I start to head upstairs, but my father's voice stops me.

"Listen, Goose." He runs one hand over his dark stubble. "We haven't had an opportunity to talk about things."

I grab a strand of my hair between my fingers, but I don't look at him. "I think things are pretty self-explanatory."

His eyes widen. "You do?"

"You're so disconnected from your old life. All of you. You don't get that this isn't the way the real world works."

"Hey now, I don't necessarily think that's fair to say."

I know I'm taking out my annoyances on him, but it's as if I'm the only one who doesn't think this entire situation is absurd. "Then why are they here? Because you're overcompensating for your loneliness? You had Aunt June. You had *me*. But you think you don't have anyone but these people who understand what it's like to feel the same way you did."

The light is gone from his eyes. "Kira—"

"Now it's like you're all hiding out here. You're not ready to let go of whatever bullshit positivity and rainbows they fed you at that ranch—"

"*Kira.*" He says my name with more authority now. "I know I've let you down in the past, but if I didn't believe I was ready to be a responsible father figure for you, I wouldn't be here."

I stare down at my bare feet. I don't understand why he couldn't have been a responsible father in the first place. Everyone experiences grief, sadness, hurt. Nobody can expect life to give you a free pass when it comes to that.

"You have to realize that when adults make horrible decisions, the repercussions are a lot heavier." He waves a hand to the backyard. "None of them have a support system right now. I've been blessed with a house that's big enough to take care of all of us. It's a temporary situation."

"Temporary? Until when? Until you're sent back after relapsing?"

My father sighs. He looks older, more tired than before. "I promise you that's not going to happen. I know you don't understand—"

"Of course I don't understand!" My voice is a rising tide that swells and swells until it breaks. "I'm not like you."

There's a pause. He has nothing to say.

I leave. I go into the living room where I turn on a recorded episode of *Crime Boss* and try and lose myself in the dramatic clangs of the theme song. A part of me almost expects him to come watch in silence, but he doesn't. Instead he turns and goes back into his bedroom, the sack of peppermints sitting like a white flag on the counter.

When the episode ends, I get up and dump the entire bag into the trash.

TEN

I'M RIDING IN THE PASSENGER seat as Peach drives my car to the DMV on Saturday morning. My dad was called in to Cedarville Elementary to fix the faulty sprinkler system, so Peach volunteered to take me in his place. Considering how our conversation ended last night, it's probably for the best.

I'm plugged into the music on my iPhone to avoid any type of small talk. I only agreed to go with Peach because I can't stand not having my own car. If I get this over with, I'll have my freedom back. Starting with booking it to Raegan's as soon as we get home.

Peach pulls into a parking spot and turns off the engine. I yank off my headphones and get out before she has the chance to say anything.

"You must be so excited," Peach says as she catches up to me. I don't know how, considering she's wearing strappy red heels paired with another one of her long Mary Poppins skirts.

"I am," I tell her. Excited to finally come and go as I please.

Sharing the house hasn't exactly been blissful. If I want to take a hot shower I have to wake up at six in the morning instead of my usual seven-thirty routine. Otherwise I'm stuck with cold water, thanks to Nonnie and Peach. Then I have to pretend I'm interested in my daily horoscope that Saylor insists on reading to me every morning when I really just want to eat my cereal in peace. I'm also almost positive that I have Queen's greatest hits memorized thanks to Nonnie's continual obsession with playing the CD at every given opportunity.

Excited might be a bit of an understatement.

The cool blast of air conditioning hits us as we enter the DMV. It smells like body odor and cleaning supplies. There are dozens of people sitting in the plastic chairs in the waiting area, but we have to wait in line for our ticket before we can join them.

"Are you up to anything fun today?" Peach asks.

I keep it brief. "Going to a friend's."

Peach smiles. "How fun. Your dad talks so highly of your friends." When I don't respond, she continues. "Did I tell you I might have found a pastry chef opening near Claremore? I'm stopping by to chat with management later on this afternoon."

I watch the people in front of us talk to the woman at the main information desk before taking a ticket out of the machine. "Oh," I say distractedly. "Is that where you used to live?"

She sits up a little straighter. "Yes."

I don't say it, but I want to ask if that's where she'll go if she gets the job.

When it's our turn to step up, Peach leans over and tells the woman that I'm here to register for a Texas license. I'm a little annoyed by her authority, but I let it slide. The woman asks me if I have my current out-of-state license, birth certificate, and social security card on hand. I do, so she quickly types something into her computer and tells me to take the ticket out of the machine.

Peach follows me into the waiting area and sits down next to me. An electronic voice calls numbers over the loudspeaker while we wait. I pull out my phone and send a text to Raegan, telling her that I'll be there in half an hour. She responds with a grinning emoji followed by a dozen exclamation marks.

"Everyone looks thrilled to be here, huh?" Peach says.

I look around at all the glum, bored faces. She's smiling when I glance back at her, like she's told a really excellent joke.

I turn back to my phone. "Ecstatic."

"My mother used to say that waiting at the DMV could have been one of Dante's nine circles of hell."

I wonder if another layer is living with three annoying people I barely know.

Peach takes a deep breath. "I know how it feels," she starts, "to have someone you love pass away at a young age. My mother died when I was seventeen."

I stiffen. I don't want to talk about Grams with anyone, especially Peach. *Especially* not at the DMV.

My dad's struggle with alcohol fluctuated after Grams passed. I told my social worker that because it was true. When he first started AA, he seemed like he was doing better. He'd take me to school and came to see me dance at all the football games, but that slowly changed. Even after Aunt June flew in as reinforcement, my dad became withdrawn, lonely. It hurt that he wouldn't talk to me like he used to.

I can feel Peach's gaze on me, but I don't say anything.

The electronic voice calls my number a few minutes later. I launch out of my seat and walk over to the proper booth. Peach follows closely behind me and sits next to me as I fill out my paperwork. I give the woman my documents and pay the fee with my dad's debit card. After taking an updated picture, I'm given a temporary license and told I'll receive mine in a week or so.

Peach is quiet as we walk back to the car. Relief floods my chest as I hold on to my tangible piece of freedom.

I'm in a much better mood as she drives us home. A part of me wants to ask her how her mother died and why she's so nice to me and why she insists on making me my lunch in the morning. But I don't.

Once we get to the house, she hands over my keys with a quick "congratulations" before walking inside and shutting the door behind her.

Hanging out at Raegan's house is less of *hanging out* and more of a nonstop assembly line of work.

I wish I was kidding.

We're sitting on her porch in her backyard armed with pencils, rulers, paint pens, and glitter glue. The swampy heat makes it hard to grip my paint pen. Raegan has us working on Spirit Week posters because she doesn't trust the cheerleaders to get them done on time.

I quickly discovered that there's no talking sense into Raegan when she has a one-track mind on her presidential duties. Whitney is using a pen to create bubble letters since she has the best handwriting while Lin and I fill in her letters with red paint. When we finish, Raegan outlines them in gold glitter glue.

"It's so hot out here," Whitney whines as her hand curves the letter O. "Why can't we do this inside?"

Raegan rolls her eyes. "My dad's afraid the fumes will harm the baby."

When Raegan's mom answered the door when I'd arrived, it looked as if she were hoarding a beach ball under her stretchy maternity dress. Even though Lin told me she is due in November, I was still a bit surprised.

"Kira!" She gave me a quick side hug. "It's so good to have you back."

"Thank you," I told her as I stepped inside. "Congratulations on your expectancy."

"Only two more months." She patted her stomach gently. "But Lord, I'm ready any day now."

Now Raegan wipes her brow with the back of her hand. "Did this really have to happen during my junior year? I don't know how I'm supposed to study for the SATs if she'll be crying all night."

"Typical," Lin comments. "You're worrying about problems that don't even exist."

Whitney and I laugh. Our eyes meet briefly, but she's quick to turn back to her work.

It's hard to not take offense to the obvious distance Whitney's placed between us. She hasn't exactly been super forthcoming whenever we're together. Even though I'm back on the team, she doesn't seem like she really cares. It's as if she'd rather have me back in Portland, and that hurts.

"Ohmigod." Whitney whips her head up, a sly smile playing on her lips.

"What? Did you mess up?" Raegan leans over to examine her work. "I told you to use a pencil—"

Whitney rolls her eyes. "No, chill." She sits up a little straighter. Her glossy brown hair is pulled back into a perfect ponytail. "I was only wondering if y'all heard what happened in Mrs. Donaldson's class yesterday?"

I freeze, the paint pen hovering over the Y I'd been coloring. I had been trying to put the Radical Races mishap behind me, but it sounds like my incompetence is already circulating through school.

My heart sinks. It isn't fair. I was the target of gossip last year after the intersection incident with my dad. Do people really have to talk about the fact that I can't solve an algebra problem? I bet there will be rumors on Monday that I'll have to be put into remedial math. Which—*no.*

"Mrs. Donaldson's class?" Lin repeats as she colors the A in MONDAY on the slick poster board.

I stare at Whitney, silently begging her not to tell our friends.

But my telepathy doesn't work because she goes on. "You know Alex Ramos?"

Wait...Alex?

Raegan shakes her glitter pen. "Yeah. He's always late to homeroom."

I tilt my head, eyebrows furrowing in confusion. I don't understand. I was *there*. What does he have to do with anything? Alex solved the problem while I couldn't. Unless he made fun of me behind my back when I stormed out of class.

Oh god. Please, please, please *don't let that be the case.*

Whitney's eyes light up like they do when she's the first to spill gossip. "Okay, well, apparently he was up at the board doing those algebra races Mrs. Donaldson makes her class do sometimes. But instead of solving the problem he solved for the square root of 'SUCK IT.' Like, that's *literally* what he wrote on the board! Can you believe it?"

My anxiety drains from me. Did he really write that? I'm not sure. I never looked at his answer. But if Whitney's telling the truth, then the class wasn't laughing at me. They were laughing at him.

Lin's eyes widen in amusement. "Are you serious? I hate Mrs. Donaldson, too, but I would *never*."

Raegan shakes her head in disapproval. "Why would he do that?"

Exactly. Why *would* he do that? Was he pissed because Mrs. Donaldson caught him sleeping? It's safe to say everyone hates Radical Races, but he has to put up with her wrath for an entire year. I don't know why he didn't just solve it.

Unless.

Unless he knew I couldn't work the problem out for myself. But that doesn't make sense. Why would he willingly put an unnecessary spotlight on himself? That's unlike him. Besides, it's not like he has a reason to be nice to me.

Lin looks at me. "Aren't you in that class, Kira?"

Everyone is staring at me now. I open my mouth to reply, but I don't want to tell them why I booked it out of there.

Whitney shrugs. "That's what I heard from Kayla Walsh, anyway."

Kayla is in my class. She's not one to spread unnecessary gossip. I decide she's a trustworthy source. "Yeah, I am," I say. "It was unexpected."

Raegan draws a few swirls with her gold glitter glue. "People shouldn't disrespect teachers like that."

Whitney playfully throws a marker at her. "Oh, lighten up. It was funny."

Raegan ignores her. I focus on filling in the rest of my letters, still wondering why Alex would do that. He's the type of person who generally stays under the radar—aside from his asthma attacks. But that hasn't happened since fifth grade gym class. And he runs with the drama crowd, which means he has to keep up a certain GPA or become at risk of being suspended from theater activities. So why would he intentionally get on Donaldson's bad side?

The back door opens. Mrs. Mahoy waddles out, shaking a carton of lemonade.

"I figured you girls must be thirsty." She smiles. "Can I pour y'all a glass?"

"Sure," Lin says, and I nod in agreement.

"Do we have any that's not from concentrate?" Raegan asks.

"No."

"Then no, thanks."

Her mother sighs, then pours three glasses for the rest of us. "You

know, soon enough you won't be the only princess in this house."
She lays a hand over her belly.

"Trust me, I know."

Her mom laughs. "The posters look great."

"Thanks," I say. "Even though Spirit Week isn't until early October."

Raegan glares at me. "Do you know how much I have to do
before then?" Her mom takes this as her cue to leave, most likely well
aware of what her daughter has to do before then. "Help organize
the pep rallies, make sure the team has our routine down—oh, *and*
help out with the homecoming parade. Plus there's everything I have
to do for Spirit Week."

Lin gives me a deadpan stare. "Look what you've done."

"Where's the off switch?" Whitney says, playfully tapping Raegan's forearm.

Raegan just gives us the finger.

When Lin and I finish our third poster, Whitney passes us another
one. This one reads, WEAR YOUR MUMS & GARTERS WITH WILD PRIDE!
GET PSYCHED FOR GAME DAY!

"Ugh, I hate this dumb tradition," Lin says as she starts filling in
the *W*. "It's worse than Valentine's Day."

I don't know how the tradition began, to be honest. Every year
on homecoming girls wear fake chrysanthemums given to them
by their dates. Guys typically wear garters. Both are decorated in
school-colored ribbons, tacky bells, and other obnoxious trinkets
that dangle down from the base of the flower, which is worn pinned
to your shirt, bra strap, or worn around your neck—depending on
the weight of it. The bigger and tackier, the better.

The mum I received from Jay seemed thoughtless, even though I would never tell him that. A few limp ribbons dangled from the base. There weren't any colorful tassels or long strands of beads. Nothing sparkled. But I smiled and told him it was great, even though I'd spent *hours* at the craft store choosing heart cut-outs to include on his garter.

"I'll make you a mum," I say, knowing I'll be dateless this year. "I'll even get one of those music boxes from the craft store and make it play our fight song. Oh, and those twinkling lights that you can turn on and off."

Lin grins. "Only if you staple three mums together, not one. I'm a three-mum kind of lady."

"Duh."

Whitney isn't laughing, and neither is Raegan. I know they're all about school spirit and tradition, but they can't deny that it *does* single out all the singles.

I need more lemonade before I pass out from dehydration. I grab my empty glass and stand up at the exact time Whitney does. She must have the same idea because her glass is empty, too. We glance at each other for a moment before starting toward the back door.

We're both quiet as we enter the kitchen. Raegan's parents have always kept a spotless house. It's a staging habit from her father's realtor career. There isn't a single crumb on the large granite island. The kitchen appliances are neatly aligned near the sink along with matching folded dish towels.

Her parents aren't around, but I can hear the faint sound of TV coming from upstairs. I make my way toward the fridge and pull out the lemonade.

I know I should bring up Jay. I don't want to, but I also don't want things to continue to be tense between us. Making amends with her is part of my twelve steps, and dancing around the topic of Jay won't get us anywhere.

"So, um," I start, pouring the lemonade over melting ice. "You and Jay."

Her hand tightens around her glass. "Me and Jay," she repeats.

She's making me do all the hard work. I take a deep breath. "Look, I know I wasn't a good friend while I was gone. I get that everyone's lives went on without me, but...I don't know. I guess I want to say it's okay. I mean, that *I'm* okay. With you and Jay."

Well. That didn't come out as smoothly as I hoped.

Whitney stares at me, her expression unreadable. Finally, she takes the carton I set down and fills her glass.

"I know it was hard being sent to Portland after everything you went through with your dad, but we're your friends." She sets the carton down a little too forcefully. "We wanted to be there for you. *I* wanted to be there for you. I tried."

Guilt twists in my stomach. "I'm sorry—"

"I had no idea if we'd ever see you again, and you were my best friend." I note her use of past tense. It stings. "What was I supposed to do? Keep reaching out so I could get more silence in return?"

I shake my head. "It was hard for me, okay? I felt really alone out there."

"We never wanted you to feel that way," Whitney says, her voice rising in the way it always does when she gets emotional. "It's like... you didn't even appreciate the friends who cared about you."

"That's not how I felt," I try.

She puts the lemonade back in the fridge, letting it shut loudly behind her. She looks right into my eyes as she carves out her next words. "But that's how it felt to *me*."

Without another word, she turns and goes back outside.

I take my glass in my hand, shocked by her honesty. She's right. I did take them for granted, especially when they wanted to make sure I was okay. It's what my dad did to Aunt June and me when she came down for Grams's funeral: Shut us out, immersed himself in his own loneliness. It was so frustrating seeing him turn into a closed-off stranger. Yet I'd done the same thing to my friends and blamed it on my own misery.

After June convinced my dad to go to AA meetings, she used to tell me how strong I was for getting through this hard time. We would talk about the happy memories we had with Grams, remembering her hidden stashes of Reese's and how she'd read us her collection of Dr. Seuss books when we were younger. I told myself I was nothing like him.

Now I'm not so sure.

I stare at my lemonade glass until condensation beads slip slowly down my hands and onto the pristine floor.

ELEVEN

NONE OF US END UP spending the night at Raegan's house. Her dad didn't want us stressing her mom out with the baby on the way even though she kept insisting she was fine.

Raegan walks us outside, clearly not happy about it. "She's already getting her way and she isn't even *born* yet!"

Lin turns to me. "We can continue the sleepover at your house? If you wanted?"

The question catches me off guard. I don't want to stumble through a vague excuse and have them think the worst about my dad and home life. Even though they're my best friends, I can't let them know about the recoverees. What if it somehow got back to Margaret? This secret is too big of a risk to let anyone else know.

I make my voice as cheerful as I can. "My dad got the carpets cleaned today, so I doubt he'd be thrilled about me having a group over when everything is still wet."

Not my best excuse, but luckily none of them seem concerned by it.

Instead, Whitney unlocks her car. She won't meet my eyes, probably assuming I'm specifically blowing her off. "It's fine. I think Jay
wanted me to come over, anyway."

I can't tell if she wants that to sting, but it does.

Lin, on the other hand, gives me a quick hug. "We'll plan for
another time."

Raegan smiles. "Yeah, it'd be good to see Mr. Seneca."

A knot of worry forms in my stomach, so I keep it noncommit-
tal. "Yeah, for sure."

I drive back home, trying not to feel bad about lying to my
friends. It's for the best. And I really, *really* don't want to get sent back
when I just got here.

The first thing I notice when I get home and open the front door
is music. It's not Queen, thank god. It sounds like something that
you'd hear at a serene water garden.

Confused, I step into the living room—which does not look
like a living room anymore. Our beige couch and leather recliner
are pushed against the wall, and our coffee table has been moved in
front of the stone fireplace. The only thing in the middle of the room
is our olive area rug and, dead center, Saylor, who is sitting cross-
legged with his eyes closed.

"Uh, hey," I say, making sure my voice is clear over the music.
"What are you doing?"

Saylor's eyes snap open. "Hey!" He leans over and turns down
the music on my old boom box. "I was just meditating."

I blink. *That's* why he reconstructed our living room?

"O-kay," I say slowly. "Well. I'll leave you to it."

Saylor sits up a little straighter. "You're welcome to join me if you want." He stands up, pulling his palms together over his head. His cluster of leather bracelets drop down toward his elbows. "You become attuned to the world around you."

I nod, not sure what to say to that.

He must sense a subject change because he goes, "Peach says you got your Texas license?"

"Yeah." I can't help but smile. "Feels good to drive a car that's mine."

Saylor lowers his arms. "I bet. Oh, hey! I got a job at the 7-Eleven down the street. I'll be the night clerk."

I debate asking him about those graphic design jobs, but he looks so proud of himself. Then it hits me. Maybe this job is the way to complete step 11: getting him out of here.

I choose my next words carefully. "That's, uh, really great." Pause. "So . . . this job. Does that mean you're moving out?"

It comes out more bluntly than I intend, but if Saylor notices he doesn't show it. He closes his eyes, as if returning to his previous meditative state, and says, "Perhaps. It's hard to say. I have nowhere to go at the moment."

I remember what my dad told me about him the other night, but that sympathy doesn't quite shield my disappointment. "Great," I mutter. "I'm gonna go shower."

Saylor nods. I leave the room and dart upstairs.

I shower quickly, not minding the lukewarm temperature after sweating all day outside. I use a few different kinds of body wash and soap to try and scrub the red paint off my hands, but nothing completely removes it. I give up, turning off the water and wrapping myself in a towel before heading to my room.

After I change into a pair of shorts and an old Cedarville Middle School shirt, I check my phone. There's a picture text from Lin. I open the image and see Lin's face twisted into a scowl. She's holding one of her red hands in the air. I read her text that follows.

LIN: Doesn't it look like we committed murder??

I laugh, then take a picture of my hand.

ME: i went all Lady Macbeth in the shower. out, damned spot! didn't work.

LIN: lolol

There's a knock at my door. I let out a deeply annoyed sigh. I hope it isn't Peach wanting to cook dinner together or Saylor wanting to talk me into yoga again. I wrap my towel around my hair and open it.

My dad stands in the hall, a smile on his face. His left hand holds up a twenty-dollar bill. "I thought I'd stop by to give you your allowance early if your room is clean."

I open the door a little wider so he can see inside. He takes it as a cue to come in instead.

"I'm still putting away laundry," I explain as he stares at the piles of clothes on my desk. "Sorry. School's been draining with homework and stuff already."

My dad nods like he understands, then takes a seat on the edge of my bed. I sit on my desk chair. I feel a little shameful about how our conversation ended last night, but it wasn't like I said any of it to be hurtful. It was the truth.

"You got your license okay?" he asks.

"Yeah. Oh, I have your debit card." I grab my purse from the ground and pull it out of my wallet. "Thanks," I add.

"You're welcome."

There's a small pause of awkward silence.

He looks at me, then takes a deep breath. "Listen, I know you're not ready to forgive me for what happened, but I want to tell you again how sorry I am."

It was all in his letters. The mournful apologies, the guilt-ridden sentences. It's not that I don't believe he's sorry, because I do. But I'm not sure if I'm ready to forgive him yet, even though I'd written in my personal twelve steps that I should.

"I want you to know—*really* know—that I know how much I screwed up. If anything had happened to you...if my actions had harmed you in any way—" He swallows, shakes his head. "I would have never forgiven myself."

I stare down at my bare knees. Grams had been gone two and a half years prior to the intersection incident, and in that time I knew my dad was slipping farther into his alcoholic haze. I was too terrified to do anything but deny it. Even when June would call and check in, I'd pretend like everything was fine.

Once I caught on to how intoxicated he'd become before going to work, I started asking Lin for rides. I made excuses. *My dad started an earlier shift,* I'd say. It was easily believable. Nobody questioned it.

There was only one time when my friends became concerned. After school, Whitney, Raegan, and Lin came over to work on a biology project. My dad's car wasn't in the garage, so I assumed he was still at work. But when we walked into my kitchen, we saw the remains of plates scattered across the scuffed tile. Hundreds of pieces were deliberately smashed in every direction, the aftermath of another episode.

Nobody said anything. Not even me. It was Whitney who suggested we go to her house. I agreed, fighting back a lump in my throat as we walked back out the door.

When I came home that evening, my dad was passed out in his room. The TV was blasting some sitcom on full volume. The laugh track mocked me as I swept up the glass pieces in the kitchen, knowing he wouldn't remember this in the morning.

Whitney texted me later that evening. I hadn't wanted to talk about it at her place, and nobody pushed me on the topic. She told me not to be mad, but she'd told Jay. She was worried, she said. But I lied. I said it was fine, that we were fine.

Later that night, my phone chimed with a text. I'd expected it to be from Jay, but I was surprised to see it was from Alex.

ALEX: just finished the season 7 finale of crime boss. WTF.

I stared at the blinking cursor, attempting to form a response in my head. Without thinking about what I was doing, I typed a reply.

ME: can you meet up?

Alex didn't hesitate.

ALEX: 7-Eleven?

ME: i'll be there soon.

From what I could tell, Alex hadn't pursued Lacey after the Sadie Hawkins dance. Our friendship had evolved into what it used to be, but I was still surprised that he was willing to meet me at 7-Eleven on a Saturday night.

Alex was already waiting for me when I arrived. He held out a cherry Slurpee for me, then motioned to the side of the building so we'd be out of sight since it was past our curfew.

I slumped to the ground, sitting with my back against the wall. He did the same.

"I'm sorry." I mashed my straw against the ice. "My dad...he's just..."

When I didn't finish, Alex said, "You don't have to be sorry for how you feel."

My fingertips were chilled from the plastic cup. This is why I'd texted him. He was always so kind, so willing to listen without judgment.

So I went on. "He has his bad days, you know, because of..."

My throat tightened. I couldn't stay Grams's name without feeling a terrible ache in my chest.

But Alex nodded. He knew my situation.

"Anyway." I took a long drink, hoping the cold would force back my tears. "It wasn't exactly a good night."

"Do you have someone who can help?" Alex asked after a moment.

I thought of Aunt June. "Yeah," I told him. "My aunt would come if I asked."

His brown eyes found mine. "You should. I mean, if you wanted. It's just—" he broke off for a second. "You shouldn't have to go through it alone, you know?"

I nodded, relief flooding my chest. I don't know if it was his words or his presence or something else entirely, but I felt a little better.

"You know what Ana used to do when I was sad?" Alex said, a hint of a smile on his face.

Ana was his sister who was a year older than us. "What?" I asked.

Alex adjusted his position so that he was sitting in front of me. Then, ever so gently, he placed his fingertips on both sides of my head. The unexpectedness of his touch made me shiver.

"One, two, three, four, now you're not sad anymore!"

He removed his hands. I laughed.

"I should have clarified that we were, like, six," Alex said with a smile.

I found his gaze, feeling my heart lift. "I think it worked."

We stayed there until midnight discussing *Crime Boss* and our summer plans and arguing over the best Slurpee flavors. It was Alex who finally suggested we head home, but not before walking me back to my street.

When I got back, I saw Jay had texted me. **U ok?** was all it said. I knew I should have opened up to him, but I was fine now. So that's what I told him.

I look back at my father. I don't want apologies. I want a do-over. I want to go back and change all the awful things that happened in the past for a more favorable future.

My fingers twist around my lotus necklace.

"I'm mad at you for not being better," I say, surprised at how easily the words erupt from my mouth.

"I'm mad at me for that, too."

"And I'm not ready to forgive you," I continue. "It's going to take a lot more than getting a job and cooking dinners and small talk to get me to trust you again."

My dad nods. "I know that."

I pick at a piece of my chipped desk. "So when are they leaving?"

He looks right at me, his eyes softening. "Your Aunt June took you in when you had nowhere else to go. Granted, I know that was one hundred percent my fault. But she still took you in."

I'm quiet for a long moment. I know Aunt June didn't have to open up her home to me, but the other option was foster care. There was no way she would have let that happen.

"I know it's hard for you having them here, but their lives fell apart, too. They know they're the ones responsible for their actions, but I want to believe in second chances. Not just for me, but for other people, too. And if I can offer them a second chance here, just temporarily, then I hope I'm helping in a small way. Does that make sense?"

I nod. I understand where he's coming from, but he could have at least run his plan by me before I came home.

We sit in silence for a moment. He hands me my twenty dollars, and I take it from him.

My eyes find my twelve-steps list folded in the corner of my desk. I told myself I'd learn to forgive my dad, but it isn't as easy as writing it on a scrap of paper.

The front door opens from downstairs. I hear a set of shoes enter through the front hallway followed by a loud . . . bark?

I glance over at my dad, eyebrows raised in question, but he looks as puzzled as I am. We jump up at the same time and rush down the stairs.

Nonnie's standing by the front door. She's holding a large grocery bag in one hand and in the other, a leash. A leash attached to a
huge, black Labrador retriever.

"Oh, hello." Her voice is intentionally sweet. The big dog laps at
her hand, then thumps his tail on the ground in excitement. "Do we
have room for one more?"

TWELVE

AS IT TURNS OUT, IT'S hard to say no to a kindhearted lady who is old enough to be your grandmother, so the dog gets to stay.

"His name is Wallis," Nonnie told us as she scratched behind his ears. "He's been at the Cedarville shelter for almost three years! Can you believe that? How could no one adopt this darling?"

I wouldn't exactly use the word *darling* to describe Wallis. He is basically a small horse. His paws are nearly the size of my own hands and every time he pants, globs of drool drip on the floor.

When I was little, I used to beg Grams for a puppy. I swore on my favorite pajama bottoms that I'd take care of it—including cleaning up its poo.

But Grams always objected. "When you learn to make that bed of yours every mornin', maybe I'll believe you."

She was right. I couldn't even last one stinking week without forgetting, and she was always there to remind me.

"If you're not responsible enough to make a bed, then how on earth are you going to take care of a livin' creature?"

I screamed at her—told her I hated her—and slammed my bedroom door. Of course my dad made me apologize later. And I did, because I could never, ever hate Grams for long.

"When you're older, I promise we'll think about it," she'd told me.

I stare at the slobbery beast in front of me. This is not what I'd had in mind when I wished for a puppy.

Nonnie and Saylor spend Sunday trying to teach him basic commands out in the backyard. Peach hangs outside with them and reads one of her romance novels in the hammock. She's not wearing heels, but she *is* sporting a long magenta skirt paired with a cream-colored blouse. It's very 1950s of her. I don't know how she doesn't suffocate from the heat.

I spend most of Sunday finishing my homework and texting Lin. She's helping organize Earth Club's first "Pick Up the Park" this Saturday at Winsor Lake. I was able to use my limited Photoshop skills to design flyers that we're going to hang around school tomorrow morning.

Everyone gathered downstairs to watch a movie later in the evening. It sounded like a comedy judging by the amount of laughter coming from the living room. I knew I would be welcomed if I went downstairs to join them, but I didn't. I still felt like a stranger in my own home.

On Monday, I get up extra early to get ready for school. It rained last night and clouds still hover thick in the air, which means it's going to be a sticky, humid day. I pull on my favorite pale-yellow button-down paired with my floral purple skirt and slide into a simple pair of flats. Then I grab my book bag and keys before

I step out of my room, grateful to have my own transportation to school.

I'm coming down the last few stairs when I hear the pounding of feet against the wooden floor. This is followed by a deep *woof!* Before I can turn back around, Wallis comes barreling toward me. I back up a step, but that doesn't stop him. He jumps up and tries to lick my face, his muddy paws staining the bottom of my shirt and the entire front of my skirt.

"No, down!" I stumble under his weight, grabbing the banister for balance. "Bad dog!"

Of course, he doesn't listen. His tongue flops out of his mouth as he continues to paw at me.

Saylor and Nonnie rush into the hall. Saylor grabs Wallis by his new collar, but the damage is done. Mud prints and clumps of dirt are smeared down the front of my carefully chosen outfit.

I. Am. Livid.

"Sorry!" Nonnie says. She has those giant curlers in her hair and her pink zebra-print bathrobe wrapped around her. "I was letting him out back—it's really muddy out there—but he barreled inside before I could stop him. He's a big people person."

My blood boils. I stare down at my ruined shirt. Saylor is struggling to hold Wallis back, but it's clear he's ready to lunge at me again.

"Just get him out of here," I snap.

"He doesn't know any better," Saylor mumbles as he turns back down the hall.

Really? The *dog* is getting sympathy? I suppress the urge to roll my eyes as I run back to my room. I find a clean skirt and a pale-blue top in my closet and cinch it with one of my brown belts. I adjust my lotus necklace in the mirror before heading back downstairs and out the door.

My mildly pissed off attitude spikes to high levels of annoyance as the day wears on. At lunch, Breck mentions having a party at his place this weekend since his parents will be visiting his older sister in Boulder. Then Jay says he can get these college girls to bring the beer because—and I quote—they are "obsessed" with him. This earns a well-deserved shove from Whitney, but he doesn't apologize.

"What?" He feigns innocence. "Do you not want beer at a party?"

Whitney glares at him. "That's not the issue."

Jay shrugs it off, even though his tiny, overconfident smile reveals his awareness of the issue.

It's weird. Even though he wears the same basketball tee and familiar pair of worn jeans, it's like he's grown into this new level of smugness that radiates some serious douche canoe vibes. I think back to when I'd caught him staring at Jana's cleavage last week in history. I wonder if he's still the type of guy who types out sweet late night texts or spends time building the classic model car kits he used to love.

I wonder if I even know him at all.

It doesn't get better after lunch.

"Miss Seneca," Mrs. Donaldson says as soon as I step foot into Algebra II. "Will you please join me at my desk?"

My heart sinks to my toes. I know this is about Friday. As much as I'd love to bolt again, I don't. I adjust the strap of my book bag and walk over to her.

Mrs. Donaldson ignores the students filing in the classroom. She pushes a blue slip of paper in front of me. No no no NO. This can't be happening. My dad will *kill* me if I have detention.

"You are not allowed to rush out of here before the bell or before I dismiss the class," Mrs. Donaldson says. "Furthermore, you are not to be wandering the halls without a pass while classes are in session."

I don't bring up the fact that there were only two minutes left of class on Friday when I bailed. Instead I mumble a faint, "Yes ma'am."

"I expect to see you in detention at three thirty on the dot." She leans back in her desk chair. "No exceptions."

I swipe the slip from her desk and walk toward my assigned seat. Crap. Not only is my dad going to kill me, but I'm going to miss Earth Club with Lin.

My heart hammers with nerves as I sink into my desk. That's when my eyes catch a blue slip sitting on top of the desk beside me. I look over to see Alex pulling his textbook out of his backpack. He glances over when he sees me staring, his eyes wandering to my own blue slip.

"Mrs. Donaldson didn't go easy on you, either?"

I shake my head. It's silly, but I feel like I might cry. I've never had detention before, and this is definitely not the way I want to start off the school year.

I can still feel Alex looking at me, so I preoccupy myself with pulling out my notebook. I can feel the tears well up behind my eyes.

"Hey," he says gently. "It's okay."

I don't say anything. I'm afraid my voice might break if I try.

Mrs. Donaldson walks in front of the board and begins to talk about linear equations. I can feel Alex's gaze lingering on me for another moment before he turns to his spiral and begins scribbling down notes.

I try and absorb the information in front of me, but I'm too upset over receiving detention. The numbers and steps are a scrambled mess of incoherence. I write down notes anyway, hoping I'll be able to make sense of them when I do homework tonight.

In my peripheral vision, I see Alex's hand moving as he copies Mrs. Donaldson's steps. He doesn't look as tired as he did last week. No red eyes or dark circles are apparent. His dark curls are still effortlessly tousled on top of his head, but they look a little tamer today. Did he get a trim over the weekend? I'm not sure.

I'm also not sure why he decided to go all *Rebel Without a Cause* on Friday. I overheard a few students talking about it in the halls this morning but other than that it seems like it's old news, which is completely fine by me.

My blue detention slip stares at me from the corner of my desk. I hope it doesn't affect my spot on the Wavettes. What if Coach Velasquez finds out and decides I'm a troublemaker? I *can't* get kicked off the team. This is going to help bring me closer to Whitney and Raegan.

I suffer through my last three classes and when the final bell rings, I book it toward A hall before anyone can see me sneaking into the detention classroom.

Room 112 is a craphole. This is where all the unloved, broken teaching materials are collected and left behind. There's a large crack in the whiteboard that hangs on the wall. Nearly all the desktops have been vandalized with some kind of sharp object, declaring things like *Mr. Harris sucks old man balls.* Even the clock is permanently stuck at 2:14. Probably as some kind of mental torture to make our time here feel even longer.

The classroom is empty except for Alex. Mrs. Donaldson motions me to come to her desk and when I do, she hands me a thick packet. The front page reads: *Algebra II Practice Problems.*

"I expect you to complete as much of this as you can," she tells me.

Great. More math. I take a seat a few desks away from Alex and set my book bag on the ground, then I start digging around in the front pocket for a pencil.

Mrs. Donaldson stands up. She heaves a canvas bag over her shoulder and looks between the two of us.

"I need to make copies for tomorrow's lesson," she tells us. "I'll be right around the corner in the teachers' lounge. You both are to stay put and work on that algebra packet. Do you understand?"

Alex and I mumble "yes ma'am" and bend over our work. I think of what Peach told me about her mom. How she said the DMV had to be one of Dante's nine circles of hell. I think another layer includes being stuck in this classroom doing algebra for all of eternity.

I try and concentrate on the packet. Most of the problems are from lessons we learned last week. I'm able to get through a few of the easy ones, but the majority of them stump me.

I glance at Alex. He's bent over his work, his thick brows furrowed together like he's deep in concentration. But I notice he completes each problem relatively quickly. It must come easy for him. He's already on the second page of the packet, which means he could have easily beat me in Radical Races on Friday.

So, why didn't he?

I set down my pencil. Loudly. "Why'd you do it?"

Alex stops writing, then slowly turns to look at me. He has this expression on his face like it's obvious, but obviously it *isn't*.

He takes a moment before he speaks. "I don't know...you choked." He folds his arms and shrugs. "And, I don't know."

Humiliation sweeps over me. I can feel the heat starting in my stomach and rising to my cheeks. I shouldn't care what Alex thinks of my intelligence, but I do.

"So you felt sorry for me? Because I'm stupid?"

Alex sighs. "You're not stupid."

I don't let up. "Then why?"

Alex unfolds his arms. Picks up his pencil. Taps it on his desk. Then he looks at me again. "I was in your algebra class. Freshman year, remember?" I do. We didn't have seat assignments, so I sat in the back, whispering back and forth with Whitney most of the time. "And no offense or anything, but you weren't very good at those races then, either."

So he does think I'm stupid. Shame eats away at me. Why couldn't I come back from Portland smarter and more sophisticated?

"And I hate how Mrs. D puts us on the spot with those races. She never asks if anyone needs clarification or if we want to run through more examples." Alex leans over and grabs his beanie from his backpack. He places it on his head. It tames his mass of curls, making his brown eyes seem a little rounder. Softer. "So yeah, maybe I wanted to prove a point. I knew I could deflect the attention away from you if I did."

I let out a hot breath of air. How *dare* he think of me as charity. I don't need anyone's help, especially not in frigging algebra class.

Alex studies me. "You're mad."

"You're observant," I snap.

He holds his hands up in defense. "I was just trying to help."

"Well look where your help landed us."

"No." Alex's tone is harsh now. "This is where *your* decision landed *you*." He leans over in the seat. "You never even saw my answer. You ran out too quickly."

Dammit. He's right, and he knows it. This would be so much easier if I could just blame him. Instead I say nothing.

We go back to our work. I can't help but run his words back through my mind. *I just wanted to help.* Why? Especially after I ignored his text message all those months ago.

Unless those feelings never went away?

I keep my head down, peering at him through my peripheral vision. He has a pencil in one hand. The other is propped up on his chin as he studies his packet. He's distant, not exactly the eager freshman who'd find any excuse to talk to me during classes and text me after each new *Supernatural* episode.

I'm overthinking this. Of course he's moved on.

"Thank you," I say.

Alex looks over at me.

I take a breath. "You're right. I didn't know what I was doing up there, so... thanks."

The corner of his mouth lifts.

I turn to my packet. A moment later, I hear him riffling through his backpack. When I look over he goes, "You hungry?"

I give him a confused stare.

Alex sits up in his seat. "Go long."

He tosses a ball of foil toward me. I catch it.

"*Oh,*" I say. "Is this—?"

He stands up and moves a few desks closer to mine. As he sets his bag down, I peel away the foil. Inside is pan dulce—a sweet bread his mom always had ready at the restaurant.

"I haven't had this since—"

I stop myself. I was about to say since Grams bought some from Rosita's Place for my birthday two years ago, but I don't want to bring her up. I don't want Alex to think that I'm giving him an opening to talk about her. It's still sometimes hard to talk about her without getting emotional.

Luckily Alex doesn't mind my unfinished thought. "My mom and I made them this morning."

Alex's family owns Rosita's Place—an authentic Mexican restaurant right off Main Street. The recipes are from his great-great-grandmother and have been a huge success in Cedarville.

He unravels the foil on his own pan dulce and sticks a hunk in his mouth. I do the same.

"Oh my god." My tongue is coated in sugar and carbs and it's the best thing ever. "I missed these."

Alex smiles.

I wait until I'm done chewing before saying, "Wait, you made these this morning? Like before school?"

"Yeah, it was my idea. I was up early helping her make tamales, anyway. It's kind of a long process, but we finished this morning. My mom's running a special this week."

"Do you work there now?" I ask. "At Rosita's?"

His face flushes. "I, uh. Just recently. My mom needs a little more help right now."

I can tell I brought up a sore subject for whatever reason, so I change course. "Thanks for sharing," I say as I polish off the last of mine. "Do you normally carry pan dulce with you in your backpack?"

He crumples up his foil into a ball. "Only on theater days when I don't have time to go home and eat."

"So your mom thinks you're doing theater stuff?"

Alex shrugs. "What she doesn't know won't hurt her."

I laugh. "I wish I had an excuse. My dad's going to kill me when he finds out."

Alex stares at me like I've sprouted another head off the side of my neck. "So . . . don't tell him?"

"Oh." I blink a few times. He already thinks I'm at Earth Club with Lin. I don't necessarily need to tell him otherwise. "Um. Wow, yeah. That could work." I give him a sideways glance. "Who knew you had a bad side?"

He shrugs. "I don't make a habit of it."

What does that mean? Am I an exception?

I stare at him a beat too long. He looks away.

I try to go back to my work, but I'm officially stuck. I've skipped around and completed all the easy problems. I'm completely blindsided by the ones that have strings of letters attached to them. Why does algebra contain so many letters? Aren't numbers complicated enough?

Alex leans over in his desk, his eyes focused on my packet. "What'd you get for thirty-two?"

I stare down at my work. "Uh, I sort of skipped around." Then I shoot him a playful glare. "Why are you asking me anyway? I suck, remember?"

Instead of answering my question, he reaches over and flips my packet toward his line of vision. I watch him study my work, suddenly feeling extremely self-conscious. I don't know why. It's not like my algebra struggle is a secret. It's why we're both here.

I take the opportunity to study his profile as he scans my worksheet. He has a really great chin. I don't tend to notice people's chins, so I don't know why I notice his. It curves neatly into a sturdy plane, jutting out slightly as he concentrates.

"Okay." His liquid brown eyes meet mine. "You're hopeless."

"W-what?" Shame coats every bone in my body. Am I really that bad? How the hell am I going to survive the rest of this year?

Alex laughs. "I'm joking, sorry! You're not hopeless." He leans in closer. He smells nice, like spicy boy deodorant and laundry detergent. "It looks like you haven't gotten the hang of a few steps, that's all."

"Great," I say, defeated.

"To tell you the truth, I'm not much better. Ana's been helping me with my homework. She had Mrs. Donaldson last year."

I remember Alex's two older sisters, Ana and Marlina. Marlina graduated last year, but Ana's a senior this year. I first met them in the sixth grade when I went to Alex's house to complete our Ancient Egypt history project.

"She tutors, you know," he continues. "She's starting back up this week in the library if you ever need extra help." I feel my face warm again. I think he picks up on this because he goes, "If I didn't get to bug her at home, I would go. I wouldn't have passed math these last two years without her."

I smile at him. I don't know why he's being so nice to me after what I did to put us both here, but I appreciate it.

Footsteps click down the hall. Alex slides out of the seat next to me and hands me my packet. Then, quietly, he walks over to his desk. I bend over my worksheet and pretend to work.

Mrs. Donaldson returns with a stack of papers in her hand. She sets them down on the desk and says, "Packets, please."

We hand them to her. She glances over them briefly before saying, "Thank you. You're free to go."

The two of us gather our things and head out the door without a word. When we're a few feet down the hall Alex says, "How much do you want to bet she'll look over our work tonight as a bit of late night pleasure reading?"

The corners of my mouth lift into a smile. Somehow we've fallen in step together as we make our way to the parking lot. "She probably dreams of polynomials and parabolas."

"Instead of counting backwards to fall asleep, she counts backwards from the square root of fifty."

I laugh. It feels nice, talking and joking around like we used to. Alex holds the door for me and I step outside. Our cars are some of the few left in the junior/senior lot. Everyone else has gone home.

Alex turns to me. "Here." He pulls a piece of candy from his jeans pocket. "For the ride home."

I don't recognize the bright-yellow wrapper, but I accept it anyway. "Pulparindo?" I say, reading the label.

He raises his eyebrows. "It's very good."

I curl the packet into my hand. "Thanks," I tell him. "For... everything."

From the way he smiles at me, I can tell he understands.

I think about confronting him about the text to complete at least one of my steps, but my nerves stop me. We walk our separate ways to our cars. Once I'm inside, I unwrap the packaging and tear off a bite. And—it's not what I expect. The texture is like sandpaper, but the flavors are a mixed medley of sweet, spicy, and tangy.

I send off a quick text.

ME: starbursts still hold the #1 place in my heart

His reply comes quickly. I look over to see if he's left the parking lot. He hasn't. His truck is still sitting there.

ALEX: blasphemy.

Then:

ALEX: glad you liked the pan dulce :)

I slide my phone into the cup holder and put my key in the ignition. I find myself enjoying the spicy, sticky sweet taste that lingers on my tongue the rest of the drive home.

THIRTEEN

VOICES ECHO DOWN THE HALL as soon as I step through the door. I wander into the kitchen and find Peach placing something in the oven while my dad chops vegetables beside her. He must have said something funny because she's laughing, and then he's laughing. Their heads lean close. It's all so natural, like they've known each other for years.

I wonder just *how* close they became at the ranch.

It wasn't completely out of the ordinary for my dad to date sporadically when I was younger, but he never committed to anyone. I was always his first priority, he said. No one was around long enough for me to wonder what it'd be like if our family expanded, and that's not what I want now. Peach seems nice, but shouldn't he be focused on fixing *our* relationship?

Another burst of laughter erupts from the kitchen. I can't remember the last time I heard my dad laugh like that. It might have been when Grams would use words wrong and call e-mails "computer letters" or maybe when he'd pranked me into drinking pickle juice on April Fools'—which I spit out *everywhere*. Watching their moment, I feel strangely left out.

My dad spots me standing there. "Hey, Goose!"

Peach smiles at me. "You're right on time. We're making home-made pizza for dinner."

I stare at them. Surely they can't expect me to play along while they slowly take over my normal life.

My dad sets down his knife and looks up at me. "How was Earth Club?"

"Good." I'm surprised at how easily the lie comes out. I'd texted Lin earlier to apologize for ghosting on the meeting, and she said it was fine as long as I showed for the cleanup on Friday.

Peach sets the timer. "Everything will be ready in about ten minutes."

She looks so comfortable in our kitchen. It makes my stomach churn. I mumble a quick, "I'm not hungry," and race upstairs, almost bumping into Nonnie as I round the corner in the hallway.

She's wearing a blouse patterned with bright green giraffes and her signature turquoise glasses. Her hands adjust the frame of one of our family pictures. Wallis sits next to her, thumping his tail in excitement when he spots me.

"Stay, Wallis," Nonnie says. Miraculously, he does. "Ha! Wish I'd realized he knew that command this morning."

I stare at the pictures. "What are you doing?"

"Oh, Wallis knocked into the wall as he was running toward the guest room." Nonnie waves her hand over the collection of pictures. "I noticed a few were crooked, so I'm realigning them."

I look at the dozens of frames hung along the wall. It's funny. They've been there for so long that I sometimes forget they exist. Most are of me growing up—toothless kindergarten pictures followed by awkward elementary school photos and overly enthusiastic middle school snapshots.

There are a ton of us as a family. One is from our camping trip in Blanco State Park. Another is from a ski trip my dad and I took a few years back. But so many of Grams. She poses with me after my first ballet recital, where she'd learned how to work a video camera just for that evening. In another, we're lying side by side in a field of blue bonnets on our road trip to Austin. There's another of us wearing red, white, and blue at Cedarville's annual Fourth of July parade.

All my friends had moms who were dependable, but I thought I'd always have Grams. These pictures are another reminder of one more thing I've lost.

"Take them down," I tell Nonnie. Then I say it louder. "The ones of her. Take them down."

Nonnie follows my stare to the pictures of Grams. Understanding washes over her features. I move past her and Wallis and walk into my room, but she follows me before I have a chance to shut my door.

"Kira?" Her voice is gentle at the edge of my bedroom. "May I?"

I set my book bag down on the ground. I'm too tired to fight her on this, so I shrug and sink down on my bed.

Nonnie walks all the way inside. Wallis takes a tentative step behind her.

"I know it doesn't help," she says, "but I'm sorry."

A tightness squeezes hard in my throat. Slowly, she comes and sits down next to me on the bed. I notice she smells strongly of patchouli and rose petals and hairspray.

"Sometimes life throws us balls and forgets to hand us a bat." She's quiet for a moment. "You miss her. That's completely natural, you know."

I don't say anything, afraid of the emotions that might come flooding out. I remember my list and how I'd committed to learn how to be a family with her gone, but it's difficult to do when the memories of her hang in every corner of the house.

"It's hard. Experiencing loss in one form or another." Nonnie runs her hands over her slacks. I stare at her chunky collection of turquoise rings—one on every finger. "But it's the way you handle it that reveals the type of person you are."

I shrug, unsure of what type of person that makes me.

After a pause she asks, "Do you know why I left New York?"

I assume she thinks my dad has told me, but he hasn't. I shake my head.

"My husband left me for another woman. Nearly twenty-five years ago. Rayanne Summers—even her name was prettier than mine."

I pick at my thumbnail. I thought losing Jay to Whitney was hard, but I can't imagine how it would feel to have a marriage end because your husband wanted to be with someone else.

"I'm sorry."

Nonnie's eyes brighten. "I'm not."

I'm confused. "You're not?"

"Having Charles leave me was the best thing that happened to

me," she says. "Oh, it was hard. And it hurt. It hurt because I still
loved him, and those feelings were terrible to try and process."

I nod, picking at my pinky nail.

"But one night, when I was trying to get back to Brooklyn, Freddie Mercury stepped right into my subway car."

I snort. There's no way I believe that. I sincerely doubt Freddie Mercury would take New York public transportation.

Nonnie smiles at my disbelief. "Of course, it wasn't the *real* Freddie Mercury. Only an impersonator. There are a lot of people who'll entertain you on your route home for tips." She waves a hand dismissively in the air. "But he had a speaker, and I listened as he lip-synched 'Don't Stop Me Now.' It was silly, but considering what I'd gone through it was also quite empowering. I gave him every cent in my wallet for his Queen CD."

I feel the question erupt before I can stop it. "Why?"

She pauses for a moment. "I married very young. I'm not sure if I had myself figured out. And although I loved Charlie, he'd held me back in a lot of ways. He was always more conservative in his mannerisms and in the way he dressed. I thought respectable attire and droll conversations were all a part of my journey into adulthood." Wallis comes and rests his chin on her leg, and she gives his head a few gentle strokes. "It turns out that's not the way it works. You have to be true to yourself. That's what the faux Freddie reminded me of that night."

I glance at Nonnie. I assumed her flamboyancy and ridiculously bright clothing were for attention, but now I'm not so sure.

"And when people stare at me or ask me why I wear the things I wear, do you know what I tell them?"

"To shove off?"

Nonnie cackles with laughter. "No, no. I tell them, 'dullness is a disease.' You know who said that?"

I take a wild guess. "Freddie Mercury?"

"Exactly." She grins. "I lost Charlie, but I spent more time becoming the woman I wanted to become." She adjusts her turquoise frames. "Now, there were mistakes I made along the way—I never intended on ending up at Sober Living—but that's all a part of life. You always have to forgive your own mistakes. Otherwise they'll eat you alive."

We sit in silence for a moment, but my mind is elsewhere. I'm transported back to Merciful Heart, where I was begging to see Grams, but my dad said no, that I don't want to remember her in her unconscious state while the doctors did everything they could to help her heart. It would only upset me, he said. And like I did that day when Grams told me I couldn't have a puppy, I repeated those same words to him.

I hate you.

He said he was sorry. He said it over and over, but it didn't matter. What mattered is the only mother I'd ever had was gone.

" 'See you later,' " I say aloud. "That was the last thing I said to her. To Grams. I was running late for school. I don't even remember what she said back."

Nonnie lets this sink in. "You've been through a lot, losing your grandmother, losing trust in your father . . . but you're still here."

I stare down at my yellow throw rug. "It wasn't my decision."

"But you're here, aren't you? Working hard in school, giving your dad another chance. That makes you the strong one."

A swollen sadness spreads through my chest, filling the hollowness within me. Tears sting behind my eyes. I never thought of myself as strong. That word was always reserved for other people: Raegan's go-getter strength, Grams's unconditional support. Never for me.

I wipe away my tears before they can fall. Nonnie pretends not to notice. I silently thank her for that.

"The pictures," I say. "You don't have to take them down."

Nonnie rests her cool hand over my own. "I wasn't going to."

It's a kind gesture, one that fills me with unexpected comfort. I realize that, at this very moment, I have an opportunity to attempt to convince Nonnie to leave as part of my list. I can easily do it, but I don't. For the first time since they arrived, I don't mind her company.

From downstairs, Peach hollers that dinner is ready.

I turn to Nonnie. "I ate earlier."

"Well, I surely can't say no to pizza." Her gaze focuses on Wallis, who is spread out on my area rug. "C'mon, boy. I'm sure there will be leftovers."

Wallis rolls over onto his back, making himself even more comfortable.

"Wallis," Nonnie warns.

Wallis's tongue flops over the side of his mouth.

"It's okay," I say. "Really. He can stay in here."

Her eyes widen. "You're sure?"

My eyes find Wallis's. It's not his fault someone left him, too. So I nod and with one last glance at the both of us, Nonnie leaves.

The tension in my chest eases, although I can't explain why. I feel like I should be angry at Peach and my dad for acting like everything is fine, but I'm not. I just feel sad. And more alone than I did before.

Wallis watches me from the rug as I spend the next few hours reading chapters for history and getting on and off the internet to see what my friends are up to. I google a step-by-step breakdown of my algebra homework before giving up and brushing my teeth.

As I'm walking back to my room, I spot something propped up against my door.

Confused, I bend down to pick it up. It's a CD case. *Queen's Greatest Hits.*

I've had to listen to this every morning for the past week. Nonnie is basically giving me the power to trash this, but I know I won't.

Even though I've memorized all the songs, I slide it into my laptop's CD drive. I play the album softly as I climb into bed. I want to be the strong person Nonnie seems to see in me, but the truth is I'm not sure that's who I am.

FOURTEEN

COACH VELASQUEZ HOSTS AN EARLY morning Wavettes meeting on Tuesday, and as I'm leaving the dance room, I spot Breck studying pages of his chemistry book outside of the gym.

"Riveting stuff?"

He looks up, then grins. "Ah. Yeah. Not so much."

"Hey, so, what's with you wanting to join the decathlon?" I fold my arms. "And you better not tell me it's to mess with Lin."

"Why would I want to do that? I like Lin."

He sounds genuine, but I wait for more.

"Okay, fine." Breck groans into his hands before looking back at me. "I want to prove I can be good at something other than basketball because...I'm not sure I want to play in college."

This wasn't the answer I was expecting. "You don't?"

"Nah. Don't get me wrong. I'll do it if I get a sick scholarship—money is important. But, you know, my brain *is* pretty dope." He taps the side of his head, smiling. "And I think competing with the decathlon team could be fun."

I study him, somewhat surprised. Breck likes partying and basketball as much as Jay, but Jay never took his grades super seriously. He was fine being average. And from what Lin told me about Breck's GPA, he works hard. Really hard.

"I'll talk to her."

He closes his textbook. "You will?"

"Just don't let her down," I warn. "You already have basketball, but this team is important to her."

"I won't," Breck says, and I can tell he's being earnest. "I swear."

I glance at the clock. The bell is a few minutes away from ringing. "I'll see you at lunch."

Breck waves, and I turn down the hall and head to my locker. I need my English textbook for first period, although I wish I could skip it and consume my stress about my chemistry test in the form of glazed donuts.

"Did it work?" A voice says from behind me.

I turn around. Alex is standing there, the sleeves of his black undershirt pushed up to his elbows. The gray T-shirt he wears over it has an upside-down stegosaurus printed on it. I'm not sure what it means, but knowing Alex I can only guess it's a film logo.

"Did what work?"

He smiles. "The excuse. From yesterday?"

"Oh." I move out of the way so he can access his locker. "Yeah, it did, actually. Thanks."

Alex opens his mouth to say something, then closes it. I follow his gaze down the hall. Lin sprints toward us, stopping when she sees me.

"This *sucks*. I stopped by the Pick Up the Park sign-up sheet and only *five* people have signed up so far! Five!"

Alex shuts his locker, then turns toward us. "I don't want to tell you how to run things." Lin looks over at him, a curious expression on her face. "But maybe next time schedule the cleanup on a Saturday? Most people have things going on after school."

Lin's eyes widen, like she can't believe she didn't think of that. "Oh! You're so right. I need to tell Andrea." She tucks a loose piece of hair behind her ear. "But you're still coming, right?" She looks at Alex. "And you, too? I saw your name on the list, I think."

"Yeah," Alex tells her. "I need volunteer hours."

"Awesome." She turns to me. "See you at lunch!"

I watch as she practically skips down the hall. "You just made her entire morning."

His eyes light up when he looks at me. "Did I?"

I pull a cheesy grin. "There's a heart of gold beneath that rebellious spirit."

Alex cringes, then yanks his beanie down over his eyes. "I can't even look at you right now. That was awful—like a really bad movie tagline."

I snort out a laugh. "What? You mean you wouldn't go see it?" I pretend to think about it. "Maybe I can make a career out of this."

Alex unveils his eyes. "I hate to break it to you, but no."

"Oh! What about this, *braving true triumph is the key to her heart.*"

"God, no."

"The ultimate courage requires the ultimate sacrifice."

"I think these are actually causing me physical pain."

I forgot how easy it is to talk with him. If he's still upset about my non-response to his text all those months ago, I can't tell. I know I need to talk to him about it, but the next words out of my mouth aren't a confrontation.

"You're here early."

Alex gives me a questioning look.

"I mean, Raegan says you're usually late to homeroom."

He studies me for a moment, a hint of a smile on the edge of his lips. "Yeah, I guess I am. My mom didn't need help in the kitchen this morning."

"Did you tell her both me and my stomach greatly thanked her for the pan dulce?"

"Yeah, she was stoked." He grins. "I also told her how much you loved the Pulparindo."

"Love is a strong word, frankly. It's a solid B-plus."

"Your tastes just aren't as refined as mine."

The warning bell rings. I glance at the clock to make sure it's right. It's unlike me to lose track of time.

I look at him. "I better get to homeroom."

"Me too," he says. "You know, to surprise Raegan with my ability to be on time."

With a quick wave, he departs down the hall. I watch him for a moment. He didn't have to write that stuff on the board during Radical Races, but he did. There's a part of me that's glad for the familiar comfort of his friendship, but there's an even bigger part of me that feels like I don't deserve it.

———————

"Can anyone tell me the nickname of Roosevelt's political advisors?"

I'm sitting in AP History armed with two pens. I use the blue one every time Mr. Densick mentions something that could be on the AP exam, and my black one scribbles the notes that will be covered on our first exam. If I'd known this class would give me early onset carpal tunnel syndrome, I'd have seriously reconsidered.

I take a short break to massage my wrist, but being a leftie my elbow accidentally knocks into Jay's. He looks up at me. Today he's wearing a pale blue polo shirt under his letterman jacket. (Mr. Densick likes to crank up the AC so no one falls asleep. Freezing us out seems like the better option to him, apparently.) It's a good color on him. I think I've told him that before. Then I wonder if he's wearing it because I've told him that before.

I force those thoughts to an abrupt halt. No. I am not going there. I'm a better friend than that.

Sorry, I mouth, then point to my limp writing hand.

Jay smiles, then shrugs. He makes sure Mr. Densick is preoccupied with talking about the current slide on the board before flipping open a fresh sheet of paper in his notebook. He draws a tiny hangman game in the corner. There are twenty spaces for letters underneath it. Then he raises his eyebrows at me, hinting I should play along.

I freeze. This is the second time he's initiated this in class. It doesn't help that he looks immaculate today. His short brown hair is styled, like he took time this morning doing it. I tell myself not to look at his most attractive features (eyes, lips, hands) because I *have* to put a stop to the fluttering inside me.

At the top of the hangman Jay writes MOVIES in block letters.

Okay. This is not a big deal. I keep building it up because I want it to mean more than it should. But to Jay, it's just a way to pass time in class. Besides, we're friends. And I'm supposed to be in the process of reconnecting our friendship, according to step 6 on my list.

I shift my spiral over an inch so he can read. *A?* I guess.

Jay fills two *A*'s in the blank spaces.

"Who can tell me," Mr. Densick is saying, "What the very first agreement for self-government in America was called? We went over this yesterday."

"Mayflower Compact," Jay calls out.

"Thank you Mr. Valenski, but next time please raise your hand." Mr. Densick writes *Mayflower Compact* in huge letters on the board. "I would highly advise you to familiarize yourself with this."

I go back through my notes and put a star next to where I've written about the Mayflower Compact. I flip back over to my page and guess: *T?*

Jay grins. There are three *T*'s.

His movie ends up being *The Fast and the Furious,* which I guess near the end, but I stump him with *Shrek.* We play back and forth for the rest of class, stopping occasionally to scribble important information from Mr. Densick's slides.

With ten minutes of class left, Jay draws up another hangman board. On the top he writes NAMES.

I guess *O, I, E, T, S, D,* and *A* before I finally lose. Right before the bell rings, Jay fills the rest of the blanks in for me: *Kira Kay.*

I don't realize I'm smiling until Jay looks at me. I try not to read into it, but how can I not? That was his old nickname for me. The nickname he gave me *when we were going out.* But we are *not* going out anymore. So why would he write that?

The bell rings. It seems to jolt Jay from his thoughts, and he slams his notebook shut with more force than necessary. He doesn't look my way once as he gathers up his things and leaves the classroom.

———————

I run into Whitney as I'm walking to my car after Wavettes practice.

"Oh!" she says, after nearly colliding with me as she cuts through a row of cars. I'd gone to the locker room to change into my purple boatneck top and jeans, but she's still wearing her red Wavettes tank top and black dance pants. I thought she'd left by now, but maybe she stayed after to talk to Jay. "Um. Sorry."

It's the first time we've been alone together since making posters at Raegan's house. She looks distracted, like she'd rather be anywhere else. I think back to my twelve steps. I know I have to try to make amends for the both of us, and I know it won't be easy. She's made that much perfectly clear. But I have to keep trying for the sake of our friendship.

"Hey, so," I start. "I was thinking, do you maybe want to hit up the mall before Breck's thing on Saturday?"

Cedarville's mall is nothing spectacular, but when we were in middle school we spent way too much time there. We'd split an overpriced cone from Häagen-Dazs and spend the rest of the time wandering in and out of stores only to end up watching guys from the high school at the indoor skate park.

"My mom's making me go to my grandpa's birthday brunch," she says.

Disappointment drapes over me. "Oh, well—"

She looks toward her car. "I should get home."

"Okay." I give her a small wave as she begins to head in that direction. "See you."

Just like that, I am dismissed. It hurts more than I want it to.

I'd told Lin what happened in Raegan's kitchen on Saturday, and she'd told me to give her time. But a part of me was angry. I know I'd been unresponsive, but she wasn't exactly Miss Communicative when she started dating Jay.

I'm walking to my car when I pass Alex's beat-up Chevy. My insides twist with guilt. Alex has three more detentions to complete for what he wrote on the board. If I hadn't choked during Radical Races, he probably wouldn't have done it.

I stare at his dented bumper. The green paint is fading from sun damage, and the door to the bed of the truck is completely missing. It's easy to tell that this car has been loved for a long time. He's not even embarrassed by it. I watched him pull into the parking lot yesterday morning with the windows rolled down.

With nothing but homework to do, I jump into my car and drive to 7-Eleven. I'm in the mood for a Slurpee, and since the summer days are dwindling down to fall, I decide to take advantage of it one more time.

I walk to the back and pour myself a cherry slush. As I make my way toward the register, I pause at the candy aisle. Before I can think about what I'm doing, I pick up a pack of my favorite candy, Starburst, the tropical kind. I used to carry a handful in my backpack in eighth grade, and Alex and I would use the discarded wrappers to write notes to each other during class. He even taught me how to make a bracelet out of the wrappers, learned courtesy of Marlina's crafty side. His was red and mine was yellow.

I pay for my sugary loot and head out the door.

When I'm back in the car, I make a right instead of a left and drive back to the school parking lot. Alex's car is still there. Good. I pull into the empty space beside him and fumble for a Sharpie in my book bag. On the candy packaging I write, *From my refined taste buds, to yours.*

I hop out of my car and slide the stick of Starburst under his windshield wiper. I don't leave my signature. I have a feeling he'll know who they're from.

FIFTEEN

WEDNESDAY ROLLS AROUND, AND EVEN though it's almost officially fall, the weather is still a swampy eighty degrees. That doesn't
stop most freshmen from wearing cozy sweaters and riding boots—
as if they aren't a walking sweatbox.

I feel proud about one thing in particular, though. After a long
conversation with Lin, she decided to give Breck a chance on the
decathlon team.

"If he misses even *one* practice or does anything to ruin our
chance at state," she told me in the parking lot before school, "I will
bake him a cake filled with laxatives."

I let Breck know his bowels are on the line, but he swears his basketball schedule won't conflict.

I end up giving Nonnie back her Queen CD later that evening.
She's sitting at the kitchen table reading the comics from Sunday's
paper. Her hair is wrapped in giant curlers and she's wearing an
embroidered gown with bright-red flowers. I know Freddie Mercury is her savior, but he's not mine.

With Saylor now working night shifts at 7-Eleven, Nonnie vol-
unteering at the shelter, and my dad working late, our schedules
aren't aligned anymore—which means I haven't been subjected to
more uncomfortable dinners where everyone compliments Peach's
cooking and pretends like this entire situation is completely normal.

Peach continues to dish out kindness like she dishes out her from-
scratch casseroles. She also continues to make my lunch, wash everyone's laundry, and keep the kitchen tidy. While I appreciate all she
does, I can't help but wish she'd focus more on getting her own life
back on track and not putting it off by staying here. Every day that
they stay here is a risk. Even though I haven't had another phone call
from Margaret, there's still a paranoid part of me that thinks she'll
somehow find out.

Then there's the fact that Peach continues to spend so much time
with my dad. It sends me into a fit of blind anger. Sometimes they
go out front and sit on the porch swing and, I don't know, *talk* for
like . . . *hours*. I can hear them laughing from my room. He looks hap-
pier than he has in years.

Which makes it hard for me to manipulate everyone into leaving.

The only upside to the week is when Peach goes to buy groceries. My dad joins me on the couch and we watch the latest episode of
Crime Boss. He even makes us a plate of what he called his homemade
nachos, which are just chips sprinkled with shredded cheese that he
pops in the microwave for a minute. It's nothing fancy, but it doesn't
need to be. We take turns trying to guess the murderer and for the
first time in a while, it feels like it's only the two of us.

Aunt June calls me later that evening when I'm in my room.

"Hey, sweets," she says when I answer. "I just wanted to check in. How are you?"

I consider telling her about the recoverees living here. I know my dad hasn't said anything to June because she would have already brought it up. It seems like something he would have mentioned to her, but I don't know. Maybe he thinks she'll get the wrong idea.

"Good," I tell her. "I miss you. And those mini pretzel bagels you used to get from that coffee shop."

She laughs. "Lord knows I've eaten enough of those for five lifetimes." She clears her throat, and her voice suddenly grows serious. "Listen, doll, I was wondering how your dad is doing? Honestly?"

I grip the phone tighter. I could tell her the truth. She could maybe figure out a way to get these people out of here so that things can go back to normal.

But what if it doesn't happen, and I'm sent back to Portland?

"He's good," I say. "Honest."

I hear her exhale. "Well, if you need anything—"

"I know. Thank you."

And just like that, I'm keeping my father's secrets all over again.

On Thursday, I'm stressing over the fact that Algebra II is still kicking my ass. I haven't been called up for any more Radical Races, but I'm getting C's and D's on most of my homework assignments. Maybe I'll find Alex's sister in the library next week, even though going in for tutoring makes me feel more insecure than I already am.

Alex received my package of Starburst, though. Yesterday he

made a production of stealthily eating them in class, grinning at me like he knew I was the mysterious candy bearer. When I caught his eye and grinned back, he dropped a few in the palm of my hand, along with an empty wrapper.

I won't say it's the best, but it's close.

I use another wrapper to write back.

You have questionable taste.

After he reads it, he gives me a playful glare, tossing a mango square at my head.

"Mr. Ramos!" Mrs. Donaldson scolds. "If you know this material well enough to become distracted, then perhaps you can lead the class in an example?"

I give Alex a look of sympathy. The last thing we both need is another detention from this class. But before Alex slides out of his seat, he glances over at me.

Worth it, he mouths.

I'm about to walk into art history when Lin pulls me aside.

"Raegan's mad at us," she says.

My good mood instantly deflates. I really don't need another friend mad at me right now.

"What? Why?"

Lin rolls her eyes. "Because we're going to Breck's party this weekend and she's not."

I throw my hands up. "So why doesn't she just come?"

"Because she's President of Leadership Council and doesn't want to"—Lin uses air quotes—"'tarnish her reputation.'"

I sigh. At least it's not my fault. I'm actually looking forward to his party. For one, it'll give me the opportunity to drop the sympathy stigma in front of most of our classmates and show them that my life is totally normal. It'll also give me the opportunity to hang out with my friends as a group and work on the goals of my twelve steps. But it makes it hard to focus on being a better friend to Raegan when she's upset that we're going in the first place.

When school lets out later that day, I go to my locker and grab the change of clothes I packed. There's no way I'm picking up trash in jeans, especially in this insufferable heat. Thankfully, Raegan scheduled our practice on the field at five thirty—going over and over our routine in the afternoon sun is never something I look forward to the day before a game.

Alex walks up just as I'm closing my locker. He smiles at me and like a reflex, I find myself smiling back.

"Are you still going to the Earth Club cleanup?" I ask.

"Yeah, for sure." He opens his locker. "Want a ride? Carpooling seems like an approved Earth Club activity."

I shrug. *Why not?*

"I'll meet you in the parking lot," I tell him, holding up my change of clothes.

"Sounds good."

I head into the girls' bathroom and lock myself in a stall. I send a quick text to Lin and tell her I'll be there in a few, and then I pull on an old, faded tank top and my black dance shorts. I throw my hair up into a ponytail, grab my bag, and walk outside.

Alex is sitting in his truck, windows down. As I walk closer, I hear jazz blaring from his speakers.

I open the passenger door and climb in.

"Interesting music choice. Are you sixteen going on sixty?" I joke, then want to kick myself. Way to kick things off by making them awkward.

Alex jabs a finger at the dial, but I notice his face flush. "Ha ha. No. This thing's stuck."

I try and keep my voice even, playing it off. "To a jazz station? That's unfortunate."

"Tell me about it." He puts the truck in drive. "But it's made me well-versed in jazz musicians. You know, in case I'm ever on *Jeopardy!*"

I laugh and just like that, the tension breaks.

His Chevy is just as worn on the inside as it is on the outside. There's a large crack running down his rearview mirror and chunks of leather are peeling away from his seats. The vents don't blow any air, which is probably why the windows are rolled down, but he taps his hands on the wheel like it's a brand-new BMW.

I notice he's not wearing his infamous double shirts, but a plain white tee paired with black soccer shorts. Pieces of his dark curls fall over his eyebrows when he glances at me. I quickly look away, flustered. I don't want him to think I've been, like, *gawking* at him.

This would be an ideal time to bring up his text.

i know my timing is off...

And yet, I can't bring myself to start that conversation. Not when we've been getting along so well as friends. Besides, it's *Jay* who I want to reconnect with. Even though he's adopted a slightly full-of-himself attitude, he's still the same Jay from freshman year. A person can't change that much.

At least, that's what I tell myself.

"Hey, so," I begin, "wasn't today supposed to be your last day of detention?"

"Yeah, but it turns out Mrs. Donaldson loves Lin. She was a star student in her geometry class last year," he explains. "When I told her only five people signed up for the Earth Club cleanup and that Lin was bummed about it, she gave in and let me go do this instead." He picks up a piece of paper from his console. "All Lin has to do is sign this to tell her I was there. For proof."

I give a playful gasp. "You used my best friend as an excuse."

"I didn't, I swear." He glances at me again. "I told you I was going to do this anyway. Even before detention. Besides, I need volunteer hours."

"For what?"

"College apps. I figure I better start now so I'm not attempting to cram it all in my senior year."

That's a good point. Why hadn't I thought of that? I've barely thought about college, let alone the SATs.

"Do you know where you want to go?"

Alex grows quiet for a moment. "I think I might stay fairly close. UT Austin or Rice, maybe the University of Oklahoma." I notice the lack of excitement in his voice. "They have a good film program."

I raise an eyebrow. "Want to try that once more, with feeling?"

Alex meets my gaze for a moment. He looks surprised that I've called him out, but what he doesn't realize is that I am the queen of lackluster replies. I perfected my technique in Portland when I told my classmates I transferred due to my mom's job. It was easier than explaining the truth. Besides, I've known Alex long enough to know that he's wanted to attend film school in southern California since forever.

"It's complicated," is all he says.

I know that feeling well enough, so I don't push him.

Alex pulls into the parking lot across from the lake. We don't say anything as we get out and head toward Lin's designated picnic table. Earth Club's President, Holly Macintyre, is pulling on a pair of plastic gloves as Lin opens a box of trash bags.

Aside from the four of us, there's Colton. Lin had to bribe him by buying him three slices of pizza at lunch, but he's here. Well, physically here anyway. He's wearing his headphones, no doubt daydreaming of playing stadium tours.

"Hey!" Lin says when she spots us. She takes a few steps away from Holly and whispers, "This turnout is *awful*. I'm so glad you're here."

"Don't worry about it," I tell her as she hands us a pair of gloves. "The next one will be better."

She gives us an unsure smile.

Holly divides us into two groups. Alex and I will take the west side of the lake, and they'll take the east. Lin reminds us to stay hydrated, gesturing to one of the water canisters they've borrowed from the football team. Then we split up.

There isn't much trash on the picnic side of the park, so we wander to a secluded area of trees. That's when we stumble upon an array of smashed beer cans, stained napkins, and forgotten tubes of ChapStick.

The west side of Winsor Lake is where the seniors come to party. They have to wander pretty far into the woods to avoid gaining attention from the cops with all the noise and music. Whitney used to say she couldn't *wait* until we were seniors so we could party here, but I don't see the fun in standing around in the middle of the forest watching everyone else get trashed. It's not that I'm against everyone having a good time. I mean, I've tried my fair share of cheap beer and spiked lemonade. I'm just not exactly comfortable watching other people get *wasted*—probably because I've watched my dad do the same thing too many times.

Alex takes in the stretch of discarded beer cans. "I never understood why Marlina loved coming here."

I glance up at him, surprised. It's as if he read my mind.

"Right?" I add. "Why can't it be cool to keep hanging out at Sonic or something?"

"Probably because you can't have sex in the back of your car at Sonic."

"Valid point."

I forgot that this place is also an STD landmine. As we toss away more crumpled aluminum and loose beer caps, I find myself wondering how far he went with Lacey. Heat fills my face. I shouldn't care. That was freshman year, which feels like forever ago.

Jay and I did everything but. I always pictured him as my first. If I'm being honest, maybe that's another reason why it's so hard to see him with Whitney. But is this the new Jay—the one who brags about girls bringing him beer at parties and who flirts a little too openly and obviously despite having a girlfriend—someone I *still* want?

"So," I say after a minute, searching for a new topic. "Ana..."

"Alex," he corrects.

I shoot him a playful stare. "*Ana*. Your sister?"

"I doubt she parties out here, if that's what you're thinking." Alex discards an empty chip bag. "She knows our mom would wring her neck if she came home drunk."

"No, that's not it," I say. "I was hoping to visit her."

Alex's thick brows furrow in confusion.

"In the library. For tutoring," I clarify.

"Oh, for sure. I'll let her know you plan on stopping by."

Relief eases inside my chest. "I feel like I'm drowning in that class."

"She can help. Like I said, she's the only reason I'm able to understand my homework."

I appreciate that he's not making fun of me. "I sort of let my grades slide when I was in Portland. I can't afford to do that this year. Not if I want to go to a decent college."

This captures Alex's attention. "Where are you thinking of going?"

I toss another empty can in my bag. The truth is... I'm not sure. Ever since I've been back, all I can think about is attempting to fix this odd situation. I know I can apply wherever I want, but there's a tiny, insecure part of my brain that wonders if I should go away to college. What's my dad going to do? And what if he relapses and I'm not there to help this time?

"I don't know. Things at home are... kind of weird."

Whoa. Where did that come from? I've already admitted this to

Lin, but she's one of my best friends. Maybe it's because of the way he's looking at me. His eyes aren't full of the sorry sympathy I was used to receiving from people. I can tell I have his full attention and it feels, I don't know ... *nice?*

When I don't say anything else, he goes, "This probably doesn't help, but my home life has been weird, too. It was just Marlina, Ana, and me last year, but then Marlina left for college and my two little cousins from Mexico moved in." He tosses an empty cigarette carton in his bag. "One is eight and the other is five. They just started at Cedarville Elementary, but they're really struggling with English."

I thought moving to Portland was a huge change. I can't even imagine moving to an entirely new country where I don't even speak the language.

"That must be hard."

"Tell me about it." Alex scoops up another crushed beer can. "I'm used to being the youngest, so having two little kids in the house is kind of nuts. There isn't much room for them. Emilio—that's my five-year-old cousin—has to share a room with me. And he wakes up a lot crying for his mama. My mom feels bad because sometimes it'll happen a few times a night, and then there are some mornings where I help her out with the restaurant..." He glances over at me. "Sorry. I'm talking a lot."

"No." I don't want to discourage him, but it does explain why he's looked run-down in class most days. "Why are your cousins here? If you don't mind me asking."

"Their dad needed surgery, and my aunt couldn't properly take care of both him and the kids. So my mom said they could spend a school year here."

"That's nice of her."

"It is, especially since she already takes care of us. It's why I don't mind waking up early to help her out with the restaurant." Alex wipes his forehead on the sleeve of his shirt. "They're in ESL classes, but I've also been giving them extra English lessons every night. Emilio is picking it up faster than Jose, but they're both making good progress."

I catch myself smiling. This is the Alex I've always known, the guy who'd do anything for family even when he didn't have to. It's nice that he hasn't changed.

I glance back down to the mess before us, then I take a deep breath. "It's been weird being home, to be honest. My dad is like . . . this completely different person. But I don't know. I know he's really trying. For me. And for himself. But things are just—they're not the same."

Shame finds its way to the pit of my stomach. I haven't even told Lin that much about my dad, so why is it so easy to confide in Alex?

I look up to find him staring at me. "For what it's worth, I'm really sorry." He shifts his weight from one foot to the other. "You didn't deserve that."

I used to hate it when people would tell me that they were sorry about what happened. It wasn't their fault my dad spiraled. But it was something people said because they didn't know what else to say. Somehow it feels different coming from Alex. It's sincere, not like he's throwing words into the wind.

It almost makes me want to tell him about my overcrowded house. About Peach and Saylor and Nonnie and all the changes that I've had to experience in the last few weeks. I so badly want someone to agree that it's a messed-up situation. For a second, I almost tell him.

But I don't.

Because, well, what about my twelve steps? I've been doing so well, especially with things that aren't on the list. I've been invited to an actual social event this weekend—even if it *is* a party thrown by Breck. Things are slowly beginning to come together like they were before. That's all I really want. To be close again with all my friends and not worry about coming home to my dad binging.

If I tell Alex the truth about the recoverees, there's always a risk of it somehow getting back to Margaret. It happened at the intersection incident when I told Lin, who told Jay, who told Jay's mom, who *then* told Margaret. And while I know that was a dire situation, I still can't risk her thinking that my dad letting the recoverees live with us is unusual behavior. I know it's not. He hasn't even been near alcohol, but still...if she somehow found out, I don't think she would hesitate shipping me back to Portland with Aunt June until my home life became more stable.

I trust Alex. I do. But I can't take that chance.

Alex grabs something from the ground. "Did you lose something?"

He's holding up a sock. It's filthy, but it's also patterned in tiny pineapples.

I feel my mouth curl into a grin. "You remember."

"Oh, c'mon," Alex says. "You wore that pineapple scrunchie every day of fourth grade—"

"Not *every* day!"

He shoots me an incredulous look. "And on your birthday, you'd bring in pineapple cupcakes with cream cheese frosting that your Grams made."

I can't believe he remembers that. When I turned fifteen, Jay had his mom make me a German chocolate cake, even though it was *his* favorite dessert. I pretended to like it anyway, but the texture was dry and tasted crumbly in my mouth.

I watch him toss the dirty sock in his trash bag. "Well," I finally say. "Whoever lost it has good taste."

We both work in silence for a few more minutes before I proclaim that I need a water break. We walk over to the cooler together. I pull down one of those paper cones and fill up.

When I turn around, I see Alex yanking off his T-shirt. His brown skin is smooth, uninhabited by freckles or birthmarks or scars. But that's not what captures my attention. No—it's the toned curves of his back muscles. The taut slopes of his shoulders.

I suddenly can't move. I've gone completely catatonic.

It's clear Alex got taller, but *this*. This is not the wiry fifteen-year-old I remember.

Water accidentally dribbles down my chin. My hand flies to my face, and I brush it away before he can see.

Alex wipes the sweat off his forehead with his T-shirt. I step aside so he can get to the water jug, but I'm suddenly self-conscious. I've practically sweated all my makeup off, and I can feel pools of it on my hairline. I must look like a complete greaseball. And—oh, no. Did I put on deodorant? I must have, right? Will he notice if I do a sniff test? He will. *Don't do it, Kira.* I take a tiny step away from him just in case.

Alex moves the water cup away from his lips. And now I'm looking at his lips. I've noticed his lips before, but not the shape. How the bottom sticks out slightly farther than the top. I imagine they're soft lips. Kissable lips.

Wait, what?

WHAT is happening?

I must be having some sort of heatstroke. Can the heat make your hormones flare up? That's why they call it *flare* up, right? That must be it. The sun is the sole cause of my suffering. But I can't leave, because then Lin would kill me. I have to find a way to *make it stop.*

Without thinking, I toss the rest of my water in his face.

Before he can react, I pick up my trash bag and run back toward the west side of the lake. What is *wrong* with me? He's going to think I'm unhinged. But a second later, I hear footsteps coming in fast. It's Alex. Trying to catch up. When I glance backward, I'm relieved to see he's smiling. Oh, good. So maybe he doesn't think I've completely lost it.

Then I notice that he's still carrying his water cup.

When I stop under the grove of trees, he slows his pace. I'm thankful to see he's pulled his shirt back on. I can't handle any more distractions right now, and I cannot, *cannot* be attracted to Alex Ramos.

Because, well, aren't I holding out for Jay?

I watch him lift the cup over his head, coming closer to me.

I hold my hands in the air. "Truce?"

He just smiles. "Why don't we make it even?"

Before I have a chance to run, Alex tips his cup. Ice-cold water soaks the top of my head and runs down my neck. Well, good. Maybe this is just what I need to nip my temporary loss of control right in the bud.

He laughs. I laugh, too. "You suck."

Alex only shrugs, but he looks proud of himself.

We spend the rest of the time picking up trash and talking about trivial things. He argues that the second season of *Crime Boss* is the best, but I think the fourth is the clear winner. We take turns trying to imitate Mrs. Donaldson's nasally voice and wonder if Cedarville's new football team will be good enough to go to state this year, which leads us to discussing our favorite concession foods. (Alex prefers hot dogs. I prefer nachos.)

We don't talk about his text.

I know I can easily bring it up, but I can't seem to let the words form on my tongue. He deserves to know I got the message. Yet every time I consider opening my mouth, I remember how it felt when he told me he was going to Sadie's with Lacey. The unexpectedness, like losing your footing in front of a large crowd, was mortifying. Bringing up his text from so long ago only for him to stumble out with "Oh! That. Yeah, I don't feel that way now" is something I don't think I'm ready to hear.

Maybe, *maybe* I'm afraid of being denied by Alex Ramos again.

When our time is up, we walk back to the picnic table. Our steps fall in sync together. It's nice. Peaceful. I take a moment and stare up at the sky.

"I used to wish my eyes were blue," I say. "I'd tell my dad I wanted them to be the color of the sky. Brown is boring."

"Nah, I like brown." Alex's gentle gaze falls on mine, making my heart race unexpectedly. A beat passes. Then another. "It suits you perfectly."

SIXTEEN

I HAVE UNINTERRUPTED TIME IN the bathroom as I get ready for Breck's party Saturday evening. We won the game against East Meadow yesterday, which put us all in a great mood. Raegan didn't even complain about Breck's party once.

I pull on my new cream-colored top, wrap my hair into a messy bun, and because I'm feeling festive, I slip into a pair of strappy wedges and slather on a bold, red lipstick. For the first time in weeks, I feel good. Confident.

When Alex gave me a ride back after the cleanup yesterday, I was tempted to ask if he was coming to Breck's party. In the end, I didn't. I knew it wasn't exactly his type of thing. At least that's what I tell myself. The honest part of me knows it's because Jay will be there, and *perhaps* I don't want to admit my feelings toward Alex are slightly complex.

I still don't know what came over me yesterday. I blame the heat.

I grab my purse and keys from my nightstand. I'm a few feet away from the stairs when Nonnie whirls around the corner, Wallis at her heels. When he spots me, he begins to pounce toward me.

"Stay!" I shout.

Wallis turns his wet nose to me, then back at Nonnie. He flumps his butt on the ground.

I let out a breath.

Nonnie takes in my attire. "Oh my, where are you going?"

I didn't expect to run into anyone as I was leaving. Earlier I told my dad that a few of us were going to hang at Breck's house and that, yes, parents would be home. Other than having to check in twice, either by text or by call, he was okay with it. The less he knew, the better.

"A friend's." I don't elaborate.

Nonnie grins. "There'll be boys at this party?"

I fold my arms. "I said I was going to a friend's."

"Oh good lord, child. I was born at night, but not *last* night. Just be careful of those young fellows. At your age, they don't exactly think with their brain, if you know what I mean."

Wallis gives a resounding *woof!* as if he's a part of this conversation.

I slide by her, antsy to leave already. "I will."

I blast my music loud as I make the short drive to Breck's house. It's a beautiful, cloudless Texas night with the slightest stirring of a breeze. The stars are bold freckles on the sky, brighter than I remember them being in Portland. Once I park, I grab my purse and head inside.

Surprisingly, the party is pretty low-key. There can't be more than three dozen people here, including a majority of the boys' basketball team. I say hi to a few girls I know from the Wavettes as I step through the doorway, moving past a small group chugging from red Solo cups.

I spot Colton first. He's wearing a black skull T-shirt with his headphones around his neck, and he waves when he sees me.

"Glad you showed," he says, and I notice he's traded his green braces bands for black ones. "Whitney and Lin are outside."

I almost say a quick thanks and leave, but I remember my list and the fact that he's number 9. Colton and I were never close, but we were friends. I don't want to dismiss him so quickly.

"How's band practice going? Don't you have a show coming up?"

He looks surprised that I remembered. "Actually, yeah. Two Fridays from now at the Pit. You should come."

"For sure," I say. Even though Colton's music isn't my particular taste, I still want to support him. "Let me know?"

He grins. "Rad."

I turn toward the sliding doors and head into the backyard. This is Breck's mother's pride and joy. A few summers ago, she built a wooden porch with an overhanging terrace. Fairy lights are strung above it, giving the patio a soft, magical vibe. The rest of the yard consists of perfectly manicured grass and an abundance of strategically placed planters, pots, and patio furniture.

Lin grabs my attention first. "Kira!"

I wave, then head over to the farthest corner of the porch where they're standing. Whitney's armed with a plastic cup and a lazy smile. She's wearing a navy dress that enhances her cleavage in what has to be a purely intentional way. Lin stands next to her wearing a Peter

Pan–collared blouse that's patterned with cherries, paired perfectly with a black skirt. She has on her signature purple cat-eye glasses, and a bright-pink color is slathered on her lips.

Even though Whitney is adamantly disinterested in rekindling our friendship, I'm still determined to make things right between us.

"Are we being antisocial?" I say, gesturing to the exclusiveness of the corner.

Whitney brushes a piece of stray hair away from her face. "We're avoiding Jay. He's being a dick."

My eyes widen in surprise. Not only because she directly answered my question, but at her blatant insult toward her boyfriend. I look to Lin for clarification.

She sighs. "He had Jennifer buy them beer."

"He *knows* I don't like her!"

"Wait," I say. "Who's Jennifer?"

Whitney takes a long chug of her drink.

Lin sighs. "Jennifer White? She hangs out with that other girl, you know, Jessica?"

Oh. Right. The college girls who are "obsessed" with Jay.

"Then she hung around for like, *thirty* minutes," Whitney says. "You should have seen her. She was all over him, and he was eating it up."

I'm surprised at how much she's confiding in me. I think back to my list. Maybe we're actually making progress. But then she swigs what's left of her drink and I realize that must be the source of her sudden chattiness.

I'm not a prude when it comes to alcohol. Back when we were

freshmen, Whitney would insist on going to house parties she heard about from sophomores. I always preferred more cranberry than vodka in my drinks, but I never got *wasted*. And when my dad's addiction became increasingly worse, I lost interest in drinking. With everything I'd been through with him, it didn't seem worth it.

She shakes her empty cup. "I need a refill," she declares, then walks back inside.

I want to get more details from Lin, but before I can she turns to me. "Want to go in?"

I shrug, so we do. Breck has his Spotify playlist blasting in the kitchen, so almost everyone is sitting in the living room so they can talk without shouting. From across the room, I see Whitney has propped herself up on a beige love seat next to Breck, who polishes off the rest of his beer. I don't see Jay, which is weird. He was never one to disappear at these kinds of things. He likes the attention too much.

"How are decathlon practices going?" I ask Lin.

Her eyes find Breck on the love seat. "You know, not terrible. Breck is pretty smart—but don't tell him I said that. His ego is big enough already."

"Massive."

"Right! At first, I thought he was only in it for the scholarship money if we win—which, I mean, I think we all are in some way. But I genuinely think he enjoys it?" Her voice heightens at the end. A question. "Anyway, the rest of the team is happy with him, too. We may have a solid chance at winning state this year."

"That's great," I say, and I mean it.

"It is," she agrees. "Hey, I miss this. One-on-one time, I mean."

Relief eases through me. It feels good to have one of my best friends back.

"I do, too."

"You should spend the night soon. Like old times."

"Only if we can Netflix an obscure movie we've never heard of and reenact all the cringeworthy scenes."

She laughs. "Absolutely."

My hand slides to my pocket, which is empty. I quickly check my purse. Crap. I left my phone in my car. If I don't text my dad to check in, he won't hesitate to revoke my newfound freedom.

"My phone's in the car," I tell Lin. "I have to update my dad or I'm at risk of being grounded."

"That's very authoritative of him."

"I know," I say, but for some reason I smile. "I'll be right back."

Lin raises her cup. "I'll be in the kitchen."

I wander down the hallway and toward the front of the house. When I open the front door, I freeze. Jay is standing on the porch, but so is another girl I don't recognize. He takes an automatic step back. The other girl appears unfazed. Her honey-blond hair is perfectly straight despite the humid evening, and she's wearing a top that's tighter than a lid on a pickle jar.

"Kira." Jay fiddles with his left earlobe. It's a nervous tic. I noticed that he did it a lot during tests our freshman year. "Jennifer stopped by with more beer." He holds up a twelve-pack.

Oh. *This* is Jennifer.

"I better go." She eyes me like I've interrupted something. "I didn't realize I was holding you up."

I don't want Jay to think I was looking for him, so I let my keys dangle from my fingers. "I left my phone in the car."

I step around them and walk down the porch steps toward the driveway. When I glance back, Jennifer is still standing there talking to him. The whole image makes my stomach churn. How long has he been out here? Why was he nervous? I mean, it's not like they were *doing* anything, but it doesn't exactly seem innocent.

I haven't talked to Jay since Tuesday's history class when he put my name in that hangman puzzle. I feel guilty. I know it wasn't my fault, but still. If Whitney is overreacting about Jennifer, she would definitely overreact if she saw my name written in his notebook.

And since when did Jay start talking with older girls? And when did he start accepting *beer* from older girls? He's always had a reputation for being a star student and star basketball player. Breck's the one who's notorious for flirting, not him.

After I grab my phone and lock up, I head back to the house. Jay is still on the porch, but there's no sign of Jennifer. He gives me a small wave as I come closer.

"So," I say, raising an eyebrow. "You're on beer duty?"

He shrugs. "I thought we could use more. The night is young."

I'm not standing very close to him, but I'm close enough to smell his cologne. It's a little overpowering, something that's musky and unfamiliar. He's wearing a black button-down with a pair of jeans. I don't think I've ever seen him in a nice shirt before. It's like he's stepped out of a J. Crew ad. It feels . . . wrong.

"Whitney's looking for you."

His amused expression deflates a little. "I figured," he says, opening the front door. "Better go."

He's distant again. I step inside behind him, but instead of feeling uneasy at how weird our friendship has become, I feel a little irritated. He's acting like being with Whitney is a chore. Which is annoying. Even though we're not on the best terms at the moment, Whitney is one of the most caring people I know. She's witty and kind and pretty, and if he can't appreciate all the great things about her, why does he even bother?

Jay goes into the kitchen to deliver the rest of the beer, but I make a right into the living room. Lin is scrolling through something on her phone when I come up and stand next to her.

"I ran into Jay outside," I blurt before I can think about what I'm doing.

Lin slides her phone in her pocket and looks at me. "You did?"

"He was with that girl. Jennifer."

Lin's eyes dart across the room to where Breck and Whitney are still sitting together in the love seat. Her head is tipped back in laughter, her brown hair spilling down the open back of her dress.

Lin sighs. "Don't tell her."

I frown. "Doesn't that go against best friend code?"

"Trust me. She's already thinking the worst. It's better if she doesn't have confirmation."

"They were just talking," I say, but I don't know why I defend him.

Lin looks at me like I'm as transparent as a glass of water. "Do you believe that?"

I'm not sure. It's like my life has been divided into two phases and I'm still living in the pre-Portland phase. That Jay was completely committed to our relationship. He was friendly, sure, but he wasn't intentionally flirty. I never felt like he was untrustworthy.

Now I'm not so sure.

Lin lifts her cup to her lips and says, "You see what she's doing right now, right?"

I turn my gaze back to Whitney. She has one hand resting on Breck's knee, and it looks like she's whispering something in his ear. He cracks a smile and playfully nudges her waist with his elbow. We've all been close friends for a long time, but the whole room must be seeing what I'm seeing. And what I'm seeing doesn't appear innocent.

"They're stuck in some type of jealousy loop," Lin says. She adjusts her frames before turning back to me. "I don't think they've cheated on each other, but it's like...I don't know. Some kind of validation?"

I'm so confused. "What do you mean?"

Lin thinks for a minute. "It's like they're sending each other a message saying that they could each easily be with someone else, but at the end of the night they'll leave together. They always do."

I run my tongue across my bottom teeth. That doesn't seem very healthy, but it's not like I have the right to judge other people's relationships. All I know is that was never how I felt with Jay, like I had to prove myself. Whitney shouldn't have to, either. She deserves better.

My insides turn cold. If I think she deserves better, then why would I want Jay back at all?

The question immediately dissolves when I hear Whitney yell, "Kira! Lin!" from across the room. Lin gives me a strict look that says, *this stays between us.* I nod, even though I feel weird about the whole thing.

"Comeer," Whitney giggles, motioning us closer. She's clearly drunk because this is the most enthusiastic I've seen her act toward me since I came back. "Hey!" She says way too loudly once we're standing next to the armchair.

"That's it," Breck says, attempting to take her cup away from her. "I'm cutting you off."

Whitney pulls her arm away just before he can grab her drink. "Nope."

I look around, but there's still no sign of Jay.

"Hey!" Whitney says again, snapping her fingers in front of my face. "I was try'na tell Breck . . . remember that one night in fourth grade when we spent the night at your house? And played truth or dare?"

I'm so surprised she's directly acknowledging me that it takes me a moment to think back. There were a lot of those times, so I nod like I know which one she's talking about.

"And you dared me to eat a whole box of Thin Mints? Remember I did it?" She turns to Lin. "Remember?"

"She *so* didn't," Breck says, egging her on.

"Shut up!" she squeaks. "I totally did. Tell him, Kira!"

Now that she's mentioned it, I do remember that night. Whitney, Raegan, Lin, and I moved the couch and coffee table to separate corners of the living room so we could spread our sleeping bags across the area rug. It was my idea to play truth or dare. We made Lin eat ice cream with ketchup on it and Raegan had to ding dong ditch Mrs. Riley from across the street. Whitney didn't follow through with her dare, though. She left half a roll of Thin Mints behind before falling asleep.

I can't tell if Lin remembers this, though. She stays quiet.

Pieces of stray hair are stuck to Whitney's forehead. Some of her mascara is smudged, but she doesn't seem to know. Or care.

I think about what Lin said about the both of them trying to prove themselves to each other. It makes me sad. I wish she didn't feel like she has to do this, but Jay obviously isn't worried about finding her anytime soon. It's like they're playing these stupid games to test each other's commitment.

Then a thought occurs to me. What if she's testing *me?* I know what she wants me to say, even if it's not the truth. But maybe that's what she needs from me for us to be close again. And that's what I wanted, right? To make amends with her, to finally be best friends again.

So I take her side.

"She did," I tell Breck. "I was there."

Breck looks impressed by the lie. Whitney gives him a smug grin. I know this was the right answer, but somehow I don't feel like I've won.

SEVENTEEN

THE NEXT WEEK IS A whirlwind. Even though The Wavettes have taken over my after-school schedule once again, it's nice to have something familiar to focus on. Plus I get to watch Raegan's co-captain skills in action, which are much tamer compared to watching her lead the school with her presidential duties.

Surprisingly, my house is much tamer, too. It helps that Peach finally landed that bakery job in Claremore, which is a twenty-minute bus ride from Cedarville. She wakes up at four o'clock every morning to be at work at five to start prepping for the day, so my mornings are now Peach-free. This also means my dad is now in charge of breakfast, and I'm much more partial to his chocolate chip pancakes.

Because of the craziness of my Wavettes practices this week, I haven't had time to get help with algebra. On the rare occasions Mrs. Donaldson allows us to work on homework in class, Alex leans over and tries to help me. But we always end up discussing the latest episode of *Crime Boss* or getting in a heated round of *Would You Rather?* where one of the answer choices is always Mrs. Donaldson.

"Would you rather nail your own foot to the ground or live with Mrs. Donaldson for a year?" I asked him on Thursday.

Alex adjusted his beanie before answering. I decided I liked the beanie. It was strangely fitting, like the way he always wore those double shirts.

"Ugh, I'd probably nail my foot. At least it's over with quickly."

"Really? You wouldn't want to have resounding dinner debates on the latest mathematical theories?"

"Pass."

"She probably makes a mean *pi*."

He laughed. I always feel a swell of pride when I make him laugh.

I'm sitting with everyone at lunch on Thursday when Alex walks by our table with a lunch tray in his hands. He gives me a small smile when he sees me, nodding in my direction. I wave back.

Jay leans over and steals one of Breck's chips. Unlike the button-down he wore to the party, he's back to wearing his letterman jacket over a Cedarville Basketball T-shirt.

"So what are this year's Spirit Week themes?" he asks Raegan.

Raegan closes her notebook. "I can't officially announce them until next week." She throws us a smug grin. "But they're awesome."

Even though all of us went to Breck's party, Raegan doesn't seem mad. But she also didn't ask about it. I make a mental note to ask her to hang out this weekend—if she has time. It's the least I can do to put an effort in our friendship, even if she isn't holding grudges.

Breck tosses a Cheeto at her. "You're no fun."

Raegan glares at him. "Excuse me, do you know how hard it is to run an entire school while your mother's experiencing pregnancy-related hormonal episodes?"

Lin glances up from her flashcards. "You're not exactly running the *entire* school—"

In typical Raegan fashion, she ignores this. "It's exhausting. Plus, I've been YouTubing birthing videos—"

Breck plugs his ears. "I don't want to hear about the placenta!"

I raise my eyebrows. "Who said anything about a placenta?"

He points a finger at Raegan. "She was about to!"

"I wasn't, but you shouldn't be so squeamish. It's a natural part of the birthing process."

Colton looks genuinely confused. "What's a placenta?"

"Dude." Jay shakes his head, then leans over and quietly explains in what I can only imagine is the worst kind of detail.

"And people eat that?" Colton says in the middle of swiping one of Whitney's fries.

She glares at him. "*You* would probably eat it, Colton."

He freezes mid-chew. "That's disgusting."

Breck glares at Whitney. "Dude, stop talking about it."

"You're going to make some woman very happy one day," she remarks. "Especially if you keep calling them *dude*."

Lin laughs. "Who wouldn't vote for him for Homecoming King?"

I pull my water bottle away from my lips. "You're nominated?"

"I can't help that the people like what they see." Breck grins. "Beauty and brains, right, L?"

"Dear god," Lin mumbles, shaking her head.

"Get you a man who has both."

"Your narcissism is up here." Lin raises her hand above her head. "And I'm going to need you to bring it down here." She gestures, lowering it near her shoulder.

I almost forgot about homecoming. It's a few weeks away, but still. I haven't mentally prepared myself for flying solo.

I catch myself glancing over at Jay, wondering if he's regretting going to homecoming with Whitney this year now that I've returned. A twinge of loneliness flickers inside me when I remember him whispering how beautiful I looked in my gold gown the night of the homecoming dance, and how he held the small of my back when we posed for pictures together. I wonder if he misses those moments, too.

He takes a huge bite of his sandwich, and a few crumbs stick to the bottom of his lip. When he catches me staring, he gives me a perplexed look like, *What?*

I sigh. I sincerely doubt it.

───────────

There is no one in the house when I come home after Wavettes practice. A note from Peach sits on the counter, saying she's taking the late bus back from Claremore because she's catching up with some old friends. My dad is most likely working late. I have no clue where Nonnie could be, and I'm betting Saylor is working a shift at 7-Eleven.

It's quiet. Oddly quiet. I can't remember when the kitchen and living room were void of any type of commotion.

I heat up a plate of pizza rolls and watch an old episode of *Crime Boss*. I find myself wishing my dad were around to make fun of Agent Dane Lizar's soul patch or how corny the explosions are in the early seasons due to low budgets. Instead Wallis thumps his tail on the rug, watching me with bated breath as I finish off my pizza rolls.

My cell phone rings. **Margaret—Social Worker** flashes across the screen. A rush of panic envelops me as I pause the TV. My first thought is *She knows*. I don't know how, but someone must have alerted her about the recoverees. Dread overpowers the panic. What if she's calling to send me back?

I try and keep my voice level when I answer. "Hello?"

"Kira, hi! This is Margaret Garcia." Nothing about her tone seems off. "I just wanted to call for a quick check-in. How is the transition going?"

"Oh! It's good! Great!" I blurt, then quickly want to smack myself. I need to bring down my enthusiasm. I don't want to give her any red flags. "My dad really seems to be keeping his promise about getting back on track."

"I'm very glad to hear that," Margaret says. "Now, we usually schedule an in-house check-in. Just to drop by and make sure you're in a good environment."

I force myself to keep calm. I cannot, *cannot* allow her over here while Nonnie, Peach, and Saylor are still around. There's no way she'll believe that them being here is a good environment for me.

"Oh, I'd say my environment is more than good. My dad's been working back at Cedarville Elementary, and I've been getting back in the swing of things at school. And with dance, too. We've got a lot of stuff keeping us busy."

There's a pause at the other end of the line. "It's great to hear you're adjusting so well."

I hold my breath, waiting for her to continue.

"Well, you've been through a lot, and I want this transition to continue to be smooth. You know you can call me if you suspect any signs of trouble?"

"Yes. Yes, I do. And I will." I'm eager for this call to end. "Thank you."

"Of course," she replies. "Don't be a stranger. I'll follow up soon, okay?"

I tell her okay, and we both hang up. My heart pounds all the way through the end of the *Crime Boss* episode. It's not that I'm lying to her. I'm just not sharing the entire truth. Everyone here has remained sober, and I don't need to worry her, or worse, get myself sent away again when I'm only trying to bring things back to the way they were.

When the episode ends, I turn off the TV and put my plate in the dishwasher. I have a ton of homework to do, including reading the rest of *The Crucible* for English. I go upstairs, flop on my bed, and force myself to try to absorb what's happening in the play.

The front door squeaks open, interrupting my thoughts. I'm setting the book down on my nightstand when I hear two hushed voices arguing downstairs. I get out of bed and crack open my door.

"It's times like this when I could use a drink," my dad's saying, his voice heavy and sad. "I think I've moved past the pain of losing her, and then it sneaks up on me."

An uncomfortable sadness rises in my throat. I know he's referring to Grams.

"Adam." That's Nonnie, stern and unforgiving. "You do not need dependency like that, you hear?"

My dad's voice is hoarse, defeated. "It was easier when she was around. She really understood Kira. Much more than I do, and now she's so distant—"

Wallis begins to bark, drowning out the rest of his words. I had no idea my dad felt that way. Sure I was close to Grams, but we also had our own relationship. We bonded over food and *Crime Boss* and little stories about each other's day. His presence in my life is just as important as hers was.

I hear more shuffling as they enter the kitchen, so I step into the hallway so I can hear better.

There's more rustling as Nonnie pours food in a bowl for Wallis. "—and it's like we've been telling Peach. It takes time. You broke her trust."

I'm surprised Nonnie understands.

"—and you don't want to give up on her. Not when she needs her dad back. She doesn't need the kind of father who resorts to drinking when he's upset." Wallis barks again, and I hear Nonnie set down the bowl with a loud *clank!* "Heidi was a wonderful woman to you both, but it's the two of you now. You've got to heal together."

I step back into my room and quietly close the door. I knew there was a chance my dad could relapse, but I didn't realize he was still struggling. I wasn't naïve enough to believe the ranch would completely cure him, but it seemed like spending time with the recoverees was helping. He's been trying with me, but maybe I'm the one who needs to try harder with him.

Nonnie's right. We're both alone, and we shouldn't have to continue to suffer alone, either.

I'm about to walk downstairs, but I hear the front door open. "—need to clear my head, take a walk. If Kira asks—"

"I'll let her know," Nonnie says, her voice sad.

The door shuts. He's gone.

EIGHTEEN

AFTER SCHOOL ON WEDNESDAY, WHITNEY, Lin, and I agree to
help Raegan and a few other students from our year build the homecoming float for the junior class. The parade is a week from today,
but she's afraid that with everyone's schedules we won't be able to get
it done on time.

I'm surrounded by flatbed trailers that we will decorate and hitch
to trucks, most of which came from volunteer dads. Principal Lawrence allowed the trailers to sit in the back of the faculty parking lot
while we worked on this, which was good because there were nearly
a dozen floats and not much room anywhere else on school grounds.

Leadership Council decided "Sensational Swashbucklers" would be
the junior class theme, which is why there are eight of us surround-
ing our flatbed in attempt to transform it into a pirate ship. Raegan
lays out the blueprint and I try to envision how we're going to pull
this off with our unimpressive materials that consist of chicken wire,
burlap, poster board, paint, and a staple gun.

"Okay," Raegan says. Her dark hair is twisted into tiny braids and pulled back into a classy bun. She's holding two rolls of cellophane— one clear and one blue. "Before we can start on the ship, let's lay this down as the base. It'll be the water."

"I don't see how we're supposed to build this ship," Lin says, still staring at the blueprint. "It's pretty complicated."

Raegan narrows her eyes.

Lin shuts up.

The cellophane is the easy part. After scrunching and stapling layers to the base of the flatbed, it begins to look like the choppy seas. Raegan walks around the perimeter and uses the staple gun to secure a silver fringe bed skirt for flair.

Half an hour later, Whitney plops down on the asphalt and scrolls through her phone. Deciding that I need a break, I sit down next to her.

Ever since Breck's party she's been slightly warmer toward me, but our conversations are surface-level. Like what time dance practice ends and the number of essays we've had to complete for our English classes. They're baby steps, but it feels like progress.

"She was more fun when she was less tyrannical," Whitney says as we watch Raegan lecture Tyler Hornsby about using too many staples.

I don't disagree. "Do you think the baby is putting her more on edge?"

Whitney shrugs, looping her thick brown hair into a secure ponytail. "Maybe."

I glance back at Raegan. She's hovering over Tyler's shoulder, monitoring his staple usage. She's always been the take-charge type of person. In second grade she was the one who started the unofficial red rover tournaments at recess. When she decided to take up dance in middle school, she stayed committed to it. She was the only one at her studio who never missed a single class.

I immediately feel guilty. I've been so wrapped up in my own problems that I haven't even made the effort to talk to her about how *she* feels about her mom's pregnancy. Maybe staying busy with all these organizations and activities is her way of coping.

Whitney's gone back to scrolling through her phone. I wonder if she still feels weird about the whole Jay thing. She never brings him up—probably to spare my feelings—but I don't want him to be the thing holding our friendship back. It's time to start making some strides in my twelve steps. She's near the top, so I try and make a better effort.

"Have you and Jay coordinated what you're wearing to the homecoming dance?"

Even though I keep my voice casual, she looks at me in surprise.

"Uh, yeah, actually." She lowers her phone away from her face. "I found this dress? It's amazing. The embroidery is so classy. It's blue and white, and Jay bought a tie to match." She pauses, then meets my gaze. "Are you going?"

"To the dance?"

Whitney nods.

"Oh. I don't know."

She turns back to her phone. In a soft voice she goes, "I think you should."

Now it's my turn to be surprised. "Really?"

She shrugs at her screen.

"Okay," I tell her, feeling a little more hopeful. "I'll think about it."

"Well think fast. It's next weekend, in case you forgot."

We glance at the homecoming float. "Who could forget with Raegan around?"

Raegan, as if she's heard us, looks over and hollers, "We need all hands on deck."

Whitney rolls her eyes. "She's literally speaking pirate now."

I laugh, and she smiles. For a fraction of a second, the tension eases between us.

I stand up. "Tell her I'm going to grab water. I'll be right back."

She nods, waving me off.

September is coming to an end, and we're having one of those rare days that *really* feels like fall. The cool shift came out of nowhere. I had to borrow Raegan's extra Wavette sweatshirt to protect me from the slight chill in the breeze.

I'm heading toward the double doors of the school when I hear footsteps coming up behind me. When I turn around, I see Alex heading in my direction.

He's wearing his black beanie atop his head of curls. The black sleeves of his shirt are pushed up to his elbows, and I can only guess he's working on one of his many theater projects.

My lips pull into a smile as he nears. "I didn't know you were out here."

He gestures across the parking lot. "I'm helping with the theater float. They only want me for my building skills." He turns toward me, holding up an empty toolbox. "We need more nails, but I think there's an extra box in the shop."

"What's your float's theme?"

"Little Shop of Horrors," he replies, his eyes animated with excitement. "Mrs. Henson announced that's going to be our musical this year, so everyone's pretty excited about it."

I've never even heard of it, but his enthusiasm is infectious. "That's awesome."

We fall into step as we walk inside. Students have already gotten a jump-start on decorating the hallways for Spirit Week. Bright posters plaster nearly every inch of free space stating things like DEFEAT THE JAGUARS and WILDBOARS WILL WIN.

I turn to Alex. "Are you going to homecoming?"

Alex fumbles to keep a grasp on the toolbox for a moment before it slips through his grasp and onto the linoleum floor with a loud *smack*. He quickly picks it up. When he looks back at me, I notice his face is flushed.

Oh. Oh CRAP.

From the uncomfortable look on his face, I can tell he thinks I'm dropping a hint about the dance. Which, *no*.

Well, not that it would be a bad thing. Going with Alex, I mean.

Wait. Do I want to go to homecoming with Alex?

I can tell he's searching for a way to try and let me down easy. "Uh—"

I think fast, trying to backtrack. "It's just that, you know, Raegan was wondering about the head count at the pep rally. She, uh, doesn't think too many people will show up this year. Which is crazy. Everyone loves homecoming. Well, maybe not everyone. That's kind of a blanket statement, but . . . well. Yeah."

Wow, what a spectacular speech. Where's my Oscar?

"Oh." Does Alex look . . . relieved? He could at least try and hide it. Do I come off like I'd be *that* terrible of a date? "Yeah, sure. Are you performing?"

"With the Wavettes?" As soon as I ask it, I realize it's a silly question. *No, Kira, he's wondering if you'll be performing WITH THE CIRCUS.*

Alex laughs. "Yeah."

I nod. "Mandatory."

His brown eyes linger on mine a moment. "Okay, sure. Count me in."

"Cool." I'm having trouble returning eye contact. "Raegan will be happy."

Alex gives me a strange look, like that wasn't what he was expecting to hear.

"Well, I better get those nails so we can finish the replica of Audrey II."

"Aubrey who?"

He grins. "You were never a fan of musicals."

I lift my hands in the air. "Guilty."

"It's the talking monster plant in *Little Shop*," he explains. "I'm in charge of creating it, actually." His face lights up. "I can show you once it's finished, if you want. Mrs. Henson thinks we can spruce it up even more and use it in the show."

I nod, and mean it when I say, "I'd love to."

He lifts the toolbox, glancing down toward the theater wing. "I'd better—"

"Yeah," I say, feeling my face flush. God, what is wrong with me? "I'll see you later."

He smiles, then heads to the woodshop classroom. My heart pounds as I make my way toward the vending machine. I put my dollar in and retrieve a water bottle, but the thumping doesn't cease. I don't even realize Whitney's pushing through the double doors until I nearly run into her.

"Whoa." She stares at me for a moment. "Uh, you okay?"

"Yeah," I say quickly.

She moves past me, shrugging it off. I steal one last glance down the theater hallway before shoving the door open and heading to the parking lot.

NINETEEN

I'M ON THE COUCH AVOIDING homework when my dad comes home from work on Thursday. No one else is here, so I've spread out on the sofa with a bag of stale tortilla chips. There's a rerun of *Chopped* playing on TV, but I've been more focused on texting Lin about potentially going to the homecoming dance as a group.

"Feel like a burrito from Lucky's?" he asks.

We haven't had a chance to talk after I'd overheard him and Nonnie's conversation the other night. I don't want to admit to eavesdropping, but it did make me think of my list again. And the truth is, deep down, I do want to forgive him. It's the only way to go back to the way things were.

I slip my feet back into my flats. "Yes, are you kidding?"

We haven't been to Lucky's in forever. It's a customizable burrito joint twenty minutes away, but it's totally worth it because they have seven different types of salsa and the best carne asada I've ever tasted. Grams hated Lucky's burritos. She always said they got too soggy too fast and gave her heartburn. But Thursday nights, when she went to the Y to play bridge with her friends, my dad and I would make a special trip together.

He drives. Talk radio is set on low, and it suddenly occurs to me that I've trapped myself in a car with my dad for a significant amount of time. It doesn't feel as awkward as the ride home from the airport, but I still can't think of a single thing to say.

After a few moments, he turns to me. "Do you have a home or away game tomorrow?"

"Away."

I feel slightly guilty about not extending him an invitation to come see me perform with the Wavettes, but he and Grams never came to away games anyway. The drives were always too long, and she liked to be in bed by nine.

"Do you need money for dinner?"

I shake my head, but another pang of guilt stabs through me. He's being so supportive. It would be easier if he were uninterested. At least then I wouldn't feel so bad.

We drive the next few miles in silence. I watch acres of green pastures and roaming cattle fly past my line of vision as the sun dips below rich green treetops. When I was younger, I remember asking Grams why she lived here her whole life. She looked confused, like I'd just asked why there weren't eight days in a week.

But then she'd said, "Because there ain't nowhere better than this."

"I miss her," I hear myself say. My heart aches in the familiar patterns of loneliness. "I think about her every day."

My dad is quiet for a moment. I know he understands who I'm

talking about. When he glances over at me, there's a sad smile on his face. "I do, too. To tell you the truth, I still struggle with missing her."

My hands twist together in my lap. I decide to come clean. "I know. I heard you and Nonnie talking the other day."

"Did you?"

I nod. "I want to trust you again . . . I just don't want things to be like last time."

He turns off the radio. "I won't lie to you, Goose. It isn't easy, but I've been in touch with Michael."

Michael. His AA sponsor. At first, I blamed Michael for my dad's decision to go to Sober Living. He was supposed to be his mentor. Why couldn't he help him?

But now I think I understand the difference in his struggle back then and his struggle now. This time, *he'd* made the decision to stay sober. I just needed to trust he'd follow through.

"Michael recommended seeing a counselor, and I want you to know I've taken his advice."

"Oh." This isn't what I expected him to say.

"I want to make sure I'm not going to slip again," he explains. "I don't want you worryin' about me. It was never fair to put you through everything I did."

I swallow, thinking back to all the nights he spent closed off in his bedroom. All the nights my sadness ate through me like acid.

"It wasn't," I agree. "I was a bit skeptical about coming home, actually."

I expect this confession will make him mad, but it doesn't.

"You know, I can't say I blame you. Although I sure am glad you did. Your Grams—well, she was there for us. But you were there for me, too. And I let you down."

I don't say anything. We both know it's true.

"Grams was always so good to us. If she were still here, she'd—"

"—have a few choice words for you."

He laughs. "Yes, that's true." He glances over at me. "We don't have to talk about this if you don't want."

I know it makes him sad, but he's trying. Maybe I can try a little harder, too.

My lips curve into a smile. "Are you sure we don't have to *taco* 'bout it?"

He grins. "We can *guac* about it another time."

I snort. "That was awful. It doesn't even make sense."

But he's still smiling, the gesture showcasing the tiny wrinkles around his eyes. I know he's still struggling, but we're different now. Somehow I know we won't ever move back in time to when I'd keep his secrets when he drank far too much.

Trust. That's what I want most with my dad. There aren't any excuses for his addiction, but I try and think of Grams's loss from his perspective. Not only had he lost his mother, but he also lost the only other person who helped raise me. He was truly on his own.

Only, he wasn't. He had me. *Has* me.

I think of the others—Saylor and Nonnie and Peach. I remember what I overheard the other night, how Nonnie was helping my dad. I know he's making an effort to turn things around, so shouldn't I accept that they're trying to do the same?

I picture my twelve-steps list sitting on the corner of my desk. I still want them gone, but I can't deny that they encourage and support each other. And aren't those the kind of people I should *want* my dad to be around?

I'm the world's biggest hypocrite. Because I know the answer, but it's not the one I want.

———————————

Colton forgot to mention that his band is playing around the same time the football game ends on Friday, but because we suffer an embarrassingly big loss, Raegan, Lin, and I are able to book it out of there as soon as it ends. Luckily the venue is a few miles from the stadium, so once we ditch our uniforms for more appropriate going-out attire (a button-down skirt and black halter top, in my case) we hit the road.

My dad said I could go as long as I'm back by midnight, which is fair. After our journey to Lucky's last night, it feels like we've fallen back into familiar territory.

"I can't stay long," Raegan says, tapping her bright-red fingernails on her steering wheel. "I have *so* much work to do for Spirit Week."

"That's fine," I say as Lin texts someone from the backseat. They're coming with me because this is a big deal for Colton, but I'm also secretly pleased to get to hang with them outside of school.

Whitney and Jay ditched out and decided to go see a movie instead. I hate that it bothers me more than it should.

The venue is a divey little place called the Pit that's squished between a liquor store and a twenty-four-hour laundromat in downtown Keegris—a bigger city close to Cedarville. They're already playing by the time we walk inside. It's very dark, lit only by the red-and-blue lighting coming from the exceptionally small stage, where the drum kit takes up most of the space on the checkered floor. There's a humid smell of too many bodies packed into one place mixed with cigarette smoke, but when I spot Colton stage left with his guitar, he grins like he's headlining Madison Square Garden.

And, honestly, his band isn't the worst thing I've ever heard.

They're in no way the *best,* but they manage to stay somewhat on beat. The singer has a pretty decent range, too.

"Wow. It's loud," Raegan says as we shove our way forward.

Lin snorts. "What'd you expect, a symphony?"

Lin and I bob our heads to the rhythmic chugging and wailing of the guitars. Raegan eventually gives in and attempts to enjoy it. When they announce the last song, we have a contest to see who can headbang the longest. Surprisingly, Raegan wins.

After Colton churns out the last note, the singer grabs his mic and proclaims, "We are A Feast of Blood and Gore—good night!"

Lin raises an eyebrow. "What a name."

"Truly," I agree.

"He was good, right?" Raegan says, then looks around. "I'm going to grab some water."

"I'll go with you," I say.

"Bathroom," Lin says, then gestures in the opposite direction. "I'll catch up."

We part ways, then head to the tiny beverage station and order our waters. As we wait, I turn to Raegan.

"Hey, um, don't take this the wrong way," I begin, using this as my opportunity to be a better friend. She's been so busy with school-work and presidential projects leading up to homecoming that I haven't really had a chance to talk to her. "But are you okay? I've noticed you've taken on a lot this year."

Raegan smiles, but I can see the tiredness in her eyes. "I know I have. It's just—" She pauses for a moment. "Did you know my mom never went to college?"

"She didn't?"

"No, and neither did my grandma. Just my dad. So I'll be the first female in my family to go. And it's not that I'm worried that I'll get in, because *duh*. I'm bound to get in somewhere."

I smile at her confidence. "Obviously."

"The thing is, I *want* to go to a good school and I *want* to get a scholarship, but... I also want to be around to help my mom with the baby. I'm finally going to have a sibling, but after next year I'll be gone." She meets my eyes. "So, yeah. I guess I'm worried they'll both need me."

A girl with bright-pink hair hands us our waters. I quickly thank her, then turn back to Raegan. "She'll be fine. They both will."

"Yeah?"

"Yeah. They have your dad. And it's not like you'll never visit. Plus, this baby is going to have, like, the best big sister role model on the planet." She laughs. "But you have to live your life, too."

As soon as I say it, I remember the conversation I had with Alex. How I was worried about leaving my own dad when I go off to col-lege. Why is it easy to give someone else this advice when I'm wor-ried about the exact same thing?

"Look who I found!" Lin announces as she walks over to us, Colton right behind her.

"I'm so stoked you made it." His smile is bright enough to light an entire city.

Raegan playfully nudges his elbow with hers. "You were great, seriously."

"Remember us when you're famous," I add.

Colton blushes, but before he can get another word in, two girls rush up beside him. One has dirty blond hair and is wearing a leather jacket with a delicate silver quill necklace, and the other has straight black hair that matches her black skater dress and Converse high-tops.

"Way to kill it tonight," the blond girl says.

Colton modestly shrugs, then turns to us. "This is Elsie and Devon. They go to East Meadow High. And this is Kira, Raegan, and Lin."

"My brother's the singer," the black-haired girl—Devon—explains. "You know, the one with awful taste in band names."

"Very descriptive," I say.

"A little *too* descriptive," Elsie replies. "We were talking about going to Waffle House. Y'all feel like joining?"

"We actually have to get going. Curfew." I glance at Colton. "Maybe next time?"

He grins. "Yeah, that'd be rad."

We say good-bye, then find our way to Raegan's car. She drops Lin off first, then swings by my house. I want to tell her she doesn't have to worry so much, that things will be fine. But how can I promise her these things if I don't know for sure?

"You know, this was fun," Raegan says. "We should do it more often."

My mood lifts. "Definitely."

As I'm getting out of her car, I hear, "Kira?"

I turn.

"Remember to wear your spirit color on Monday."

I give her a thumbs-up. As I walk inside, my cell chimes with a text.

JAY: how was the show

Jay. Jay is texting me. It's a little surprising, considering he's with Whitney. I debate on texting back right away, but ultimately I end up crafting a reply.

ME: should've come to see for yourself! but they were great.

JAY: yeah, really should've. the movie blew.

JAY: where you at? meet at Sonic?

I pause, uncertain if I want to hang out with Whitney and Jay right now. It'd be one thing if Whitney was the one reaching out since things are still off between us, but on the other hand, the two of them *are* 3 and 6 on my twelve-steps list. At this point, I can't afford to say no if I really want to make progress.

ME: not too far. see you in a few.

Since it's 11:30, I send another quick text to my dad, assuring him I'll be home within the hour. But when I drive up to Sonic, I spot only Jay sitting on a red plastic picnic table. Hesitant, I pull my car into an empty space, then get out to meet him.

"Where's Whit?" I ask as I walk up.

"Hello to you, too," he jokes, slurping on his drink. "Took her home after the movies. Said she had a headache."

"Oh," I reply, suddenly feeling weird. I don't want Whitney to think I'm hanging out with Jay behind her back and get mad. I mean, I *did* assume she'd be here. It's not like I can be at fault for that, can I?

His finger hovers over the order button on the menu board. "Want anything?"

On the other hand, Jay asked me to come here specifically because he knew we'd have one-on-one time. Since I'm trying to reconnect with him, I should at least see where it goes.

Right?

I sit down next to him. "Fries?"

As Jay places the order, a few freshmen at another picnic table catch my attention. They're wearing Cedarville colors, and one of the guys hooks an arm casually around a girl wearing a festive red ribbon in her hair. He whispers something to her, and she bursts out laughing.

It reminds me of my freshman year with Jay. The unexpected wave of nostalgia hits me hard and fast.

"So," he says. "Colton's on the road to fame and glory?"

"Seems promising." I spare a quick glance at him. He's wearing a simple white shirt and basketball shorts, and his hair looks slightly neater than the day before. "Is that a blue raspberry slush?"

He shakes his cup. "Nope, got tired of those. It's a chocolate shake."

"Oh."

It's odd, but the slight change of his drink option feels like a

betrayal. I tell myself it's all in my head. Jay's welcome to order whatever he wants.

But still.

The fries are delivered, and I set the carton between us so we can
share. We eat in silence for a few moments. When the breeze shifts,
I catch a faint scent of the body spray he wore when we dated. Even
though he's changed so much since I left, I can't help replaying the
good moments over in my head. Our kisses in dark theaters. The
thinking of you texts.

Jay shakes his empty milkshake cup, gesturing to a garbage can
sitting a few feet away. "Think I can make this into the trash?"

"You're on the basketball team. I *hope* you can make it."

He grins. "Rude."

"How is that rude? That's a fact."

Jay aims, then glances over at me. "How about a little support?"

"Does your ego need it? Is that you, Breck?"

"Oh, fuck off." He flings the cup perfectly into the bin with a
satisfying thud. "Nothing but net."

I laugh, shaking my head. "Two points."

"That's clearly three."

"Whatever makes you feel better."

He scoots closer to me, an easy smile spreading across his lips.
Then his hand is on my bare knee, and my heart jumps in my throat.

Jay's eyes lock with mine. "You look nice tonight."

I want to tell myself it's an innocent compliment, but when his
hand ever so slowly creeps higher up my thigh, I know it's not.

My smile disappears as I immediately shift both of my legs away from him. Because even though there are spurts of moments where being with Jay feels so natural, *he's with Whitney*. Whitney, who is part of the reason I agreed to come here in the first place. And what does this say about Jay, who's clearly trying to make a move on me *while* he's with Whitney?

"No." There's firmness in my tone. "I don't think—"

Next to the carton of fries, Jay's phone chimes with a text. Because I'm both nosy and curious, I glance down, which is how my eyes read: **hey, if you're coming, bring beer.** From Jennifer. The same Jennifer that was at Breck's party, I'm sure.

Jay doesn't waste time texting back. "Winsor Lake," he explains, obviously aware I read it. "Got a fake ID last weekend. They want me to come party. And bring more booze."

"A true hero," I say, but even I hear the joke fall flat.

"Something like that," he mumbles.

A pang of annoyance stabs me in the chest. Why? Why have I been pining after someone who's clearly chosen to hang out with me, his ex-girlfriend, behind his actual girlfriend's back? Someone who he'd *then* ditch out to pick up beer for a party? Maybe that's who Jay has become. The one who's always searching for the next best thing.

"I should go, anyway." I can't shake away the weirdness that's been slowly encroaching on me. "Thanks for the fries."

"Oh—uh, no problem." I feel him watching me as I hop off the table. "Um, hey?"

I turn back to him, wondering if he's going to say he'd rather stay here with me, that spending time together sounds way better than some party at the lake. Because *that's* the Jay I know. The guy who'd pick me over boozing it up in the woods.

Instead, he tosses me my car keys. "Can't really go anywhere without those, right?"

"Right." I force my lips into a tight smile. "Have a good one."

An uneasiness sits in the center of my chest as I walk away. I can't quite explain it. It's not until I brush my teeth and slide into bed that I'm able to pinpoint my feelings a little more clearly: Maybe it's impossible to reconnect with someone who's not who they used to be.

TWENTY

I DO NOT, IN FACT, remember to wear my spirit color on Monday.

It's first day of Spirit Week, but I'm not in a peppy mood. It's another reminder that homecoming is a few days away. I'll be dateless, which shouldn't be a big deal, but it feels like it.

The theme today is Class Colors. Juniors were encouraged to wear green, but my black Earth Club shirt with a minimally green recycling sign paired with my plain jeans did not impress Raegan, who sat down at lunch looking like a leprechaun threw up all over her.

"You could have made a bigger effort!" she huffed. "The winning class gets to exempt a final at the end of the year, you know."

I did know. I just didn't care.

I'm still slightly annoyed by my interaction with Jay on Friday. At lunch, Whitney didn't seem fazed when he talked about winning four rounds of beer pong at the Winsor Lake party, nor when he reenacted how Breck projectile vomited in the back of Hudson King's pickup. I gave up finishing my ham sandwich after that story, but I couldn't quite shake missing the Jay I thought I knew freshman year.

Coach Vasquez pulls me aside after Wavettes practice. She tells me if I can't bring my Algebra II grade up to a C, I'll be suspended from performing at our next game. I should feel motivated to work harder, but a tiny part of me wouldn't be disappointed if I were kicked off the team.

The thought takes me by surprise. Wasn't this one of the things I desperately wanted? To bring me closer to Raegan and Whitney?

I tell her I'll work harder, but my feelings toward the Wavettes do nothing to lift my craptastic mood.

As I'm walking across the parking lot to my car, I spot Alex. My heart flips dangerously. He's lying in the bed of his pickup on his back with his eyes closed, his earbuds plugged in. What a weird place to hang out. Why is he still here?

I'm in no hurry to go home, so I wander over to him. My shadow falls over his face, indirectly gaining his attention. When he sees me standing there, he smiles.

"Sunbathing?" I ask as he pulls out his earbuds.

"Ha, no." He sits up. Today he's wearing an olive-green T-shirt over his typical black long-sleeve shirt. "I'm waiting for my little cousins. They have an extra hour of ESL after school."

I glance across the street at Cedarville Elementary. "That's nice of you. To wait for them, I mean."

He shrugs, pushing a few untamed curls away from his face. "They like walking home, but my mom doesn't like them crossing that busy intersection off Rosewood and Main." He squints up at me, studying me for a second. "You okay?"

The question throws me off momentarily. I'm surprised that I'm so transparent, but then again, Alex has always been able to read my moods.

"Sorry," he adds. "You just look, I don't know ... deflated?"

"Oh," I say. Then, "Yeah, I don't know."

Alex is still staring at me, and I know he's willing to listen. I don't want to tell him about Coach Vasquez and my D in Algebra II, because then he'll just ask why I don't go to Ana's tutoring sessions in the library. And I need to. Desperately. I also don't want to tell him about things at home, either.

So I keep it vague. "I'm trying to get my life back, I guess. Coming back isn't what I thought it'd be."

Alex doesn't respond right away. Instead he scoots over on the bed of his truck, making room for me. I sit down next to him. A breeze shifts, and I catch the familiar scent of his laundry detergent.

"I mean, I should be happy to be back on the team, right?" I hear myself saying. "I shouldn't dread going to practice."

"Ana quit Debate Club her sophomore year. She said it wasn't as fun as it was freshman year. Things change, I guess."

"It's just—" I shake my head. I don't know if he'll understand. "I made a lot of mistakes when I went to Portland. I dumped Jay and stopped talking to all my friends. My grades dropped. I wasn't involved in *any* activities, and I had, like, no family." When I look at Alex, I'm relieved to see he's not giving me a pitying look. "I want the life I had before all that happened. I know it won't happen overnight, but I'm trying to get there."

"Well, all your friends love you. And you're practically over-involving yourself in school stuff. I wouldn't worry too much."

I glance down at my jazz flats. Untrue. Whitney is still tentative around me, even though *she's* the one who went behind my back when she started dating Jay.

I blink. Where did that thought come from? I'd never let myself dwell on that fact too much, but I feel like I do have the right to be upset about it. We used to tell each other everything.

I push thoughts of Whitney aside. "It's not only that. My dad and all the re—" I catch myself. No one knows about the recoverees living with us, and I don't want to change that. I backtrack. "All the, uh...problems we've been through together." I pick at my thumbnail. "It feels off."

Alex looks across the parking lot. "I know. I mean, I don't *know* how it is exactly, but I know with my dad gone it's...different."

I glance over at his profile. "Your dad's not here?"

Alex's mom and dad opened Rosita's after they gained their citizenship here, before Alex or his sisters were born. From the way Alex talked growing up, Rosita's was his parents' pride and joy. They're also the hardest working people I've ever met.

Alex doesn't speak for a moment. Silent seconds tick by. I'm wracking my brain for a subject change when he says, "He's been in Mexico trying to sell property—the original Rosita's restaurant. We could really use the money, especially with Ana going off to college next year. But the whole selling thing is more complicated than we thought."

"I'm sorry," I say earnestly. "That sucks."

He nods his head in agreement. "The hardest part is not knowing when he'll be back. It's...I don't know. I guess I see so many kids here take their parents for granted. My friends are like, *you're so lucky you don't have your dad breathing down your neck all the time!* But I want him to come see the sets I build for the theater shows and be there for Ana's academic awards and, I don't know, be at dinner with us every night." He glances down at his paint-stained Converse. "I wish I had that, you know?"

I lick my bottom lip. I do know. I know because *I* have that now with *my* dad—because he's trying. I also have Nonnie's pep talks. Saylor offering to teach me yoga. Peach's kind gestures of making my lunch and driving me to the DMV and asking me about my day.

Why do I want them to leave? Because I magically expect my life to go back to normal when they do? Because if they leave, my relationship with my dad will be better? None of that is guaranteed.

My throat is tight. I have to swallow a few times so my voice doesn't break. "I know," I say, feeling like a gigantic hypocrite all over again.

We're quiet for a moment, absorbing each other's silence.

Finally Alex turns to me. "Is this what you want?"

I'm confused. "What do you mean?"

"The old life you're trying to re-create," he clarifies. "Are you sure it's what you really want?"

I feel my lips part, but I can't think of the right words to push out. I *am* trying to re-create my old life. And for what? Because everything will automatically be better? It wasn't better before my dad left for Sober Living, so why am I so willing to believe my twelve-steps list will make me happy?

Alex's phone alarm beeps. He shuts it off, then looks across the street. "I better go get them."

Oh, right. His little cousins. I slide off the bed of his truck. "I should get home," I say. We're both well aware I haven't answered his question.

I hear Alex's engine start as I walk to my car. I slip into the driver's seat, but I don't start it right away. Once I see his truck disappear in the elementary school parking lot, I start the engine. But I can't seem to shake Alex's words from my mind the entire drive home.

Is this what I really want?

TWENTY ONE

THE NEXT DAY IN HISTORY class, I don't spare myself any glances at Jay. At least, not until he taps on my arm, asking to borrow a pen after Mr. Densick hits us with a pop quiz on the Revolutionary War.

I hand him an extra from my bag, noticing he has a dried smear of toothpaste under his bottom lip. Those were the lips I'd imagined kissing over and over while I was living in Portland. I fantasized about him grabbing my hand in a dark movie theater, and how my stomach would flip whenever his steady blue eyes fell on mine.

But then I remember those small memories that tugged at my brain over the past few weeks. He'd never checked up on me when I was in Portland, not even through text. Then there were trivial things, like how he hadn't put any effort into my Christmas gift and homecoming mum when we were together. Plus, at Breck's party . . . it was like talking to a stranger. Not to mention Friday night at Sonic, when he made a not-so-innocent move on me and then *ditched* me to get drunk at Winsor Lake.

A funny emptiness sits in the pit of my stomach. That's when I know—it's different now. I don't feel like my nerves are on fire when I look at him. Those overwhelming feelings have diminished. There's a small pang of sadness in my chest, but I know it's not because he's with Whitney.

It's not until after class that I realize—maybe this is what it feels like to fall out of love.

———————

I text my dad after school to let him know I'm staying a little later to watch Lin's decathlon practice, where they're having a mock competition to prepare for the Super Quiz, which is an event open to the public that doesn't happen officially until early next year. But, as Lin says, preparing ahead of time in front of an audience doesn't hurt.

Mr. Densick is the teacher in charge of the team, so everyone meets in his classroom after school. They've managed to rope in two other students to observe, and for the next forty-five minutes they do their best to answer a series of challenging questions Mr. Densick has prepared.

Lin second-guesses herself a lot, and I know the pressure of the time limit doesn't help. Surprisingly, Breck answers a good amount of them correctly. I can tell he's proud of himself, too, especially when Mr. Densick compliments him at the very end.

Once they wrap it up, I see her breathe a sigh of frustration. Breck must notice as well, because he holds up his hand in a high five, which Lin dejectedly meets.

"Don't be so hard on yourself," he's saying as I walk over. "You did good."

"*You* did good," Lin replies, and it's not at all sarcastic. "I'm the one who sucks."

"No negative attitudes allowed in this room," Mr. Densick says, shuffling through papers on his desk.

I give her an encouraging smile. "Breck's right. Also, you both were great."

Lin gives me a quick hug. "Thanks for sticking around." She turns to Breck. "Honestly? And don't get an even bigger head, but I'm glad you're on the team."

Breck lets out an exaggerated gasp, clutching his chest dramatically. "Did everyone just *hear* that?"

"Okay, I literally said—"

"LIN PHAM IS GLAD I'M ON THE TEAM."

I wave good-bye to both of them. "I should get home."

She's trying not to smile at Breck's enthusiasm, but cracks. "Thanks again for com—"

"LIN THINKS *I'M* THE BEST."

"Don't twist my words!"

I can't help but grin. It makes me happy to see them succeeding with Breck's contribution to the team.

When I get home, I don't go inside right away. I sit in the silence of my car and scroll through old photos on my phone, stopping when I find the section of selfies I'd made Jay take with me after a football game freshman year. We're both in uniform making silly faces, except for the last one where we're both cracking up over something.

My heart remains still in my chest, not fluttering even once.

It feels so weird. Final.

I pull the keys out of the ignition and walk inside. Wallis bounces around me in his familiar enthusiastic greeting, but once he gets the attention he desires he pads away.

I set my book bag down by the stairs and wander into the kitchen. Peach is sitting at the kitchen table, my dad's laptop perched in front of her. She's wearing thin frames as she studies the screen. A pile of opened mail sits beside her.

"Hey!" she says. "I brought home some cupcakes from the bakery. If you're hungry, there's stew on the stove."

I'm about to thank her when my eye catches the piece of mail at the top of the stack. It's addressed to my dad, but I notice the return address reads CEDARVILLE HIGH SCHOOL. I pick it up, realizing that it's my progress report.

I'm immediately infuriated. "Did you go through my *mail?*"

Peach glances up, startled. Then she notices the envelope in my hand.

My dad emerges from his room. "What's going on?"

I cross my arms, glaring at her. It's not enough that they're infiltrating my home. She has absolutely no right going through my personal items.

My dad takes my progress report from me as Peach tries to explain. "Your dad wanted me to help him get some things in order. I'm filing all of it for—"

"Kira, you have a D in algebra?"

There's anger in his voice, but I'm too mad to worry about that. Instead I turn to Peach. "You can't just go through my stuff whenever you feel like it."

"It was in your daddy's name, I just assumed—"

My dad steps in. "That's okay, Peach. I know you're trying to help."

I can't believe it. My dad is actually *defending* her. I thought we were on the verge of a breakthrough after we talked the other night on the way to Lucky's.

My face heats up, and I feel my defenses rise. "It's *not* okay. What about this is okay?"

I can tell by the look on my dad's face that my outburst is not welcome, but I don't care.

"Grams used to take care of the finances," he says. "I needed a little help getting organized, that's all."

Peach stands up. "I—"

"No." I don't want to hear it. I'm tired of her always hanging around, worming her way into my life. "I don't care what my dad says. I don't want your help—I don't want you here. You're *not* Grams, and you're not my mother."

Silence.

Dead. Silence.

I can't look at my dad. I know he's furious, but he's not the only one. I don't even know *why* he wanted me to move back here in the first place. Not when he has his Sober Living friends that apparently make his life *so much better* now.

"Kira, please apologize."

His authoritative tone is back. I ignore it, taking the stairs two at a time, already aware that I'm going to be in huge trouble, but I don't care. I close myself off in my room. All I wanted was a normal life with my dad. *My* dad. Nobody else. I don't need anyone taking Grams's place.

Wallis scratches at the door. Sighing, I get up and let him in. He sniffs around my bed skirt before nudging my hand with his nose, urging me to pet him.

I remember Nonnie mentioning that she was the fourth person to adopt Wallis. It's weird, because even though his prior families abandoned him, he still has this automatic trusting demeanor. He's been cast aside so many times but gives each new person another chance.

A voice in the back of my mind says, *You're the one not giving them a chance.*

It says, *You're being too hard on him. On everyone.*

Wallis paws at my bed. I let him jump up, which causes the mattress to creak and sag under his weight. I'm still convinced he's part Shetland pony.

I don't do my homework. Instead I walk over to my desk and unfold my twelve-steps list. My dad and I need to learn how to make a life for ourselves, and that means he can't use them as a safety net anymore.

It's time for us to start being our own family, just the two of us.

TWENTY TWO

AFTER LAST NIGHT, I PLAN to leave for school without interacting with anyone. I'm still not in a stellar mood. It's one thing for my dad to let the recoverees stay here, but to let them meddle in my life? That's a boundary I'm not about to let any of them cross.

My dad is buttering a piece of toast when I walk into the kitchen. I brace myself for some type of scolding, but I'm surprised to see the softness in his expression when he meets my eyes.

"Goose, about last night." He sets the knife down beside the plate. "I understand why you're upset. I don't want you to feel like anyone is trying to fill Grams's shoes."

The defensive side of me begins to dissolve. Could he actually understand why I'm upset about involving them in our personal life?

"But I'd still like you to apologize to Peach. It wasn't fair to lash out like you did."

And there it is: The proof that he doesn't really understand. Because to him, it's more important that I apologize when *I'm* the one whose life has been completely derailed not only by his addiction, but by inviting these people here and expecting me to act like everything is perfectly fine.

I grab an apple from the fruit bowl. "I'm going to be late."

Then I leave. I tell myself it's not as harsh as it feels.

My lunch period was spent listening to Raegan discuss Leadership Council plans for the homecoming dance while Whitney ran through her hair, nails, and makeup appointments with Jay, who seemed like he was only half-interested. But when Jay mentioned his "brilliant idea"—his words—of having the guys' basketball team moon the Homecoming King and Queen during the first dance, Raegan almost snapped the pencil she was holding before going off on him. After my recent revelation, I was certain that any feelings I may still have had toward him had completely evaporated.

I'm pulling into the driveway after the homecoming parade—which was organized flawlessly, all thanks to Raegan—when I spot a black sedan I don't recognize in front of my house. I slide the gear in Park and step out as Margaret emerges from the car.

All the blood in my body freezes.

She's smiling happily as she walks over to me, her tall heels clacking on the pavement. When she removes her Audrey Hepburn–style sunglasses, I'm relieved to see that she doesn't have any concern expressed across her face.

"Hello, Kira!" she says, her tone friendly. "I know this is unexpected, but I was in the neighborhood and thought I'd swing by."

I try and keep the panic off my face as a million different thoughts churn in my brain at once. Does she suspect something? Did the neighbors report unusual behavior of us having too much company here? No, that couldn't happen. Because even if they did, how would they know Margaret is my social worker?

"Oh, well, I guess you have good timing." I hold up my dance bag. "I'm just getting home from practice."

She nods, looking toward the front door. "Mind if I do a walk-through?"

This is a nightmare. I can't outright say no, because then it'll *definitely* look suspicious. I also have no idea who's home right now, waiting to give away all the big secrets I've conveniently left out of my conversations with Margaret. Despite fighting with my dad and Peach over my grades, I wasn't ready for this moment. I'm happy here. I *can't* be sent off again.

I do my best to give an easygoing shrug. "Sure."

We walk up the front porch, and my hands shake as I unlock the front door. When I start to open it, there's a booming *woof* as Wallis comes charging toward us.

I take hold of Wallis's collar, but don't put too much effort into stopping him from jumping on Margaret. Maybe Wallis's enthusiasm will make her uncomfortable, therefore getting her out of here quicker.

"Well, this is certainly a new addition."

"Yeah, he's our rescue." Wallis rubs his nose over her pencil skirt, and she takes a tiny step back. "He's good. Just extremely friendly."

"Mmm." Her eyes wander down the hall that leads to the living room, and I'm relieved to see that no one's occupying it. Still, I can't let go of the anxiety in my chest as she moves onward. If anyone is here, I hope to whatever higher power exists that they don't choose *now* to come out and say hello.

"Your father isn't home?" Margaret says once she's surveyed the kitchen.

His car wasn't in the driveway, so I know he's not here. It's a miracle that no one else is home, and I don't need anyone walking in *right this second*. I have no idea how I would explain.

"Still at work," I tell her, still trying to figure out how to end this as quickly as possible. "Sometimes they need him to stay a bit later."

She nods. It's hard to read her expression, but she doesn't seem troubled. "I have confirmed that your father is continuing his AA meetings."

This doesn't surprise me, especially since he'd told me he was in touch with Michael. He really is committing to his sobriety.

"And counseling," I add, hoping she can't sense the anxiety in my voice.

"Good, good." She takes another look around as Wallis sniffs at her ankles. "I was hoping to check on him, but seeing you was really the goal. Let me ask you this, though. Have you picked up on anything that could be considered out of the ordinary for him? Any unusual behaviors?"

The truth gathers on the tip of my tongue. What if I told her, admitted everything about the recoverees living here? She might be able to use her power to kick everyone else out *without* sending me back to Aunt June. It's a tempting thought, but one I'm not willing to risk.

I shake my head.

"We've been good, really. But I have your number and, honestly, I appreciate you being here for me."

It's blatant sweet talk, but not necessarily untrue. Still, Margaret looks pleased. "Of course, of course. I'll get out of your way." She gives Wallis a reluctant pat on the head, and the touch of affection causes him to happily roll over onto his back.

As we're walking out to her car, I spot a familiar figure walking down the sidewalk in the distance. No, no, *no*. It's Saylor. My heart pounds as Margaret digs through her purse for her keys. If she sees him come inside, then it's over. Done. She'll find out I lied and will call my dad and—

A short beep sounds as Margaret unlocks her car, then slides inside. I look back down the sidewalk to see Saylor's an uncomfortably close distance away.

"Again, call me anytime you need me," Margaret says.

"Sure. Will do." I hope I don't sound as distracted as I feel.

With a small wave, she shuts her door and starts the engine. Saylor's only a few feet away when she shifts into gear and drives down the street. I hold my breath, waiting for her to circle around, but she doesn't. After a few more seconds, the car disappears from sight.

I let out my breath.

"Hey," Saylor says. "Who was that?"

"No one. Don't you have to work?" It comes out more accusatory than I want it to, but I'm still stressing from that uncomfortably close call.

If Saylor notices, he doesn't show it. "I mixed up the schedule. I don't work again until tomorrow."

He opens the door. I'm about to pull a disappearing act to my room when he says, "You know, I'm pretty good at algebra."

Heat boils inside my chest. Peach must have told him about my D in algebra. I can't have any sort of privacy around here.

"I'm working on it," I say, avoiding his gaze.

Saylor just shrugs. "All right, then."

I head to my room and change out of my dance clothes. It's annoying that Saylor's forcing himself into my business. He should really be focusing on saving up the money for his yoga profession or whatever.

I plop myself down at my desk, determined to finish all my algebra homework. We've only started learning about quadratic functions, but of course Mrs. Donaldson assigned the hardest problems in the textbooks (all even numbered so we couldn't cheat and get the odd answers from the back index). Lin and Raegan are in pre-calc, so we don't even have the same textbook. And I definitely don't want to text Alex for help, because then he'd ask why I haven't gone to see Ana. It's not that I don't want to—Ana is great—but Wavettes practice this week has been even more demanding with the homecoming game on Friday.

I sigh, slamming my book closed. Frustrated with my own incompetence, I walk over to my window. Saylor is lying in the hammock reading a book, the hood of his sweatshirt covering his long ponytail. Before I can change my mind, I begrudgingly grab my textbook and go downstairs.

"You know anything about quadratic equations?" I yell from the porch.

Saylor looks up from his book. The tree leaves above him rustle. "I know a good amount, yeah."

He gets out of the hammock, and I feel a tiny surge of relief as he follows me back inside. I lay out my textbook on the kitchen table and point to the cluster of problems.

"Give me a sec," Saylor says, scanning through the previous lesson. "It's been a minute since I've done this."

I nod, grateful not to feel forced to fill this silence. I sneak a glance toward the living room, but Peach isn't there. That's weird. She's usually here by now. A small part of me feels guilty for the relief that eases in my chest.

"Right, so you first have to make sure the equations are set to zero before you can solve." Saylor takes my pencil and begins writing down the first problem. "Also, keep in mind that the square of a negative will always be positive. Here, let's walk through this one."

I watch as he successfully completes the first equation, but then he lets me take the reins on the second problem. He has to remind me of a few steps, but once I do them in the correct order, I'm able to plot the right intercepts on the graph.

"See? You got this," he says, and I'm even more relieved that he helps me through every problem until my assignment is done.

"I wish stuff like this came naturally to me like it did to Grams," I say, surprising myself with the mention of her name.

I'm thankful he doesn't take this as an opportunity to talk about her. Instead he says, "Well, I bet other people wish they could dance as well as you can."

"That's different. I'm decent at best, and that's only because we have practice every week."

Saylor grins, tapping a finger on my textbook. "So if you practice more of this, you should be decent at best."

I roll my eyes, but I feel a smile come through anyway. I walked into that one. "Mrs. Donaldson makes sure we get *plenty* of practice, as you can see."

Saylor stands up, stretches, then looks back at me. "Well, if you need any more help, you know where to find me."

"Thanks," I say, my voice small. I know he didn't have to help me in the first place.

Saylor grabs his book from the table—*The Spiritual Journey of Yoga's Healing Powers*—and flips through to his dog-eared page. His dozens of leather bracelets collapse upon each other from the movement.

"Why do you wear so many?"

Saylor looks down, then smiles. "They're intention bracelets. I branded them myself, but I don't know...I guess they've been good reminders for me."

A few of the words catch my eye. *Focus. Strength. Trust.*

My gaze lingers on the last one a little longer. I take a deep breath. "Where's Peach? Isn't she usually here by now?"

When Saylor's eyes meet mine, there's a certain sadness in them. "Uh, your dad drove her to get some of her belongings. Her daughters aren't really...well, they're not ready to forgive her yet. I guess."

I expect to feel angry—that means Peach is going to stay here longer, which is not part of my twelve-steps plan—but I don't.

Instead I feel sort of bad that I yelled at her yesterday. The last thing I want is to make things harder on her.

"Oh," is all I can think to say.

"Well," Saylor says after a beat. "I'll see you in the morning."

I nod. "Yeah, okay."

The back door closes, and I begin gathering up my books. That's when my eye catches something sitting near my extra pencil, and I realize it's one of Saylor's intention bracelets. When I turn it over, I read the word that's been branded into it: *Forgive.*

I'm not sure if he purposefully left it here or if it fell off, but before I can think about it too much, I fasten the thing around my wrist. I don't know what draws me to it, but even so, I have a feeling Saylor won't mind if I keep it.

TWENTY THREE

BECAUSE I REALLY DO WANT to raise my algebra grade, I end up in the library with Ana on Thursday. She'd agreed to stay an hour later than usual because of my Wavettes practice, which is nice of her. I find her sitting near the reference desk when I push through the double doors.

I'm a little intimidated as I walk over to the table she's claimed for us. Ana has always been effortlessly gorgeous. Her dark-brown hair hangs down in a braid over her shoulder, and she sits upright with perfect posture.

When she spots me, she smiles. "Kira! It's great to see you. It's been too long."

I'm reminded why she's popular in her grade. She can easily make anyone feel welcome.

"It really has." I take a seat next to her, setting my book bag in the chair beside me. "Thanks again for helping me out."

"It's no problem. Alex caught me up on what's going to be on your test next week."

I pull my algebra textbook and flip to the chapter we covered today about radical functions. "I should warn you that I'm pretty hopeless."

She waves that aside. "I doubt it. Let's see what you're struggling with."

For the next forty minutes, Ana patiently breaks down Mrs. Donaldson's most recent lesson. By the end, I've even managed to solve a few homework problems on my own.

"See? I knew you could do it." She smiles at me. Her eyes are the same shade of soft brown as Alex's, and it catches me off guard for a moment. "Sometimes it helps when someone else explains it in another way."

Relief breaks through my chest, even though I know I have a long way to go. "Thank you, seriously."

She dog-ears one of my textbook pages and taps her pencil eraser on the remaining practice problems. "Come see me a few more times before your big test and do these over the weekend so you don't forget. If you get confused, just text me." She writes down her number on my spiral.

I glance up at her. "I really appreciate it."

Ana shrugs like it isn't a big deal. "I had Mrs. Donaldson last year. I know how she can be."

"Yeah, but you're way smarter than me."

She laughs modestly. "No."

"Seriously. Alex told me how you guys are up super early to help with the restaurant, and you're in a ton of clubs and volunteer with tutoring—"

Ana flushes. "Alex told you that? About Rosita's?"

I try to backtrack. "Well, I mean, yeah he mentioned it once." Now I'm the one blushing. I don't want to offend or embarrass Ana. She's so sweet. "Sorry, I didn't mean—"

"No, don't be sorry." Ana studies me for a few seconds. "You know, I'm not surprised. He's always been really open with you."

If Alex's former crush was obvious to me, then I'm sure Ana and Marlina were also aware. Alex didn't seem ashamed when he told me about helping his mom out at Rosita's. Then again, it'd always been easy to talk to each other. But that had slowed when—

Right. When Lacey asked him to Sadie Hawkins and in a weird fit of unannounced jealousy, I quit speaking to him as much.

"I have to get going." Ana closes her spiral, giving me another warm smile. "But like I said, text me over the weekend if you have any more questions."

"I will," I say.

With a small wave, Ana grabs her backpack and walks out of the library. I pack up my things and head toward my locker to get the books I need for my homework tonight. As I'm walking past the auditorium, there's a loud *bang* as the doors slam open. A bunch of kids emerge from the theater, including Alex.

My breath sticks in the shallows of my throat.

"Kira, hey!"

He begins to walk over to me. Somehow I find my voice.

"Hey." My tone feels a few octaves too high. "I just finished tutoring with your sister."

If Alex notices, he doesn't say anything. "How'd it go?"

"Really good."

He grins. "Good."

A beat of silence falls between us, and I find myself wracking my brain so this moment doesn't have to be over.

"We're running through the first act," Alex says. "For the fall play. All-hands-on-deck mode. I have to move a few props during scene breaks."

"Oh! Okay. Yeah." This is where I should turn to go, but I don't. Instead I stand there like a massive dork.

He gestures toward the auditorium. "Do you, um...want to come watch?"

I'm surprised at the invitation. Aside from the holiday program the Wavettes put on, I've never been in the auditorium for a theater performance. But I want to be backstage with Alex. I'm suddenly grappling with this urge to spend time with him.

"Yeah, is it okay? For me to be in there, I mean?"

"Definitely." He tugs on the back of his beanie. "You can watch from backstage with me."

And just like that, I'm following him into the auditorium. Mrs. Henson, one of the theater instructors, is giving commands to a few actors on stage. Aside from her, the rest of the seats in the theater are empty.

Alex leads me down a small hallway that loops backstage. It's mostly all juniors or seniors in this cast, but no one pays me any mind as we walk by. They're running lines with each other or discussing costumes with the senior costume designer, who looks a little stressed out.

Alex stops at the right wing of the stage. It's cluttered with a white dresser on wheels and a small office desk with a lamp on top of it.

"I kinda just wait here until scene break. Super exciting, right? But it's cool seeing them improve." He moves the lamp to the ground, then takes a seat on the desk. He pats the empty space beside it. "Here."

My nerves thrum through my veins as I climb next to him. We're sitting so close, and I'm so, so aware of him. The soft flops of his dark curls. The calluses on his hands from building props in the workshop. The slight overlap in his two front teeth when he looks over at me and smiles, like I'm the only person here that he cares about.

My heart beats deeply, an erratic rhythm in my head.

I think back to what Ana said. *He's always been really open with you.* But he wasn't the only one. Even though Alex wasn't part of my immediate circle of friends, I'd still told him about my dad. I talked to him about it more than I ever talked to Jay.

Is it possible that our friendship has evolved so naturally that I've barely noticed?

He shifts. Our hands almost touch. I swallow and swallow and swallow. I imagine what it would be like if we made even the slightest contact. My skin would ignite. I would burst into flames.

I inhale sharply.

Then I panic.

This feels *way* beyond friendship.

"Sorry." Alex's voice is abrupt. Insecure. "This is boring. I—"

"No." I interrupt. My synapses crackle with electricity. Does he feel it, too? "I like it. I feel very VIP."

He breaks into a grin, but I catch his chest exhaling in relief.

"Why tech theater?" I ask, hoping talking will calm down my spasmodic heart rate. "Doesn't everyone want to act?"

"Nah," he says as we watch the actors run through blocking. "I'm better at designing and building. Besides, I get to watch it all happen from back here."

I flick my gaze to the set on stage. The current scene takes place in a kitchen, but from the way the painted wooden walls are tri-folded together, I can tell it's easily able to transform into a whole new room for a completely different scene.

"You used to write screenplays," I say. "In middle school, remember? They were *Supernatural* episodes you wished existed. Oh, my god, remember the one with the murderous poltergeist?"

"Oh." He glances down, embarrassed. "Man, those were awful."

"They weren't!" I mean it. "Do you still want to go to school for screenwriting?"

"I do, but I don't think it's such a smart idea."

This surprises me. "Why?"

He keeps his gaze on the stage. "Because, I don't know. That whole industry...it's so risky—and it can be pretty unstable, from what I've read. Both my parents worked really hard to make sure we have everything we need. I should major in business, you know? Get a job where I can have that stability they were able to give us."

"Is that what you really want?"

It's the same question he asked me. I can tell he remembers, because he meets my gaze.

"No." I'm surprised by his honesty. "But it's the responsible thing to do. I want to make my parents proud. I don't want them to have a son who's in debt and who can't find a job because I risked it all in a creative industry."

"Alex." His name sounds so sad in my mouth.

But he just shakes his head. "I—"

I don't know what he's going to say because it falls quiet on stage. The lights dim, casting darkness in our small corner.

Alex leans back ever so slightly, his shoulder brushing against mine. My stomach flips. Was that intentional? No, I'm reading too much into it. This desk is so small. It was an accident.

Right?

In the darkness, my eyes find his chest. His breaths accelerate. *In-out-in-out-in-out.* Does he feel it, too? Am I the only one who feels this undefined friction between us? I don't know. I try looking at him, but I can't read his expression in the dark.

I focus on the stage. The only source of light is the spotlight that pours down on the two actors on stage. Alex adjusts his posture, leaving a bigger gap of space between us. The hopeful expansion in my chest immediately deflates. I'm imagining this. I'm overreacting to everything.

That's when the lights go completely dark, startling me. Scene change. It must be. We both move to get off the desk at the same time, but I stumble. He quickly grabs my shoulder to stabilize me. The warmth of his hand penetrates through the sleeve of my shirt.

He doesn't let go.

Not immediately.

Alex's touch isn't the VOOSH of raw energy I felt with Jay. It's stronger. His contact is a gravitational pull, tilting my universe off axis. My skin is made of stars, and I am spinning, spinning, spinning through space.

"Are you okay?" he says, reeling me back to reality. I'm dizzy in a way that has nothing to do with the darkness. "I should have warned you." He lets go, and it takes everything in me not to protest. "I have to move these real quick."

I watch as his silhouette positions new props on stage. All I can do is stand there, trying to figure out what just happened.

But if I'm being honest with myself, I already know.

Alex disappears from the main stage just as the light filters back on. He's smiling, adjusting the back of his beanie as he heads toward me.

"Try not to look so impressed. Those things can't move themselves."

I laugh, but it comes out strangely. My throat is dry, and I've suddenly lost the ability to string together an intelligible sentence.

He scratches his neck. "I won't make you stay. You probably have better things to do."

The thing is, I don't.

I can't think of anywhere I'd rather be.

"No," I tell him. "I want to stay."

It's hard to tell because it's so dark, but I swear I catch him smile.

That's when I know.

Oh god.

I like Alex.

TWENTY FOUR

TODAY IS HOMECOMING, BUT INSTEAD of meeting my friends in homeroom I've been sitting in my car for the last several minutes. Groups of freshmen snap selfies outside of the gym while flaunting their mums like badges of honor. Red-and-white ribbons billow in the breeze and entangle their legs as they parade through the double doors.

My freshman mum from Jay is still hanging in my closet. I remember when he gave it to me, and how most of the ribbons were wrinkled and glue-gun spiderwebs hung from the fake petals of the mum. Even the lettering of my name was crooked. I knew it was a haphazard disaster, but I was so enamored with him that I didn't care.

Jay had walked me the long way to my English class that day, specifically maneuvering past the gym so the basketball guys could see us together. When I sat down at my desk, Alex was looking at me like he was trying not to laugh.

"What?" I'd snapped.

He was eyeing my droopy mum. I'd spotted Lacey in the hall earlier. It was easy to tell he'd put some effort into hers.

"Nothing," he'd said. "He walks with you like you're some show dog."

I rolled my eyes and brushed it off, telling myself he was jealous. But once we were at Breck's house party after winning the game that night, I couldn't help feeling like I *was* his Wavette accessory—that I could have been easily replaced by another girl on my team.

Maybe this is what happens when you fall out of love with someone. You begin to realize all the times you were let down. All the times you brushed something aside because your heart was too preoccupied by the what-ifs and what-could-bes. That maybe you should have listened to the nagging part of your brain when it said you could do better.

I run my hands over my steering wheel. I don't want to go inside and watch as Whitney's treated mediocrely by someone who'd rather flirt with some college girl who spends Saturday nights bringing beer to a high school party. There was one point in time where Whitney and I valued each other's honesty, but I know that's changed. If I brought it up, she'd think I was jealous. I don't want another fight—especially since I'm still walking on unstable ground with her.

I'm putting my keys back in the ignition right as a truck pulls up beside me. I immediately recognize the deep-green paint job and the rusting bumper.

Alex.

Nervous energy tingles in my fingertips. I spent another hour with him backstage yesterday after they finished the first act, and in between scene changes we studied for our Algebra II test. We'd spread out on the dirty theater floor, reading our notes beneath the glow of our cell phone lights. Whenever he leaned over to compare answers, delicate prickles of energy would explode like tiny fireworks in my brain.

He's the only part of my twelve-steps list that I haven't actively worked on. But if I don't confront him about the text, I'll never know.

Before I even consider what I'm doing, I walk around to the driver's side and tap on the glass.

As Alex lowers his window, I notice he's wearing his typical attire: a black long-sleeve shirt with a green DEEP FLAME PRODUCTIONS T-shirt over it. His black beanie sits atop his head, and his mop of dark curls appear springier than usual as they peer out underneath.

He grins at me. "Fancy meeting you here."

"Do you want to skip with me today?" I blurt.

He looks surprised. "Sure," he says without question. "Hop in."

My insides flood with relief. I walk around and climb in the passenger's side. As soon as my door closes, Alex puts the car in Drive and we flee from the parking lot, away from all the gilded mums and past memories that hang over my head like heavy clouds on the verge of a thunderstorm.

"Where are we going?"

We've been driving in silence for a few minutes. I open my mouth to give him a destination, but I blank. I only know I didn't want to go to school. I hadn't thought where we'd go instead.

Alex must sense my hesitation because he says, "I know a place."

His sense of control puts me at ease as I settle back in the worn seat. We drive another block before Alex pulls into the donut shop a few stores down from 7-Eleven.

I smile. This is the place where my dad would buy éclairs for my birthday. He'd also get me a carton of chocolate milk until one day in sixth grade when I told him I was "too old" for it and wanted coffee instead. After one sip of the bitter tar-fluid I immediately regretted it, but I was too proud to tell him I preferred chocolate milk.

Alex holds the door open for me. I'm greeted with the warm scent of freshly sugared pastries. The glass case before us holds dozens of frosted options.

I choose a strawberry sprinkle. He chooses a chocolate glaze. On a whim I grab a carton of chocolate milk from the door of the glass cooler. Alex doesn't make fun of me. He even pays, even though I insist I should.

"I'm the one who asked *you* to skip," I say as we walk out. "I should at least buy you a donut."

"It's not like you had to try hard to convince me." His warm gaze finds mine. "I wanted to come with you."

My cheeks flush, and I turn into the same sugary, frosted goo that coats my donut.

When we get back on the road, Alex's hand finds the radio knob. "Music?"

Sensual jazz music flows from its permanent speaker prison.

"Oh god, no," I laugh as I release my donut from its bag. "It sounds like the sound track leading up to a bad sex scene."

Alex accidentally taps the brakes, jolting us.

I turn twelve dozen shades of red. *Why* would I say *that?*

Alex lets out a nervous laugh, and I'm thankful when he changes the subject. "I don't think you've skipped school a day in your life."

I give a small shrug. "There's a first time for everything."

From the way he glances at me, I know this is his roundabout way of fishing for information. He skipped with me, no questions asked. He deserves to know what's going on.

"It's like . . . ever since I've been back I've felt like I've been walking on one of those fun house bridges. The ones that try and throw off your balance, you know? And every time I feel like I'm making it closer to the end, the bridge shifts and I'm trying to keep myself from toppling over." I trace my finger around the edge of the door handle. "If that makes any sense."

He's quiet for a moment. "You told me the other day that you wanted the life you had before everything with your dad happened."

"Certain things," I admit, thinking of my list. I'd give anything to have Grams back. Of course, I still want the recoverees gone. "But the more I try and force it, the more distant I feel."

"Maybe that's the problem."

"What?"

"Forcing things to be the way they were before. I know people make mistakes, and I won't pretend like I'm an expert in what's going on in your life, but even when people give us second chances it doesn't mean it's going to be the same."

My mind lingers on that word: *second chances*. Despite me ignoring That Text, he'd easily fallen back into the rhythm of our previous friendship like nothing happened. My non-response must have hurt him, just like ignoring Lin, Whitney, and Raegan had hurt them. But he'd stood up for me in Mrs. Donaldson's class, and here he was cutting class with me.

My heart flutters. Could *he* be giving *me* another chance?

"So you think someone should embrace a situation they're put in?"

"Yeah, if it's good." Alex glances at me. "I know working with my mom and sister at Rosita's isn't glamorous, but it's going to help us pay for college."

I study him. He's never been afraid to be fully himself. Most students I know still complain that their parents are so embarrassing, yet Alex talks about working with his mom and sister in his family's restaurant so casually. With pride.

That's when a twinge of guilt strikes me. Because I haven't been accepting of the recoverees. They're people who are trying to change for the better, like my dad. And despite my crummy attitude, they've been good to me. Even after my outburst about my progress report, Peach still makes my lunch every day. Saylor's helped me with my homework, and even though Nonnie's been better at giving me space, she'll still check up on me from time to time to make sure I'm doing okay. They don't have to do any of that, but they do.

Alex starts to merge onto the highway.

"Where are we going?"

"On an adventure," he says, grinning. "You look like you need one."

TWENTY FIVE

ALEX DRIVES US TO CANTOR Creek, a slightly bigger town thirty minutes down the road. Tons of seniors always make a trip here before prom because their mall is bigger than ours, which means there's a larger dress selection. Even though the dilapidated buildings and charming storefront displays are similar to Cedarville, it feels different. Nobody here knows who we are.

Alex parks the truck on Main Street, which is double the length of the Main Street in Cedarville. It's a chilly day—a reminder that Halloween will be here before we know it—but I don't mind. Because even though it's brisk, the sun is shining and I'm feeling good. Great, even. Better than I have in a while.

We walk past a few beaderies and bookstores before entering a particularly dusty antique shop called Memaw's Attic. An enormous tub of skeleton keys catches my eye. I pick one up.

"I wonder what doors these unlock."

Alex reaches for one with an ornate handle. "Remember the time you lost your keys on the class trip to Austin?"

I set the key back in the pile. Eighth graders at Cedarville Middle get to go on a class trip to see the capitol and watch an educational film in the neighboring Imax theater. On the bus ride there, my purse had toppled over and my house keys had made their great escape.

I freaked out after lunch when I was searching for my pack of gum, discovering my keys weren't there. Whitney came back on the bus with me to help me look. Alex was already inside grabbing his sweatshirt from his seat. I remember he'd asked why we were on our hands and knees and when I told him, he started crawling on the gross, dirty floor with us. Whitney was the one who found them a few seats down from ours. I was so relieved.

I don't think I ever thanked Alex for helping.

"I almost forgot about that," I say.

He holds my gaze. "I didn't."

Shame trickles down my spine. I'd rejected him in middle school when I ignored his obvious feelings toward me, and I'd moved on to Jay when I knew I didn't have a chance with Alex at the Sadie Hawkins dance. Yet after all of that, he's still willing to be my friend.

And maybe more?

I want to show him that the times we spent together were meaningful to me, too.

"We did that project. At your house," I find myself saying. "The Ancient Egyptian one?"

He picks up an antelope saltshaker, grinning. "I had to give Marlina *and* Ana my allowance money that week. Otherwise they would have never left us alone."

He's not even bothering to hide how he felt before. I set down another key and look at him.

"Alex—"

"I know." He adjusts his beanie—his nervous habit. "I know you didn't feel the same way about me, but it's not like I was very subtle."

I shake my head, confused. "I just—I don't get it."

He looks amused. "I didn't think my feelings were that complex."

I take a deep breath. There isn't a better time than now.

"No, I mean, I wasn't a good friend. Back in middle school? I hurt you. I knew you liked me, and I didn't even acknowledge it. And I never replied to that text you sent before I left for Portland. I feel like I always mishandled your feelings. Even after not hearing from me for so long, you're still here, being a really good friend to me. It's more than I deserve."

I don't expect him to appear surprised, but he does.

"Says who?"

Now I'm confused. "What?"

"Who says it's more than you deserve?"

Is he trying to make this hard for me? I grow frustrated. "You weren't the only one I stopped texting when I left. I didn't even keep in touch with Raegan or Lin or Whitney, and Whitney's *still* mad about it."

"Kira." His voice is serious now. Quiet. "You were going through a really hard time. Of course, I understood why you didn't text me back."

I look up at him. His face is sincere.

"After I sent it, I honestly thought it was an unfair thing to do to you. You had enough to deal with already." He leans against the crate. "Plus, isn't Whitney dating Jay now? I don't get why she's mad at you when she would do something like that knowing what you were going through."

This is something I'd thought about, too, but I thought it was selfish of me. It's not like my friends had ditched me. They were constantly trying to make me feel included even though I was thousands of miles away. Couldn't they understand why it was hard for me? And yeah, maybe it was unfair that Whitney didn't tell me about Jay, but I always thought we'd had a solid friendship—one that boys and bouts of silence couldn't break.

But it's not Whitney who understood that. It's Alex.

"I was going to ask you to Sadie's freshman year," I admit.

"Really?" Alex blurts, disbelieving.

"Yeah. Until Lacey did."

"And you went with Jay."

He doesn't say it in an accusatory way. He's stating a simple fact. I nod. "Yeah."

We stare at each other for a moment. I wonder where we'd be if we could rearrange bits of our past. If he said no to Lacey. If he said yes to me. If I replied to his texts. If I kept in touch with my friends.

If, if, if.

We're quiet as we exit Memaw's, but I can't stop thinking of what he said. Am I justified in my feelings of annoyance toward Whitney? Don't I have a right to be upset with her for hiding such a big secret from me?

We wind up meandering into an unusually warm gift shop. I watch Alex push up his long sleeves, and the sight of his lean forearms leaves me momentarily dizzy.

I swallow. "Alex?"

He turns to me, his eyebrows raised in question.

"What's with the two shirts?"

"Oh. It's for theater rehearsals. I have to wear all black when I'm moving props, so I wear it under my shirts so I'm not carrying around a change of clothes."

I smile. "It's very trademark of you."

"My signature style. I bet you had no idea I was so fashion forward."

I laugh, then pick up a bottle of lavender aromatherapy room spray and spritz it in the air. Alex scrambles backward.

"Sorry," he tells me, standing a few feet away. "My asthma. I, uh, have really weird triggers."

"Oh!" I quickly cap the spray and wave my hand in the air, trying to make it evaporate. "Sorry! I forgot! You had that attack in PE class in fifth grade."

Alex groans, pulling his beanie over his head like an ostrich burying its head in sand. "I wish people didn't remember that."

The nurse, the vice principal, *and* the principal rushed to the gym when Coach Mendez paged for Alex's emergency inhaler. When his inhaler didn't work, they had to call 911 and then his parents. Everyone was talking about it at school the next day. To make it even worse, his mom wrote a note that said Alex had to sit out running the mile in PE, but that only made him stand out even more. Lacey even tried to fake an attack to get out of running and when that didn't work, she made fun of Alex for the rest of the week.

What did he ever see in her, anyway?

"I've gotten better, but I try and stay away from things that trigger it," he says as I lead us out of the shop. "Perfumes, hairspray, scented lotions—"

"Living with two sisters must be so fun."

He laughs. "Actually, they let me have my own bathroom for that reason. It's pretty awesome."

"Ugh, that must be nice." Then I stop myself. Alex doesn't know about the recoverees, and he knows I don't have any siblings.

He throws me a confused glance, but doesn't push it.

We get ice cream for lunch even though it's in the sixties. When I shiver, he takes off his beanie and places it on my head.

"Sorry I don't have a coat on," he says.

His smile is enough to fuel the warmth inside me.

We keep walking. He swings his arm next to mine and talks about continuing to build the gigantic Audrey II plant model for the spring musical. He helped make the shell for the homecoming parade, but he has the mechanics all planned out. He created a giant gap in the back to control the movements of the plant's mouth by using a series of pedals and pulleys to open and close it. As he explains his pulley system, all I can focus on are his hands and the rush I felt when he carefully stabilized me in the dark theater.

We're almost back to his car when his phone rings. He gives me an apologetic smile before answering, "Hey." I watch as the color drains from his face. "Okay. I know, okay? It's fine. Okay . . . *okay*. See you." He hangs up, then turns to me. "Ana noticed I wasn't at school today."

Dread seeps through my veins. "This is my fault. I shouldn't have—"

"Kira." He steps toward me, his eyes deliberately falling on mine. "You didn't make me do anything I didn't want to do."

His words launch me halfway to the moon.

"But we should get back." He checks the clock on his phone. "Don't you have to be at the pep rally before the game?"

I let out a string of curse words. He laughs. I'd almost forgotten about homecoming.

"Are you going to the game?"

He stares at me. "Do you want me to go?"

"I mean... if you wanted—you don't *have* to." Now I'm having a hard time meeting his gaze. Jeez. What is wrong with me? I look up, take a deep breath, and find the word I was searching for. "Yes."

"Okay then." His smile is a promise. "I'll be there."

———————

Alex drops me off at the back doors of the gym, then goes to find a parking spot. Even though it's Friday, everyone is still here to partake in the homecoming festivities. I pass through a sea of glitter and ribbons and mums, but they don't bother me like they did before.

My heart is racing as I maneuver my way to the locker room. I can't erase the image of the way Alex looked at me in the shop. How he remembered the details of times we spent together.

How he remembered *me*.

Nearly all my teammates are dressed in uniform by the time I enter the locker room.

Raegan's the first one to pounce. "Where were you today?"

I pull my poms out of my dance bag. "I didn't feel well," I lie. "But I'm okay now."

"Well, good." She gives me an odd look. "What are you wearing?"

My hand flies to the top of my head. Alex's black beanie. I forgot I still had it on.

"Nothing," I say quickly. I don't know why I'm lying to one of my best friends. I stuff it in my bag before peeling off my clothes and changing into my uniform.

Whitney comes up to me as we're heading to the gym for the pep rally. I notice she isn't wearing her mum, but seeing as we're about to perform that obviously makes sense.

"You're here." She says this as if she expected me to bail on our routine. "Does my lip liner look off?"

"It's perfect," I say, because it is.

She still double-checks herself in her front-facing camera.

Raegan leads us into the gym, which has been decorated in a sea of red and white. Nearly everyone in the stands is wearing their RED OUT shirts, the ones students get at the beginning of the year to wear to games to show school pride. We take the center of the floor and perform our Rihanna routine. I try to scour the crowd for Alex, but I can't find him. My heart sinks.

We have an hour and a half to kill before the game. The Wavettes' moms made us sandwiches and brought us bags of chips as a quick dinner, so Whitney, Raegan, and I take one corner of the room and sit down to eat. But instead of making idle conversation, Raegan begins intently reading something on her phone.

Whitney sighs. "Please don't tell me you're on that SAT app again."

"No, I'm reading pregnancy tips," Raegan says, not looking our way.

"For the last time," Whitney says. "You. Are. Not. The. One. Having. This. Baby."

Raegan rolls her eyes. "I *know*, okay? But my mom isn't exactly young anymore. There can be more complications when you're older." She points to her phone. "Swimming! I should have thought of that. It's good for joint pain. I need to tell her." She starts tapping out a text on her phone.

Whitney rolls her eyes, but I understand. Raegan can't control her mom's pregnancy like she can control one of her Leadership Council projects, and that scares her. Plus, I know she wants to be involved in her future sister's life as much as possible, despite the fact that she hasn't entered this world just yet.

While Whitney yammers on about some celebrity couple, I sneak Raegan a text.

ME: your mom will be fine. don't worry xo

I follow up with a few of the dancer and party horn emojis to get her pumped for the game, and she gives me a half smile. I know she won't stop stressing—it's ingrained in her nature at this point—but I want her to know she has friends who care about her. It's the least I can do for all the supportive texts she sent me in Portland. The ones I didn't bother replying to.

We make our way outside at six thirty. Because the homecoming court is being announced at halftime, we perform our second routine before the opening kickoff. My switch leaps aren't the best, but for the most part we nail it.

When the game begins, I casually lean over and scour the rows of students, hoping to spot Alex.

"There," Whitney says, nodding toward the right side of the bleachers.

I freeze. Am I that obvious?

"She's there. By Colton?" She's pointing at Lin, who's flipping through a book while Colton bobs his head to the music in his headphones next to her. Breck and Jay are the only two actually watching the game.

"Right," I say, focusing my gaze on the field. I don't want to continue to be obvious, but I'm dying to know if Alex stayed.

We're winning twenty-one to seven when halftime rolls around. I cross the field with the rest of the Wavettes to cheer on the homecoming court. Breck escorts Genevieve Jackson, who's also in our grade. It's tradition for the court to arrive in formal attire, and they both look captivating in their elegant gown and suit. We stand patiently on the sidelines as the senior court enters, then wait to hear the final tally of votes. There's a wild round of applause from the juniors when Breck is announced Homecoming King, and an even louder round of praise when senior Natasha Collins wins Homecoming Queen.

Raegan turns to me. "How long do you think he'll demand us to call him King Breck?"

I laugh. "I'll bet a solid month."

When the third quarter starts, I jump up. Third quarter is the only time we're allowed to leave the field for a bathroom and concession break.

"You guys want anything?" I ask Raegan and Whitney.

They decline, and I rush over to the massive concession line. I'm not hungry, but I'm using this as an excuse to run into Alex—if he's even here.

My stomach churns with nervous energy. I *hope* he's still here.

I'm at the end of the concessions line when I feel a presence behind me. I turn around, expecting to find Alex, but it's not him. It's Lin.

Her bright-red lips pull into a smile. "Good job out there."

"Thanks," I tell her, still glancing in the stands for Alex. "Are you doing anything after the game?"

"Jay's trying to get everyone to go to this party." She rolls her eyes. "But I'm just going to head home. Curfew and all that."

"Right," I say, just as my eyes catch a glimpse of Alex in the stands. He's sitting with a few of his theater friends. Heat flushes through my entire body. *He stayed.*

Lin gives me a weird look. "What?"

"What?" I repeat, tearing my eyes away.

She just shakes her head. "Text me tomorrow?"

"I will," I promise.

We end up winning twenty-eight to fourteen, which means the Wavettes take the field to do twenty-eight celebratory high kicks. Whitney disappears with Jay shortly after, so Raegan and I walk back to the junior/senior lot together.

"Want to go over our chemistry homework on Sunday?" Raegan asks, unlocking her car.

"Sure," I tell her. "Text me?"

"Will do." She gives me a quick hug. "See ya!"

I find my car, my heart a little heavy that I didn't spot Alex in the chaos after the game. I'm texting my dad to let him know I'm on my way home when I hear a loud tap on my window, like a pebble hitting the windshield. Then another. And another.

I glance around until I see Alex's truck a few feet away. His window is rolled down, and he's tossing Starbursts in my direction.

Grinning, I roll down my window. "You're wasting perfectly good candy!"

He pops one in his mouth, then throws his head back in mock ecstasy. God, he's such a dork. I notice his curls are blowing loose and wild in the wind—and then I realize why.

"I still have your beanie!"

He smiles. "Keep it!"

I watch him pull away, and it's not until I'm in my driveway that I realize my smile stayed with me the entire drive home.

TWENTY SIX

EVEN THOUGH THINGS ARE STILL shaky between my dad and me, he agrees to let me spend the night at Lin's on Saturday. We debated going to the homecoming dance, but in the end decided to skip it in favor of a long overdue sleepover. We did, however, help Raegan set up the decorations in the gym while blasting Beyoncé, which was more fun than I expected. She even ordered pizza and wasn't *too* controlling about how the streamers were hung.

We're decompressing in Lin's room, and I'm painting my toes a bright shade of yellow I bought only because it was called *Pineapple Paradise*.

"David was brilliant, of course." Lin swipes a splash of coral polish on her pinky. She was at another mock decathlon competition this morning to prepare for the real one in January—the first one of the year. "But I kept second-guessing myself. I felt so dumb. Also, Breck sort of killed it? Especially with the science questions."

I hold my foot carefully over my paper towel. Her room looks

more like a hotel than a teenage haven. She has thick, navy cur-
tains that match her bedspread, which is tucked and smoothed over
so tightly someone could probably suffocate under there. There is
nothing on her desk aside from a lamp with a depressing gray lamp-
shade. Her mom makes her keep all her textbooks in her closet to
keep her room from looking disorderly. She'd probably have an
aneurysm if she came in here and saw us with the nail polish.

"First of all, you're not dumb," I tell her, because it's the truth.
She's in the top twenty percent of our class. "Try and let go of your
nervousness, you know? You'll be more confident next time."

"True. I'm always nervous when we first start practicing." She
caps the coral polish. "God, I'm starving. I want pizza rolls. And a
Slurpee."

Lin's parents don't believe in junk food. Their pantry is always
stocked with healthy snacks like mixed nuts and dried seaweed. It's
one of the reasons she hates having sleepovers at her place. That, and
we're not allowed to leave the house after ten.

It's ten thirty now.

"Let's go to 7-Eleven," I say. "Stock up."

She checks her phone. "Yeah, right. They won't let us leave."

I stare at her. "But if they don't know we're gone—?"

"Sneak out?" She looks uneasy. "Really? For food?"

"They'll never know. We'll make it a ninja mission."

She laughs. "Some girls sneak out to go to parties, and we're
sneaking out to get snacks."

We wait until our nails dry. I use her laptop and open iTunes, then
I click the first artist and let it play on low. Too much quiet will make

them suspicious, so I set it close to the door. They hardly ever come in to check on us, which is why I think Lin is okay with this plan.

I pull on my black sweatshirt and zip it up to my chin, then I yank the hood over my head. "Ready?"

"Out the window?" She says it like we'll be scaling a fourteen-story building.

"You're on the first floor!"

"There's still a *drop*."

"Oh my god. It's like, two feet."

I climb out first. She follows. Five minutes later, we're giggling like five-year-olds as we sprint down the sidewalk and around the corner out of her neighborhood.

"I've never done that before!"

Laughter bursts from my lungs. "We should really get you out more."

It's a perfect autumn evening. There's a crisp chill in the air and even though it's dark, the streetlights illuminate the fact that the oak trees around us are changing colors. It's funny—autumn used to be my least favorite season. Now I'm finding I don't mind it.

The door to 7-Eleven chimes when we walk in. I breathe in the sticky scent of artificial syrup and leftover glazed donuts. Lin walks toward the back to grab a Slurpee. I'm about to make my way toward the candy aisle when I hear someone call my name.

I freeze.

Oh no.

No no no no no.

I turn and face the register, but I already know who's standing behind it. Saylor. He's wearing his starchy uniform shirt and plastic name badge. And waving. Enthusiastically. In my direction.

I give a pathetic half wave before ducking into the candy aisle.

Crap. How could I be so careless? Of *course* Saylor is working tonight. He works almost every night shift.

This is bad. This could blow my entire cover.

I don't know what to do. If I duck out now, Lin will be forced to interact with Saylor when she pays for her food. He could bring up the fact that he knows me—that he's been living in our house for the last two months. And I can't let anyone discover that piece of information. I already had a close call with Margaret and Saylor, but if the fact that they're staying with us gets back to Margaret, I can lose my dad, my friends, and my life all over again.

Lin finds me frozen in the candy aisle. "Aren't you getting anything?"

Her arms are loaded with snacks. I grab the first thing I see— chocolate-covered pretzels. "Um. Yeah, this."

Lin raises an eyebrow, but she doesn't say anything as she walks toward the register. I follow her, looking anywhere but at Saylor.

She sets her loot on the counter.

Saylor begins ringing her up. "This looks a lot better than a dance."

Lin glances up, then continues to pull out bills from her wallet. "Yeah. We think so."

Okay, this is fine. We clearly look like high schoolers who are not at the homecoming dance. It's a completely normal comment.

Saylor looks at me. "I wasn't much of a dance guy, either. Drove my mom nuts. She practically had to force me to go to the prom."

I let out an unintelligible, choked noise just as Lin drops a handful of change on the ground. "Aw, crap."

I'm sweating. Profusely. I have to get out of here, so I start pulling out bills from my back pocket. "Here."

"I got it," she says from the ground.

Saylor scans her chips. "Oh man! Sweet Jalapeño flavor? I should bring some of these home." He looks at me. "You think your dad would eat them?"

All the blood in my body freezes. Time stops.

Lin stands back up, pushing the handful of her fallen change toward him. "Why would her—?"

"My dad! Yes! He would!" My words are too clipped. Too loud. "You should tell him the next time he comes in!"

Saylor throws me a peculiar look.

"You know what?" I set my chocolate-covered pretzels aside. "I'm not in a chocolate mood. Uh—" I pat my stomach. "Too much pizza earlier."

Now it's Lin's turn to throw me a confused stare. "Are you sure?"

"Yes!" I'm itching to get out of here. One more close call and my carefully concealed lie could unravel. "Totally."

Saylor hands Lin her receipt. He won't look at me. Maybe he's hurt that I'm pretending not to know him, but whether I want to let him in my personal life is my business. I already had a close call with Margaret. I'm not about to let that happen again.

I quickly head out the door.

Lin jogs to keep up with me. "Do you know that guy?"

"Um," I say. "Kind of. My dad goes in there a lot."

It's part of the truth, anyway.

"Oh." She looks back. "He seems kinda weird. Did you see all those leather bracelets on his wrists?"

"They're intention bracelets," I say without thinking.

Lin raises an eyebrow. "How do you know that?"

I freeze. *God, Kira. Just shut up.*

"Uh. Because he's usually working when I stop by after school sometimes. And I asked."

"Oh," she says again.

We fall quiet. I hate lying to her, but I can't risk telling anyone about them. Especially now that I'm on the verge of getting my best friends back and reconnecting with my dad.

And maybe, *maybe* Alex has something to do with me wanting to stay.

We're rounding the sidewalk back into her neighborhood when I say, "Can I tell you something?"

Lin grins. "About how you totally skipped school with Alex Ramos yesterday?"

My mouth drops open. "How did you—?"

"David told me. He was in the parking lot and saw you guys drive off together."

"Why didn't you say anything?"

She shrugs. "I wanted you to bring it up, I guess. You tell Whitney and Raegan everything because you're with them all the time, and I'm always the last to know stuff."

My gut twists with guilt. That happened a lot freshman year, but now it's different. She has to know it's different now.

"It's not really like that," I say. "I don't know...I don't feel as close to them anymore, especially Whitney. I feel like it's my fault."

Lin sips her Slurpee and casually says, "It's not."

I'm surprised to hear this. "What do you mean?"

She passes me her cup, and I take a swig of the cola flavor she chose. "I see you at lunch. You try really, really hard to make the whole situation not awkward. Whitney still doesn't tell you how she really feels about everything. She probably doesn't tell you anything about her relationship with Jay because she feels guilty." She pulls a piece of stray hair behind her ear. "And all of Raegan's energy is in her presidential duties. She doesn't have time for friendship. Don't take it personally."

I want to laugh. And cry. Because she's right. She's *so* right. We're all not as close as we used to be, but it's not for my lack of effort.

"Do you think we're drifting apart?"

She falls quiet for a moment. "Sometimes, yeah."

This sends a wave of sadness through me.

"But not because we don't care about each other," she explains. "Just—I don't know—maybe we have different priorities right now."

I think back to middle school when we wouldn't even think of spending a weekend away from each other. Shopping trips, birthday parties, movie nights, sleepovers—we always had something planned. It seems so far away now, like it's impossible to get back to the way things used to be.

Lin links her arm through mine. "But anyway. Are you going to tell me about Alex?"

I immediately grow flustered. "I—I don't know how it happened."

"Oh, come on." Lin stares at me. "Really? He's had a crush on you for ages."

"I know," I blurt, then shake my head. That sounded vain. "It's just—I haven't treated him very well."

I tell Lin about his text confession all those months ago, and how he was so kind when we talked yesterday. I tell her how he's been so understanding and patient with me over the years, and how my feelings have unexpectedly started to grow stronger for him, too.

"What about Jay?" she asks.

Hearing his name used to send my heart soaring. It's strange— not feeling anything for someone you once felt so much for. Like listening to your favorite song on repeat for too long. It loses the magic you once felt in the beginning, but it's not terrible. You're just indifferent toward it.

"He's not the person I thought he was, I guess. It's like we're both two totally different people now. I don't know," I hear myself say. "I feel like I've moved on."

"Wow, that's big."

Is it? It feels like a gradual change, not like I woke up and— *bam!*—my feelings were automatically gone. They trickled away like sand in an hourglass. I still care about him, but not the same way as I used to.

Lin takes another sip of her Slurpee. "Alex is a good guy."

That's what I'm worried about. Do I really think I deserve someone like that when I'm attempting to be the person I was eleven months ago? I've hurt him before. He doesn't deserve to have that happen again.

The sidewalk is illuminated by the orangey glow of the over-hanging streetlamps as we round the corner to her neighborhood. We walk in silence, arms linked, keeping each other warm from the chill. There are no crickets tonight.

When we get back to Lin's house, we climb back through the window, laughing at ourselves. Lin swings her leg back inside, knocking a few picture frames off her nightstand. They land on the floor with a loud crash, but miraculously they don't shatter.

I snort out a laugh as she closes the window only to hear footsteps coming down the hall.

"Crap!" Lin hisses, diving for the laptop that's still playing music in front of the door. I shove the stash of junk food under the bed, careful not to knock over her Slurpee. We hold our breath, listening as the footsteps grow lighter as they come down the hall.

Lin lets out a breath. "I could have been *so* grounded."

"But you're not," I say, tossing the bag of sour jelly rings in her direction.

She smiles, and I can't tell if it's because she's proud of herself for getting away with it or because she enjoyed the whole excursion. I hope it's both.

TWENTY SEVEN

I'M FINISHING UP ANOTHER TUTORING session with Ana after school on Tuesday when Alex texts me.

ALEX: are u still around? want to meet me in the workshop?

My heart swells. I fire back an *okay* before I even question it.

Ever since we skipped school together on Friday, I've been finding any excuse to talk to him. In Algebra II, I ask to borrow a pencil even though I have six sitting in the bottom on my book bag. Heat gathers in the pit of my stomach when he waves in my direction in the halls. I consider it a small victory when he texts me first, because at least that means he's thinking of me, too.

Ana turns my notebook back toward me. "You got those last two equations right."

I let out a small breath of relief. It's so much easier when she breaks the steps down for me.

I begin packing up my books. "Thank you. My dad wasn't exactly thrilled when he saw my progress report."

Ana smiles. "I'm here anytime."

I'm standing up, about to say good-bye, when she adds, "Your performance was great on Friday. Alex thought so, too."

Heat rises to my cheeks, a mix of flattery and fluster. "Oh, um—thank you."

She grabs her book bag, grinning like she knows something I don't. "See you next week."

I wave good-bye, but my mind is replaying what Alex said on Friday: *I didn't think my feelings were that complex.* We were so out of sync back then, between Lacey, Jay, and my dad. But things are different now.

Could our timing finally be right?

I walk into the tech workshop, not surprised to see Alex is the only one working late. He's wearing his double shirts with the sleeves pushed up to his forearms, and a few loose curls fall into his face as he reaches for a screwdriver.

A nervous *zing* courses through me. God, he's *gorgeous.*

My heart stumbles. I catch my breath.

"Hey."

He looks up, a grin spreading quickly across his face. "Hey!" He steps to the side, then gestures to his creation. "I wanted you to meet Audrey II."

I'm floored. Alex has really brought this life-size monster plant to life. The shell of the Venus flytrap body is coated in a glossy green paint, and vines twist along the outside of the base. The enormous mouth contains dozens of sharp wooden teeth—painted white—that give her a truly menacing personality.

"I still have some tweaks to work out. I want to make her look more waxy than shiny, but I've finally got the pulley system working."

He walks around to the back, and I follow. There's a large, gaping hole in the back of the plant-body, and a small bench, and Alex's slender frame slides in with ease. His right arm reaches for a rope to his right while his feet press down on two different pedals. In an instant, Audrey II's giant mouth widens.

I marvel at the mechanics of it all. "That's amazing."

He eases his grip on the rope, and the mouth closes. "Wanna try?"

"Can I?"

Instead of exiting the gap, Alex scoots over to make room for me. My heart bangs against my chest as I slide in next to him, leg against leg, shoulder against shoulder.

"Okay," he says, his soft breath tickling my neck. "Press down on both of those pedals and pull the rope at the same time. You'll feel it give."

Our fingers touch as he hands me the rope, and a rush of heat fills my body. I blink away the persistent pounding in my ears, using all my strength to pull. I feel it give, just like Alex said.

"You're a natural."

I find my voice through my nervousness. "I'll add it to my list of many talents: *Life-sized Botanical Puppeteer.*"

Alex laughs, and the vibrations of his body course against mine. When he stops, he looks right at me. His gaze is so intense, so immediate. My chest rises and falls in quick motions, but his does, too. His soft brown eyes are still searching mine, deciphering. Deciding.

I so desperately want him to show me exactly what's on his mind.

He reaches toward me, his thumb trailing down my jawline. Chills and yearning and desire burst through my chest. Slowly, carefully, he tips his head toward me. His bottom lip brushes mine, a motion that sends raw electricity spiraling through my veins. I take in a sharp breath, closing my eyes as his lips fully cover my own.

That one spectacular motion sets me off.

I devour the sensation, breathing him in. His hands are still cold, but the heat from my body could start a fire between us. I run my hands down the fabric of his shirt, pulling him closer, and his breath hitches in surprise.

All I can think is *Alex, Alex, Alex—this is Alex.* How long have I wanted this for, and how long have I been denying that I've wanted this? His lips are so urgent on mine, but his hands are so gentle. I shiver, tangling my hands through his loose curls before we both gasp, pulling away.

Oh *god.* We're still at school. What were we thinking? I mean, clearly we weren't, but anyone could have walked in. We're both on thin ice with Mrs. Donaldson. We don't need to get on anyone else's bad side.

Alex is flushed, and I imagine I am as well. His hair is rumpled but his eyes are glowing, and I ache to dive back in.

As we collectively try and catch our breath, he turns to me. "Can I ask you something?"

I wonder if he can see the warmth on my cheeks. "Go for it."

"Would you rather live in this gigantic Venus flytrap for the rest of your life, or give Mrs. Donaldson a pedicure?"

A burst of laughter escapes my lips. I'm still shaky from his kiss, but I try and keep my voice steady. "I'd stay right here." His hand is still on my knee and when he notices, he blushes. I don't want him to remove it, but I know it's probably best to extinguish the flame for now. "God, I don't even want to imagine touching her feet."

Alex laughs. "Me, either."

I sigh. Everything has changed, but it feels so right. So easy.

I turn back to him. "Can I ask *you* a question?"

He nods.

I take a deep breath, then blurt out what's been on my mind since we talked about it on Friday. "Why don't you look into applying to a film school? Or somewhere that has a stronger focus in screenwriting?"

He's quiet for a long moment. "I don't know. Ana is already set on attending Stanford, and Marlina's already thinking of transferring to Kansas State. It just seems selfish, I guess." He shrugs. "It feels like I'm ditching my mom."

"Does she feel that way?"

"Well, no—"

I give him an encouraging grin. "Then why not go for it? You designed this set for *Little Shop of Horrors*. You've finished screenplays—"

"I was twelve when I wrote those. And they were terrible."

"They weren't, but you're going to write your own pilot someday. And it's going to be great." I look at him. "You're talented, Alex. You should really go for it."

He looks down at the pedals. "It's hard, I guess. Maybe it wouldn't be so hard if I wasn't the youngest."

"Your mom knows how to adapt to change," I say. "She'll be okay."

He glances up at me. "What about you?"

"What about me?" I repeat.

"I still remember our conversation from that day in the parking lot. You were miserable when you came from practice."

I stare down at my hands. Caught.

"I think … a part of me doesn't want to be on the Wavettes," I admit. "The part of me that stays only wants to in order to be close to Whitney and Raegan."

"So why don't you quit? It's not like you'll lose their friendship."

It's true. It's scary how true it is, and yet I continue to be the biggest hypocrite. Because this not how my twelve-steps list is supposed to go. I'm supposed to want to be on the Wavettes with my best friends, to earn back their friendship. I'm supposed to want to reconnect with Jay, but I'm falling for someone completely different.

"I guess being part of the team makes me feel like I'm part of their lives again, like I was back in freshman year. Even if it doesn't feel the same."

"But … you're sticking it out until it does feel the same?"

I shrug, not quite committing to a yes or a no.

"Don't take this the wrong way," he says. "But why try so hard? To get back to a point in time that maybe wasn't so great for you?"

My phone chimes with a text. Dad. **Almost done with tutoring?**

Ever since my outburst with Peach, he's been keeping a closer eye on me. I've caused the walls to go back up between us, but I know the only way to break them down is to apologize to both him and Peach. I still haven't, and I know that hurts him more than he'd ever admit.

I'm thankful to use my dad as an excuse to exit this conversation. "I should get home."

His features sink with disappointment. "Yeah, okay. It's getting late anyway."

He climbs out of Audrey II, then extends a hand to help me.

I'm reaching down to get my book bag when he says, "Listen... I, uh. It's just that, if you ever need another Slurpee night, I'm available. You can text me anytime."

I know his words are coming from a good place, but they fill me with unexpected guilt. Here I am again, avoiding his hard questions by looking for an escape when he's simply trying to be there for me. And after we *just* kissed. I hope he doesn't take it as a rejection, because it's not.

It's definitely not.

He's asking the questions I should have been asking myself all along. "Thank you," I say, and I hope that he knows I mean it.

He smiles, but his face doesn't light up like it did before.

With one last glance, I do the only thing that comes easy. I leave.

TWENTY EIGHT

THE NEXT TWO DAYS OF Wavettes practice are exceptionally awful. Coach Velasquez plays a recording of our homecoming performance from her phone, ripping our form to pieces. Because we were off our A-game, we run through our main sequence dozens of times and stay thirty minutes later than we usually do for a longer cool-down.

By Thursday evening, I'm so sore and exhausted that I fall asleep on the living room couch. When I wake up, it's somehow already nine o'clock. I sit straight up, already in a full-blown panic. I have a *ton* of homework due tomorrow that I haven't even started.

My sudden motion startles Saylor, who's sitting on the love seat across the room watching Animal Planet with Nonnie.

"Shit," I say. "Shit, shit, shit."

Nonnie rubs her cat slippers together. "That's quite the amount of expletives."

I rub my eyes. They're raw and itchy—no doubt my mascara

is smeared everywhere. My skin feels dry from falling asleep with makeup on. I'm going to regret it when I break out later this week.

"I have an English paper due tomorrow." I dig through my schoolbag that I'd left by my feet. "I haven't even started. I'll be up all night."

Saylor eyes the textbooks I'm piling on the coffee table. "I can help."

"Thanks, but—"

"Seriously, I don't mind. I'm not working tonight." He motions upstairs. "Go get your laptop."

My brain is too scrambled to come up with any better ideas, so I go and grab my computer. When I bring it back down, he takes it from me and opens a blank Word document.

"What are you—?"

"Get your book and tell me your thesis," he says. "You think, I'll type."

My stress level begins to dissolve. It takes me a moment to remember the prompt for my essay. "I have to write if I think John Proctor is a hero or an anti-hero. From *The Crucible*."

"Ah, I know that one," Nonnie interrupts. "Shakespeare?"

Saylor and I exchange a horrified look.

She stands up, patting me on the arm. "You know, maybe I'll grab us some snacks."

As she disappears into the kitchen, her teal curlers bobbing as she walks, Saylor turns to me. "I've read it," he assures me. "What's your stance?"

I talk, trying to remember what I'd thought when I finished the play. John Proctor isn't a hero. Not really. He chose to die rather than continue living a lie, because his reputation and name would be tarnished going forward.

Saylor's typing everything I'm saying, and it hits me that he's helping me even though I pretended not to know him when I saw him at 7-Eleven with Lin. I never apologized for that, but I never felt like I had to. It's my business what I choose to tell my friends, isn't it? I shouldn't feel bad about that.

Nonnie comes back with a bowl of frozen grapes, and when Saylor reaches for one I allow myself to look at him. Why is he being so nice to me? Peach too, even though she hasn't been around much the last few days. She definitely deserved an apology that never came, and yet they haven't held any of this against me.

By the time I'm done making a compelling argument, Saylor just stares at me.

"What?"

"Nothing," he says, but he doesn't look at me as he hands my laptop back to me. "You have a very interesting essay, that's all."

The front door unlocks, and a second later I hear my dad call hello. Once a week he's agreed to take later janitorial shifts so he can meet with his therapist in the morning.

Wallis is the first one to the front door, greeting him enthusiastically.

"We're in here!" Nonnie hollers.

When my dad sees the three of us sitting in the living room, he smiles. "Has Kira convinced you all to start watching *Crime Boss*?"

"I missed it," I admit. "My quick nap turned into a four-hour coma. Saylor was just helping me finish an essay."

My dad doesn't hide the impressed look on his face. "That was nice of him."

"Thank you," I blurt, turning to Saylor. Because he's right—it was nice.

"It's no problem, but I'm going to head to bed," Saylor says, shooting me another strange look. "I'll see y'all in the morning."

It's not until I read it over the next day that I realize why Saylor was looking at me strangely. My essay *is* interesting, but only because I was never talking about John Proctor living out a lie. I was talking about myself.

TWENTY NINE

WHITNEY AND I ARE THE last ones in the locker room after rehearsal on Tuesday. I know she's killing time waiting for Jay to be done with basketball practice. It's what I used to do, which is why I'm taking advantage of this rare one-on-one time I have with her.

"Whit?"

She glances at me in the mirror, carefully applying her lip stain.

I sigh. "Will things ever not be weird with us?"

She considers my words for a moment. Ever since I didn't show up for the homecoming dance, she's been treating me like she's better than me. At practice, she'll only talk to the seniors, leaving Raegan and me to break on our own. And the other day at lunch, when I said I was thinking of dying the ends of my hair purple, she sneered and said, "It'll clash with our uniforms."

When she wasn't looking, Lin glanced at me and rolled her eyes.

But that's the thing. I don't want Whitney to be someone I roll my eyes at behind her back. She was someone I told *everything* to, including my crush on Alex freshman year. Our one-sided friendship isn't just frustrating, it's infuriating.

When Whitney speaks, her voice is soft. "I don't know."

This is not the answer I wanted to hear, but if I'm being honest with myself, it was the one I expected.

I don't try and hide my annoyance. "Okay, well when you do know ... you know where you can find me."

I walk out of the locker room before she can say anything else. It doesn't feel good, but I've already apologized. Her insecurities are out of my hands.

I'm pushing open the double doors to the junior/senior lot when I spot someone standing by my car. My heartbeat quickens. He has a different beanie on today—this one's dark blue—but I'd recognize him from across a football field.

"Hey," Alex says, his smile warming me to my core. Before I can reply, he gently takes my hand and drops something inside.

I immediately open it. There are three strawberry banana Starbursts, the best kind.

The corners of my lips turn up into a smile as I start to unwrap one. "You saved them for me."

"You sound surprised." He smiles. "But actually, I was just about to text you. Want to stop by the restaurant for dinner?"

I nearly choke on the candy. Alex looks startled. I hold up a hand to tell him I'm fine, but I'm not sure if I am. Because I know he's talking about Rosita's, his parents' restaurant. So does that mean Alex is asking me on a date? Or is this, like, a casual oh-we're-just-getting-burritos thing?

"Sure," I say, trying to keep the nervousness out of my voice.

I used to go to Rosita's with Alex in middle school to do homework. The last time I remember going with him was freshman year when we were working on an English essay, but something tells me that we're not going to work on algebra.

Alex smiles at me, and a slow tingling spreads from my belly to the tips of my fingers. It's been a week since our kiss, and I haven't been able to forget it. I want to tell him I feel the same way, that I want our friendship to be something more, but I can't seem to find the opening words.

"Cool." He unlocks his truck, which is only a few spaces over from mine. "I'll drive?"

The fluttering returns, because going *together* actually feels like it could be a real date.

On the way over there he fills me in on the fall play and the upcoming *Little Shop of Horrors* auditions and the finishing touches he needs to put on Audrey II. I listen, my gaze falling on his mouth every so often.

But suddenly the sun is dipping below the skyline and we're at Rosita's. Everything I want to say becomes stuck in the back of my throat.

When we walk inside, I spot Alex's mom refilling drinks for a couple sitting near the window. Her face brightens when she sees me.

"*¡Mijo!*" She gives Alex a quick squeeze before enveloping me in a bear hug. I let myself relax, hugging her back. "*¡Te ves bien!* You've been well?"

"Yes! Thank you," I say, smiling. It's the less complicated answer, anyway. "It's great to see you."

"Vamos a comer," Alex says, then switches back to English. "I'll help you close later."

His mom gives him a grateful look. *"Sí, sí, necesitas comer,"* she says, then goes back into the kitchen.

"Food?" I guess.

He grins. "Hope you're hungry."

"Starving, actually."

"Good. If you recall, she doesn't exactly hold back."

Alex and I sit down at the bar. "It looks exactly how I remember it."

"Not much has changed. But hey, my dad might be coming home soon. Hopefully by December. We think we might have a buyer for the restaurant."

"Alex." His smile is contagious. I'm really happy for him. "That's amazing."

"My mom could really use help with my little cousins. Ana and I switch off evenings closing here, but she's buckling down with her college apps. She shouldn't have to be distracted."

I can't help staring at him. He's so selfless. He's not the only one who has more people living under his roof, and he's never complained about it. Not once.

Alex meets my gaze. "What?"

I blush, looking away. I've been staring too long. "Nothing," I say, then reconsider. "Actually, promise me something?"

"Depends, but go ahead."

"Finish a screenplay by next summer."

Alex looks surprised. "I don't—"

"What do you have to lose?"

He thinks for a moment. "I guess I'll have more time with my dad back."

"You will," I insist.

His mom returns with a platter of food for us. Chips and salsa, tortillas and rice and beans, and plenty of beef tamales. She sets the spread down in front of us, and we offer our thanks before she heads back into the kitchen.

"You're going to have to roll me out of here," I say, looking at the plate in front of me. I smile at him. "I'm going to eat everything."

"I'm sure she has pan dulce back there, too."

I dramatically clutch my chest. "Obviously we have to eat that, too."

He grins. "Obviously."

I'm about to dig in when I hear the door open. To my surprise, Lacey Woodward walks in. Her blond hair flows elegantly behind her, something straight out of a shampoo commercial. My insides immediately coil in defense. What is she doing here?

Alex puts on his typical good-natured smile when he spots her. "Hey, here for pick-up?"

"Yup," Lacey chirps. "Mrs. Henson is having us run lines until nine tonight, but, whatever, she's buying us dinner so I guess that makes up for it."

"Let me grab my mom, one sec." He hops off the barstool, leaving me alone with Lacey.

I try sitting up a little straighter, pulling my shoulders back. No wonder Alex went to Sadie's and homecoming with Lacey. She's straight out of a Disney movie with her petite frame and endearing spackle of freckles across her nose. Compared to her, I'm a frump with frizzy hair.

I take a deep breath. *That was two years ago. Why are you worrying?*

"It's good to see you," Lacey says. "I mean, I know I've seen you at rehearsals and stuff, but I just meant here. Like, back at school."

My jealousy toward her dissolves, just a little. "Thanks. I did miss it here."

Alex reappears with two carry-out platters wrapped in a plastic bag. "Go forth and feed the masses."

"Cool, I'm starving." Lacey hands over the credit card, and Alex quickly rings up the transaction. "See y'all later."

I watch as she leaves. When I look back, Alex is staring at me. Smiling.

"What?" I ask, embarrassed and defensive at the same time.

"You don't have to worry about Lacey."

"Who said I was worrying about Lacey?"

Ugh, my attempt to be cool about this is quickly backfiring. Even *I* can hear it.

Alex stares at me, raising an eyebrow. "You do remember that you're the one I kissed the other day, right?"

Heat flows through my body, creeping up the back of my neck as I remember the gentle desperation of his lips on mine. That's not a moment I'm likely to forget.

We finish our meal and then, as promised, Alex brings a variety of pan dulce for us to share as dessert. I'm lost in our conversation. His eyes never leave mine as I bring up memories of all the notes we wrote to each other on Starburst wrappers we eventually turned into bracelets. He admits to keeping them, and I tell him I have mine, too. We switch to discussing ideas for his screenplay, and I scribble down notes on a napkin, growing warm as he leans closer to watch me write.

In the quiet, I hear a soft buzzing noise. My phone. I dig through my book bag and find it buried at the very bottom. And crap. *Triple crap.* There are fourteen missed calls from my dad. I check the screen: 9:43 p.m. I'm never home this late. He must be wondering where the hell I am.

Alex looks at me. "Everything okay?"

"Yeah," I say, trying to keep my voice calm. I fire off a quick text to my dad to let him know I'm on my way and that I'll explain when I get home. "I forgot to tell my dad I was going out. I should get back."

"I can take you back to your car," he insists.

"Actually," I say, feeling brave. "Want to drive me home?"

I want this to feel like a first date—one that doesn't end in me abruptly leaving. I can always get a ride to school in the morning.

"Sure," Alex replies, nervously fumbling for his keys.

I spend the entire ride home wondering if Alex will kiss me goodnight, or if I should be the one to make the first move. But when he rounds the corner onto my street, I immediately realize my mistake. Because they're there. All of them—my dad and Nonnie and Saylor—gathered in my front yard for the entire world to see.

THIRTY

"WHO ARE THOSE PEOPLE?" Alex asks.

I'm frozen in my seat. I blink once. Twice. But they're all still standing there. Nonnie in her cat slippers and her zebra-print bathrobe and Saylor, barefoot, in his familiar black yoga tank and loose ponytail. My dad looks angrier than I've ever seen him. His arms are folded across his navy work polo, his eyebrows narrowed. He's no doubt making assumptions as to why I'm not in my own car and why, exactly, I'm riding in a beat-up truck with a boy this late at night.

Who are those people? How do I even begin to answer that? I can't. Not with anything that isn't the truth, and if the truth comes out—

This is my fault. I promised myself I wouldn't let anyone come close to finding out and the one time I'm not careful, everyone is right outside my house. I should have driven myself, should've told Alex I'd see him at school tomorrow. But I wanted to pretend nothing was out of the ordinary, that I was just a girl on a date with a boy she likes. Someone who has nothing to hide. Now it's too late.

Nonnie steps back onto the porch and walks inside the house, but that doesn't make anything better, because Alex sees her go. I can see him attempting to put the pieces together.

"Hey, are you okay? Do you need—?"

Heat burns through my cheeks. I have to get out of here.

I grab my bag from the ground and reach for the door handle. "I should—"

I don't finish that sentence. As soon as I'm out the door, Wallis lunges for me. Saylor calls him off before he can pounce on me, which would have furthered my humiliation. I wish everyone would go back inside, but I realize it doesn't matter now. The damage is already done.

"Where the hell were you?" my dad says as soon as I'm within earshot. Angry wrinkles appear between his brows. "I expected you home *hours* ago. You told me you'd be home after practice."

From behind me, I hear Alex's truck rumble as he drives away. I want to be relieved, but I'm not sure if what he witnessed could somehow get back to Margaret.

"I'm sorry." My voice is small. "I lost track of time."

"That's not a valid reason. We expected you home for dinner and you didn't come, and now there's some guy dropping you off after dark. Do you know how worried we've all been? You didn't call—"

"It was just Alex," I murmur, but I know that's not what he

wants to hear. This is my fault—I should have called or texted or *something*—but I don't need him giving me the third degree about it. "I'm sorry, okay?"

I head inside, hoping they follow. It's bad enough Alex saw them. I don't want his yelling to draw attention from our entire neighborhood.

My dad is at my heels. "Peach is driving around looking for you. We were all worried sick."

Nonnie's standing by the stairs with a concerned look in her eyes. I glance away. Maybe I don't have a right to be annoyed, but I am. I didn't ask for everyone to care about me. I was able to take care of myself all those months before my dad was admitted to Sober Living.

I stop in front of the dining room. "Well, tell her I'm fine."

But my dad isn't done. "You can't just come and go as you please. It's not acceptable, leaving without telling us."

"*Us?*" Hot anger slides through my veins. I don't owe anyone here an explanation except for him. "Last time I checked, *you* were my only parent in this house."

"Do not use that tone with me," my dad warns.

I'm trembling in quiet rage. This isn't fair. How is he questioning his trust in me when he's the one I couldn't trust for so long?

"Why do you even care?" I throw up my hands. "For months you didn't care. Then you left and made this—" I reach behind him and grab a ceramic dish from the cabinet, one of the ones he'd produced from the last rehab he'd gone to. "This stupid pottery and your stupid Small Successes and your stupid ranch equestrian training."

"You will not talk to me like that in this house, do you understand?"

I ignore him. The feelings I thought I'd processed erupt to the surface. All I wanted was for my twelve steps to get me my normal life back, and now Alex knows something's up—the whole neighborhood knows by now, probably—and my dad doesn't care. He doesn't see that them being here is a problem, not a solution.

Nonnie and Saylor have disappeared.

Good. It's about time they learned to leave.

I look down. The ceramic is cold in my trembling hands. "You're not the only one who lost Grams, and when I needed you, you couldn't be there for me. You put more effort into this than you did with *me,* Dad. For *months.*"

And then I do something I don't expect.

I drop the dish.

The noise startles me as it shatters into a thousand tiny shards on the tile floor. For a moment, neither of us moves. I've shocked my father into silence.

My breathing is staggered, but I find my words. I find the feelings I've kept from him for so long. "If I had the choice to come back and live here without you, I would have done it in a heartbeat. It wasn't only you who left, you know that, right? Because of you, I had to leave my friends, my boyfriend, *everything* behind. And I come back and my life is just—just fucked up now! And it's your fault. Then you invite these strangers into our home and—honestly? I've been covering for you because if Margaret found out, she'd want you back in rehab. And we both know where that would leave me. So yeah, I hate that they're here. Don't you get it? It's not *normal.*"

His face crumples, and I know I've irreversibly hurt him. The fight has left his eyes.

I pass by Nonnie and Saylor on my way upstairs, but neither of them try and stop me. I know they heard my outburst, but I can't find the strength to care.

It's my dad's turn to pick up the pieces.

THIRTY ONE

NOBODY BOTHERS ME FOR THE rest of the evening, and the next morning I wake up early enough to get ready before anyone is awake. I don't want to face them. It's cowardly, but I'm still rattled from my outburst last night. As soon as I hear Peach lock herself in the bathroom, I walk to school with an entire hour to kill.

I avoid Alex for the first half of the morning. I don't stop by my locker, and I take a different route to history so I won't run into him as he's leaving theater. I have no idea what I'm going to tell him, or how to answer the questions he'll undoubtedly ask. He sent me a worried text once he was home—**is everything ok?**—but I didn't reply. I didn't know what to say.

When lunch rolls around, I buy two slices of pizza and slide into my spot next to Lin. Everyone is sitting at the table, except for Colton, who is mysteriously absent.

"Halloween weekend is almost upon us," Breck announces, then nudges Jay. "And we got the invite to a senior party at Winsor Lake."

Raegan snorts. "Trashy."

Ever since Breck was voted Homecoming King, his confidence has been at an all-time high. Lin explained that she's been letting him ride this wave only because it's given him a boost in decathlon practice, which he has apparently been crushing.

Whitney glares at Jay. "You weren't going to tell me?"

Lin gives me a look like, *typical*.

Jay immediately looks uncomfortable. He clears his throat. "I don't even know if I'm going—"

"Dude!" Breck interjects. "You said you would."

Whitney rolls her eyes. "Whatever. Have fun in that STD cesspool."

"Hey, guys!"

I turn toward the voice. Colton is striding toward us. He's wearing a typical band T-shirt with a dark green and gray flannel shirt over it, but it's his smile that's different. His braces are gone.

He takes in our blank stares. "It's me, Colton."

"We know that, dork." Whitney laughs. "You're still recognizable without a metal mouth. Congrats, by the way."

"They took them off this morning." Colton slides in the seat across from Jay. "I'm a free man."

"Does this mean you're giving up toothpicks?" I ask.

Colton shoots me a playful glare. "Hey, toothpicks are good oral hygiene."

"They're also disgusting," Raegan adds.

"Kira?"

My smile fades at the sound of my name. I turn toward the voice, my stomach twisting into knots as I see Alex standing a few feet from our table. Despite the six pairs of eyes currently focused on him, his worried stare finds only mine.

I feel the shame swell over me again. I know why he's here. He wants to make sure I'm okay, because that's the type of guy he is. I should feel grateful, but instead I feel my defenses rise.

"Hi," I say, but it comes out colder than we both expect.

He's clearly uncomfortable, tugging on the back of his beanie. "I just wanted to see how you were."

It's a kind gesture, but I inwardly cringe. Because if he's going out of his way to come over here to check in on me, then he knows something's wrong. The last thing I need are his questions. It's a stinging reminder of how awful I acted toward my dad last night.

"Fine." I say quickly, hoping he can read my expression and drop the entire thing.

He nods. I expect him to tell me he'll see me later and go sit with theater friends, but he doesn't.

"Who...uh, who were those people?"

Everyone at the table is listening closely, and I suddenly realize why. Aside from Lin, my friends don't know how close I've become with Alex. Not once have I invited him over here, yet he's making an effort because he cares.

But I can't answer him truthfully, and I don't have any reasonable excuse to use as a cover-up. So I do the first thing that pops into my head and deny everything.

"What people?"

Alex's brows furrow. "Last night? At your house?"

I'm weighed down by stares. I'm sinking faster than I can swim.
And then I ruin it.

"Why does it matter?" I snap.

His eyes widen. "I just—"

"Just stay out of it, okay? It's none of your business."

My words are sharp. Hurt crushes his features. I immediately want to take it back, but I can't. Before I can say anything else, he shakes his head and walks away.

I close my eyes. I am the worst.

Whitney turns back to glance at him. "Was Alex at your house last night or something?"

I shake my head. Lin aggressively slams her flashcards on the table. She knows I'm lying. Alex knows something's up. I'm stuck in this terrible, sick cycle that I can't seem to break.

I backtrack. "Sort of. He gave me a ride home."

"He's cool," Breck says. "Gave me a jump the other day in the parking lot when my battery died."

Lin's disapproving look cuts me deep. That's when it hits me: My twelve-steps list will never, ever work. You can't create a set of goals to make your future more like your past. That's not how you move forward. Instead I've twisted everything into a giant lie that I've been attempting to live out, and keeping up with it is exhausting. I'm destroying everything good around me.

I turn to get Alex's attention, but he's not sitting at his usual table. When I do a quick sweep around the room, I notice he's not there. He's already gone.

THIRTY TWO

I'M GROUNDED, WHICH ISN'T SURPRISING given the way I acted last week, but my grounding extends over the weekend of Halloween. So on Saturday when everyone goes to Colton's house for a horror movie marathon, I'm stuck at home.

I've trashed my twelve-steps list, tearing it up into tiny pieces and watching them fall in the wastebasket in my bedroom. When I went back and read through the twelve steps, I realized I'd written a list that was meant to fix important relationships for the sake of re-creating the past *I* wanted. The twelve-step program doesn't guarantee life rewinds back to how it was before the addiction. The addict has to do a lot of work evaluating their own behavior while accepting that life won't be exactly the same as before, in order to make a better future for themselves.

That's what I need to do, too. I don't have control over certain things that've happened in my life. Dad's addiction. Gram's passing. Moving in with Aunt June. Living with the recoverees.

Because you *can't* control life's misfortunes. They're inevitable. You can only control how you react to them, and how you move forward.

I'm in my room braiding and rebraiding my hair as the sun is just beginning to set. It casts a hazy purple glow over the costume-filled streets. I almost wish Nonnie would turn *Queen's Greatest Hits* on to drown out the happy screams from the trick-or-treaters outside my window.

A mixture of boredom and desperation kicks in, and I wander downstairs and into the kitchen. A warm, sugary scent hits my nose. Peach and Saylor are making candy apples. There's a hint of spice, of autumn. It reminds me of all the times Grams would make her sweet apple pie for our Thanksgiving dinners.

Peach spots me first. "Hey, Kira." Her voice is gentle, but not quite as chipper as usual, which makes my stomach burn with guilt. I've given her such a hard time, yet she continues to reach out. "Saylor has never made candy apples, can you believe that? So I'm teaching him. Care to join us?"

Saylor doesn't meet my eyes. He's wearing a fleece pullover that conceals all his bracelets. He looks incomplete without them.

I can tell he doesn't want me here, and for some reason that hurts. He's always had a soft soul, but now there are no signs of empathy.

Not that I deserve any.

"No thanks," my voice comes out small. Ashamed.

My dad appears. He's wearing his old glow-in-the-dark jack-o'-lantern T-shirt that he always brings out this time of year. There's an enormous plastic bowl of candy in his hands.

He turns to me. "Feel like takin' on candy duty tonight?"

Instead of hanging around the kitchen where I'm not wanted, I figure this is the next best thing. "Sure."

I take the bowl outside and sit on our porch swing. At least this way I won't have to listen to the doorbell ring all night.

It's a chilly evening, the kind that reminds me that winter is right around the corner. I'm wrapped up in my oversized Cedarville sweatshirt and a worn pair of sweats. The first kid I hand candy to asks why I'm not wearing a costume. I pull my hood over my head to hide my lack of effort, and he scampers back to his parents.

A few minutes later, the front door opens. Nonnie stands there dressed in full Freddie Mercury attire. She's wearing a white button-down and slacks with a fur-lined red cape draped over her shoulders, a magnificent jeweled crown resting on top of her head.

"Can I sit down?" she asks.

I nod, surprising myself that I'm eager for company.

We're quiet. A trio of little girls dressed as the Powerpuff Girls come up to get candy. I give them each a handful.

When they walk away, I turn to Nonnie. "Are you always Freddie Mercury for Halloween?"

She folds a hand over her chest. "It would be a sin if I weren't."

I feel the corners of my mouth turn up.

"Aha!" she exclaims. "There it is. I was wondering if I'd ever see you smile again."

Shame trickles through me. "My dad hates me."

"Oh, child, no, he doesn't." Her voice is heartbreakingly gentle.

It makes me feel even worse. "Your father cares about you so much. You gave us all quite a scare the other night, that's all."

We're interrupted by another group of trick-or-treaters dressed in various Marvel superhero costumes. I give them each a generous amount of candy and watch them run over to the next house.

"Sometimes genuine concern can come off aggressively," Nonnie says. "That's only the panic talking. Trust me. I spent years thinking my brother despised me."

"Your brother?" I repeat, a little surprised. I didn't know Nonnie had siblings.

"Oh yeah." She leans back on the porch swing. "He took me in when I was living in New York. Thought he'd find me dead in a gutter if he didn't. I was reckless when I drank, and every time I came home obliterated he'd scream at me. Sometimes until he was hoarse." She pats my knee. "But that's because he was overly concerned about me, especially since I don't have the greatest track record."

"Why?" I have a hard time imagining someone as confident and carefree as Nonnie depending on an excess of alcohol as a release.

She's silent for a moment. "It was an easy way to escape my self-hatred." Her hand smooths over the fur lining of her cape. "It never made things better."

I nod, knowing—in a sense—how she feels. It never helped my dad escape his depression after losing Grams.

"I didn't meet that faux Freddie on the subway until years after Charles and I divorced," she continues. "I didn't cope well with his affair in the beginning. I blamed myself. I drank to try and feel good again, but I was slowly spiraling out of control. I said awful things to my parents—to my brother Paul—but he never gave up on me. Not until the day he died."

It's strange. In the back of my mind I knew Nonnie was at Sober Living for the same reasons as my dad. It's hard to picture her as that person.

"That's why I won't give up on Saylor. I never had a chance to reconcile with my parents, but he does. He will. Forgiving someone isn't always easy, but it's possible."

I pick at a loose strand of fabric on the rocker. I remember what she told me that night we talked in my bedroom. *You always have to forgive your own mistakes. Otherwise they'll eat you alive.*

I know what I should do.

I pull my knees close to my chest. "I'm sorry," I whisper. I feel my throat tighten. "I didn't mean what I said that night."

"Of course you did," Nonnie says gently. "And that's okay, I promise you that. Emotions are what keep us alive. It's what needed to be said, and I know it's what you needed your father to hear. While I accept your apology, I want you to know I don't blame you."

I feel tears fall down my cheeks. She's being so *kind.* So understanding. I don't deserve it.

"Coming home late with a boy wasn't your smartest move, but granted, your father never did give you a chance to explain, did he?" She shrugs. "We all make mistakes. It's what keeps us interesting, but it also shouldn't destroy the relationship you have with him."

My chest tightens with emotion. I don't want to be on bad terms with my dad. I know he didn't leave me to go to rehab for selfish reasons—it was his choice to get help. Not just for himself, but also for the people he cares about. For *me*. And if I'm being honest, I didn't only come back for my friends and my normal school life. I also came back for him.

"Nonnie?"

She glances down at me.

"Thank you."

She pats my leg. "Freddie said he liked to be surrounded by splendid things, and I agree." She smiles. "But you know what? You're one of them."

My tears fall faster. "I've been horrible."

"Darling, no." She places her arm around the bench and leans closer. "You've been human."

We pass out candy until the streets grow quiet, but I can't shake the shame that sits in my stomach. Part of my twelve steps was to get Nonnie and Saylor and Peach out as soon as possible. I wanted the life I had before they came. I still don't know what would happen if Margaret found out, but now that I know them, I'd willingly defend them as good people, just like my dad. What I'd created was a set of guidelines to get my life back to how it was, when what I really need is the courage to move forward.

Alex was right. I am scared of change.

If I really wanted to better myself, I'd be kinder, like Nonnie. I'd learn to be patient, like Saylor. I'd be generous, like Peach. These were all things worth accomplishing, not a petty list designed with the intention of bringing my life back to the way it was a year ago. Because despite what I thought, struggling to live with an alcoholic father and no maternal support wasn't ever going to be normal. Living in a house with people who actually care about you...that's more normal than anything else.

Nonnie stands up. "C'mon, let's go rot our teeth on Peach and Saylor's candy apples."

I hesitate. She notices.

"Don't be worried," she tells me. "They're human, too."

THIRTY THREE

ALEX REFUSES TO ACKNOWLEDGE MY existence. He completely ignores me in Algebra II on Monday when I try and talk to him, and when we meet for Earth Club after school, he leaves before I have a chance to explain myself. I know he's probably going to work on Audrey II in the theater wing, but if he's not talking to me here then why would he talk to me there?

"He was sure in a hurry," Lin says as the door closes behind Alex. She raises an eyebrow at me. "Everything okay?"

I swallow the lump in my throat as I stare at the closed door. I've disappointed so many people on my twelve-steps list, but Alex feels like the worst. He's someone who's always been there for me. How could I be so awful to him? Especially after he was vulnerable and open about his feelings toward me. I know he was only trying to make sure I was okay that day in the cafeteria, but I was scared about my secret getting out.

Still. It's not an excuse.

No wonder he doesn't want anything to do with me.

I haven't apologized to anyone aside from Nonnie. I'm too consumed by shame. But despite how horrible I'd been, everyone has been kind. On Halloween, Peach saved me a candy apple and my dad let me watch *Nightmare on Elm Street* with everyone even though I was technically still grounded. He even made popcorn the way I like it—with M&M's mixed in—and Wallis curled up next to my feet throughout the whole movie.

I've hidden so much already. I'm tired of hiding.

I tug at the end of my gray sweater and glance at Lin. "There are some things I should tell you."

I explain everything. About how well my dad is doing and how he's trying to fix things between us. About Alex and our kiss and all the time we've spent together since I've been back. I tell her about Peach, how she gets up ridiculously early to work at the bakery. I talk about Saylor and his yoga habits, how he's patient with me when he helps me with my homework. I tell her about Nonnie and her neon safari animal obsession and how Freddie Mercury saved her life. I explain how worried I was about Margaret finding out about them and possibly sending me back to Portland. I talk until my throat is dry and my voice is cracking and a tiny piece of weight is released from my chest.

Lin sits on top of one of the empty desks and listens. When I finish, she's quiet for a moment. I worry I've disappointed her, too.

"Wow," she finally says. "They don't sound bad at all."

I glance up at her. "Really?"

She widens her eyes like, *duh*. "You said Peach wants to run her own pastry business? That's pretty cool, right?"

I nod, realizing it is.

"Saylor does yoga? I've always wanted to try that."

"He loves teaching."

She goes quiet again. I watch as she cleans her lenses on her shirt that's patterned with little white daisies.

"I know you probably don't want to hear this," she says while adjusting her frames on the bridge of her nose. "But it was really cool of your dad to let them stay."

I honestly didn't expect this reaction, but I'm not mad. It's a relief that she's being so understanding. "You think so?"

"Yeah. I mean, it wasn't fair the way you found out, but he seems like he's trying a lot harder than he was before."

"He is." I pick at a loose thread on my sleeve. "But I was afraid Margaret wouldn't understand if she found out, and that she'd send me back to Portland."

"Margaret, your social worker?"

I nod. "She called me the first night back and was like, 'if there's any unusual behavior with your dad, call me and we'll send you back to your aunt.' And him inviting all these people to live with us was unusual for me, obviously. So I felt like if I wanted to stay here, no one could know."

She thinks for a moment. "She probably just meant if he was drinking again, right? Or if you suspected anything like that? But I guess it must have been a shock to find out they moved into your house while you were gone. And you couldn't have known the very first night that they weren't going to be a problem."

"No," I agree. "I guess that's why I was scared. That if anyone found out, they'd think living with four alcoholics wasn't a good environment. Then it would get back to Margaret and my life would be uprooted again."

"Of course. But . . ." She considers her next words. "I mean, how was Alex supposed to know all that?"

I blink. That night seemed so strangely bizarre. In my head, it was a huge deal to see everyone standing out in the open outside. And the fact that Alex seemed concerned and asked if I was okay, like I needed help, made me think that he was already thinking the worst. But in reality, how *was* he supposed to know the entire situation?

Lin slides off the desk and reaches for her backpack. "You shouldn't have been so hard on him, but I guess I get why you were. It's a lot to deal with."

She's giving me an excuse for my lousy behavior. She's always been a good friend in that way—but still. I know I don't deserve it.

"It was really crappy of me," I say as we walk out of the classroom. I notice Raegan has already hung blue and silver posters throughout the hallway to promote the winter formal. "I feel like I've ruined everything."

Lin slips her thumbs under the straps of her backpack. She's had the same pastel pins stuck on them since eighth grade: a cartoon lion's head, a daisy, one with chevron stripes. "I can see why he's upset. He's been into you for so long."

Heat flushes through me, but the feeling of regret is more potent.

"And he's one of the good ones—it's obvious he cares about you. Like, really cares. If someone I had strong feelings for snapped at me like that, I'd retreat, too. But listen, I don't think it's too late to fix it."

We've reached the double doors that lead to the junior/senior parking lot. Instead of opening them, I face her. "You don't?"

She shakes her head. "We both know Alex is a really sweet guy, and he's always worn his heart on his sleeve around you. It's not going to be easy. I'd hate to be in your shoes, to be honest. But if you really care about him, you have to try."

I let my arms fall to my sides, exasperated. "I've tried all day!"

Lin rolls her eyes. "All day? Kira, do you really blame him for not immediately forgiving you?"

As much as it hurts to hear it, I know she has a point. It's not like I stole his favorite T-shirt or something. I'd basically slammed a door in his face, choosing to be cold and ruthless instead of opening up about the parts of my life I'd been trying to hide. Alex has never judged me, and neither have my friends. What am I so scared of?

I remember the gentle press of Alex's fingertips as he pulled his beanie on my head the day we skipped. I think of the way his eyes crinkle when I make him laugh, how he always gives me his full attention when I'm talking to him instead of browsing through his phone. I remember the comforting smell of his boy deodorant and clean laundry scent. I think of what he said at the restaurant—*You do remember that you're the one I kissed the other day, right?* He was vulnerable with his feelings toward me for the *second* time, and then I go and push him a million miles away.

Lin's right. I can't give up yet.

"Is he worth it?"

I don't hesitate. "Yes."

She shrugs, opening the door to the expansive parking lot. "Then try harder."

THIRTY FOUR

BY WEDNESDAY, ALEX STILL ISN'T responding to any of my texts. I'd tried my best to summarize the situation, not fearing the consequences of Margaret anymore. I wish he'd let me explain everything in person, but he avoids his locker at all costs and he won't look in my direction in algebra. When Mrs. Donaldson catches me leaning over to get his attention, she smacks her dry erase marker on her desk.

"One more word out of you, Miss Seneca, and I'm sending you down to the office."

Then she pairs me with Peter Thompson—one of the smartest kids in our grade—for a Radical Race. As punishment, probably.

Of course I don't win.

But I think of what Lin said. *Try harder.*

Alex isn't the only person I need to try harder with, though. There are other people in the house who deserve better than what I've given them. I haven't exactly shown that I've appreciated everything everyone has done for me. Not only Peach, Saylor, and Nonnie, but my dad, too. He's spent months trying to earn my forgiveness, and what have I done in return? Behaved selfishly. Screamed awful things at him. But he hasn't given up, and neither has anyone else.

I stop by the grocery store after school and pick up some ingredients. It's been a while since I've made a pizza from scratch. My dad and I used to have pizza Wednesdays where we'd make our own pie and watch the newest episode of *Crime Boss*. He was always in charge of the crust while I made the sauce, but I figure it shouldn't be too difficult. Plus, I want to extend a kind gesture to everyone tonight— a first step toward an apology.

No one is downstairs when I get home, which I was hoping for. I pull up a recipe on my phone and get to work.

It's a fairly straightforward process. After I knead the dough, I start on the sauce. Once both are prepared, I flatten, spread, and top with shredded cheese, oregano, and some sun-dried tomatoes. Then I pop it in the oven, setting the timer before I flop over on the couch. I feel good—like I've accomplished something.

I waste time browsing through channels since a new episode of *Crime Boss* isn't on until eight. I'm about to settle on watching a ridiculous reality show when the fire alarm blares—no—*pierces* through the entire house.

CRAP. I jump up and run to the kitchen, flinging open the oven. The sun-dried tomatoes are charred black, and the edges of the pizza are curling with smoke. I flip the oven off, hop up on the kitchen counter, and wave a dishrag in front of the alarm, hoping it will make it stop.

"Kira?"

Peach appears in the kitchen, her eyes wide with worry.

Thankfully the alarm falls silent, and I climb down from the counter and set the dishrag down, feeling tears well up behind my eyes. Why did I have to screw this up, too?

Nonnie is suddenly behind Peach, waving her hand in front of her face. "Is everything okay?"

I nod, my throat tight. "I, uh." I swallow. "I was trying to make dinner. For everyone."

Nonnie beams at me, but I can't meet her eyes. If I do, I know I won't be able to stop my tears.

Peach takes my creation from the oven and waves my abandoned dishcloth over it. "Do you have more dough?" she asks, her voice kind.

I nod, gesturing to the bowl.

Her magenta lips pull into a gentle smile. "Do you want to try again?"

I meet her gaze. I know she's talking about the pizza, but it doesn't stop the tightness in my throat and sting of tears behind my eyes. I can't seem to find the right words, so I nod my head and hope she understands.

Nonnie squeezes my shoulder. "I'll help."

Peach walks us through the steps. The first crust I made was too thin on the outer edges, which is why it burned so quickly. She shows me how to spread it evenly, and I put more effort into it than I did before.

"See, you're getting it." Peach says. "You know what would go good with this? My chocolate peanut butter cookies."

Nonnie grins. "I won't say no to that."

While I'm put to work gathering ingredients, Peach explains that they might offer her a full-time position at the bakery. They've been impressed with her ideas and management skills so far. I find myself congratulating her alongside Nonnie, but not because it might mean she'll be able to leave soon. Because I *am* happy for her.

We're mixing the cookie dough in a large bowl when my dad comes home.

"Something smells amazing," he says.

"Kira made us dinner," Peach tells him.

"I had help," I add.

My dad smiles at me. It's the first real smile I've seen in days.

We fall into a familiar hum. Nonnie gets out plates and sets the table while Peach finds vegetables in the fridge to prepare a salad. My dad takes a pizza cutter to our second creation.

"Save some for Saylor," I say, knowing he's working at 7-Eleven late tonight.

Once everyone's sitting at the table, I redirect the attention my way. "Listen, there's an away game on Friday in Little Pine. I wanted to invite you guys . . . if you want to come."

My dad's entire face lights up. "I'd love to see you perform, Goose."

Peach and Nonnie say they'll be there, and my dad starts talking about my old performances. He even gets out his phone and pulls up a video of my first routine back in freshman year. Normally I'd groan, but I like seeing him so happy. When Peach compliments my technique, he grins.

I know a pizza and an invitation won't fix things, but at least it's progress.

THIRTY FIVE

BEFORE I HAVE TO BE on the bus to our away game after school on Friday, I take a detour down to the theater workshop. I figure if I catch Alex off guard, I'll finally have a chance to explain myself.

I stop in front of the workshop door, take a deep breath, and then push it open.

Nobody pays attention to me as I walk inside. The ground is covered in a thin layer of sawdust, and a few techies are crowded around a hand-painted set, arguing about blocking and props. They don't bother giving me a second glance as I walk by.

Audrey II is sitting in the back corner of the workshop, fake vines spilling from all sides of her. My heart swells. Alex has done a phenomenal job. The base of the Venus flytrap is layered in different shades of green felt, and the lips of the plant are painted a waxy red. The mouth is gaping, huge, with sharp wooden teeth that have been carefully painted white and screwed into the gums. It's easy to tell how much work he's put into her.

Then, to my horror, the mouth begins to slowly close. I jump back—startled—and scream just as the jaws clamp shut.

A few students glance my way, giving me a weird look. There's a rustling behind Audrey II and a moment later, Alex emerges from the depths of the contraption. When he sees me standing there, his brows furrow in confusion.

"I know you don't want to talk to me, but I wanted to explain."

His eyes harden. I may have taken him by surprise, but that's not enough to wash away his anger toward me.

"It doesn't matter." The warmth is gone from his voice.

An ache fills my chest. *You don't matter* is all I hear.

Alex steps in front of Audrey II. I think back to all those texts we exchanged, how excited he was to be working on the mechanics of his creation. I want to tell him how amazing it looks, but I know it's too late for that. I hope it's not too late for this.

"I really care about you," I finish, hoping he hears the longing in my voice.

He laughs in this cruel, anti-Alex way. "Really? Because the way you treated me in the cafeteria? It didn't exactly feel like it."

My eyes lower down toward his paint-spackled Converse. "I shouldn't have acted like that."

He crosses his arms, two black sleeves pulled tightly across his body. "I like hanging out with you, Kira. I *more* than like hanging out with you. But when I really thought about it, I realized I was like . . . your secret."

Now I'm confused. "Wait, what?"

"I didn't see it at first. But then I did. We'd only spend time together if it was only the two of us. I know I'm not cool like Jay or whatever, but I didn't think you were ashamed of me. And then at lunch you just flipped a switch and—I don't know—shut me out."

I feel my eyes go wide in shock. "I'm not ashamed of you."

"Really? Where are we now?"

He wants me to prove his point that we're in a secluded part of the theater, but I can't. How could he think I'm embarrassed by him? We had dinner at Rosita's. I've been trying to gain his attention at school all *week*.

I take a small step closer. "You don't understand."

"I don't understand? I told you everything about my family, Kira. *Everything*. About my cousins and my parents and my sisters. God, I told you how I felt about *you* . . . I put myself out there, then you shut me down in front of your friends. Slammed the door just when I thought—" He shakes his head.

"I'm sorry." I try and blink back tears, but they betray me.

He shakes his head. "Forget it." He won't look me in the eyes. "You didn't have to tell me anything about that night in the first place. It's not like we were . . . anything."

Those words stab like knives straight into my chest. A rush of emotions flood through me. I rewind back to feeling his hands stabilizing me in the dark theater. The way he glanced at my profile as he drove us out of the school parking lot and to the donut shop. The smiles he saved for me as we walked by each other between classes. Maybe we weren't anything, but I still want to be something. I want his friendship. His trust. *Him*.

I wipe at my face, attempting to compose myself. "I was scared. I didn't want anyone finding out about them, but you were so—"

Alex's eyes cut away from me. "You don't owe me an explanation."

Translation: *I don't care.*

I watch as he walks away, disappearing around the massive body of Audrey II. This time, I don't go after him.

THIRTY SIX

MY DAD'S WATCHING THE LOCAL news when I get home from the game against Little Pine. When he sees me, he smiles and mutes the TV. "Goose! Your performance was so great. We were all so excited to see you shine out there."

The happiness in his tone makes me smile. "Thanks. Where is everyone? I didn't see your car outside."

"Saylor took them all out for milkshakes, even though I warned him Sonic gets crowded on a Friday night."

Even though I'm officially ungrounded, I still feel awful for the things I've said to my dad. He's been trying so hard, just like I've been trying with Alex. I now know how it feels, if only a little.

I join him on the couch. There's an enormous bag of peppermint patties on the coffee table. I take one, fiddling with the silver wrapping until I can find the right words. "I'm sorry... for what I said that night."

His tired eyes find mine, but they're not full of disappointment.

"I'm the one who owes you an apology. I should have asked you if you'd be comfortable with them staying here before I even offered."

"I would have said no." I shrug, because that's the truth. I would have. "But I'm glad they're here."

He takes a long look at me. "Grams would be proud of you, you know."

I snort, thinking of my trashed twelve steps and Alex and Whitney and everyone else that I've hurt. "No. She wouldn't."

"She would." He says this with confirmation in his voice. "I'm sorry, Goose. I didn't realize how hard it would be to leave your friends—your life here. I thought I was doing you right, but I didn't put you in a great situation. Having to leave, well, that wasn't fair to you, was it? I sure didn't make it easy. But you're handling coming back as best you can, and I know Grams knows that."

I nod, feeling hot tears well up behind my eyes. "I miss her."

My dad puts an arm around me, and I feel myself leaning into him. "I miss her, too."

We fall quiet, and I know we're both thinking of her. For as much as I miss her, I don't think I ever let myself openly grieve. But here, with my dad, I don't try and stop the tears that fall.

After a minute, he hands me another peppermint patty. "Do me a favor, though?"

I glance up at him.

"No boys." He reconsiders this. "No boys until you're thirty."

"*Dad.*"

"Thirty-five."

twelve steps to normal

I crack a smile. "I'm sorry I didn't tell you I was with Alex."

"Well, there's a name I haven't heard in a while."

I want to say he won't be hearing much more of it, but I don't.

We watch a few minutes of *Crime Boss* before he turns back to me. "I was thinking of having a barbecue here with everyone on Sunday. Are you okay with that?"

I nod in affirmation, realizing I don't really mind having these people around. They're helping not only my dad, but each other, too.

"Dad?"

He looks at me.

"Did the twelve-step program work for you?"

He thinks for a moment. "Not at first...but I think it's only because I wasn't allowing it to work, if that makes sense? I'd get stuck on steps for what I now realize are very obvious reasons, like I didn't admit my problem to myself. Or I didn't feel like I owed someone an apology. And a part of that was because I was too stubborn and prideful, but not enough to not want to fix myself."

"I tried to make a list for myself when I came back," I admit. "But it sort of backfired."

My dad smiles. "You know, there's a step—step nine—that says 'Make direct amends to such people wherever possible, except when to do so would injure them or others.' Even if you don't realize it, both of our apologies accomplish just that."

I remember my promise to fix my relationships with everyone. Those weren't bad steps to take, but it's about time I accepted my life is different now. Not in a bad way. I've gained three extra people in the house who really care about me. About Dad. And I know even Grams would be grateful for that.

I lean into his shoulder. "I'm glad you came back."

He smiles, then wraps me into a hug. I hug him back. We don't say anything, but we don't have to. For right now, this is enough.

THIRTY SEVEN

"YOU'RE BURNING MY BUNS!"

Nonnie playfully snaps the grilling tongs close to Saylor's face. "Oh, trust me, if I were burning your buns, you would know."

It's a perfect day for a barbecue with a gentle, crisp breeze in the air and miraculously low humidity. Both Saylor and Peach have the day off and since Nonnie doesn't go to the shelter on Sundays, my dad decided to grab burger meat and veggies from the store so we could enjoy the day together.

"Don't take offense to this," I tell Nonnie as she wraps her rainbow, iguana-patterned shawl around her. "But do you know what you're doing?"

Her turquoise frames slip down the edge of her nose. "Of course I know what I'm doing."

Smoke billows from the grill.

She suddenly looks unsure. "Okay, go get Peach."

Smiling, I walk back inside. Wallis stays at my heels, but he doesn't jump. He's gotten better at controlling his enthusiasm, which I appreciate.

I find Peach standing at the island, knife in hand. "Nonnie needs some assistance. Preferably before she sets our lawn on fire."

"I'm on it." She gestures toward the tomato she was chopping. "Want to take over?"

I do, attempting to carefully slice them using her same perfect method. That's where my dad finds me as he rounds the corner out of his room.

"Now here's something I've missed," he says, ruffling my hair. "You and me in the kitchen."

"Don't look so impressed. I'm only slicing veggies." I gesture out back. "Peach took over the grill. I think she has it handled."

My dad looks around, then grabs his apron. "I guess I'll start preparing my World-Famous Potato Salad."

I finish chopping the vegetables and put the platter in the fridge so they stay cold. Then I begin helping my dad peel potatoes over the sink.

"The secret ingredient is cumin," he tells me.

"Should we post it on the internet and make millions?"

"Maybe we'll keep it in the family, like those baked beans," he says. "This was always a hit at Grams's Fourth of July parties."

Back then, Grams would invite her work friends over and tell me all my friends were welcome to join us. Of course I'd only invite Whitney, Raegan, and Lin. They were the only ones that mattered. Since we didn't have a pool, my dad would let us set up the Slip 'N Slide, and Grams always said it was a miracle no one ever broke a bone on that thing.

After eating, we'd walk down to the Cedarville public park. There was a huge hill that gave a perfect view of the city's fireworks, and the four of us would spread our towels into one giant square and eat the popsicles my dad had carried for us in the cooler. I remember smelling like sunscreen and bug spray and smoke from the grill. It smelled like happiness.

"Dad?"

He glances at me.

"Can we make those chocolate lava cupcakes later?"

"Yes, oh—" His eyes gleam. "And if they come out good you can take a selfie of them for your Instagram."

I crack a smile. "That's just called a picture."

"I can't keep up with your lingo these days."

As he begins to launch into a conversation about a phenomenal grilling app he discovered, the doorbell rings. He starts to take off his apron, but I stop him. "I'll get it."

I wipe my potato-y hands on my jeans and run to the front door. When I fling it open, Jay is standing there.

"Hey," I say, surprised.

He's wearing a pair of black basketball shorts and a red Cedarville T-shirt. He's sweaty, as if he just got back from playing ball.

"Sorry." Jay suddenly looks embarrassed for being here. "I tried texting you."

"My phone's charging upstairs," is the only thing I can think to say.

"Oh. Right." He shakes his head. "Sorry, I didn't mean to just show up."

I blink at him. Once. Twice. This is weird. I mean, at lunch Jay practically acts like I don't exist. It's not supposed to be like this. Him, showing up here, like he did when we were dating. It feels like a betrayal to Whitney.

"So, uh," I start, "is everything okay?"

"Not really." He looks at his Nikes. Then back at me. "Whitney broke up with me."

I feel my eyes widen. That's not what I expected to hear, let alone from Jay. If anyone, I would have heard it from Whitney first.

My stomach tightens. Well, I would have if our friendship was like before.

"Did she say why?"

"She didn't think I was that into it. Which, I don't know, maybe I wasn't."

I want to tell him she's probably insecure over the fact that he openly flirts with every female in his vicinity, but I don't. It's not my place.

"She says she doesn't want things to be awkward. You know, like at lunch. But I don't know." He shrugs. "I feel like it will."

"It can't be more awkward than eating lunch with you both after I discovered you were together."

I don't mean to blurt it out, but there it is. We lock eyes for half a second before bursting out laughing.

"Man," he says. "I'm sorry. That was kind of shitty."

"*Kind of?*" I throw him a grin. "What about when you hit on me at Sonic?"

His ears go red, and he has the moral conscience to look apologetic. "That *was* shitty."

"Well, it's all in the past," I find myself saying. "I mean, we weren't that great for each other, were we?"

He's quiet for a moment. "Yeah, I guess. I felt like you never let me all the way in. You were private about a lot of things, and I get that. But I told you over and over that I'd be there if you needed me, and I always felt like you were pushing me away. Or just pretending things were okay when they weren't." He looks directly at me. "But I could have tried harder, too. There were a lot of times I could have reached out and didn't."

A mix of emotions sink in my chest. I knew I treated him that way, but I've never heard him admit it out loud. When it came to discussing the hard things, Alex was the person I was comfortable confiding in, and now he doesn't want anything to do with me.

"I'm sorry," I say. "I wanted to pretend I was living a normal life."

Jay laughs in surprise, but from his expression I can tell it's not mean-spirited.

"What's so funny?" I ask, curious.

"I mean, it's just that nobody's life is ever really normal, you know?"

I nod. It's true. I've been judging things for how I wanted them to be, not how they actually were.

I take a deep breath. "Sometimes I feel like...like I don't know who I am," I admit. "But...I know who I want to be. Does that make sense?"

"Yeah," Jay says. "It does."

Before I can say anything else, the door swings open from behind me. Wallis comes bounding outside and nearly knocks Jay over. Saylor rushes out and grabs him by the collar.

I expect my natural reflexes to rise and wait for my body to go into panic mode, but it doesn't. After confiding in Lin, I'd also told Whitney and Raegan about the recoverees, and neither of them saw a need for concern. They agreed that if everyone in the house was only helping and supporting each other, there wasn't a reason to worry. At this point, that fear has dissolved. I have nothing to hide.

"Wallis!" Nonnie says, poking her head outside. Her rainbow shawl billows around her neck. "Get back here, you naughty thing."

"Sorry," Saylor says to Jay as he attempts to usher the dog back inside. "He's still learning how to control his excitement toward other humans."

"That's okay," Jay replies. "I was about to take off, anyway."

"Saylor, Nonnie." I gesture beside me. "This is my friend, Jay."

"Great to meet you," Nonnie says, extending a hand. "There's a ton of food here if you want to join."

"Actually, I should get home. But thank you."

Saylor nods. "Of course. Nice to meet you."

When the door closes, he turns back to me. "Your dad is doing okay, then?"

"He is." It feels good to admit it. "More than okay, actually."

"It's nice to see him having friends over. Being social and all."

"They're friends from the Sober Living place. His fellow recoverees." Explaining this to Jay doesn't feel like a huge deal after telling my friends.

"And you're fine with them being here?"

"Yeah." It wouldn't have been my answer a month ago, but it's true. "They're good people."

Jay's expression softens, and I'm relieved to see he doesn't seem apprehensive. "Seems like it."

For the first time in a long time, I feel positive about things. I'm not tempted to escape the confines of the house, and somehow—even with everyone here—it's begun to feel more like home.

I don't mind that I have every lyric on *Queen's Greatest Hits* memorized. I don't mind the small gasps Peach makes during the most predictable moments of *Crime Boss* when she sits down to watch with my dad and me, and I don't mind when I find Saylor quietly meditating in the middle of our dismantled living room, making odd humming noises. Because Saylor helps me with my English essays even though he doesn't have to and Peach does my laundry because she knows my schedule is crazy during football season and Nonnie shows me wild pictures from her old life in New York.

It's nice to have people showing they care about you.

Maybe they're not perfect, but they're not encouraging bad behavior. And even though I don't quite understand it, they're recovering together. I can see the light in my dad's eyes every time they admit their Small Successes at dinnertime and how he's trying, really trying, to make this easy on me.

I'd be lying if I said I wasn't glad that I'm part of it.

Jay's giving me a sideways glance.

"What?"

"Nothing. I don't know. You just look happy, I guess."

I turn to the closed door. When I go back inside, I know I'll be greeted with a slightly charred hamburger bun and Nonnie's awful dance moves and the gleam in my father's eye when he tells everyone I helped him make his World-Famous Potato Salad. I find myself wanting to go. To be part of it.

"Yeah." I feel my lips pull into a smile. "I think I am."

THIRTY EIGHT

WHETHER IT'S OUT OF FEAR or discomfort, Jay eats lunch with the rest of the basketball team on Monday. Breck joins him, which makes Colton the only guy at our table. He hardly seems to notice, paying more attention to the music in his headphones than our conversation.

"*He's* the one making it weird," Whitney interjects, her gaze over at the basketball table. "I told him nobody here would care."

I don't offer up the fact that he came over yesterday. It doesn't change anything—it's not as if we're getting back together.

Raegan waves a hand in the air. "It'll blow over. You guys were basically in the same place, anyway."

Whitney glances over at me, then looks away. So she's talked to Raegan about it. That doesn't surprise me. It's not like we talk about things like that anymore.

Lin looks up from her history notes. "But you're okay?"

Whitney shrugs. "Yeah."

"Oh," Raegan turns to me. "You said one of your dad's friends has a dog?"

"Yeah." I'm surprised she remembered. "Wallis."

"Do you think I can borrow him?"

"Uh, why?"

She stares at me like it's obvious. "Because I'm going to be a sister."

Lin and I exchange confused glances.

"We just established that Wallis is a *dog,* right? You were mentally present for that?"

Raegan waves away my sarcasm. "Of course. That's why I need all the practice I can get. I figure if I'm good at taking care of a dog, then taking care of a baby should be no big deal. They're both big responsibilities. And my mom is supposedly due this weekend."

I make a note to never tell Raegan's future sister that she was once compared to a dog. I know there's no talking Raegan out of an idea she feels strongly about, so I say, "I'll ask Nonnie tonight. I'm sure it'll be fine."

"Your mom must be so excited," Whitney adds.

"She is. She's not worried at all." Raegan sits up a little straighter. "I think everything will go well."

"It will," I assure her.

She smiles back at me.

I think back to what my dad had said about getting stuck on certain steps in the twelve-step program. He'd mentioned number 9 stated to make amends with people you've harmed. Even though the theory behind my own list wasn't perfect, I was glad I'd made the effort to be a better friend to Raegan and Lin and Whitney. Things may not be like they were, but at least I hadn't let those friendships go. The list was good in that sense.

After lunch, Lin and I walk to my locker. I linger there longer than usual, hoping Alex will come around. But of course, he doesn't.

"Don't worry," she says, giving me a quick hug. "It'll work out."

I want to believe her, but it's seeming more unlikely every day. Especially after our last conversation. I can't blame him for being hurt at the way I acted in the cafeteria, but *I'm* hurt that he could even think I was ashamed of him. Between exchanging notes written on Starburst wrappers in Mrs. Donaldson's class and having a very public dinner at Rosita's, plus all the times we'd walk together in the halls or meet up after school, I don't understand how he could possibly think that.

Lin agrees with me, but she seems to think time is the answer.

I wish I were a more patient person.

When I get home later that evening, Nonnie is watching TV on the couch while simultaneously trying to instruct Wallis how to shake hands. She has her giant rollers in her hair and is wrapped in her usual zebra-print robe. I flop on the armchair beside her, sore from practice and tired of stressing about Alex.

"Saylor might be right," Nonnie sighs. "I don't know if you can teach this old dog new tricks." She looks at me. "How are you, darlin'? You're home pretty late."

"Practice ran long." I glance around. "Where is everyone?"

"Working or working late." She strokes Wallis's fur. "Peach left us a casserole for dinner."

Wallis flops out his big tongue, his drool dribbling onto the carpet. "Why Wallis?" I hear myself ask. "I mean, out of all the dogs in the shelter, why him? I would want to try and save them all if I could."

At the mention of his name, Wallis rolls onto his back. Nonnie rubs the coarse fur on his belly. "I know they all need love, but he just seemed like he needed it more. Can't quite explain it. Those other families gave up on him, you know? I guess I felt like the poor thing needed someone who wouldn't."

Wallis thumps his tail on the floor, like he can tell he's the topic of conversation. I wonder if Nonnie felt that way about her parents before they passed away, like they gave up on her. She mentioned her brother hadn't, but he'd also passed. I hadn't thought about it this way until now, but maybe we're the family she'd been looking for— the one who wouldn't give up on her even after knowing how much she'd struggled.

I hold out my hand, not even flinching when Wallis gives it a giant lick. "He's lucky to have you."

"Nah," Nonnie says, peering at me from behind her turquoise frames. "He's lucky to have us."

THIRTY NINE

MRS. DONALDSON HAS US COMPETING in Radical Races on Tuesday in preparation for our final, which is a nice distraction from Alex. At least it forces me to pay attention. Thanks to Ana, I'm a little more confident each time I'm called up there—even if I only have two Jolly Ranchers on my desk while most of the class has five or six.

I'm staring at the back of Alex's beautiful curls, trying not to be too wistful as he races against Audrena Jones, when there's a knock at the door. A moment later, Principal Lawrence sticks her head in.

"I'm sorry to interrupt," she tells Mrs. Donaldson. Her eyes find mine. "Kira? Can I speak to you for a moment?" She gestures for me to gather my belongings.

I feel the stares of everyone in the class as I grab my things. Every horrible thought crosses through my mind: My dad has relapsed. He's been taken down to the station again. Cedarville Elementary has fired him for showing up drunk.

Panic rises in my chest. I don't want to have to call Aunt June about this.

Once we're out in the hallway, Principal Lawrence shoots me a sympathetic glance. "I'm sorry to be the one to bring you this news, but your grandmother is in the hospital."

I'm hit with a sudden wave of déjà vu. No, that can't be right. Grams was in the hospital more than two years ago. She must have me confused with another student.

Principal Lawrence must sense my bewilderment. "Your... Nonnie? I assumed it was your grandmother, but—"

My blood freezes. I forget how to breathe.

"What hospital?"

"Merciful Heart," she says. "We can write you a pass."

I can't find the words to form a coherent reply. Instead I turn and head down the hallway, breaking into a run as soon as my feet hit the pavement of the school parking lot.

There's no way. *No way.* Nonnie can't be in the hospital. I mean, I know she's older—she can't run around the yard with Wallis like Saylor can—but she's fine. We talked last night. She was *fine.*

I miraculously make every green light on the way to the hospital. When I walk through the sliding doors of the emergency room, I'm relieved to see that Peach and Saylor are already here. He looks devastated.

"Your father is on his way," Peach says, her voice small.

I blink back tears. "What happened?"

"Stroke. One of the volunteers at the shelter called her an ambulance and rode with her here."

Saylor sits back down. He covers his face with his hands.

I turn back to Peach. Her lips are uncharacteristically nude, removed of her typical magenta lipstick. "What's going to happen? Is she okay?"

"We're not sure. She's . . . not conscious right now."

I feel myself nodding. Peach guides me to a chair. She repeats things the doctor has told her. Nonnie experienced an ischemic stroke. One of her blood vessels blocked the flow of blood to her brain. They don't know the extent of the damage just yet, but her doctor will come by and see us when they have any further updates.

I sit in the chair beside Peach and wait, but it doesn't feel like I'm here to see Nonnie. I saw her this morning. She was sitting on the kitchen stool while Saylor toasted her Pop-Tart and Peach ranted on about how she couldn't believe they were eating Pop-Tarts when she brought back fresh bakery items from her shifts.

My dad shows up a half hour later. I wrap my arms around him as Peach tells him everything we know. Then we go back to waiting in silent agony.

An hour goes by. Then two.

When Nonnie's doctor finds us an hour later, he tells us she's conscious. My hope deflates as he continues to say that she's not in the best condition. We can expect to see physical impairments in her face. She's having trouble speaking and seems to be very confused. He believes seeing familiar faces might help, but he says we shouldn't overwhelm her. He tells us it's best to visit two at a time.

Peach and Saylor go in first and when they come back forty minutes later, Peach's eyes are red. Saylor looks like he's having a hard time holding it together.

"Just be prepared," Peach tells us softly. She has her arm around

Saylor. "I'm going to drive him home to get a change of clothes. He wants to stay here tonight."

My dad nods. "We'll see you soon."

I follow my dad down the long hallway until we reach her room in the ICU. My heart clenches as we step inside. This isn't Nonnie. She's dressed in a drab gray gown. No glasses. No chunky turquoise jewelry. Her hair is flat, so unlike her typical robust curls. Worse, the left side of her face isn't even. Her mouth is pulled down in a terribly unnatural way, almost like a Picasso painting.

My throat tightens into a knot. I swallow, but it refuses to dissolve.

My dad speaks first. "Nonnie," he says gently. "You gave us all quite a scare."

Nonnie blinks, like she's struggling to put the pieces of my father's words together. She looks tired. Exhausted. Finally, she simply nods.

"Saylor and Peach will be back," he continues, walking over to her and taking her hand. "Saylor's bringing your Queen CD and a few changes of clothes for you. But you have to rest up so we can bring you back home, okay?"

Nonnie blinks. Several minutes pass before she says, "Freddie."

My tears are falling freely now. "We'll blast Freddie so hard we'll annoy everyone in here."

Nonnie's eyes fall on me, as if she's just now recognizing that I'm here.

"Ma," she says.

I look to my dad, but he only squeezes my hand.

She continues to stare at me, as if wanting reassurance that I'm her. "Mama?"

My emotional barrier collapses. The doctor warned us she would be confused, but I didn't expect it to hurt this much.

Nonnie's crying now. It's hard to understand what she's saying. She struggles to enunciate. "I-I'm sorry. I'm so sorry."

I break into a thousand shattered pieces. Nonnie never cries. Not strong, beautiful, confident Nonnie. An uncontrolled sob bursts from my lips. She's not there. This isn't her.

My dad puts an arm around me. I can tell I'm upsetting her. More tears fall down her face.

"I forgive you," I say, trying to make my words even. I don't know why she thinks I'm her mother, but I hope giving her closure will help. "Don't worry, I forgive you."

Her mouth tries to smile. She reaches for me, but it's a struggle for her. I step closer and clasp her hand. It's so cold.

My dad and I leave when Saylor and Peach come back. Saylor's brought Nonnie's favorite neon cheetah scarf and her worn kitten slippers, but I can't tell if Nonnie recognizes them. I hope Freddie Mercury will be a comfort for her tonight.

I don't feel like driving back home alone, so my dad tells me we can swing by and get my car in the morning.

My dad takes a deep breath. "Nonnie's parents died several years ago. She was still drinking at the time. One of her biggest regrets was not asking them for forgiveness."

I think of what she told me a while back. *You always have to forgive your own mistakes. Otherwise they'll eat you alive.* I didn't think of it then, but I know now. She was speaking from experience. Nonnie never forgave herself for not making peace with her parents. It breaks my heart knowing it broke her.

"She talked about them a lot in Sober Living," my dad continues. "Her counselors told her over and over that her parents would be proud of who she's become."

I wipe my eyes on my sleeve. "There's no one else like her."

My dad gives me a sad smile. "No one."

We're quiet the rest of the way home. I wish I'd taken the time to get to know her better. When she gets out of the hospital, I promise myself I will. I've been so self-centered with my own problems, but she was always there to comfort me. Even after I said all those horrible things, she still forgave me. I didn't think it meant much before, but I was wrong.

It means everything.

FORTY

TWO DAYS LATER, NONNIE PASSES away in her sleep. The doctor warned there was a chance this could occur, but I thought Nonnie was stronger than the odds.

Saylor and Peach were with her. Peach explained she'd been wearing her favorite headscarf, listening to her favorite music with some of her favorite people—that she really believed she was finally content. I believed that, too, but it isn't enough to repair the slow ache of her loss.

I don't go to school on Friday. Saylor holes himself up in the guest room with Wallis, and nobody disturbs him. I sleep on and off, hoping to wake up into a different world where I'll see Nonnie and her sky-high hair rollers and with her red Freddie Mercury cape wrapped around her. I have to believe she's somewhere good now. I hope she's met the real Freddie Mercury. I hope he's everything she imagined.

My dad and Peach make funeral arrangements over the weekend.

I can't seem to be in the same room with them without crying. Saylor quits his job and continues to isolate himself, not wanting to contribute to the funeral. He's still in denial. We all are, I think.

Wallis keeps Saylor company, but he knows something's wrong. I find him whining in front of the guest bedroom door, Nonnie's room. When I open the door, I wish I hadn't. I wasn't ready for her familiar scent of rose and patchouli. It's another aching reminder that she was here, and now she's not.

Later, when I pass by the guest room, I notice Wallis has curled himself onto her hand-knitted blanket. His ears perk up when he hears me pass, but he lies his head back down when he realizes I'm not her.

My heart breaks for him.

The night before the funeral, I can't sleep. When I close my eyes, I see Nonnie's blue ones beneath her turquoise frames. I hate that I didn't get to know her better, especially when she was so kind to me. She admitted her faults and hardships without hesitation, and all I tried to do was send her away.

Guilt and sadness cling to me like summer humidity. I've been stupid and selfish toward the people who care about me.

I wish I could talk to Grams.

Being back at Merciful Heart brought up the devastating memories of losing her all over again. She was such a huge source of comfort, and the deep expanse of loneliness without her here is gutting. There wasn't a tough situation she couldn't handle. I'm not sure how I'm supposed to be the strong one without her.

My phone reads 1:03 a.m. Since the dull emotional ache in my chest won't dissolve, I decide to creep quietly downstairs. After Grams died, Dad put her clothes and linens in weatherproof storage containers and kept them in the garage. And right now, I want to be as close to her as I can.

I try not to make too much noise as I move aside my dad's toolkits and boxes of Christmas decorations. The navy containers are toward the back, but something clinks loudly when I begin to pull the first one out. I discover the source of the noise, spotting a large handle of vodka rolling on its side.

Hot anger snakes through me. I have no doubt it belongs to my dad—a ghost of his past life he attempted to hide. It's dusty and unopened, which makes me think he must have forgotten about it when he came back from the ranch.

Still, I can't shake my anger and resentment. I was *there*. I was there for him the *whole time*. He didn't have to drown his loneliness when he had me. We could have gotten through our grief together. I was his daughter, his support system, but he'd chosen this instead.

I'd spent the first month in Portland wondering if I should have reached out to him more or tried to talk to him more, despite Aunt June telling me otherwise. I was so sure I could have prevented his addiction. But that wasn't true. No matter what different scenarios I created in my mind, the result would have still been the same.

Thinking about it makes me furious. After everything with Grams, it wasn't fair that I had to watch my dad spiral.

How could he do that to me, knowing I was grieving for her just as much as he was?

I ignore the vodka, opening the tops of Grams's storage

containers. I'm hit with a scent that was remarkably *her,* and my anger is instantly replaced by tears. The memories of her—her cashmere sweaters and crocheted blankets and flannel button-downs—are here, abandoned and alone. She's not coming back, just like Nonnie. This is all we'll ever have.

The sorrow and guilt and shame lie thick under my skin. Maybe I couldn't have done anything to change my dad's trajectory, but I *could* have cared more about Nonnie. I didn't have to give her such a hard time whenever she reached out. Her heart was so big, and I acted so terribly. Not only to her, but toward Saylor and Peach. Toward Alex. I was cold and ungrateful. Cruel, even. Nobody deserved the way I treated them.

Knowing I'll never get another chance to get to know Nonnie or tell her how much I appreciated her brings back the bitter ache I'd felt when Grams passed. The anguished, miserable feelings I never thought I'd have to endure again.

The reality of it stings.

I slide into a sitting position on the concrete floor, then pick up the handle. When I crack open the top, the cheap, sharp smell hits my nose. But I don't care. I don't want to think anymore—about anything. Not Grams or Nonnie or Alex. I wish things had been different with each of them, but I can't change the past. I can't change anything.

Closing my eyes, I take a drink. My immediate reflex is to gag. This *burns,* and not in the good way. I lose grip of the bottle's cap and it clangs to the floor, rolling away. I let it go and force another sip down. Then another.

"Kira?"

Before I can even think about putting the bottle back in its hiding place, Saylor steps out from around my dad's car. I watch his expression drop as he looks from my eyes to the handle of vodka.

I feel all my defenses rise, but he surprises me by calmly sitting down next to me. "What's that going to solve?"

My brain already feels foggy as I try and process my answer. "Not feeling like this."

"Sad? Angry? Guilty? Confused? Lost?" Saylor rattles off everything I haven't expressed. "I've been there, too. We all have."

"Well I have *more*." My grip tightens on the bottle. "Grams is gone. Now Nonnie is gone."

There's sympathy in Saylor's eyes. "I know, and it's unfair. But this?" He gestures to the handle. "It doesn't help. You know it only makes things worse."

"I'm fine." I wish he would just leave. "Seriously."

"You're drinking alone on the floor in a dark garage," Saylor replies. "I'd hardly say that's fine."

The emptiness in my chest expands, numbing my somber thoughts. I'm not acting like myself. This isn't how Grams would want to see me coping—and neither would Nonnie.

"How are you okay with this?" My voice cracks. "She's gone."

"I'm not okay with it." His eyes are heavy with sadness. "Are you?"

"No."

His next words come out softer. "I didn't know where I was going to go after Sober Living. When your dad extended the invitation to come here for a little while, I said yes because I knew Nonnie was coming, too."

I hug my knees to my chest. "Why?"

"Our stories paralleled, in a way. We'd ruined relationships with nearly everyone around us, and we were all out of second, third, fourth chances." He thinks for a moment. "She saw herself in me. That's what she said. Wanted to make sure I succeeded in the ways she didn't—not until the very end, at least. I knew if I came here, came with her, that I wouldn't be tempted to go back to substance abuse. Because she made me believe in myself."

Tears sting behind my eyes, making my nose run. I wipe it on my sleeve. "But what about now? Now that she's gone?"

"Just because a person is gone doesn't mean their impact is gone, too." Saylor places a hand on the storage container. "The way you still feel your Grams's love? I still feel Nonnie's strength. Her resilience that encouraged me to be better. I'll always carry that with me."

Now I let my tears fall freely. "She meant a lot to you."

When he looks over at me, I notice his eyes are red. "She did."

We fall into silence, absorbing the comfort of each other's company.

"It took me a long time to realize that you don't have to go through the tough and terrible things alone," Saylor finally says. "And your dad and Peach and I are here to help you through this, you know?"

I nod, trying to swallow the painful ache in my throat. He's right. Sitting here in the dark with this giant bottle makes me feel horrible for abusing it in the same way my dad used to.

Saylor produces the vodka cap that had rolled away. "I'm not going to lecture you anymore. You already know everything I want to say about this."

I take the cap from him. "How did you know I was out here?"

"I heard you. I couldn't sleep, either." He stands up, then offers me a hand. I take it. "Let's go pour that out."

I follow him into the kitchen, bringing the handle with me. I tip it over into the sink and watch as the clear liquid disappears down the drain. When it's empty, he tosses it into the recycling. He doesn't falter once, not even when he could have drunk it with me in the garage. His strength brings shame to me all over again.

It's strange how, at one point, I wanted nothing to do with them. Despite what I thought, they've changed me in the very best ways. I didn't know Nonnie for very long, but I'm glad I knew her at all. If she's taught me anything, it's that you should take time to get to know the people you care about.

I gesture outside. "Have time to talk?"

Saylor nods, and we walk to his hammock in the backyard. There's a slight chill in the air. I tuck my hands into the sleeves of my sweatshirt.

"Please don't tell my dad," I say, my head fuzzy from the liquor.

"I won't...as long as you promise to talk to one of us in the future."

"I swear." The tightness in my throat makes my voice small. I'm grateful and embarrassed, but if Saylor notices he doesn't say anything.

"We can talk about her," he says gently, "if it helps."

I think back, wishing my dad had asked me if I wanted to talk about Grams after she passed. Instead he'd clammed up and turned to alcohol, just like I'd tried to do. And I don't want to be the person he once was. I want to talk.

So I do.

"Was Nonnie her real name?"

Saylor tucks his hands behind his head. "No, but that's an interesting story."

He tells me her real name is Nancy and that she never had kids of her own. When her brother's kids had kids they sort of adopted her as another grandmother. Nonnie's part Italian, and *Nonnie* is Italian for grandmother.

I bet she made a pretty great faux-grandmother.

We stay out there a few more hours, lying side by side on the hammock. He tells me more about Nonnie—how she wore her Freddie cape to the top of the Empire State building. How she always told him she'd break a bone if she tried to do yoga. How she wanted to buy a house of her own so she really *could* save every dog in the Cedarville shelter.

I don't ask about her life before Sober Living. That's not the Nonnie I want to know, and that's not the person she'd want me to remember. It doesn't matter anyway, because in the end she was the best person she could be. That's what counts.

I prop myself up a bit so I can see Saylor better. "I never apologized to you. About...how I treated you." I take a deep breath. "I'm sorry. For everything. You've been so good to me, and I've been awful."

Saylor just looks at me. "Kira, I already knew how you felt—I knew you were sorry."

I furrow my brows in confusion. "You did?"

"Your essay that I helped you with? About *The Crucible*? You weren't talking about John Proctor. You were talking about *you*. And despite your existential crisis that's clearly unrelated to John Proctor, I knew you cared about us." He looks right at me. "And Nonnie knew, too."

I sniff, and my next words come out watery. "Why have you always been so nice to me?"

Saylor leans back in the hammock. "We don't just learn how to recover in Sober Living, you know. We learn how to be better people in general." He gives me an amused look. "Plus, you're like the younger sister I never had. I hope I don't make your life too miserable."

"I acted that way at first," I admit. "But I don't feel that way now."

And for the first time in days, Saylor smiles.

Nonnie's funeral takes place on Sunday, and it's as unbearable as I thought it would be. The weather has shifted, bringing in a biting wind. I don't know most of the people who attend, but my dad and Peach make sure to introduce themselves. I don't feel like joining in on the politeness, not even when the casket is lowered into the ground and Queen's "One Year of Love" plays.

I sit outside with Saylor and Wallis during the memorial afterward. I can't make myself go inside and see all the pictures of Nonnie and meet the people who were in her life before me. It still makes me feel guilty. I should have tried to know her better.

"I'm going to head home," I tell Saylor as we begin to see more and more people leave. "Do you want a ride?"

He shakes his head. He must be freezing, but he doesn't complain. "I'll wait for Peach, but thanks."

When my dad was making funeral arrangements, I was afraid it would bring back awful memories of losing Grams. That was the trigger that made him seek absolution in alcohol. I kept a close eye on him, but he remained focused the entire time.

Trust.

I'm walking to the car when I hear a screech of tires in the parking lot. I look up, surprised to see Lin's mother's Explorer hurtling in my direction. Lin jolts to a stop beside me, then rolls down the window.

"I'm sorry!" she says, her voice rising in panic.

It's unlike Lin to be in such a frenzied state. It puts me on edge. "Is everything okay?"

"Yes—well, sort of. Raegan's mom is in labor!"

I feel my mouth fall open. I'd nearly forgotten her due date was near. "It's happening?"

"It's happening!" she practically shouts. "I tried to get ahold of you, but—"

I shake my head. I'd left my phone in my room before we came because I didn't feel like being connected to technology today. Raegan must be freaking out. I can't even imagine. She's been anticipating this day for so long.

I run around to the passenger's side. "I'll go with you."

Lin speeds all the way to the hospital. My stomach drops when she pulls up to Merciful Heart. It's the largest hospital in Cedarville, so I should have expected Raegan's family would be here, but it doubles my pain of losing Nonnie.

Lin parks and we run into the building, then we take the elevator up to the maternity ward. Whitney is standing in the waiting area, waving us over.

"They went back there half an hour ago. It shouldn't be too much longer, I think." She turns to me, taking in my black dress. Before I can comprehend what's happening, she wraps me in a quick hug. "I'm sorry."

When Whitney breaks away, Lin quickly says, "I'm going to find some coffee."

I turn to Whitney, surprised by her warmth and sympathy. "Thank you."

"I'm been so prideful and stupid," she says, tears filling her eyes. "You've apologized and tried not to make things weird, and I held all that against you. And now you lost someone, *again,* and . . . it makes me so sad. It's so unfair."

I'm shocked at her confession. "It doesn't matter, okay? We both messed up, but we're here now."

She sniffs, wiping her eyes. "God, sorry. I'm blubbering all over you when you're the one going through a hard time." She meets my gaze. "Are you okay?"

"Not really," I admit.

She hugs me again, this time not letting go as quickly as she did before. I let myself hug her back. I know she's flawed—we both are—but I miss her. Even if we aren't as close as we used to be, even if we've grown apart, I still want her to be my friend.

When we break away, I ask, "How's Raegan?"

"Absolutely freaking out. She snapped at a nurse for something I didn't understand. She must have done more research than we thought."

"Shocking."

"Right?" Whitney looks around. "Poor Lin. Does she even *like* coffee?"

I laugh, knowing the answer and appreciating her giving us our time.

"I know it's not my place to say this," Whitney says. "But knowing you and your dad, I have to know that Nonnie had a great last few months of her life with you guys."

I think of Nonnie laughing out in the backyard as Saylor toppled over in his headstand. How she paraded through the house in the Freddie Mercury cape. How she teased Peach's overly polite southern mannerisms and taught my dad all the words to "Bohemian Rhapsody." How she was never going to give up on Saylor—or me.

I have to believe she loved it here, too.

"Thank you," I tell her. "That means a lot."

Lin returns a moment later, and I tell them all about Nonnie. It feels good not having to pretend with them anymore. I never should have in the first place.

An hour later, Raegan bursts through the doors.

"I'm a sister!" she exclaims. "She's so tiny. And beautiful. My mom's okay, although this one nurse poked her three separate times before sticking an IV in. But they say she handled the pregnancy very well for her age."

A wave of relief rolls through my chest. "That's *so* great."

Raegan turns to me, squeezing me tight. "Thank you for being here."

I try and return her smile. "Can we see her?"

"Yes!" She's swelling with pride. "She's in the hospital nursery. Follow me."

We follow her past the double doors and around the corner of a long hallway. Raegan stops in front of a long window where half a dozen babies are resting in beds that resemble high-tech shopping carts.

"That's her," Raegan says, pointing to the farthest bed on the right.

My eyes land on this tiny bean of a human, small and safe, gently wrapped in a soft white blanket. She's beautiful, already so loved by so many in this world. In Raegan's eyes, she's perfect—but she'll make mistakes. It's impossible not to. But I can tell by the way Raegan is gazing at her, she'll love her through anything. And maybe that's all anyone can ask for.

FORTY ONE

EVEN THOUGH MY DAD TOLD her she didn't have to, Aunt June flies into town the next day. She says it's not a big deal, that she has time off to spare. I can't say I blame her, though. My dad wasn't exactly okay the last time he lost someone.

When I pick June up from the airport, she wraps me in a huge hug. I squeeze her tight, overcome by waves of emotion.

"Oh! I've missed you," she says as we walk to my car. "I know it's only been a few months, but you just look so grown."

I feel a smile tug on the corners of my lips. "I sort of feel that way, too."

She waits until we get in the car before she goes, "Your dad told me everything, about his friends staying at the house, although I wish you would have. I'm so sorry to hear about Nonnie."

My chest tightens. I don't know if I'm still in denial about it, but it's like a fresh wound every time I hear her name. "We're all... sort of getting through it together."

She sighs. "When he told me about his friends living here, I'll admit I was a little worried. I can't imagine how you reacted to that homecoming. But after talking to him for a long while, it seemed as though they're good people and, more importantly, they haven't relapsed and put you in any danger. After all you've both been through, I know he'd do anything to keep your environment safe and stable."

"I haven't ever felt threatened by them. Honest," I say. "But I was afraid Margaret would react badly and send me back to live with you."

Aunt June's eyes fall soft with sympathy. "And you just wanted to be home."

I nod.

"Well, I'm sorry to visit under unfortunate circumstances, but I'm looking forward to meeting them. I'm glad your father has this support system, you know."

"I am, too," I say, and I mean it. Because they're not only his support system, but mine, too.

"And I'm glad you're happy here, doll."

"It doesn't mean I *don't* miss you."

"Ah, I know." She smiles. "But it's nice to hear it."

As I'm pulling in the driveway, I notice a strange, multi-colored something hanging from the mailbox. My brain automatically jumps to Nonnie's love for rainbow extravagancies, but I know that can't be it. After helping June with her suitcase, I start down the driveway.

"Just a second," I say.

I open the mailbox all the way, freeing a Starburst bracelet made from only the tropical wrappers. There's a note attached, but I already know who it's from.

> I KNOW YOU'RE GRIEVING, AND I WANTED TO SAY I'M SORRY. I DIDN'T WANT TO BOMBARD YOU WITH TEXTS OR ANYTHING. IF YOU WANT TO TALK, I'M HERE.

I clutch the bracelet in my hand. This is the first time I've heard from Alex in over a week. Does this mean he could be open to forgiving me?

I swallow, remembering our conversation in the workshop. He's probably just offering his condolences. Like Lin said, that's who he is—a nice guy.

"Anything good?" June asks as I'm unlocking the front door.

I stare down at the bracelet. "I hope so."

Wallis bombards June as soon as we walk through the door. I use her suitcase as a blockade until my dad runs down the hall, grabbing him by his collar. Saylor is on his heels, apologizing profusely.

"I'll let him outside," he says. "I'm Saylor, by the way. It's great to finally meet you."

"Likewise," June says, and I can't help but think how surreal it is that she's here.

Wallis *woofs* as Saylor takes him away. He wanted to keep him, and he'd asked us if that was okay. I remembered when Nonnie said she wasn't going to give up on him. I know Saylor won't, either.

Peach steps into the room. "Oh, June, it's such a pleasure to meet you." She wraps her in a hug like they've been friends forever, and to my surprise June returns it. She says something to Peach that I can't hear, but when I see Peach nod mournfully I can guess what it's about.

"Come on in. You must be exhausted," my dad says, placing her suitcase near the stairs.

June wraps my dad in another hug. "You look so good. How are you doing?"

"We're holding up as best we can, I think," my dad answers earnestly. "It was unexpected."

While they sit in the living room, I walk into the kitchen where Peach is reheating some leftover soup for June. She gives me a tired smile when she sees me.

The guilt I've held on to for the last few months blankets me. Before I can think, I blurt, "I—I'm sorry . . . I've been meaning to say it for a while now, but I haven't."

Peach gives me a light squeeze on my shoulder. "Oh, Kira, I know."

I'm surprised by this. I acted so horribly, yelling at her over a progress report. "You know?"

"Well, your pizza was a nice gesture, but Nonnie told me," she explains. "She was really in tune with everyone's feelings around here. And quite honestly, I did overstep some boundaries. I didn't mean to pry into your personal life."

I shake my head. "You were trying to help. All of you were. And you did." I glance toward the living room. "My dad hasn't been like this—like himself—in a while."

"We all got some much-needed help at Sober Living," Peach says. "But I do want you to know that I'm trying to work things out with my own family, and I know Saylor is trying really hard to move forward with his career. I'm not sure how long we'll be here, but I want to respect you and your space."

I know I can't take back my next words, but I also know I don't want to. "You can stay here as long as you need."

When she smiles, there are tears in her eyes.

"Thank you. It's a lot, especially with the holidays—" The microwave beeps. She blinks away her tears and stirs the soup. "Anyway, I appreciate it. Saylor and I both do."

I step forward and give her a small hug. Surprised, she stands there for a moment before hugging me back. It feels nice, and I realize Nonnie was right. You have to forgive your own mistakes. I hope, somewhere, she knows that I have.

My dad walks into the kitchen as Peach is taking the bowl of soup to June.

"I'm proud of you, Goose," he says. "I haven't made this easy on you, but thank you for understanding."

I nod, glancing back toward the living room. Dread sinks into my stomach when I realize there will come a time when June will go back to Portland and Saylor and Peach will move forward in their own lives. Things will go back to the way I wanted, and it'll be just the two of us here. Only I'm not sure if I want that anymore. I'm scared of what will happen when they do leave.

"We're going to be okay, right?" I look up at him. "Whenever it's just you and me again . . . we'll be okay?"

I know he hasn't been reliable in the past. Life has hurt us both in so many ways, but in these last few months, it's healed us, too. It's helped us move on. We've both changed and adapted and survived.

My dad wraps one arm around me, then kisses the top of my head. "We're going to be just fine."

This time, I believe him.

———

Later, when everyone is finally asleep, I lie in bed, staring at a text message I'd carefully composed a few minutes earlier. I finger the Starburst bracelet around my wrist. Then I hit send.

ME: i got your note. i know it's late, but can you meet at 7-Eleven?

Thankfully his reply comes quickly.

ALEX: give me 10 minutes

I'd been thinking of everything I wanted to say to him all evening. I'd been hurt that he didn't forgive me right away, but then again, I don't feel like I deserved immediate forgiveness. I'd been cruel, and he had a right to stay mad. He didn't even have to reach out when he discovered Nonnie had passed, but he did. He did because he's a good person. He's someone I want in my life.

Someone I might love.

I pull on my navy hoodie and tiptoe downstairs. Wallis is in the guestroom with Peach, thankfully. June is on the couch, but her deafening snoring means she's out like a light. I feel bad for sneaking out without my dad knowing, but I'll be back. There's no reason for him to worry.

The quick walk to 7-Eleven feels like it takes ages. The crisp night air stings my cheeks, but my thumping heart keeps my body heat regulated with nerves. I assume I'll be the first one to arrive, which will give me time to mentally prepare, but when I round the corner of the building I'm surprised to see that Alex is already there.

His eyes meet mine. All kinds of emotions explode inside me. It's been so long since he's even looked at me, and the weight of his gaze makes me flush. He looks good. *So* good. His curly hair peeks out from underneath his beanie, and he's wearing a faded denim jacket over a black T-shirt.

When he hands me a waxy, plastic cup, my breath catches in my throat. It's a cherry red Slurpee. My icy fingers reach out and take it.

Alex keeps his gaze on me. "Want to talk in my truck?"

I nod, realizing that's how he got here so fast. Once we're inside, protected from the wind, I set my Slurpee in his cup holder and take a deep breath.

"I'm sorry—"

Alex turns to me, and I'm relieved I don't see harshness in his features. "No, listen—you've apologized so many times and I just...I wanted to say some things."

My heart sinks, but I nod for him to continue.

"*I'm* the one who should be sorry. I got too in my head about you and Jay, which made me weirdly, um...insecure?" He flushes, but meets my gaze. "I don't think you're ashamed of me. I guess maybe I—maybe I wanted you to open up to me like you used to. But just because I tell you stuff about my life doesn't mean you have to do the same, you know?"

I watch him tug on the back of his beanie, a little stunned at his upfront apology.

"I want to. Open up to you, I mean," I say quietly. "I was scared for a lot of reasons. I didn't want to have to leave a second time... and leave you. I want to finish what—"

I cut myself off. Finish what? Finish something that never began?

"I know," Alex says, then shakes his head. "I mean, not fully. But I understand you wanted to do everything in your power to keep your dad from relapsing and from being sent away again."

I look down at my hands. That's all true.

"I shouldn't have been so harsh toward you when you came to apologize. I was still hurt, I think, but that's not an excuse." He looks right at me. "If you want to talk about stuff, I'm here. I've always been here. And I won't ever judge you. I, um, I guess what I'm trying to say is... I want to be your friend."

A lump rises in my throat. *Friend*. He wants to be my friend. Nothing else. It's hard to hear, harder than I expected. And I know it's because I wanted us to be more.

I can't stay here. I reach for the handle of the door.

"What are you doing?" Alex asks, confused.

A chilly breeze rushes through the crack. "Leaving?"

To my surprise, Alex smiles. "Kira, I don't want you to leave."

Now I'm confused. "You don't?"

He laughs. "No! Of course not. We had a fight. You apologized, and I also wanted to apologize for how I acted. But, um...I don't want our friendship to be over."

Disappointment tugs at my heartstrings. I think of our kiss back in the workshop, of our endless conversations and the intoxicating way he always smells like his familiar laundry detergent, like *him*. But

I know this is my fault. I set us back again. Of course I'd need to earn his friendship before he could even see me as anything more.

But then Alex does something I don't expect. Alex, the mostly shy, caring person that I've known for the last ten years, reaches for my hand.

My skin sparks with electricity.

"I also . . . I don't want *us* to be over."

I can't help the tears that fall down my face. "You don't think I screwed this up?"

"No." He looks right into my eyes. "Kira, I care about you. A lot." Then his body is angled toward mine, his hands delicately on my shoulders. "We've danced around the idea of being together for so long and, um . . . well . . . I want to be. Together, I mean."

He's nervous, but my own nerves burst with happiness at his words.

I can't help but smile. "I want that, too."

Alex smiles back, running his hands all the way up my shoulders until they gently cup my face. I'm not sure which of us leans in first, but we meet. Heat fills every inch of my body, a quiet flame that builds and builds. His lips are soft and cold and taste like cherry flavored syrup, and I want to live in the depths of this moment for eternity.

Suddenly, Alex backs away. "Oh god, I'm so sorry. I mean, I'm sorry to hear about Nonnie." Alex is stuttering now, nervous. "I don't want you to think I'm, um, taking advantage of your grief or—"

I immediately shake my head. "No, I know you're not."

I feel him let out a sigh of relief.

Then I hear myself saying the things I've thought about since the funeral. "I wish you could have met her. She was really great. Sometimes strange. Well, a lot strange. But in her own way, you know? I wish I could go back and do it all again—introduce you and Lin and everyone. She gave me a lot of great advice."

Alex raises an eyebrow. "Yeah?"

"Yeah." I smile, remembering. "One time she met Freddie Mercury on the subway." I stop. "You probably don't want to hear about that."

"No," Alex says. "I do. Whenever you're ready . . . we have time."

I'm transported back to freshman year when we shared laughs in the backseat of his mom's car. I think of all the shy glances that turned into meaningful gazes. I remember how devastated I was when he went to Sadie Hawkins with Lacey, and I can only imagine how he felt carrying around his feelings for me when I showed no signs of returning them—or how he felt when I left Cedarville without a good-bye. Despite all of that, he'd always been there. Always cared. And even though it had taken me longer to find my way back to myself, even with my twelve-steps list, I realized just how much I cared, too.

I lift my eyes, meeting his gaze. "I'm ready."

He smiles. A beat later, he slides his hand back in mine. I realize he's right—there is no rush. We have time.

So I start from the beginning.

author's note

LIKE KIRA, I GREW UP with a father who suffered from alcoholism. While his character arc was one that was familiar to me, I didn't want to explore the negative aspects of this horrible addiction. That's hard to relive in any context. So I chose to focus not only on Kira's journey, but on the hopefulness of her father's recovery—a process I watched my own dad go through.

I began writing this book in 2014, when my dad was still alive, but it wasn't until he passed away early in 2016 that I realized how close to home this book was for me. While Kira's story is not my own, it is one I wished my father and I could have had. I hope I've written something he would be proud of.

However, I know not all stories end happily like Kira and her father's.

Loving an alcoholic is painful and heartbreaking. Addicts' behaviors not only affect themselves, but their friends, families—their children. And when someone in your family has an addiction, it's hard not to feel a wide variety of emotions, including shame, anger, depression, or helplessness. Watching someone struggle is an incredibly difficult burden to take on, but it's something that shouldn't be kept secret.

There are people who can, and want to, help you. Alateen provides a safe space to talk to sponsors and other teens concerned with someone they love who's experiencing a drinking problem. There are also support programs, such as Hazelden Betty Ford Foundation, designed to educate you on these diseases and provide a safe space to cope with any pain and difficulties you've experienced. You can also find information on the websites for the National Association for Children of Addiction and American Addiction Centers, with specific information for teens linked below.

National Association for Children of Addiction
nacoa.org/just-4-teens/
American Addiction Centers
americanaddictioncenters.org/guide-for-children/
Alateen
al-anon.org/newcomers/teen-corner-alateen/
Hazelden Betty Ford Foundation
hazeldenbettyford.org/treatment/family-children/childrens-program

acknowledgments

There have been a lot (A. LOT.) of people who've graciously listened to me talk about writing books, comforted me through rejection, and celebrated the publishing journey with me, and you all deserve a year-long vacation on a tropical island with a never-ending supply of cookies. Instead, I hope this sincere thank you will suffice.

A heartfelt thank you to everyone at New Leaf Literary. Sara Stricker, thank you for your brilliant notes and guidance. I am so grateful for my incredible agent, Suzie Townsend, who plucked me from the slush pile and continued to believe in me throughout these last several years. Suzie—my god—you've read SO many versions of this story and really helped me shape it into something great. You are a phenomenal person, and I am a better writer because of you. Thank you a million times over for your endless support.

To my amazing, hardworking team at Little, Brown/JIMMY Patterson Books: Thank you for reading my words and loving them enough to want to publish them. I am so lucky and fortunate to work with such exceptional people. Thank you to everyone who had a hand in bringing this book to life: Linda, Sabrina, Pat, Erinn, Scott, and everyone involved in the sales, design, and production. Many hugs, thanks, and praise to Sasha Henriques and Aubrey Poole for your extremely helpful edits—and for simply being wonderful.

I am also beyond thankful for my editor, Jenny Bak, who worked tirelessly to not only make this story stronger, but to give it *so* much more heart. Jenny, YOU ARE A DREAM. Your passion and enthusiasm for this story means more than I can express. Thank you, thank you, thank you for loving this book. You are savvy and lovely and dedicated, and I am so lucky to be on Team JIMMY with you!

I want to extend an endless thank you to James Patterson. It's still surreal to me that you've read and loved this book! Thank you for championing Kira's story, and thank you for giving it such a spectacular home. I am so appreciative to you and what you've built at JIMMY Patterson Books. You've helped make my dream come true.

Writing can often be a lonely profession, so I am incredibly grateful for my Los Angeles writer friends who've offered their support and friendship over the years, especially Julie Buxbaum, Jeff Garvin, Charlotte Huang, Kerry Kletter, Kathy Kottaras, Adriana Mather, and Nicola Yoon. You all are a wealth of knowledge and genuine treasures. I am so lucky to know you.

Extending enormous *thank you*s to the following authors who've been encouraging, kind, and supportive: David Arnold, Bree Barton, Stephanie Garber, Melina Marchetta, Maura Milan, Bridget Morrissey, Adam Silvera, Josh Sundquist, Jessica Taylor, and Jeff Zentner. I admire each and every one of you.

Sending every single heart emoji to Candice Darden, Lara Parker, and Pablo Valdivia for reading this book in its roughest form and providing notes and feedback that made it better. I am so thankful to have you in my life.

Thank you to the kind, smart, and fantastic debut authors who make up the Electric Eighteens. We did it, y'all!

I can't even begin to state how grateful I am to every single blogger, vlogger, bookstagrammer, bookseller, and librarian out there. And YOU, reader. Yes, you! THANK YOU.

I am overwhelmingly appreciative to the National Association for Children of Addiction, Alateen, American Addiction Centers, Hazelden Betty Ford Foundation, and the many other organizations who provide help, compassion, and support. To everyone out there who has had alcoholism affect your life in some way: You don't have to go through this alone.

Many thanks to Hector Bagnod for encouraging me when I couldn't find my words, for comforting me through all the rejections, and for believing in me when I didn't believe in myself. You always knew.

To all of my wonderful, caring friends, especially Drew Melton, for being the best bad influence on me, and to Sandy Melton, for being the sweetest. Big *thank you*s to the always-supportive Bagnod family. I'm also grateful for my ladybabes, Colleen D'Agostino and Serena Gustafson, whose drive and passion I'll always admire. And the Leslie Knope to my Ann Perkins, Corrie Shatto, you poetic, noble land-mermaid. I cherish your friendship so much.

To my incredible C-Town crew: Britney Cossey, Lauren Davis, Frank Herpin, Shaun Ngo, Kim Patel, and Sophia Shah.

I've cherished our conversations, laughs, and most importantly our friendship. Thank you for putting up with me for the last ten years. I hope you'll stick around for the next ten (or twenty) more.

To my *BuzzFeed* family, especially everyone in LA Editorial. I am so lucky to have the privilege of working with an incredible, talented, and exceptional group of coworkers that I am proud to call my friends. You all kept me smiling during a hard time in my life, and I am forever grateful for you.

To each and every person in my big, loving, supportive family: Pam, George, Keres, Katie, Kent, Laura, Erik, Rebecca, Tim, Angela, Sarah, Jeff, Elaine, Dave, Shawnee, Brendan, Denay, Jaymie, Dan, Deanna, and Joseph. You all bring so much brightness into my life. Very special thanks to Kathy and Greg Roche for your love, generosity, and kindness in housing a struggling writer trying to find her path.

Thank you to my grandmother, Carol Bishop, whose selflessness and strength I will always admire. I don't know anyone else who has a heart as big as yours. Also, I am certain my love for reading came from you.

To my dog, Gizmo, for being the best companion I could ask for. He can't read this, but I think he knows.

So much love to my favorite sister, Cianna, who is stunning both inside and out. I may be older, but you're definitely wiser. Thank you for answering all my weirdly specific questions about high school that I'd blanked on. More importantly, thank you for all the laughs—and for being you.

My mom, my rock, Debbie Penn. Thank you for the overwhelming support you've continued to give me growing up. I told you my dreams, and you said *Yes, go get them.* Thank you for not freaking out when I changed my major three times and for being there every time I have an emotional breakdown. You are smart and beautiful, and you've taught me so much about compassion and strength. If I can be only a fraction as incredible as you, I'll consider myself lucky. I love you.

Finally, this book is dedicated in memory of my father, Richard Penn, and my grandmother, Clara Penn. I love you and miss you both.

about the author

FARRAH PENN was born and raised in a suburb in Texas that's far from the big city but close enough to Whataburger. She now resides in Los Angeles, California, with her gremlin dog and succulents. When she's not writing books, she can be found writing things for *BuzzFeed* and sending texts that contain too many emojis. *Twelve Steps to Normal* is her first novel.